ENDURE
The Pain

THE MAURA QUINN SERIES BOOK TWO

ASHLEY N. ROSTEK

Endure the Pain

Edited by Alexandra Fresch of To the Letter Services

Cover design by The Dirty Tease

Formatting by Dark Ink Designs

This is a work of fiction. All names, characters, places, and incidents are the product of the author's imagination or are used fictitiously. Any resemblance to actual persons, living or dead, organizations, events, or locals is purely coincidental.

BOOKS BY ASHLEY N. ROSTEK

Maura Quinn Series

Embrace the Darkness

Endure the Pain

Endurance

Escape the Reaper

WITSEC Series

Find Me

Save Me

Love Me

Free Me

For M & L—
My everything.

BEFORE YOU READ

The content in this book may be triggering to some. The trigger warnings below will contain spoilers. If you don't want anything spoiled and you're comfortable reading triggering content, stop reading this page, flip to chapter one, and happy reading <3

Endure the Pain contains descriptive violence, killing, drug use, alcohol, sexual content, sexual assault, and loss of pregnancy. There's a lot of foul language.

After reading the previous trigger warnings and you still wish to continue reading, welcome back to the world of Maura Quinn :)

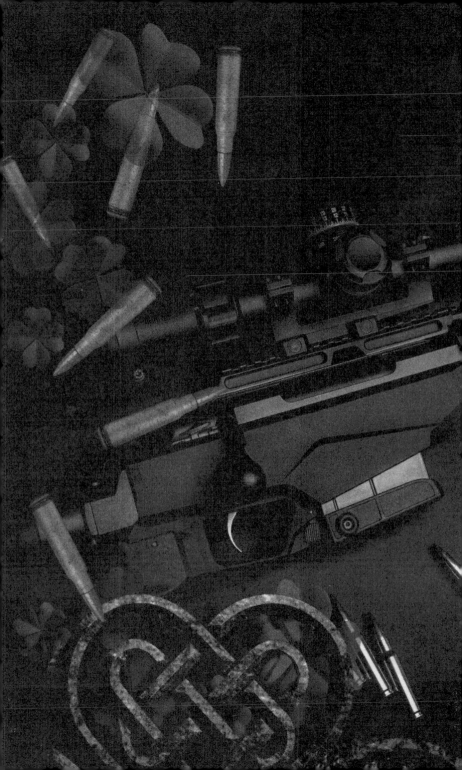

CHAPTER ONE

I f someone had told me a month ago that I'd be returning to my childhood home, back into the thrall of drama that was my family, and end up employed in my father's criminal empire, I'd have laughed in their face and returned home to Tom, my cheating ex-boyfriend. Not that I'd known he was unfaithful at that time or that he'd been sleeping with my best friend, Tina —both of whom were hopefully rotting in hell.

But all that had happened. And more.

"I love you, Jamie," I said into the phone before shots whizzed past my head. Dropping the phone, I threw my body over Rourke, who lay unconscious on the floor, bleeding from where he'd been shot. The gunfire stopped and was followed by the sound of grunting and rustling behind me.

"Maura, behind you!" Dean yelled out.

I leapt over Rourke's body, twisted around on my knees, and came face-to-face with a man sporting a pale blond mohawk. I only had a moment to take him in and the scene going on behind him. He was wearing tight jeans and a black hoodie and was holding a silver Glock. My attention caught on the red ribbon forming the letter *A* with a black swastika shadowing it, tattooed on his neck. Only members of the Aryans—a white supremacist gang—had that tattoo.

Glancing past him, I could see Asher fighting off a man, another Aryan I assumed, holding a knife. Dean had his back against the door that led to the stairwell. He was struggling to keep it closed. Shooting me a worried look, he seemed torn as to what he should do. Hold the door? Or come save me? Our eyes locked and I shook my head, making the decision for him. If he came to help me, more of them would get inside.

The Aryan standing before me lifted his Glock and aimed it at me. I frantically scooted backward until my back hit a wall.

"Hold still, Princess. I'll make it quick," he said, smiling evilly as his finger hovered over the trigger.

I didn't blink.

I didn't breathe.

I watched as his finger curled around the trigger. My heart skipped a beat when the gun fired, but not before a giant blur tackled the Aryan to the floor.

The giant part was my first clue that Asher had been my savior. The two wrestled on the ground. Asher moved fluidly to maneuver himself behind the Aryan, putting him in a headlock. He yanked the Aryan's gun out of his hand, sending it flying. My eyes followed as it skidded across the floor and I dove for it. My fingers closed around its grip and I pushed myself to my feet.

They both looked up at me as I aimed the gun in their direction. I didn't hesitate in pulling the trigger. The Aryan's head jerked backward, and blood poured from his eye. Shoving the lifeless Aryan off of him, Asher took a moment to ease his labored breathing before getting back on his feet. He appeared more banged up now than when we had all crawled from the wrecked Escalade upstairs. The side of his face was beginning to swell, and he was hugging his ribs on his left side.

His eyes dropped to my abdomen before narrowing. "Were you shot?"

I glanced at my canary yellow blouse that was drenched with red and saw I had a steady drip of blood flowing from the hem to the floor. I was bleeding more profusely. Probably due to all the jolting around I'd just done. I didn't let my concern show as my gaze lifted back to Asher.

The sound of banging and Dean grunting pulled our attention to the door. His feet were sliding on the floor, slowly losing purchase as he struggled to keep the enemy out.

I held out the Glock. "I'm fine. Go help Dean."

Asher took the gun and ran to help hold the door closed. I'd intended to return to Rourke's side but could barely put one foot in front of the other. I felt weak. The act of breathing was a chore and all I wanted to do was lie down.

Pain flared at my knees. Looking down, I realized I had fallen to them. Then the room started to spin. I closed my eyes, attempting to blink the dizziness away, but once they were closed, I found it impossible to open them. The urge to let go and fall into oblivion was as strong as a siren's song.

I could feel my body falling. My already pain riddled head hitting the ground was the jolt I needed to snap my eyes open once more. The lights on the ceiling were sliding back and forth, making it difficult to focus on any one thing.

Why is it so cold?

"Maura!"

Jamie?

Warm arms cradled my body and I was slightly lifted off the freezing floor. For only a second, I saw beautiful hazel eyes until the urge to close my own won and everything ceased to exist.

3

My nightmare was always the same. Or should I say, was always of the same person. I could never see her face fully, but that didn't seem to matter because I had a sinking feeling I knew who she was.

I walked through the halls of Quinn Manor late at night. Glancing in the mirror hanging in the hall as I passed, I saw that I was the child version of myself. I appeared to be seven or eight years old. My red hair was twisted into two braids that barely passed my shoulders, a large cluster of freckles dotted the tops of my cheeks, and my green eyes were large, doe-like, and filled with fear.

The sound of a woman screaming had woken me and pulled me to my father's study. As I quietly approached it, I could see that the door was slightly ajar. The screaming had stopped, only to be replaced by a man and a woman shouting. The man sounded like my father. I found that strange because my father never raised his voice. He didn't have to. His presence alone was enough to capture everyone's attention.

Creeping silently to peek through the slightly open door, my entire body jumped and froze when two shots rang out.

The woman had let out another blood curdling scream, before yelling, "What have you done?"

Taking the last step forward, I peered into the dimly lit room to find my father standing over a bleeding man. The man was dead. I could tell by his vacant, unblinking eyes. A woman was draped over his body, crying into his chest. Her hair was fanned out like a wild mane. The tangled strands looked like they had been dipped in black ink because her roots were red as blood.

The light reflecting off the gun in my father's hand drew my attention, and the realization that it was him who had killed this man made me gasp. My father's head whipped in my direction. His eyes found me right away. The feral anger carving his expression cemented my feet to the floor. I had never seen him so mad, but he quickly smothered it with an emotionless mask. All I could do was watch as he came toward me with such poise—like the ruthless king I'd always thought him to be. It was equally reassuring as it was frightening, given who he was and what he had just done.

Opening the door all the way, he grabbed my arm and pulled me into the room. My father ushered me to stand before the sobbing woman and the dead man. My bare feet stepped into something wet and my eyes dropped to the floor. To my horror, I was standing in the dead man's blood. The thick liquid squished up between my toes and covered my sparkly nail polish. It was such a terrifying sight that I barely even noticed that my father had taken my hand and placed his gun in my palm.

My fingers instinctively closed around its grip and he guided my hand to point the barrel at the sobbing woman. I looked up at him, questioningly. His forest green eyes locked with mine. There was such an intensity to his stare that I thought I could see pain, sadness, and rage waging war against his self-control behind those eyes. Then he blinked and was back to revealing nothing. "Pull the trigger, Maura."

The woman's head snapped up. Her skin was covered in a layer of blood and half of her face was curtained by messy hair. Only one eye was visible. The color reminded me of gray clouds that blocked out the sun before it rained. Her one striking eye was wide, and it was staring right at me like nothing else mattered in the world. Just me.

It was unsettling to the point that I took a step back, bumping into my father. The back of my body molded to his legs. With the gun still pointed at her, my arm began to shake.

My father put his hand on my shoulder. The warmth it exuded helped ease the panic bubbling inside me. "Remember the rules of the game, Maura. Do you remember what I said about fear?"

I nodded slightly. "Fear is a tool, not a shackle."

"Very good," he said, squeezing my shoulder gently. "Now, find your strength and show the enemy they don't hold any power over you."

I closed my eyes to find the strength he spoke of, as if it might be another entity inside of me. I couldn't find it and had to settle for taking in a deep breath. When I exhaled, my trembling lessened, my racing heart slowed, and I opened my eyes with confidence.

"That's it," he assured.

"You twisted bastard!" the woman snarled at him. "You never had the balls to pull the trigger yourself! You don't deserve her, Stefan! She belongs to me!"

My free hand that was resting on my father's leg fisted the fabric of his slacks. "Daddy." My voice quivered. I didn't like how she spoke to him. No one talked to him like that. Not unless they wanted to suffer.

"Like I'd ever allow my daughter to be around a crack whore who tried to sell her at six weeks old for another fix," my father seethed. "And don't think for one second that I actually believe you're here for her. We both know it's money that you're really after. When I paid you to stay away, I warned you if you ever showed up here again or ever made your presence known to Maura, I'd make you regret it."

"This isn't about money. I know I made mistakes in the past, but I'm clean now. She deserves to know me and she's old enough to decide if that's what she wants," the woman argued.

"I think that's the best idea your coke-muddled brain has ever come up with. We'll let Maura decide." My father knelt down behind me. "Maura, do you want to stay with Daddy, or do you want to go away with this strange woman?"

That seemed like the stupidest question he'd ever asked me, and I opened my mouth to answer him, but he cut me off. "If you choose to stay with me, you are to aim this gun at her and pull the trigger because if you don't, she'll keep coming back."

I glanced back at the scary woman, then back at my father. "Is she bad?"

"She's not good to us," he answered, and I caught sadness in his eyes again.

"Did she hurt you, Daddy?" I whispered.

"She hurt me by trying to hurt you," he answered.

That was all I needed to hear. I aimed the gun with both hands and widened my stance like he and my uncle Conor had taught me.

The woman's eye widened again. "Maura, sweetie, put the gun down. I'm your—"

I pulled the trigger.

The bullet shot out and her body fell backward. The recoil from the gun made me stagger and lose my footing. My father caught me and took the gun from my hands, before turning me away from the carnage to face him. His lips moved, but no words reached my ears.Then the scene of my nightmare faded to nothing and I woke up.

CHAPTER TWO

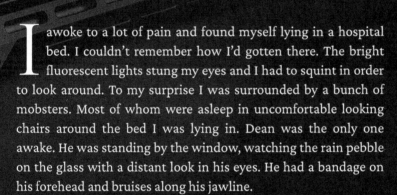

I awoke to a lot of pain and found myself lying in a hospital bed. I couldn't remember how I'd gotten there. The bright fluorescent lights stung my eyes and I had to squint in order to look around. To my surprise I was surrounded by a bunch of mobsters. Most of whom were asleep in uncomfortable looking chairs around the bed I was lying in. Dean was the only one awake. He was standing by the window, watching the rain pebble on the glass with a distant look in his eyes. He had a bandage on his forehead and bruises along his jawline.

How'd he get hurt?

Did it have to do with why I'm lying in a hospital bed?

I found myself unable to look away from Dean's battered face. Flashes came and went: blood running down the side of his face from a really bad cut by his temple and him reaching out for me to take his hand. My whole body tensed, unsettled by the nagging feeling that I recognized what I was seeing.

My gaze traveled to the sleeping Asher sitting next to him, who was just as bandaged up and bruised, and my memories of the accident and fighting off the Aryans rushed back to me. I scanned the rest of the room. Louie was asleep with his arm propped up on the arm rest and his head lying on his fist. Jamie was sitting in a chair to my left. He had a death grip on my hand and was sleeping soundlessly with his head resting on my thigh. Stefan was sitting on my right, also asleep.

I squeezed Jamie's hand. His eyes shot open, immediately meeting mine. A second passed before his eyes widened and he sat up. "Hey," he whispered, reaching toward me to swipe the tears away from my cheek with his thumb.

My voice came out low and raspy. "Rourke?"

Jamie squeezed my hand. "Alive and in a room down the hall."

I released the breath I hadn't known I was holding and closed my eyes. Jamie lifted my hand and I opened my eyes just in time to see him bring the back of it to his lips. He let everything he was feeling come to the surface. His exhausted yet relieved eyes conveyed it all. This mobster loved me.

I moved my hand from his lips to cup his cheek and tried to show him how sorry I was for the pain my cowardice had put us through.

His eyes read mine before he leaned forward. His kiss was gentle and chaste but filled with so much love that it blanketed my soul with warmth.

Breaking our kiss, he rested his forehead lightly against mine. We stayed like that, basking in the comfort our closeness exuded, until everyone in the room started to wake. They each perked up when their eyes landed on me. A hand gently closed around my right wrist, making me turn my head toward Stefan. The small movement caused my entire skull to explode with searing pain.

I groaned and closed my eyes tightly.

"I'll go get the nurse," Dean volunteered and left the room.

Slowly, I attempted to turn toward Stefan. His attire was... relaxed, with his dress shirt untucked, sleeves rolled to his elbows, and the collar unbuttoned. His tie and jacket were hanging over the back of his chair. Dark bags were starting to form under his eyes. "You almost look human."

The corner of his mouth twitched. "As opposed to what?"

"Indestructible. Powerful. The big bad boss," I answered with a sad smile. Was it strange that I held onto moments like these, where he couldn't hide what he truly felt behind an unreadable facade, as if they were gold?

"Do you remember what happened?" he asked.

I huffed. *Really? No "how are you feeling?" Or "are you okay?"* I shouldn't have been surprised. "We were attacked," I started, sounding annoyed. "They shot Rourke's enforcer and rammed into the side of our car. I wasn't wearing my seat belt. Rourke tried to grab me, but it was too late." The car rolling and me being thrown all over the place like a rag doll replayed behind my eyes. The memory made my head smart and I reached up to touch my temple as if to ease the pain, only to find that my head was bandaged.

Stefan squeezed my wrist a little. "Keep going."

"I woke up in the trunk space. Rourke found me, then Dean and Asher. They were trying to help me out of the car when bullets started flying everywhere. Rourke threw himself over me. He was shot. I felt it when it happened. Then I got hit on my side." My hand dropped from my head to my side. Through the thin fabric of my hospital gown, I could feel I was bandaged there as well. "The guys in the van gave us cover." I looked to Jamie to ask him if they were okay, but before I could ask, he shook his head. *They didn't make it.* "Did they have families?" I barely knew them, but I owed them. They had sacrificed themselves so we could escape.

"Don't worry about that right now," Stefan ordered.

I nodded. "Dean pulled Rourke and me from the car. We took off on foot. It didn't take long for our attackers to catch up with us. We'd locked ourselves in the parking garage's mechanical room. The security guards seemed to be using it as an office and they had a first aid kit, which I used to help stop Rourke's bleeding. Dean and Asher barricaded the door but two of them were able to get inside. One came right for me, but Dean warned me in time..." I trailed off.

Pushing through the searing pain, I broke down that moment, slowly. I could see Dean perfectly, standing with his back to the door, trying desperately to keep it closed. Both his and Asher's guns, empty of ammo, had been tossed to the floor. That hadn't seemed to set Asher back as he'd taken on his opponent with his bare hands. I shifted my focus back to my Aryan. He'd paid no attention to Rourke and hadn't even spared a backward glance at Dean. *Why did he come after me and not Dean?* Dean had clearly been a bigger threat and the obstacle preventing any more Aryans from getting in that room.

Hold still, Princess. I'll make this quick. I repeated the Aryan's words in my head.

"He called me 'Princess,'" I unintentionally mumbled out loud.

"Who did?" Stefan asked.

"The Aryan. He knew who I was," I answered distractedly as I remembered the Aryan zeroing in on me.

"Maura," Stefan said, trying to get my attention.

It worked. The movie that was my memories playing behind my eyes shuttered away and I was back in the small hospital room. My eyes flicked to Stefan. "Did they take the guns?"

"Yes."

"Why would they follow us down to that room? They got what they came for. Why risk pursuing us?" I asked.

The corner of Stefan's mouth lifted as he stared at me proudly. "I think the better question to ask is, if they were after the guns, why did they target your vehicle so heavily? The van carrying the guns could have easily taken off, which is our protocol unless my life or...my daughter's life is ever at risk."

"You mean to tell me the guys in the van would have just left Rourke there to die if I hadn't been in that car?" I questioned angrily. Rourke's life was worth more than fucking guns.

"If they were solely after the guns, they would have primarily targeted the men in the van, not the SUV driving ahead of it."

Oh. With all that said, if they really had been targeting me, which my gut was screaming they had, it was still speculation. "How'd they know I'd even be in that car? And why would the Aryans want to kill me?"

In one quick movement, Stefan's eyes shifted to Jamie before returning to me.

"Stefan?" I urged, but before he could answer, Dean returned.

Stepping into the room, Dean held a scowl that was harsher than normal. I was going to ask him what was wrong, but the nurse that appeared behind him gave me my answer. She was elderly with a head full of graying amber hair and purple rimmed glasses that framed her eyes. Her body moved stiffly as she made her way through the room. She glanced around at the guys, eyes full of judgment and disdain.

Only those who lived under a rock didn't know what the name Quinn meant or who it belonged to. Especially in New Haven, where Quinn Manor loomed over the city like a haunting and infamous shadow. The Quinns had ruled the New England area for generations. People either respected our family or feared and hated us. The respect came because my family, namely Stefan, took part in and donated to many charities. This hospital was a prime example. Stefan was a huge benefactor. I was sure his generosity didn't always come without strings attached. He was an Irish mob boss, after all. I could only assume that the stipulations included privilege and a certain level of discretion, like turning a blind eye to gunshot wounds that were required by law to be reported to local police. Those who feared and hated us consisted mostly of law enforcement who weren't on Stefan's payroll and people like this nurse.

The nurse went straight over to assess the IV machine I was hooked up to and typed something on the computer next to the bed. "How are you feeling?" Her tone was bland, and the question sounded forced.

"I have a lot of pain."

"You should count yourself lucky that's all you have, considering your choice of friends," she said.

I had to stop myself from gaping. "Excuse me?"

"Well, look at what they dragged you into. You were shot and almost killed. Maybe this will teach you not to hang around thugs," she chided.

If I hadn't been hurting in a hospital bed, there was a good chance I would have strangled her with her stethoscope. My mind was at odds with what it wanted to do versus what it could do in that moment. So I just blinked at her.

"I didn't know nurses were paid to berate their patients," Jamie snapped at her.

She looked taken aback for a moment before she recovered. "Let me guess, you're the boyfriend who manipulated this poor girl to join your thug lifestyle."

Louie erupted into a fit of laughter. "She thinks Jameson corrupted Maura?" he wheezed. "That's fucking hilarious."

Stefan stood from his chair and stuffed his hands into his pockets. He gave the nurse a friendly smile that was kind of eerie because his eyes read differently. They were predatory. He leaned forward slightly and squinted at her name tag. "Georgina Osman. That's a pretty name. I'll be sure to remember it. Mine is Stefan Quinn."

All the blood drained from her face and she took a step back. "Are you threatening me?"

"Whatever do you mean, Mrs. Osman?" he asked innocently. "I was simply introducing myself so you'd know who reported your unprofessional behavior to your supervisor." He then looked to me. "I know you're in pain, but I don't trust her."

I nodded with understanding.

"I don't trust you to treat my daughter. Please excuse yourself from this room before I have you removed," Stefan ordered.

"Your daughter," she gasped as if just realizing it. *Did she not read my name on my chart?* She put her hand to her neck as if to clutch her nonexistent pearls.

"In case you were wondering, that was a threat," I told her. "I'd get your ass moving, Nurse Ratched."

She huffed and stormed out of the room.

"I need to pee," I announced.

Dean and Asher beelined for the door while mumbling that they would wait out in the hall.

"I'm going to go find Brody and get you a new nurse," Stefan said and bolted.

I tightened my hold on Jamie, even though he'd made no move to leave, and I gave him a firm look that said, *You aren't going anywhere, buddy.*

He smiled and pulled off my covers, exposing the ugly hospital gown I was in and my bare legs. I unhooked myself from the blood pressure cuff that was wrapped around my arm and pulled off the thing clamped to my finger that monitored my pulse. Before I could even attempt to get out of bed myself, he scooped me up in his arms.

"Need some help?" Louie asked.

Jamie tilted his head toward the IV pole I was tethered to. Understanding, Louie rolled the pole behind us as Jamie carried me to the bathroom.

"I probably could have walked," I said as he sat me down on my feet in front of the toilet.

"You're hurting. I don't want you pushing yourself."

Louie handed my IV pole to me and they both left to give me privacy. Pain flared in my abdomen and head as I sat on the toilet and it didn't let up when I slowly hobbled over to the sink to wash my hands.

I glanced in the small mirror. I had bandaging from the center of my forehead to my temple. I was sporting a nasty black eye, and cuts and scrapes from my ear down to my collar bone. Bunching up my gown in my hands, I dared to look at where I'd been shot. What I saw left me stunned and confused.

What the hell?

My abdomen was blotched with purple bruises and patched up with bandages in multiple areas—not just where I'd been shot. What was even more shocking was the blood-filled drain tube coming out of me from under my sternum.

"Maura."

Through the mirror, I saw Jamie poke his head into the bathroom. His eyes took me in—standing before the mirror with my gown up—then he stepped fully into the bathroom. He closed the door and leaned his back against it. "You were bleeding internally. The doctor said your spleen ruptured due to the accident. They had to rush you into emergency surgery where they removed a portion of it and repaired the damage the bullet caused. You also have a nasty skull fracture."

Was that all? I almost said. As I absorbed everything he told me, I found words failing me and I numbly dropped my gown.

Jamie pushed off the door and I turned to face him. His hand slid behind my neck and gently pulled me closer. Eyes boring into mine with the slightest hint of sadness, he said, "I almost lost you."

I laid my cheek over his heart, seeking comfort while offering what I could to him in return.

The doctor showed up after I returned from the bathroom. She greeted me with a friendly smile and began looking me over. She asked how I was feeling, and I expressed how much pain I was in. The doctor called for a different nurse to bring me something to help with the pain. Then she asked if I remembered my accident. I lied, saying I didn't, and she immediately tried to reassure me that having a hazy memory wasn't uncommon with skull fractures. *That's good to know.*

Stefan was still gone, and Dean and Asher were still waiting in the hall. Jamie and Louie were with me and listened quietly as the doctor went over the surgery and the extent of the damage. The healing period was four to six weeks. Yeah, that wasn't going to work for me. I had the drug pillar to run now that my uncle was gone, and De Luca refused to work with anyone but me. Not to mention I'd go nuts if I had to be stuck in bed twenty-four-seven for weeks. Jamie must have seen something in my expression because he asked her, "What if she refuses to stay in bed?"

Louie chuckled at the not-so-friendly look I was giving Jamie.

"You need to listen to your body. If you overexert yourself, there could be complications and you'll extend the time it takes for your body to heal properly," the doctor advised.

After the doctor left, Stefan returned to my room with Brody right on his heels. Brody was barely in the room a minute before he began fussing over me. He fluffed my pillows and adjusted my blankets. Then after I told him how the first nurse had treated us, he stepped out, and demanded angrily to the first hospital employee he saw that he wanted to speak with the hospital director immediately.

"Stefan Quinn is a major benefactor to this hospital, and this is how you treat his daughter? Maybe he should pull his funding!" Brody said loudly.

"That won't be necessary, sir," the director said with panic in his voice. They were standing out in the hall, but the door was cracked, and we could hear everything.

"She's been through enough with the accident and surgery, she doesn't need some self-righteous wretch making her feel worse than she already does," Brody seethed.

I snorted trying to suppress my laughter. "Brody's going all mama bear on him."

Stefan looked up from his phone with a raised brow. "Interesting choice of words."

"I think they're quite accurate. When it came to raising me, he was more nurturing and softer. Since I already had you, I always compared him to what it'd be like to have a mother."

"I can see why you'd think that," he said and returned to whatever he was doing on his phone.

"You never talk about her," I said softly.

His fingers froze mid text before his eyes flicked back to mine. "You never ask about her."

That was true. Mostly because I was apprehensive of what he'd say if I ever did bring her up or ask the questions that weighed on me. I'd been having the same nightmare almost every night since my rape. It was amazing what someone could learn to live with when left with no other choice. But Stefan and I had been growing closer. Staring at him, I contemplated whether or not I should tell him. "I—"

I was interrupted with a knock on the door and I couldn't tell if I was relieved or irritated. Not that it mattered, because of who walked in.

Without waiting for permission, one right after the other, Detectives Cameron and Brooks strolled into my room. Dean followed in after them, looking even more pissed than when

Nurse Ratched had been here. Stefan, Jamie, and Louie rose from their chairs, all of whom didn't seem too pleased.

The two detectives eyed the mobsters surrounding me before their stares homed in on me. "Good afternoon, Miss Quinn," Detective Brooks greeted.

CHAPTER THREE

J amie scowled at the detectives. "Were you camping out in the fucking parking lot? She just woke up."

Detective Cameron squared his shoulders and glared at Jamie. "Don't be jealous, Coleman. I'm sure if I looked hard enough, I could find something to question you about."

Jamie stepped toward the detective. "We both know you won't find anything. But please, go ahead. The last time you had a hard-on for me ended so well. Failed marriage. Kids wound up hating you because Daddy missed one too many soccer games. At least you still have your fellow pigs to keep you warm in the pen at night."

Cameron's jaw clenched and his hands fisted tightly at his sides. As if foreseeing his partner's intentions, Detective Brooks put a hand on Cameron's shoulder, stopping him from advancing on Jamie.

"I understand you detectives have a job to do, but I don't understand why it can't wait. My daughter almost lost her life and is in a delicate state. The last thing she needs is for you to put her through unnecessary stress," Stefan argued.

Oh jeez. It was a chore not to laugh at his hypocrisy. The first thing he'd done was question me after I woke up. Now he was playing the role of a caring father and acting as if I was a dandelion, one gust of wind from being blown away.

"Be that as it may, she was involved in a shooting which resulted in five dead and both her and your nephew shot. There were enough shell casings in that garage to show that over five hundred rounds were fired," Brooks explained.

I sighed. "Sit down." Everyone looked down at me. I reached for Jamie's hand and tugged him backward, preventing him from arguing. "Could you also take a seat, Detectives? No offense, but I have a skull fracture and it hurts to look up at you. I'd be more than happy to answer any questions you may have but you've got to meet me on my level."

Dean skidded two chairs toward them before going to stand by the window. The detectives exchanged a look and reluctantly sat. Jamie, Louie, and Stefan followed suit.

Brooks and Cameron eyed my hand clasped in Jamie's before Brooks plastered on a friendly smile. "Thank you for cooperating."

"I don't remember much," I lied.

"Can you tell us what you do remember?" Brooks asked as he pulled out a little notebook and pen.

"I remember being in the car."

"Where were you headed?" Cameron interrupted.

I fought not to look to Stefan for guidance. Instead, I furrowed my brow as if I was really trying to remember.

Jamie squeezed my hand. "It's okay, baby. The doctor said it would take time before things would start coming back to you."

I willed tears to my eyes. It wasn't that hard because I was already emotionally spent. "I'm sorry."

Cameron's eyes narrowed and if his expression was anything to go by, he clearly felt like I was full of shit.

"It's okay," Brooks said, kindly. "Is there anything else you remember?"

I nodded. "I was talking to Rourke in the backseat. We were laughing about something."

"What were you laughing about?" Cameron asked.

"It's all hazy. I think we were talking about Jamie."

Cameron rose a brow. "Jamie?"

I pointed to Jamie. As far as I knew only his mother and I were the ones he'd allowed to shorten his name. Everyone else called him Jameson or referred to him by his last name, Coleman.

"Well, isn't that cute," Cameron mocked.

What a dick.

"With all due respect, Detective, can you save whatever beef you have with Jamie for another time? I have graciously agreed to answer all your questions because I want to help you find the people who set out to hurt me and my family. Three of my friends are dead. So please, can you do your job and ask me what it is you want to know?" I snapped.

The room went quiet. Louie snorted and Jamie did nothing to hide his smug smile. Brooks cleared his throat. "Of course, Miss Quinn. Please continue."

I went on with a very vague explanation of what had happened up until the driver, Rourke's enforcer, had gotten shot. Then I said everything was a black hole after that.

They asked me if I'd ever interacted with the Aryans before. I played completely dumb, stating that I'd never met an Aryan in my life.

Cameron frowned. "It's unfortunate that all the traffic cams and security footage in and around that parking garage were mysteriously down at the time of the shooting. All we have to go off of is what you, Rourke Murphy, Asher King, and Dean Gallagher have to say, and it isn't much."

"I wish I could be more help," I said.

When they were finished with their questions, they stood to leave, but just as Cameron reached the door he paused and glanced back at me. "One more thing...have you heard from your ex, Tom Morris?"

I shook my head. I was so grateful that I'd taken that thing off my finger earlier because my pulse rate skyrocketed. "No, I haven't."

"Have you tried reaching out to him?" he asked.

"Is there something I should know, Detective?" I deflected.

His scrutinizing eyes held mine. "I find it strange that you wouldn't attempt to reach out to him after I told you that he was missing. Despite your separation, you two were together for over a year. Weren't you the slightest bit worried about him?"

I opened my mouth to speak, but he cut me off. "Because I'm feeling *gracious* at the moment, I'll give you a few days to rest up, but I will need you to come down to the station to answer a few more questions."

I didn't respond, nor did he wait around for me to. As Detective Brooks went to follow his partner out, he glanced over at Dean. It was brief and I couldn't see his expression, but whatever it was caused Dean to look away from him with a clenched jaw.

***

"If I wasn't high on painkillers right now, I'd be going bananas. I don't know how much longer I can do this," I groaned as I slowly made my way back from the bathroom. Dean and Asher both watched as I stiffly took a seat on the couch next to them.

"Quit complaining. It's only been two weeks," Dean grumbled and turned his attention back toward the TV.

"Enjoy it while it lasts. We are. It's easier to keep you alive when confined to one room. Once you're able to rejoin civilization, all bets are off," Asher teased.

Being cooped up in my room with my goons while watching an unhealthy amount of TV since being released from the hospital had been a bonding experience, to say the least. We'd reached a point of comfortable where they'd turned into mouthy little shits. Not that they hadn't been that way before. They just didn't hold back anymore. It might have pissed me off at times, but I still respected them for it. Stefan thought it was a bad idea to form friendships with my security. He was worried about the heartache I'd face if one of them died. I understood his concern. I couldn't, however, live my life surrounded by strangers.

Besides, it was kind of hard not to get to know someone when confined to a room for weeks. I'd learned a lot. Both Dean and Asher were ex-military, which wasn't surprising. Dean had grown up in New Haven but didn't have any family left. He had been vetted by one of Conor's enforcers before they'd introduced him to Louie, who'd presented him with the offer to join the family.

"Did you know who we were at the time or what it'd mean when Louie made the offer?" I'd asked him.

He'd been caught off guard by the question and seemed to shut down after replying simply, "Yeah."

I'd reached out to him without thinking and touched his arm reassuringly. I didn't know why I'd done it and the gesture had surprised us both. "I wouldn't blame you, but do you regret it— joining the family?"

The three of us had been sitting on my couch with a movie playing on the TV. Dean had been sitting in the middle with Asher and I flanking him. Asher had been quietly watching us while munching on popcorn. He'd preferred kettle popcorn over the old fashioned butter that Dean and I liked, which was why he'd gotten his own bowl while Dean and I had shared. Dean hadn't answered right away, and I'd ended up blurting, "I wouldn't wish this life on anyone."

The harshness that usually molded Dean's expression had lessened. "Maybe in the beginning. I had different expectations then."

I'd been surprised by his honesty. "What were you expecting?"

He had shrugged. "Doesn't matter because a fiery red-head strolled in with a devil-may-care attitude and changed everything."

Asher had snorted in an attempt to stifle a laugh.

I'd rolled my eyes. "And what about you? How'd you find yourself working for Jamie's uncle?"

He'd given me a cocksure smirk. "Well, I was everything Aiden was looking for."

Dean had snorted that time. "And what does Aiden look for?"

Asher had scratched the short beard along his jaw, mulling over what he should say. "He typically seeks out someone who's ex-military or ex-law enforcement. Little to no family. Strong mentality is also a must."

My brow had furrowed. "Strong mentality?"

"Got to be okay with killing and not let it fuck you up," he had answered, tapping his temple. "Aiden's clientele is good, bad, and downright ugly. Not that any of us care. We wouldn't work for him if we did."

"And why do you work for him?" I'd asked.

"The money," he'd replied simply.

No wonder it didn't take much convincing to get him to sign a contract with me instead of Stefan after I offered to double his pay. "You must have been bored watching over me in Hartford."

His mouth had curled upward in one corner. "I wouldn't say that, doll."

I'd known what he'd been referring to. *Perv.* I could only think of one instance during the time frame he'd watched over me—my last two years in Hartford—which had been the time Tom and I had had sex in his car.

I'd scooped a handful of popcorn from the bowl Dean had

been holding and tossed it at the smirking Asher. "You're the definition of a peeping tom, you know that, right?"

Asher had howled with laughter and Dean had looked between us, completely at a loss. I'd taken pity on him and gone over my time spent in Hartford. As I'd been going over how I'd met Tom and our time spent in his car, I'd trailed off. "How long did he cheat on me?"

Asher's giant hand full of popcorn had frozen halfway to his mouth. "Are you sure you want to know?"

I'd nodded.

He'd dropped the popcorn back in the bowl and set it aside before leveling his gaze with mine. "About a month after you started seeing each other."

Tom and I had started having sex three weeks after we'd begun dating. I'd been on the pill since I was eighteen, but I'd made him get tested before I'd agreed to have sex with him without a condom. That had been three months into our relationship. It had made me feel extremely sick knowing he'd put me at risk of contracting something for almost a year. If I hadn't been tested at my annual gynecologist appointment a week before I'd killed the bastard, I'd have thrown up right then and there.

"Was he with Tina the entire time?" I'd asked Asher.

"They were only together for a month, but she was the longest he kept going back to. Most were hookups he'd met at a party or out with his friends."

Thinking back to our conversation about Tom's whorish ways made me want to take a bath in bleach. The sound of my phone ringing was a welcome distraction. I picked it up from the coffee table and my stomach knotted when I read the caller ID. It was Detective Cameron. Again.

I had never gone to the police station to talk to the detectives, which had sent Detective Cameron onto the warpath. He'd threatened to get a warrant to arrest me for reasonable suspicion.

Stefan had called Adam, the family lawyer, then assured me that no judge would sign off on the warrant. By his confident tone, I knew that these judges were either on the payroll or Stefan had leverage on them.

I silenced the phone, like I'd done the past hundred times he'd called me, and tossed it back on the coffee table. Both Dean and Asher eyed the phone but didn't say a word. They knew who it had been.

"Do you think we have Cheetos?" I asked them. "Since I have no choice but to be a couch potato, I might as well indulge in the junk food."

Asher stood from the couch. "Want anything else?"

I shook my head.

"She'll want something sweet ten minutes after she's done with the Cheetos," Dean said. I didn't dispute that because I did tend to crave something sweet right after eating something salty. I shouldn't have been surprised Dean had picked up on that, but I was and I made it a point not to show it. Even though we had bonded in the past couple of weeks, Dean had the habit of closing off if he did something nice or showed he cared. Asher nodded, also appearing nonchalant about the suggestion, and left for the kitchen.

A few hours later, I had fallen asleep on the couch due to a junk food overdose and was startled awake when Jamie came barging into my room.

"You just scared the shit out of her," Dean grumbled as he stood from the couch.

Jamie ignored him and came right over to me. "I'll make it up to you later. Right now, we need to get you in bed because Detective Cameron and his sidekick are here demanding to speak to you. Stefan is doing his best to delay them until Adam gets here, but that won't stop them from coming up here to question you."

"Here?" I sat up quickly and winced at the sharp pulling I felt in my abdomen. I had a feeling I was overdue for pain meds. "As in my bedroom?"

Noticing me wince, Asher headed for my bathroom, I assumed to get my meds because that's where they were.

Jamie offered me his hand to stand up. "Yeah, baby. Stefan told them you were given strict orders from the doctor to stay in bed and that's why you can't go downstairs to speak with them. Cameron countered, stating they'd accommodate you by coming up here."

I groaned as I got to my feet. "Any way I could shower or at least change first?" I had freaking Cheetos stains on my shirt.

The corner of Jamie's mouth lifted. "Trying to look nice for the sidekick?"

I glared at him before walking away to climb into my bed. "Don't mess with me, Jameson Coleman. I'm starting to feel the symptoms of cabin fever and I won't feel bad if I have to release the crazy on you."

Leaning against the headboard, I caught a gleam of mirth in his eyes. "You've always been crazy, Maura. I've told you this." He leaned forward and kissed my temple. "And nothing gets you moving faster than when I piss you off." He gave me a shit-eating grin, which I returned along with my middle finger. That got him to laugh and he stepped away so Asher could hand me my pain meds and a glass of water.

Just as I popped the pills in my mouth, there was a knock at the door. I didn't bother responding to the knock because I knew Stefan would just walk in like he always did. The only reason he'd knocked at all was to give us a heads up.

The door opened and first to walk in was Stefan, followed by Adam, then the detectives.

Stefan's eyes locked with mine as he made his way over to me. "How are you feeling, sweetheart?"

"I'm sore, but I just took my meds," I replied.

Stefan positioned himself next to my bed and Adam stood next to him. Jamie had made his way to stand on the other side of the bed. Dean and Asher stood silently by the couch. Detectives Cameron and Brooks strolled through my room to stand at the foot of my bed. Them being here felt like a major invasion of my personal space.

Cameron and Brooks eyed the men around the room. "Is the crowd really necessary?" Cameron asked. "We're only here to ask her a few more questions."

"Harass her, you mean," Jamie quipped.

Adam sighed. "Detective, I think you should get on with the questions you came here for."

This sucks, I thought and shifted my tangled braid off my shoulder, which reminded me that I was in desperate need of a shower. My hair was visibly dirty. It was why I had braided it this morning with the intent of taking a shower later.

"Do you know a Christina Barker?" Cameron questioned.

Well, shit. I knew where this was going. "Tina's a friend from college. Why?"

He ignored my question "When was the last time you spoke to *Tina?*"

I pretended to really think about it. "A month and a half ago. We had lunch to catch up."

Cameron made a note in his little notebook. "Did you know she and Tom were having an affair?"

I reeled back, feigning shock. "What are you talking about?"

"Answer the question, Miss Quinn," Cameron ordered firmly.

"No. I did not."

"Tina was reported missing around the same time Tom went missing. That's a pretty big coincidence, don't you think?" he asked, but I knew it was rhetorical.

"What exactly are you implying, Detective?" I asked, knowing he was tiptoeing around why he was really here.

His eyes filled with disdain. "I don't think Tom Morris and Christina Barker are missing. I'm pretty sure they're dead."

This time I didn't put forth the effort in pretending to be shocked. What was the point? I tilted my head slightly, my eyes narrowing. "Let me guess, you think I killed them?" I'd underestimated Detective Cameron. A mistake I'd never make again.

Cameron closed his notebook and stuffed it in his pocket. "I think you're a very smart woman despite what you've portrayed so far."

I was sensing a *but* coming.

"But I think you're as good of a liar as your father and everything you've told us up until now is bullshit. You knew Tom and Tina were having an affair and either you killed them or you had Daddy whack them for you, then burned down your townhouse to cover it up." His eyes flicked to Jamie, then Stefan, both of whom held blank masks.

Adam stepped closer. He was a short man with a balding head who didn't look at all intimidating, but according to Jamie, Adam was a badass lawyer. "That's clearly speculation, Detective. You wouldn't be using the words '*I think*' if you had any actual evidence to back those accusations."

Cameron's expression hardened and he and Adam began arguing, throwing threats and legal jargon that I didn't understand at each other.

I glanced at Detective Brooks, who had been quiet the entire time, letting Cameron take the lead. His eyes were roaming around my room as if he were absorbing every little detail. *Strange.* Sensing me staring, his gaze shot to me. I saw the small flicker of surprise in his eyes before he drew them away to give his full attention to his partner and Adam. I could tell he was straining not to look back at me and it wasn't long before he suggested that they leave. Cameron agreed and Adam and Stefan escorted them out the door.

Taking a seat next to me, Jamie cupped the back of my neck and softly pressed his lips to my forehead. "You okay?"

Dean and Asher took that as their cue to leave and they darted for the door.

I shrugged. "He's a good cop. It's annoying."

The corner of Jamie's mouth lifted. "He's a pain in the ass, but he won't find anything to pin on you."

I knew that. Even though I didn't know where or how he and Louie had gotten rid of Tom and Tina's bodies, I trusted them.

Oh, Louie.

He was avoiding me. He'd barely spoken to me while I'd been in the hospital. At first, he'd seemed to be fine with Jamie and I being back together, but his carefree smile had lost its brightness the longer he'd hung around in the hospital with us. Each time Jamie kissed me or touched me, Louie's jaw would visibly clench, or he'd look away. When he couldn't seem to stand it any longer, he'd stood abruptly from his chair and left without saying a word. I'd wanted to call out to him, stop him from leaving. Jamie had squeezed my hand, drawing my attention, and shaken his head. I hadn't seen Louie since.

Pulling me out of my thoughts, Jamie's fingers twiddled with my messy braid before giving it a gentle tug. I leaned closer and his soft lips covered mine. My nose filled with his delicious woodsy scent and I reveled in the sensation of his lips moving with mine. *What I wouldn't give to get him naked right now...* I was dying to take our kiss further, but the doctor had said I wasn't allowed to have sex until she cleared me.

"You smell so good," I said, sounding like a woman starved.

He chuckled. "I wish I could say the same."

I mocked shock and playfully smacked his arm. "Excuse me, sir, but I've been a good girl and have embraced the bedrest. Isn't that what you wanted? If you don't like my lazy look, don't let the door hit you on your tight ass."

A mischievous smile pulled at the corners of his mouth before he leaned in closer, making me lie back on my pillows. He shifted on the bed until he was hovering over me, caging me beneath him with his knees on the outside of my thighs and his hands resting on the bed by my upper arms. "I find sweats and Cheeto stains hot as fuck."

"Oh, really?"

"Really," he said before he kissed my jaw and ran his nose along my ear, coaxing a full body shiver from me. "You're so fucking sexy, I'd slide into you right now if I could," he whispered in my ear, then kissed me heatedly. My toes curled into the mattress. He was getting me pretty worked up, until he had to ruin it by pulling away. "But you know what the doc said."

I sighed frustratedly as he climbed off of me and the bed. "Fucking tease."

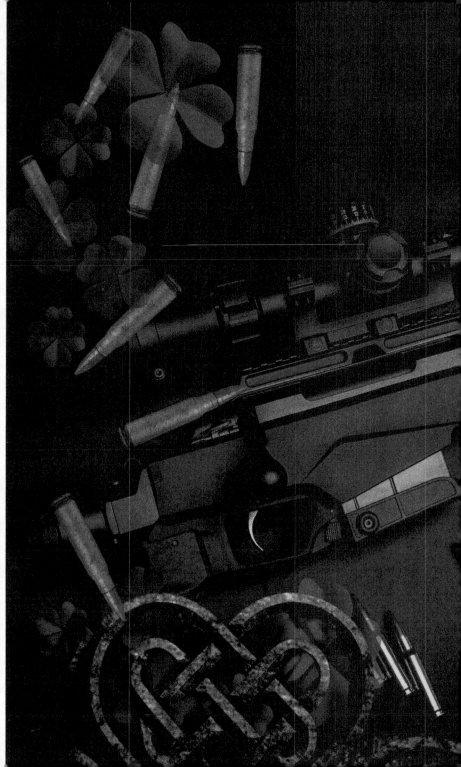

CHAPTER FOUR

It'd been four weeks since the accident and I'd reached my breaking point. The pain of boredom was worse than being shot. I was determined to escape the confines of my bedroom to attend today's family meeting. I'd heard Rourke was attending. He too had been ordered to rest up since the accident and had missed the last few meetings. Call it fear of missing out or boredom, I didn't care, but if he was going, so was I.

In order to achieve my mission, I had to find a way to occupy Dean and Asher long enough to get ready and sneak downstairs without them trying to stop me. I had yet to speak with Finnegan and Gavin, the remaining few of Samuel's inner circle I'd let live and who now answered to me. I asked Dean and Asher to go retrieve them for me. Asher was on board with the idea of getting out of the house. Dean, however, was being particularly stubborn about it. He could tell something was up, but the moment I started stripping to get in the shower, he grunted out of frustration and they both left.

I rushed to get ready after my shower by applying minimal makeup and braiding my wet hair to the side. I slipped on an emerald jersey knit dress that ended at mid-thigh and black flats.

Excitement bubbled within me as I strolled out of my bedroom. I was tempted to yell *"Freedom!'"* like Mel Gibson did in *Braveheart.*

I was feeling a lot better. Still a bit sore and I'd become a little winded by the time I made it to the stairs. The lack of exercise for the past month could explain that. Pushing on, I made sure to be careful going down the stairs.

"You should be resting, beautiful."

Busted.

I froze in my descent six steps from the bottom. Standing in the foyer with one hand in his pocket, staring up at me, was the man who I hadn't seen since I'd woken up in the hospital. I locked eyes with his beautiful sapphire blues and felt a little guilty at how my heart picked up speed.

Louie.

I couldn't stop my gaze from gliding all over him. He was in a dark blue suit with black pinstripes and a black dress shirt and shoes. Like always, he wasn't wearing a tie and his collar was left unbuttoned. He looked good. *Really good.* That thought tightened something in my chest and my hand squeezed the banister.

"You've been avoiding me," I blurted.

He looked away. "I know."

He knew? I took a step down, drawing his attention back to me. "Louie, I—"

The front door opened, interrupting what I was going to say, and in walked Dean and Asher with Finnegan trailing behind them. Dean and Asher noticed Louie first before their eyes landed on me. Both instantly turned annoyed.

"You owe me fifty bucks," Dean said to Asher. Louie took that as his moment to escape me and slipped out of the foyer.

"You should be resting," Asher said in a low chastising tone.

I ignored him and finished my way down the stairs. "Finnegan, how are you?" I greeted, stepping in front of him. He wasn't pleased to be here in the slightest and obviously didn't give a shit that he showed it either. We must have caught him at a bad time if his outfit was anything to go by. He was wearing black basketball shorts, a white T-shirt, tennis shoes, and a baseball cap on backward. He looked like he had just left the gym or was on his way to it. By the lack of smell, I assumed the latter was the case.

"Finn," he corrected, eyeing me up and down with a scowl.

"Finn," I repeated. Suppressing my urge to smile, the corner of my mouth twitched. I couldn't care less that he didn't like me. At least he wasn't regarding me with utter loathing like he'd done with Samuel and Dylan at the execution. "Where's your friend Gavin?"

"Wouldn't call him a friend," he said.

Dean leaned closer to me. "We checked his home and tried calling his cell. No answer."

Finn folded his arms over his chest. "You can't really blame him for being reluctant in coming here. You did kill his buddies in front of him."

"Actually, I can," I shot back, voice cold as ice. I'd have to deal with Gavin later. Glancing at Dean, my frustration lessened. "Family meeting is about to start. Let's not be late." Spinning on my heel, I walked out of the foyer.

Goons were already standing guard in the hall outside the chamber and they all glanced in my direction as I approached. With bigger strides than mine, Dean easily passed me to pull open the heavy, steel-reinforced door. "Were you wanting Finn to join the meeting?" he asked before I could step inside the chamber.

I looked over my shoulder at Finn, who was staring at the chamber doors with a somewhat awed expression until his eyes shifted to me and he recovered to his normal frown. I wasn't sure how the others would take to him attending the meeting. *There's only one way to find out,* I mused, and nodded.

The voices in the chamber quieted as I stepped inside and

heads turned in my direction. Stefan and Jamie's shoulders slumped as if exasperated when they saw me. Conor and Rourke were a little surprised but otherwise happy to see me. Louie was the only one who didn't seem fazed about whether I was there or not, as his expression was schooled.

"You know it's rude to stare, right? The polite thing to do is stand when a woman enters the room," I chided teasingly as I made my way across the room. Dean ushered Finn behind me quietly.

Rourke snorted. "I think you hit your head a little too hard in the accident, cuz."

I flipped him off as I approached him. He stood and we hugged. We hadn't seen each other since the hospital.

"How are you?" I asked him.

"Alive." He smiled down at me. "What about you? Stefan and Jameson look ready to lose it."

I rolled my eyes. "I'm fine," I assured him as I took a seat in my chair. I met Stefan's displeased eyes across the table. "I'm a grown woman. I know my body and all I'm doing is sitting in a damn chair. If that doesn't satisfy you, chastise me later."

"I could make you return to your room," he said with eerie calmness.

Tension silenced everyone else in the room as they looked from Stefan to me.

"You could try." A mean smile stretched my lips. "Might cause more damage than it's worth, though."

Stefan sat straighter and his expression turned cold. "You're too damn stubborn for your own good."

I huffed. "I wonder who I get that particular trait from, Daddy."

His anger seemed to instantly vanish and was replaced with shock before he quickly masked it. I gave him a questioning look at the sudden change in mood. When I got nothing from him, I glanced around the room. Everyone was staring at me like I'd grown a second head.

Conor cleared his throat. He was the only one sitting on the left side of the table, with empty seats flanking him. It was expected that Samuel's chair would be vacant, but where was Dylan? "I haven't heard her call you that since she was a wee one," Conor said to Stefan.

Oh.

Stefan had an unwaveringly blank expression, trying his best not to make my little slip a big deal. I almost laughed, wondering if this was how it was for Dean when he did something nice and I tried to be nonchalant about it. "Can we get this meeting started? Where's Dylan?"

"He betrayed the family," Stefan answered.

I bit my tongue in vexation. Yes, Dylan had made a mistake. A mistake orchestrated by Samuel's manipulation. Dylan had proved his loyalty and paid the price of watching his father's execution. If we kept punishing and alienating him...

Something in my expression must have slipped because Stefan arched a brow. "You disagree." It was a challenge. He and I were on a roll today.

"You're the Ri." It was one thing to butt heads with him regarding me but another to question his rule when it came to the family.

His eyes shifted behind me to where Dean and Finn stood. "Why is he here?"

I didn't question as to who *he* was. "Who do you think is going to help me fix the mess Samuel left behind? I can't run drugs by myself and we have a shipment coming in soon. Might as well catch us both up to speed because I don't want to track his ass down later."

Stefan continued to eye Finn. "You're Kiran O'Reilly's nephew."

I recognized the name from Finn's file that Vincent, the nineteen-year-old hacker genius with blue hair, had given me when we'd been investigating Samuel. Kiran O'Reilly was currently serving time in prison, but other than that I didn't know much else about him.

"I am," Finn replied. His voice didn't hold the usual venom. With those two words, I heard respect. *Interesting.*

Hating that he was standing behind me, I kicked out Dylan's chair and it scooted away from the table. "Take a seat, Finn."

Everyone looked at me like I'd committed some grave sin. I met their stares head on. "Untwist your panties, gentlemen. He's my guest and it's not like Dylan's using it." I glanced at Stefan. "I like to be able to look at someone when speaking with them."

"We have a code—traditions, Maura," Jamie said.

"Only your father—" Conor started but trailed off when he noticed a change in me.

My darkness surfaced. My entire body relaxed as the feral entity within me took over. I tilted my head slightly as I regarded my uncle, leveling him with a cold stare. I didn't like being questioned. There was only one person at this table I gave that right to and he had yet to say anything, which told me he wasn't going to. My eyes traveled to Jamie, then Rourke and Louie. They smartly kept their mouths shut. My gaze landed on Stefan last.

He held a proud expression. "I suggest you take that seat, O'Reilly."

Finn stepped out from behind me and slowly sat in Dylan's chair. He glanced around the table. It was obvious he was a little unsettled to be sitting there.

"Why's your uncle in prison?" I asked bluntly.

Finn glanced at everyone around the table again.

"Are you looking to them for permission or to save you from answering me?" I snapped. "I'll tell you right now, you're wasting your time and mine."

Finn glared at me. "He sacrificed his freedom to save the family," he said with a hint of pride. "Fifteen years ago, the cops ambushed a gun exchange. My uncle stayed behind to hold them off so Stefan and four others could get away. My uncle was caught and charged. The DA offered him a plea deal for shorter time served if he gave up everyone else involved. He didn't. He got sentenced with twenty years in prison and to this day, despite all the attempts they have made to get him to rat, he refuses to betray the family."

"I was among those four," Conor said sullenly.

I guess that explained why he'd looked like he'd wanted to kill Samuel and Dylan at the execution. Their betrayal had pissed all over everything Finn's uncle had sacrificed. I tapped my fingers on the table as I studied Finn. His eyes were the darkest shade of green I'd ever seen and the color of his hair reminded me of nutmeg. His lashes were enviably dark and long, and he had a tiny white scar on his chin.

Finn glared back at me. "You have a staring problem."

This time I didn't stop my smile from slowly forming.

Louie whistled. "You've got a death wish, man." Despite trying to be funny, there wasn't any of the normal lightness in his tone.

"Or maybe he doesn't realize who the fuck he's talking to," Rourke added.

"It's because I'm a woman," I told them. I hadn't known what his hang ups were at first or if they were just with me, but the more I listened to him speak and interact with everyone else, I knew. Finn glanced around the table, expecting to find support in his sexist views. It was satisfying to see him disappointed.

"I bet two hundred she turns him into ceviche within a week," Rourke said to the table.

"Him or his dick? She is *The Castrator*," Louie asked, and everyone chuckled, apart from Finn and myself.

"I'll get in on that bet, but Maura's iron-willed and gets off on torture. Three hundred he'll last at least a month before she offs him," Louie said.

Idiots.

"I bet five hundred she doesn't kill him at all."

Everyone turned to face Jamie. But he ignored them all as he stared solely at Finn. His expression was anything but kind. "Everyone at this table would've killed you along with Samuel. I would've killed you. If I see you look at her like that again, I just might."

Finn squared his shoulders in a defiant posture. "She your woman?"

Jamie didn't confirm or deny it, not that it had been secret, but his eyes narrowed sharply. "She's the Banphrionsa and next in line to take over. You will show her fucking respect."

Everyone was a little stunned. I didn't need Jamie to defend me. He had always respected that by stepping back and letting me destroy my own enemies. But I would've been lying if I'd said it wasn't nice every once in a while. Scratch that. It was sexy as hell, seeing his own dark side come out, wanting to protect me—wanting to kill for me. I could feel his desire to reach for his gun and shoot Finn right then and there.

Oh, great. I was getting turned on in the middle of a family meeting.

I cleared my throat and relaxed back into my chair, forcing my darkness down. It was a bigger hussy than I normally was. "What's going on with the Colombians?" I asked Stefan, getting the meeting back on track. "A little birdie told me they took our payment, but reluctantly."

He arched a brow. "And by birdie you mean Jameson."

I shrugged. Stefan let it go and the meeting officially started.

Once the meeting was over, almost everyone beelined for the door. It had been a long meeting. We'd gone over the shipment of drugs arriving in less than a week and how I had to come up with a plan to retrieve it and house it until I had to deliver it to De Luca. Our relationship with the Colombians was hanging on by a thread. Samuel had done something to piss them off. *Surprise, surprise.* Stefan had been able to convince them to continue doing business with us by explaining that Samuel had been *retired.* That tidbit of information had prompted them to inquire as to who they'd be working with. Stefan had been honest and said the conversation had become strange after that. The Colombians had agreed to one more shipment, but wouldn't sell any more to us until they met me in person. Stefan had agreed and invited them to the family's annual charity party held here at the house, and that was one month away.

Almost all of those who belonged to or were allies of the family were invited. It was a lot of criminals under one roof. The charity part was real and everyone had to donate to help the New England area, but it was also a way for Stefan to rub elbows and check up on the *family* that ran *business* in other cities.

I'd never been allowed to attend the party growing up. Stefan had liked to keep me hidden for my safety and kept goons stationed at the top of the stairs, preventing me from going down and anyone who might go venturing up. That didn't stop me from spying from Jamie's room. His windows had overlooked the pool and backyard where the party was always held.

"I think the party will be a good opportunity to introduce you and your new status within the family," Stefan had said.

I'd kept my expression blank. "Any way I can talk you out of that?"

Stefan frowned. "Why?"

I had more than one reason. The main one...I wasn't completely sure how I felt about being Stefan's heir. I wasn't going to tell him that, though. "People tend to act differently—honestly—when they don't know who I am. Just let me do my thing before you make any announcements."

Stefan had studied me as if not completely convinced but had relented with a, "Fine."

The topic had then switched to the Aryans. We needed to strike back at them—a task Rourke and I had fought over.

"It was my guys who were killed, Maura," Rourke had grumbled.

"And it was my guys who saved you," I'd shot back.

"Enough." Stefan had glanced back and forth between us with an admonishing expression. "You'll both work together." Rourke and I had looked at each other, seeking what the other thought. Rourke had shrugged, okay with the order.

Jamie, of course, had not been thrilled and stayed standing next to his chair when everyone went to leave. Knowing he wanted to talk to me, I stayed behind as well and told Dean to head out without me. Jamie and I waited quietly for everyone else to exit the chamber. Stefan was the last to leave and glanced at us on his way out. Just before the door closed behind him, I caught the corner of his mouth lifting.

Jamie's posture relaxed a little once the door closed. He stuffed his hands into the pockets of his slacks and said, "You didn't need to come today and you don't need to rush to get back at the Aryans. Stefan and I can handle things until you're better."

I was grateful that he was willing to shoulder my responsibilities and I loved that he worried about me. But I was over being treated like I was made of glass and he should trust me to know what I could and couldn't handle. I didn't want to fight with him and I sure as hell wasn't going to give in. Which left me one option.

I leaned forward a little and placed my hands flat on the table. Jamie had a direct view down the top of my dress. As expected, his gaze dropped from mine and heat flooded his eyes. A devious smirk pulled at my mouth. "I guess I've been a bad girl. Maybe I need to be punished."

He shook his head. "And you call me a fucking tease?"

"It's not teasing if I let you."

"Maura, you know what the doctor said—"

I pushed away from the table. "She said to listen to my body," I argued and stalked around the table, closing the distance between us. "Apart from being a little sore, I'm pretty much back to normal." I touched his forearm, reassuringly and because I needed to feel him.

He stared down at me, stubbornly still as a statue. It pissed me off. Clearly, I needed to up my game by showing him the true definition of a tease.

I yanked Rourke's chair away from the table and slipped off my shoes before sitting on top of the table next to him. I scooted back until I could bend my knees and my feet could rest on the edge of the table comfortably. The skirt of my dress bunched at my hips, flashing him my black silk panties.

Jamie watched me stoically.

I lay back on the table and lifted my hips slightly. Using my thumbs, I slowly pushed my panties off my hips, over my slightly parted thighs, and down to my ankles. I unhooked my underwear from my feet and threw them at him. They hit his chest and he quickly yanked a hand from his pocket to catch them.

I opened my legs, baring myself to him. His nostrils flared as his eyes raked over my exposed flesh. My fingers sought out my clit and did slow strokes over it. I knew it turned him on to watch.

I also knew his control was close to breaking by his hooded eyes and his quickened breaths.

"Do you want to know what I'm thinking right now?" I asked. His eyes slowly traveled up to mine. "I'm imagining it's your mouth instead of my fingers. I want you to fuck me with your tongue until I'm begging you to fuck me with your cock."

"Christ," he cursed.

The more I touched myself, the wetter I grew. I let out a wanton little whimper and he shoved my panties into his pocket. He moved quickly, lust riding him hard, and scooped me up. I was placed on my feet before I was spun around to face the table.

Standing behind me, he brought his lips to my ear. "I know what you're doing. If you want to win, you better beg for my cock." It was his ultimatum.

Grateful he couldn't see, I grinned triumphantly. "Please, Jamie. I want your cock so bad."

He pushed gently between my shoulder blades. "Lean forward and put your hands on the table." I heard the clink of his belt and the distinct sound of his zipper coming undone. He shoved the skirt of my dress over my hips. "Feet apart," he ordered. I widened my stance and sucked in a breath when I felt him align the head of his cock with my entrance. He drove into me slowly. My head fell forward, groaning loudly. It felt so good, him stretching me —filling me.

Once fully sheathed, he bumped my cervix, making me moan his name.

His fingers curled around my braid while his other hand grabbed my hip. He tugged lightly on my hair, forcing my head back. "You know what it does to me when you say my name like that." His words came out coarse and rumbly. He pulled out of me only to shove back in slowly. "I want to be rough with you," he growled, continuing his languid pace of in and out. It was driving me insane.

Seeking more, I rocked back against him, slamming down on his hard rod. He released my hair and held me firmly by my hips, preventing me from amping things up. "I won't break. Stop holding back," I snapped, beyond sexually frustrated.

He chuckled, then pulled out all the way and rammed back into me. My whole body quivered. He didn't hold back after that. He pistoned his hips at a delicious speed. It had been so long and he had me so worked up that I was already feeling that addictive pressure. The more it built the more intense the pressure was and the louder I got. I knew he was close to meeting his release as well when his hands tightened on my hips and he grunted behind me. We came together and my screams filled the chamber. That happened to be the same moment the door opened.

My head whipped in that direction and my eyes locked with sapphire blues. Jamie and I seemed to tense up at the same time. Frozen in place, both panting, we stared at Louie.

His eyes roamed over us but mostly my bent-over body with what seemed like longing. Then he blinked and closed himself off with the clench of his jaw. He looked at Jamie. "A word, when you're finished," he said tightly and stepped out of the room, closing the door harshly behind him.

Jamie slid out of me and fixed my dress before working on fastening his pants. I didn't move, staring down at the table, trapped in my thoughts. I couldn't get Louie's expression out of my head or how it tore me up on the inside. *What the hell is wrong with me?*

Jamie placed his hand on my back and rubbed in a soothing motion. "You okay?"

I forced a small smile before turning to face him. "Yes."

His eyes narrowed slightly. I was positive I wasn't revealing what I was truly thinking or feeling. After what seemed like forever, because I'd unintentionally been holding my breath, he gave me a small smile of his own and leaned down to kiss me.

47

CHAPTER FIVE

J amie and I left the chamber and found Dean, Asher, and Finn waiting in the hall. All it took was one look and it was obvious they knew what Jamie and I had been up to. Asher did nothing to hide his shit-eating grin while Dean's grumpy demeanor wavered. Finn still held the exterior of an asshole, but his eyes showed he was amused.

Jamie kissed my temple. "I'll see you tonight," he said and left to go find Louie.

I locked eyes with Finn. "I'm putting you in charge of the shipment we have coming in less than a week. It will be your responsibility to retrieve it and watch over it until the time comes to do the exchange with De Luca."

Finn's brows shot up. "Really? Why would—"

"I don't care that you don't like me," I interrupted. "You say you're loyal to this family. Stefan, Jamie—all those *men* sitting in that meeting—don't believe you. I, however, want to. So I'm giving you this opportunity to prove yourself. Don't let your personal setbacks ruin it. Because if you do, you'd be no different than Samuel and look where he ended up."

Finn's jaw visibly clenched at the clear threat behind my

words. When he eventually nodded, I knew I'd gotten through to him. "I'll take care of it, but I can't do it on my own. I'm going to need Gavin, if you decide to not kill him, but even that still won't be enough. I need a team because you *retired* my last one."

I arched a brow at him.

He quickly raised his hands in front of him. "Not saying they didn't have it coming, but we still have the problem of being short handed. I'm going to need a show of power at the docks when I pick up the shipment. We have an arrangement with our couriers, but they can be shady fuckers. With Samuel gone and Dylan on house arrest, I wouldn't put it past them to try and squeeze more money out of us. Then we got to guard the shit and I can't watch it by myself twenty-four-seven."

"Okay," I said, pleased he was taking this seriously. "I suggest you talk to Gavin and have him get his ass here by the end of today to fucking grovel. As for a new team, talk to Louie. Where are you going to house it?"

"McLoughlin's," he answered and smiled when I let my curiosity show. I knew the pub was one of many fronts we had, but I didn't think we actually hid it there. "It used to be a speakeasy during Prohibition. There's a tunnel that runs from McLoughlin's to a secret cellar underneath the building next door. Back in the day the family used to hide all the booze down there. Now, we hide drugs."

I smiled, slightly impressed. "I want to be updated every step of the way." He gave me a curt nod. "Louie should be somewhere around here."

Finn went to leave but something that he'd said made me stop him. "Why did you say Dylan's on house arrest?"

Finn eyed me as if searching for something. When he found whatever it was, he said, "You didn't know?"

What the fuck?

I walked away. Dean and Asher rushed to catch up to me as I

stormed through the house toward Stefan's study. The door was closed, but I didn't let that stop me. I shoved it open and walked in on Stefan and Brody standing close behind his desk. Brody appeared to be straightening Stefan's tie. I pretended not to see Stefan's hand dropping from the small of Brody's back. I turned around to face my goons still standing in the hall. "I'll be out in a bit," I said and shut the door.

I turned to face *my parents*. At this point, they had put some space between them. Stefan was pulling out his desk chair to take a seat while Brody went to scoop up what looked like a leather planner from where it was sitting on the other end of the desk. He was fighting not to smile and failing. He knew I already knew about his relationship with Stefan. I could see how this whole situation was amusing and I would've been fighting back my own smile at catching them if I weren't so pissed. "Why is Dylan on house arrest?"

Stefan locked eyes with me. "You know why."

I let out a heavy breath in order to keep calm. "We punished him by killing Samuel. He proved his loyalty by being willing to kill Samuel himself. You can't keep punishing him. Instead, we should be giving him an opportunity to redeem himself."

Stefan's body went still, his demeanor closed off yet ominous. I was now speaking to the boss and he was pissed. "I am the head of this family. Not you."

"Pride should never come before family," I snarled, which pissed him off more. "You're taking the pain of your brother's betrayal out on Dylan. Yes, Dylan had played a part in that betrayal, but Samuel was a manipulative bastard."

My father's usual unreadable expression melted away to reveal a scowl. "He knew what he was doing. I don't know why you're fighting so hard for him."

"Because if our roles were reversed, I don't know if I would have done anything differently than Dylan. I like to think that I would have told you, 'No, it's wrong to go behind the boss's back.' But knowing you, the master manipulator, you would have prepared for that. You would have told me all the right things to get me to do what you wanted. And I'm not going to lie, selling to Nicoli was a smart move."

"What about pocketing the money?"

"I would've been against it. There are more important things in life than money and I strongly believe forgiveness should never be bought, not that Samuel really intended to use the money for that."

"Says the girl with two million dollars in a duffel bag tucked under her bed," Stefan drawled. After I'd been released from the hospital, Dylan had shown Jamie where he and Samuel had been storing the money at the warehouse on Stone Street. Stefan had come to my room that evening with the duffel in hand and said it was my bonus for getting the money back before tossing it on the foot of my bed. Thankfully, he'd missed my feet, because two million dollars wasn't light. I hadn't been really capable of going to the bank at the time, so I'd had to settle with stuffing the heavy sucker under my bed.

I waved flippantly at his comment. "My point is that you can't fault Dylan for trusting his father. Especially when Samuel was just as manipulative as you." Stefan opened his mouth to argue but I spoke before him. "You've taught me how to spot it and how to counter it. Can you say that Samuel did the same with Dylan?" I shook my head. "Samuel would've never given Dylan the power to outsmart him."

Stefan let out a frustrated sigh and leaned back in his chair. I glanced at Brody, who had been quiet the entire time. He was staring at Stefan with a sad expression and by the way he leaned slightly in his direction, it seemed like he wanted nothing more than to comfort Stefan.

"You said Dylan is my responsibility. That's why I'm fighting you on this. If you keep pushing him away when he needs us the most, he will learn to hate us and blame us for all the bad that is happening in his life right now."

Stefan wouldn't look at me as he sat there brooding and it squelched the last of the patience I had left. I stalked behind his desk where he was sitting. I angrily started pulling drawers open until I found a Glock I knew he had hidden there. I took it out, cocked it, and laid it on the desk in front of him. "You said you'd kill me if Dylan fucks up. Well, might as well get it over with now because you're setting me up to fail."

Stefan looked up from the gun to stare at me. I met his eyes defiantly, challenging him.

Out of my peripheral, I noticed Brody take a hesitant step forward. "Maura," he said shakily. It broke the stare off that Stefan and I were in.

Stefan scooped up the gun and put it back inside the drawer. He calmly pushed it closed. "Get out." He refused to look at me, but I knew he wasn't talking to Brody. So I left.

Later on that evening, I decided to soak in the bath with a very large glass of wine. Lounging back, I was lost in my thoughts, staring at a cluster of bubbles on my knee. I didn't like fighting with Stefan. I'd told myself I wasn't going to question him about Dylan because he was the boss and it was his right to deal with him as he saw fit. And yet, I'd done it anyway.

Why do I care what happens to Dylan so much? It's not like he ever stuck his neck out for me growing up.

I sighed. Because we were family and most of all, I could see myself when I looked at him. A child of the mob. I wouldn't say the grass was greener with how he was raised. We were both dealt shitty hands. Samuel raised him to be entitled because he was male. Stefan raised me to be smart because I was female.

None of us were good people, but we were still a family. If we lost sight of what was important, then what was the point of the drugs, guns, and any other shit we were fucking risking our lives doing? Was it greed? If so, then we were no better than Samuel.

"You and Stefan are fighting?"

Jamie's voice broke my trance and I found him standing next to the tub, staring down at me. I hadn't even noticed him enter the bathroom, let alone approach me.

"What gave you that impression?" I asked as I reached for my wine from the shelf next to the tub.

He watched as I brought the glass to my lips. "You both were absent at dinner."

"I'm sorry you ate alone."

"Louie was there." He frowned. "You're deflecting and drinking when the doctor specifically told you not to while taking the meds she prescribed."

"It's wine. It doesn't count," I grumbled and took two big gulps, afraid he'd take it away.

He smiled, well aware of what I was doing, but thankfully made no move to take my glass. "Do you want to talk about it?"

I shook my head. "I wouldn't mind a distraction. Care to join me?"

His eyes moved down the length of the tub, taking in the parts of my body that weren't covered by bubbles. "I'm not really a bubble bath man. It's cramped and sounds dangerous for someone still not fully healed. I'm more of a bed man. There, I can give my girl safe but multiple distractions." He gave me a panty melting—if I were wearing any—smirk before leaving the bathroom.

I almost yelled that he'd been a table man this afternoon, but the fact he'd called me *his girl* left me stunned. I shook my head to clear it and climbed out of the tub quickly because I was pretty sure I'd been promised multiple orgasms.

Wrapping a towel around myself, I leaned against the bathroom door frame and watched Jamie as he slipped out of his dress shirt. His back was to me, which allowed me to ogle the muscles rippling under his tattooed skin. He unfastened his slacks and slid them off, revealing black boxer briefs that molded to him like a second skin. He turned a little to toss his pants on the dresser and a little smile slowly tugged at his mouth, telling me he'd finally noticed me.

"I think you've both fixed and broken me," I said and grimaced, internally kicking myself for saying anything.

He faced me with a slightly puzzled look. "Meaning?"

"I never cared for sex before you," I mumbled honestly and crossed my arms over my chest.

"You mean with Tom?"

I nodded. "Sometimes it could be fun, after I got past my setbacks and if Tom was patient enough to wait for me to get past them. The majority of the time, sex felt like a chore or an obligation. I'd lay there, internally freaking out, doing everything I could to not let it show and if it did, he'd usually pretend not to notice and continue on until he got off."

Jamie's face relaxed, showing nothing as to what he was feeling. "Do you force yourself—"

"No," I cut him off, shaking my head. "With you, I feel a sense of comfort. Maybe it's because I've always loved you or because you feel like my other half, especially when we were kids. Like it had been you and me versus everyone in this house, the family, the world. I know you'll always be there for me, no matter how low or damaged I become. It's a level of trust that when I'm with you, everything else fades away and all that's left is you and me."

His blank mask faded to show his relief. "You're not damaged, Maura. I know you don't believe me, but to me...you're perfect."

I was touched by his words, but he was right. Doubt and inse-curities were powerful emotions. Hopefully, one day I'd be stronger than them.

Jamie slowly made his way closer. "How did I fix *and* break you?"

His hands grasped my hips. I uncrossed my arms and hooked them around his neck, molding my front to his. "Well, thanks to you, I really like sex now, but also want to jump on you every time I look at you."

He chuckled. "Then you must have broken me, too." He ripped off my towel and I let out a gasp, then smiled up at him. He dropped it to the floor and ran his hands down my spine. My skin broke out in goosebumps and my whole body shivered from his sensual touch. His warm hands smoothed over my bare ass and gave it a good squeeze. Those frisky hands moved just under my butt to lift me and I locked my legs around his waist. "Having you clenched around my cock and screaming out my name is the closest thing to heaven I'll ever know. You're an addiction I never want to kick." His lips captured mine in a devouring kiss.

He walked us over to the bed and laid me down gently in the center. Bracing himself over me, he broke our kiss and his hazel eyes bored into mine. He let his love for me show in them and it made my heart rate pick up speed. "I'd choose you. I know I said I wouldn't, but if you ever ask, I don't think I could stop myself from choosing you."

He was talking about choosing me over Stefan. "I'll never ask you to choose."

"I know," he said and brushed a strand of wet hair away from my face. "I love you. So much so, I'd do anything for you."

I nodded because there was a chance I'd cry if I spoke. His lips returned to mine in a toe-curling kiss before moving down my neck. He pressed his mouth over my heart and nuzzled my breasts with the little bit of scruff on his face. Scooting down my body, he settled himself between my legs. His strong hands pushed my legs open wide before his head delved. I hissed as his tongue rolled over my clit and I tried to squeeze my legs shut when he sucked it between his teeth. My legs didn't move an inch. He wouldn't let them, and his eyes met mine in warning. I read it loud and clear. If I wanted to come, I better keep my legs open.

As he continued to worship me with his mouth, one of his hands glided down my inner thigh and his finger dipped into my wet core, pushing inside of me. Pumping it in and out a few times, coating it in my essence, he pulled it out and trailed his finger down.

I sucked in a breath and I felt his lips curling into a smile. He lifted his head and met my eyes. "Relax. Trust me," he whispered and returned his mouth to my clit. The flicking of his tongue intensified as he rubbed at my back entrance. It made me delirious, but in a good way. Then he pushed past the ring and stroked in and out.

My orgasm shot off like a firecracker, surprising me. His wandering finger in no man's land fucking got me off so fast and so hard there was no time to brace myself. No, *I'm coming. I'm coming.* Nope. I just *fucking came*! I might have even blacked out for a second.

Jamie chuckled as he watched me come undone. "That's one."

Oh, boy.

CHAPTER SIX

S tefan went to Boston *for business* the next day and would be gone for a few days. I must have really pissed him off because he left without telling me. He always told me if he was going to be gone for more than a day. This time I had to hear it from Jamie. I knew I wasn't a little girl anymore but still...it upset me. After my goons left for the day and Jamie was away doing mob shit, I might have had a little too much wine and thought it would be a good idea to text Stefan.

> I don't care how mad you are. I am still your daughter and you left without saying anything to me.

Stefan didn't respond. An hour and two bottles of wine later, I picked up my phone again.

> #Worstfatheroftheyearaward
>
> I'm mad at you took!
>
> I meant too!
>
> U boke our dear!

*Deal

U promis ed

Farter first boss second

I burst into a fit of giggles after rereading that last text I sent. *Oops.*

Then my phone rang and it was Stefan. In a panic, I sent him to voicemail.

I don't want to talk u I madder at you!

I texted quickly.

I don't want tot ear ur excuses

Ur a man liputator

U don't lobe me

Nver have

Wha I have to do?

U make e sad

I almost jumped out of my skin when there was a knock on my door. I got up and teetered a little, really feeling the effects of the wine. Using the arm of the couch, I righted myself and continued on toward the door. Josh, one of my father's goons, who monitored the control room, was standing out in the hall with a phone pressed to his ear.

He held the phone out to me. "The boss wants to speak to you."

I glared at the phone. "I don't want to talk to him."

Josh got a panicked look on his face.

"Better yet, tell him I hope the maid forgot to change the sheets in his hotel room and the previous guest had dirty, sweaty sex on them. Enjoy your trip, Stefan!" I slurred loudly, confident he'd heard me, and slammed my door closed. Despite being drunk, deep down I knew I was probably making an ass of myself. I just didn't care. It could have been the alcohol giving me the courage or it could have been that I didn't want to hold back when it came to Stefan anymore. Yes, he was the boss. He could be that to everyone else. Not me. Fuck how things were done. It was time for change. He was my father and would only be my father.

I made my way back over to my phone, debating going off on Stefan again, but saw that it was about to die and went to go plug it in by my nightstand instead. My bedroom door burst open, startling me. In walked Josh and two other goons whose names I didn't know.

"I'm sorry, ma'am. I've been ordered to confiscate any alcohol in your room and to make sure you go to bed," Josh said.

Alrighty then. If that's how it's going to be, fine. I reached under my pillow and grabbed the Glock that I had hidden there. I turned back to the goons and cocked it. The two goons I didn't know were already standing by my coffee table, getting ready to take my wine, and they froze. My eyes traveled between them with an arched brow. The three of them exchanged nervous glances.

Josh put his hands up. "Ma'am?"

"Would you like to hear a story?" I asked and didn't wait for a response. "Three goons barged into the Banphrionsa's room late at night. Little did the three goons know, the Banphrionsa was just as ruthless as her father and enjoyed killing a little too much. Let's be honest, killing can be a fucking high, especially when she gets to kill someone who's wronged her. Now, let me set the scene. There's three against one. How many can she shoot before one of them can pull his weapon to stop her from killing them all? My bet is on two. She's an excellent shot, but I doubt she's fast enough to take out all three of you. Plus, she's had quite a bit to drink tonight. So one of you will live. Well, until the boss finds out what happened. Because, no matter how upset he is with her and she with him, he will fucking kill anyone who hurts his Banphrionsa. Do you know the point of this entire story, gentleman?"

"We have orders," Josh repeated, in a pleading tone.

"Wrong. It's that parents and their kids don't always agree, and you just fucked yourselves by getting in the middle."

"Then what are we supposed to do?" one of them asked.

"Get the fuck out," I practically growled at the same time that Jamie walked through the door.

He scanned the room, lingering on the gun in my hands. His expression hardened and he turned a murderous glare on the goons. All three of them got matching panicked looks on their faces.

"Sir, she's had a lot to drink tonight and the boss is worried because she is still on medication from her accident. He asked us to confiscate any alcohol and help her get to bed," Josh explained quickly.

Jamie's glare lessened a little and he looked at me.

I shrugged. "I may have raged at Stefan through text and refused to answer when he called. Of course, he tried to show his power by sending his goons in here. If the bastard thinks I'm just going to be ordered about by his lackeys, he's fucking mistaken."

"Do you think you can get her to put away the gun so we can do our jobs?" Josh asked Jamie.

Jamie snorted and folded his arms over his chest. "Who did you plan to shoot first?" The question was clearly meant for me.

"Josh appears to be the leader. Sometimes when the leader is taken out, the followers hesitate from surprise. That'd give me time to take out the other two," I answered honestly.

Josh looked from me to Jamie. "Sir?"

Jamie ignored him. "So is that the plan? You're just going to kill them?"

"I was kind of hoping I didn't have to," I said.

"The boss gave us orders. You expect us not to follow them?" Josh snapped.

"I know you want to impress the boss, but in this situation take the road where you keep your life," Jamie said. "He won't fault you because the last thing he'd want is for his daughter to get hurt. They may be fighting, but think about it? He sent you in here because he's worried about her. She, of course, took that as him trying to control her and pulled a gun. They're too much alike. Dominant, stubborn, and proud, with mean Irish tempers. When they butt heads, it's best to just steer clear and let them hash it out. They always do."

Josh looked to the other goons, then nodded. "Let's go."

They filed out of the room, closing the door behind them. Jamie watched me slide my gun back under my pillow. "He's right to worry, you know. You're not supposed to be drinking."

I let out a heavy sigh.

"Don't get pissy with me," he snapped, stalking toward me. "I love you. That means when you do stupid shit that could get you hurt, I get to call you out on it." His hands cupped my face. "I'm not trying to control you. You're it for me. My everything. I don't care if you want to walk beside me in this life or take the lead, as long as you're with me, that's all that matters."

I nodded. "I'm sorry. I know it's no excuse, but I let my frustration with Stefan get the best of me."

"You're forgiven." He kissed my forehead. "Now, get your lush ass to bed," he ordered as he swatted said ass.

I yelped and flipped him off.

A few days later I felt strong enough to go for a walk around the property. I was still a little sore, but the meds I was on helped with that. I made a promise with Jamie that I wouldn't drink a drop of alcohol until I was off them. I had about another week left of pain meds and just a few more days of antibiotics. My doctor had noticed one of my incisions had become red and hot to the touch and put me on another round of antibiotics. I couldn't wait to be past all of this and feeling one hundred percent again.

"You doing alright?" Dean asked me for the third time as he and Asher walked with me. We were halfway through our second time walking the property line.

"Yeah."

"Stefan's coming back tonight?" Asher asked.

"Probably already home," I mumbled as I avoided looking at the house. The night of drunk texting my father was not one of my finest moments. I'd bared a lot of vulnerability and I still wasn't sure if Stefan would use it against me. At the same time, I knew our relationship wouldn't improve if one of us didn't let their guard down. It was up to Stefan now, where we went from here.

"Maura," Dean said, drawing my attention. He nodded toward the house. I gazed in that direction, and standing by the pool was Stefan. Changing course, I cut through the grass field that made up most of our backyard, toward where Stefan was. He waited patiently, wearing an unreadable expression.

Crossing my arms over my chest, I stopped with a few feet between us. Dean and Asher continued walking, with the intention of giving us privacy, but they didn't get far before Stefan spoke.

"We're having guests over for dinner tonight. Make sure

you're there." His words were curt and his tone was distant. Then, he walked away, not giving me a chance to respond.

My nails dug into my skin as I tightened my crossed arms. Biting my cheek, I turned away from the house, giving my back to Dean and Asher. I couldn't hide what I was feeling, and I wasn't entirely sure I could hold back from crying.

I supposed Stefan had given his answer. He really knew how to make someone feel like they were nothing more than an obligation. I didn't know why I'd tried so hard. I couldn't make someone love me.

A hand landed on my shoulder and squeezed. I badly wanted to accept the comfort Dean or Asher was offering, but there were eyes everywhere. I took a deep breath, burying my hurt, and plastered a smile on my face before turning around. Dean dropped his hand, eyes gliding over my face. His gaze lingered on my forced smile and his expression hardened into a frown. Asher stood next to him, staring at me as well.

"Let's head inside," I said, walking away toward the house.

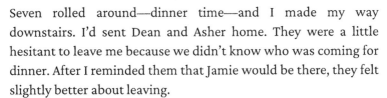

Seven rolled around—dinner time—and I made my way downstairs. I'd sent Dean and Asher home. They were a little hesitant to leave me because we didn't know who was coming for dinner. After I reminded them that Jamie would be there, they felt slightly better about leaving.

A lot of voices carried out of the dining room and my steps faltered when I walked inside. The table was full. Stefan and Jamie were present, of course. Louie was there too, in his spot next to Jamie. Aunt Kiara was sitting across the table from Stefan with Conor sitting to her left and Rourke next to him. What shocked me was that Dylan was seated next to Louie, with his mother, Aoife, sitting to his left, and his younger sister, Brenna, sitting across from him.

I looked at Stefan and found him watching me. He stood from the table, drawing everyone's attention, and the talking lowered as they watched him walk over to me.

I stared at him, desperately trying to read his blank expression.

"Family before pride," he said low enough that no one else could hear, then leaned forward to kiss the top of my head.

He listened.

I cleared my throat to rein in my emotions. "Thank you."

Stefan and I took our seats at the table. I sat across from Jamie and gave him a small smile before my attention drifted to Louie. He was already staring at me, but quickly looked away. My smile slipped before I could mask my expression. My eyes flicked back to Jamie and my stomach sank. His brows were furrowed as he studied me, then his gaze moved to Louie. They exchanged a look I couldn't decipher.

I forced myself to look away from them to glance around the rest of the table. Aunt Aoife, which was a traditional Irish name pronounced *ee-fa,* appeared to be completely zoned out and I had a feeling she had taken something. Brenna, who was seventeen, was quiet while she listened to Rourke discussing something with Dylan and Conor. It wasn't unusual. She had always been shy. Dylan actually appeared to be trying to engage with others, which I was going to take as a good sign, but I could see sadness around his eyes.

"Maura, how are you feeling, sweetie?" Aunt Kiara asked, drawing my attention.

"I'm better, Auntie. If it wasn't for Rourke, I don't know if I'd be here," I said.

Kiara smiled and patted Rourke's hand affectionately. "He did us proud by protecting the family's heir."

The entire table went quiet.

"Kiara!" Conor barked before putting his face in his palm.

"What?" she asked, looking from her husband to Stefan.

"We haven't announced it yet," he told her.

It was that moment Aoife joined reality. "You made her your heir?" she gaped at Stefan. "She's a woman! She can't—"

Dylan grabbed her wrist so harshly his knuckles turned white and she winced. "Mother, don't," he said, quieting her instantly, and she returned to her zoned out state. Dylan locked eyes with me. "What my mother meant to say is congratulations, cousin."

I didn't respond. Instead, I looked to Brenna. Her head was downcast, her eyes wide and full of panic as she stared at her lap.

The door leading to the kitchen opened and Jeana, our personal chef, and one of the new house staff who Brody had hired walked in carrying our food. The best part about the two new house staff was that one was a middle-aged woman named Ronda and the other was her son, Noah, who was around my age. Noah was working tonight with Jeana.

Dylan eyed Noah as he set a plate down in front of him. "What happened to the hot blonde?" Dylan asked Jamie.

I answered for him. "Stefan wisely fired her when she touched something that didn't belong to her."

Dylan's brows rose. "Pity." Then he looked to Louie. "You hit that, right? Was she any good?"

Of course, that made me look at Louie. He glanced at me briefly before peering down at his plate. "Uh, barely memorable. Anyone catch the game last night?"

Dylan didn't pick up on Louie's attempt to change the subject or he didn't care. "What about you, Jameson? You go there?"

Jamie looked to me like Louie had. "No. Not my type."

"And what is your type, exactly?" I asked, taking over the conversation.

Jamie smirked at me. "Beautiful, crazy, red hair, and isn't afraid to get bloody."

I smiled like a loon.

Brenna let out a little giggle next to me and put her hand on my arm. "Are you two finally together?" she asked in a low voice. She didn't look anything like her brother, with her Quinn green eyes and beautiful long blonde hair that she'd inherited from her mother.

I nodded. "How are you doing, Brenna?" I asked just as low, wanting to keep our conversation between just us.

She took a bite of food and shrugged. She thought that filling her mouth would be a good enough excuse not to answer and was hoping I'd let it go. I wouldn't. I'd just go about it in a different way.

I took a bite of my dinner as well and caught her relaxing a little, as if relieved. "How's school? It's your senior year?"

She began poking at her food with her fork. "Yeah. It's good."

"Have you thought about college?" I pushed.

"Like I'll ever get to go." She grimaced right after the words left her mouth and her eyes went wide. Looking panicked, she peeked at Dylan and her mother. Dylan was busy talking to Louie, but her mother was giving her an evil scowl that held some sort of warning. Brenna's eyes dropped to her plate. I watched her as she tugged at her sleeve until it was practically pulled down to her fingers. She went back to pushing around her food while she chewed on her lip.

I couldn't take my eyes off her sleeve as a ball of anxiety grew in the pit of my stomach. I knew what I was seeing. I recognized all the signs. I just desperately didn't want it to be true. Light caught on her lone silver ring. It was a simple band with the infinity symbol etched into the metal.

"That's a pretty ring," I said and held my hand out for hers.

She set down her fork and placed her hand in mine. I pulled

her hand closer, but not to my face. I guided her hand between us off and below the table so no one could see. Before she realized what I was doing, I tightened my hold and yanked up her sleeve to her elbow.

Bruises covered her fair skin.

Brenna quickly yanked her sleeve back down and glanced at her brother and mother to see if they'd seen. It didn't appear that they had, but I still refused to let her go.

"Did he do this to you or was it both of them?" I demanded in a whisper. Two times she looked to Dylan first, a clear indication of who she was afraid of more.

She tried to yank her arm away again, but she couldn't put a lot of strength behind it or we'd be noticed. "No one did this to me. I did it. I was sad about my father." Her words came out almost as if they were practiced.

"I can protect you," I said, still making sure no one heard me.

"Maura, please. You're going to make it worse," she pleaded.

I let her go.

I couldn't stop myself from staring across the table at Dylan and Aoife. Both were none the wiser as Dylan continued to talk with everyone and Aoife was back in fucking La La Land. My heart was racing, my anger was overwhelming, and I had to grind my teeth to keep myself from screaming.

A hand grasped my wrist. I glanced down at it and saw that I had a steak knife, held tightly in my fist. I didn't remember grabbing it from where it had been lying on the table next to my plate.

"Maura," Stefan said in a low voice. My gaze traveled up to meet his. "Let go of the knife," he ordered and went to take it with his other hand.

I found it hard to loosen my fist. I unraveled my fingers one at a time, until he was able to pull the knife away. My fingers were sore from the strain and my palm stung. I turned my hand face up, finding small cuts from my nails.

"Maura," Stefan said, but I didn't meet his gaze.

I was too ashamed.

I stood from my chair.

"You okay, baby?" Jamie asked.

I nodded. "I'm going to get some juice," I lied, needing to get out of there.

"I can get it for you, Miss Maura," Noah said. I hadn't realized he was still in the room. All I could do was pretend I hadn't heard him and dart into the kitchen.

Jeana was putting tinfoil over leftovers to keep the food warm. She asked if I needed anything as I walked by. I pointed at the pantry. I didn't have a plan and wasn't in the right state of mind to think about the best way to be alone.

Inside the pantry, I let out a ragged breath and hugged myself. *Did I do this?*

My chest felt heavy with guilt. My eyes caught on the many bottles of whiskey on the shelf and temptation gnawed at me. Remembering my promise to Jamie, I smothered the temptation and that frustrated me more.

My breathing started to pick up and my heart was pounding. I was angry. I was sad. I was riddled with guilt.

I should have stood up to Stefan sooner.

Or killed Dylan when I had the chance.

The pantry door opened behind me and I froze. "I just need a moment and I'll be right out," I said weakly without looking to see who it was.

A hand touched my upper arm. "Maura?"

It was Stefan.

Still with my back to him, I stepped out of his reach. "Can you give me a moment?"

"I'm not going anywhere," he said.

I shook my head in frustration. "I fucked up." My voice broke. "I let him live and now he's hurting her and possibly Aoife as well." Tears filled my eyes and I sucked in a wobbly breath. "I don't know how to fix this. I wanted to save him. I still want to save him, yet at the same time, I want to gut him. I promised myself I wouldn't tolerate this shit. I'd do everything I could to stop it. I never thought I'd be the cause of it." My lungs felt like they were constricting, making it hard to breathe. My tears fell rapidly as I fought to get air.

Stefan put his hands on my shoulders. "Maura, look at me," he ordered as he spun me around.

"I'm not as strong as you," I said raggedly, between gasps. I was fighting to keep it together and failing. "I just need a moment," I begged, hoping he wouldn't hold it against me.

He took in my tears with a frown, but his eyes looked torn, as if he were debating with himself. "You're allowed to have as many moments as you need," he finally said and pulled me close. His arms enveloped me in a tight hug. I caved, desperate for his comfort, and I buried my face in his shoulder. His hand began stroking the back of my hair. "I know you're strong. I have no ulterior motive. Stop holding yourself back and let go."

His words cut at my weak restraints. The tightness around my lungs let up, and I sobbed. My whole body shook as I wailed into his shoulder. Doubts, anger, and years of pent up desperation for his love came to the surface. "How can I be your heir if the decisions I make get others hurt?"

"Don't blame yourself for the faults of others. Dylan's actions are his own. As a leader, we have to make tough decisions. Fear of the worst hinders our ability to show compassion and know when to grant second chances. Don't let that fear seep in."

"What do I do about Dylan?" I asked.

Stefan's body tensed. "There's not much you can do."

I stepped out of his embrace. "What?"

"What are you going to do? Kill him? Forbid him from seeing Brenna and his mother?" He arched a brow. "If you choose either of those, the family is going to want to know why. It's no secret how women are treated. We've never tried to stop it. Hell, your grandfather encouraged it. Who's to say the majority of the family won't turn on you for taking away their right—their power. It could end with them banding together to come after us and put someone else in power, or they'll defect, leaving us vulnerable to other crime families. Do you have a plan to handle those ramifications?"

"I can't do nothing."

He sighed. "I know. You need to think of a plan. Prepare for multiple outcomes. You know how to play the game and with this, you'll need to play it better than everyone else."

"What about Brenna? She's just a kid."

"Did she ask for help?"

I shook my head. "She doesn't believe I can help her."

"Then you need to find a way to prove that you can, but until then..."

There's nothing we can do for her. I hated this. I wished I could just go in there and whisk her away. Then beat the shit out of Dylan. But I couldn't force Brenna to do something she didn't want to do. And what if I did make things worse for her?

I wiped at my face, feeling equally embarrassed and annoyed.

"I'll tell everyone you weren't feeling well. Make sure you eat something later," he ordered.

I nodded, relieved I didn't have to return to the dining room, and we both exited the pantry. Thankfully, Jeana and Noah weren't in the kitchen, because the pantry door hadn't been entirely closed. Jamie, however, was leaning against the wall right outside, with his arms crossed over his chest.

Stefan continued on to the dining room, leaving us alone.

Jamie pushed off the wall. His hands cupped my cheeks, making me look up at him. "I could hear you crying, and I thought

I might have to kill someone." Dropping his hands from my face, he hugged me tightly. "You know you can lean on me, right?"

"I know. I think it was best that Stefan talked to me. Things have been really tense between us and I really needed him to show me he could just be my father."

Jamie's hand rubbed up and down my back, soothingly. "Are you okay?"

"I will be. As soon as I figure some things out."

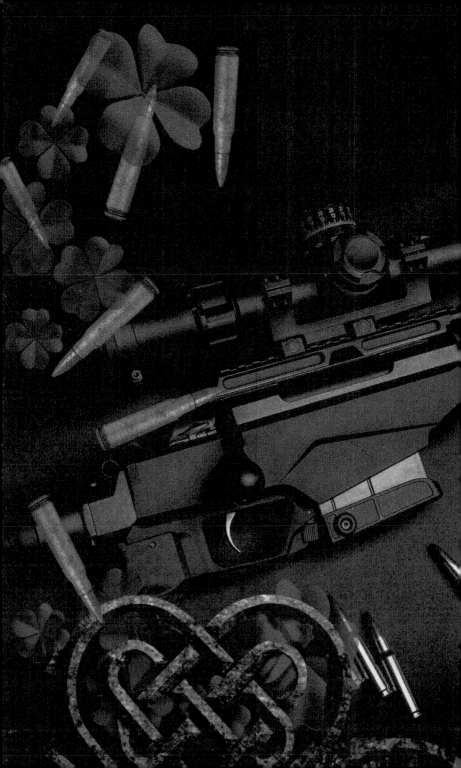

CHAPTER SEVEN

O ur shipment from Colombia was here before I knew it. Gavin had never stopped by the house to speak with me. Finn didn't have any luck tracking him down. He eventually went by Gavin's house. There was no answer. For whatever reason, Finn felt the need to break in. Good thing that he did because Gavin's place was trashed, as if a fight had broken out. He said there was blood splattered on the living room floor. I called Jamie and he went over there right away. He and Finn spoke with Gavin's neighbors and landlord. None of them had seen or heard anything.

I told Stefan. He listened quietly, sitting behind his desk, as I explained everything.

"What do you think we should do?" he asked.

I thought about it for a second. "I'd call on Vincent to work his magic and have Jamie look into any leads he comes up with."

Stefan smirked. "Vincent is good at the finding part. Jamie is very good at either killing or capturing who we're looking for. Good plan. It's what I'd do."

That was a few days ago and we still hadn't been able to find Gavin. According to Vincent, Gavin's last digital footprint was from two weeks ago when he had bought beer and cigarettes from a convenience store close to his house. After that, nothing.

I was currently on my way to McLoughlin's to meet Finn. He, with the help of Louie and a few other goons, had picked up our shipment and were transporting it to the pub.

"I kind of miss my sweatpants," I mumbled, staring out the window at the cars driving next to us. I was alone in the backseat of the Escalade. Asher was driving while Dean rode in the passenger's seat. We were all armed, with a few spare rifles in the trunk space. Driving through the city would never be the same.

"Are you in pain?" Dean asked.

"She took her pain meds before we left. They should've kicked in by now," Asher added.

"No pain. This pant suit is confining," I said. Over the past month, Stefan had been filling my closet to the brim with more new suits. Now that I was part of the business, I needed to represent. The only upside was the suits came with new shoes. I'd chosen to wear orange satin Manolo Blahnik pumps with my black suit. I kept admiring them because, well...*my name is Maura Quinn and I'm a shoe whore.*

Dean turned in his seat and caught me staring. "Those ugly shoes wouldn't look good with sweats."

My mouth fell open in shock. "That's the meanest thing you've ever said to me. Take that back!"

He gave me an incredulous look.

I glared at him. "You can kiss my pale Irish ass, Grumpy! These shoes are fucking gorgeous."

The corner of his mouth twitched, but his signature frown stayed in place. "Out of all the shit I say, picking on your shoes is what ruffles your feathers?"

I shrugged. "We all have our triggers." My phone beeped, notifying me of a new text, and I pulled it from my purse. "Finn made it to McLoughlin's with the shipment," I announced after reading the text.

"We're pulling up," Asher said, and I glanced out the window. He parked the car in the street, right in front of the pub's entrance. Dean hopped out but waited by my door until Asher was standing there too before opening it and letting me out. Asher took the lead, entering McLoughlin's first, and Dean followed behind me.

Inside, it was dim, and music played in the background. Black leather booths and wooden tables lined one side of the narrow pub and the bar took up the other side. An Irish flag was hanging on the wall behind the bar, surrounded by shelves displaying an array of Irish whiskey bottles.

Because it was the middle of the day, the pub wasn't busy. Just a few booths and half of the bar stools were occupied. I noticed Finn sitting at the far end of the bar. Louie was with him.

"Can I help you, ma'am?" the scowling old man standing behind the bar asked, drawing everyone's attention to me. Finn and Louie stood from the bar and I continued toward them.

"No," Dean answered for me, glaring back at the bartender.

"What are you doing here?" I asked Louie.

He gave me a small smile, which made me sad. I missed his bright and carefree smiles. "With Gavin missing, Finn needed the extra muscle. I was able to get you two trustworthy guys. They're watching over your shipment," he explained, words so matter of fact.

I reached out and touched his forearm. "Can you stick around so we can talk? I'll buy you a drink after I'm done looking over the shipment." Louie glanced away, a clear indication he was thinking of an excuse not to. I stepped closer, for some semblance of privacy because Dean, Asher, and Finn were standing right next to us. "You can't avoid me forever and I won't beg. So man the fuck up before you leave me no choice but to make you talk to me." I looked to Finn. "Where to?"

Finn tilted his head toward the far back of the pub, gesturing for us to follow before he started walking in that direction. Dean, Asher, and I trailed behind him as he led us into the pub's kitchen and over to a stainless-steel behemoth of a refrigerator. He pushed it to the side as far as the power cord would let him, revealing the wall behind it. There were very thin lines in the wall in the shape of a door. Finn pushed on it and it swung open easily into a black abyss.

"Watch your step," he warned before stepping inside and began moving downward into the darkness.

Asher went in first, taking a few steps down before turning back with his hand held out. "It's dark and I don't trust the traffic cones you call shoes."

Dean let out a full belly laugh behind me.

I frowned at Asher and reluctantly took his hand. We took the stairs slowly. There was a light at the very bottom, but it didn't help much. Once at the bottom we walked down a stone hallway with strung up lights that gave off underground bunker vibes. At the end of the hall was a door. It was open and inside were two goons sitting on top of a giant wooden box. The room was small. In the center was a metal table and built into one wall was a giant safe.

Finn ordered them to open up the box and start pulling out the drugs. One of the goons grabbed a crowbar that had been on the table and he used that to pry open the top. The smell of strong coffee hit my nose. I leaned closer to look inside the box and found it full of loose coffee beans.

Finn caught me peeking inside. "Colombian coffee beans. It's how we smuggle the drugs in. Once we're done unloading, we'll take the beans to the coffee shop down the street."

I watched as the goons began digging through the beans until one of them pulled out a taped up block and tossed it onto the table. I picked up the block to examine it. "I didn't know we owned the business down the street," I said as I thought back to the time Dean and I had sat in my car for hours, parked in front of that coffee shop, spying on Mark, the enforcer I'd executed at my first family meeting.

I tried to peek past the thick silver duct tape to see inside the kilo but was worried about ripping it and spilling it everywhere. So I put it back on the table.

"We don't. It belongs to a widow. Her husband used to be part of the family until he was killed by a De Luca during Giovanni's reign. We give her the beans as a way to help out. It isn't much, but it's all she'll accept," Finn explained.

That's nice, I mused and continued to watch as the goons began pulling kilo after kilo from the box and tossing them onto the table to be stacked in a row by Finn. One of the kilos in the box had a tear in its packaging and, as fate would have it, one of the goons tossed it a little too harshly. The kilo landed further than the others, on the table right in front of Dean and me. A cloud of white hit our faces. Startled, I inhaled. We both did. And everyone stared at us in horror.

"Oh, fuck," Finn said, gaping at us.

Dean and I turned to look at each other. His face was covered in white dust, making him look like a clown.

"Oops," I said before bursting into a fit of giggles. "You should see your face."

Dean glared—I meant really glared—at me. "This is far from funny, Maura. We just inhaled a fuck-ton of cocaine."

Shit, he's right. Stefan's going to kill me.

Asher and Finn took charge while the two goons stood off to the side, unsure of what to do. Dean and I were ordered not to breathe and to close our eyes while they wiped the excess coke off.

"I've never done coke before," I admitted. "What's coming? Oh, shit! I took oxy less than an hour ago."

Finn and Asher glanced at each other, exchanging a worried look. "Help me get them upstairs," Asher said to Finn and it didn't feel like a request. "I trust that you can handle the rest of this shit from here?"

Finn nodded and turned back to the goons. "Finish unloading. I'll be down here to help lock it up into the safe."

Asher and Finn ushered Dean and I back upstairs. By the time we made it into the kitchen my heart rate had picked up speed and I felt kind of euphoric. "Oh, wow."

Asher put his giant hands on my shoulders and steered me back into the pub. "Thank fuck," Asher said from behind me and urged me toward the bar where Louie was waiting. *He stayed!*

"Hi, handsome!" I beamed. Louie swiveled around on his stool. I grinned and wrapped my arms around his neck. His body stiffened for a second before he circled his arms around my back. Sighing with relief, I burrowed my face in the curve of his neck and inhaled his delicious clean scent. I'd missed him so much. Louie stiffened again and grabbed me by my upper arms to hold me away from him.

He stared into my eyes, searching. His eyes widened and drifted to Dean and Asher. Finn, I guessed, had gone back to help lock up the drugs. "She's fucking high!" Louie whisper-yelled.

Asher leaned closer to whisper in his ear, most likely telling him what had happened. Louie had yet to let me go and I took that time to check on Dean.

He was staring off into space. "I don't know what I'm going to do," he mumbled, absently. I didn't like the look in his eyes that came with those words. It was almost as if he was...scared.

I broke out of Louie's hold and wrapped my arms around Dean. I squeezed him tight. "Shh, it's going to be alright. I'll protect you, okay?" I told him. "You're one of my best friends and I kind of fucking love you. If you need me to kill someone, I will. Just tell me who."

I heard someone snort behind me. Glancing over my shoulder, I found Asher looking ready to burst. "You should see his face," he said in a strained voice. "He's stiff as a board and doesn't know how to handle your admission of love." Then Asher threw his head back laughing, unable to hold it in any longer.

I released Dean. His forehead was scrunched, and he seemed at odds on what he should do. I patted his arm. "It's okay. I don't expect you to say it back." That made Asher laugh harder.

Louie put his hand on my shoulder. "We need to get you home."

Asher sobered himself and wiped at the corner of his eye. "Come on, man," he said to Dean and steered him toward the door. The four of us made our way out of the pub. Asher retrieved my purse from the Escalade and handed it to Louie.

"You're taking me home?" I asked Louie. He gave me the slightest nod and ushered me to his car.

During the drive back to Quinn Manor, my body became really hot. Sitting in the passenger's seat, I pointed the vents at me. It wasn't enough. "Why is it so hot?" I was burning up.

"It's the drugs," Louie said.

Oh. I undid the buttons on my jacket and shed it off, leaving me in just my black tank that revealed a lot of cleavage. I smiled when I caught Louie staring. "Why have you been avoiding me?" He returned his focus back to the road and I chuckled. "What a stupid question. I already know the answer."

"You do?"

"What I really want to know, and what really eats me up with guilt because I'm *dying* to know, is how badly do you want me? Do you just want to fuck me, get me out of your system as you do with other women, or do you want more?"

Louie whistled. "Beautiful, you've always been blunt, but when on drugs...fuck."

"You didn't answer my question," I grumbled and lifted my hair off the back of my neck. I fiddled with the air vents again, pointing them at my chest and neck. The cold air hitting my damp skin felt good. I closed my eyes, groaning.

"I think about it, you know," I mumbled. "I hate myself for it, but I think about that night...what would have happened if you hadn't stopped and Jamie hadn't shown up." The forbidden thought ignited something inside of me and I was beginning to get hot for other reasons.

I opened my eyes to find his expression schooled. The tightness in his body gave him away, though. I laughed again, loving that I affected him. "If we could have one night together, what would you do to me?"

His grip tightened on the steering wheel and his voice became riddled with anger. "Maura, stop."

Someone else might have been deterred. I was stubborn and itched to see how far I could push until he snapped.

CHAPTER EIGHT

"Louie, Louie." I smiled a loopy smile. "Do you remember the story you told me about how you and Jamie fucked the same woman? I've replayed that story in my head while in the shower, only I imagine that I'm that woman as I slide my fingers between my legs." To demonstrate, I dropped my hair and trailed my hands over my clothes, down my body. I squeezed one of my breasts with one hand through the thin fabric of my tank and snaked my other between my thighs over my throbbing clit. I couldn't have stopped myself from rubbing it through my slacks even if I'd wanted to. The drugs were making me brazen and completely disintegrated what little verbal filter I did have. My dirty ministrations caught his attention and desire flared in his eyes as he watched me touch myself. "I came so hard, Louie." My breath hitched on the tail end of his name because my fingers hit the perfect spot.

He cursed, then brought the car to a stop and shifted it into park. Gazing out the front windshield, I realized we were parked in front of Quinn Manor. Louie climbed out of his car and slammed his door shut. My eyes followed him as he walked around the front of the car and ripped open my door. He reached across me to unfasten my belt, then grabbed my upper arm and yanked me from the car. I lost my footing and a little squeal slipped from my lips. He let loose a few more obscenities as he scooped me up bridal style, effortlessly.

Wanting to be an even bigger pain in the ass, I went limp in his arms with my arms and head hanging loosely. It made the entire world go topsy-turvy.

He grunted at the awkwardness. "You're not going to make this easy for me, are you?"

"Like how easy you've been lately? I had to practically threaten you to get you to talk to me!"

"You're so lucky you're hot. It makes up for your vindictive bitch streak."

I flipped him off.

Louie walked with me in his arms into the house and once the front door closed with an echo in the foyer, I yelled out, "Daddy, I'm home!"

"I'm aware, Maura," I heard my father say.

I attempted to sit up. All my limbs flailed as I failed. I snorted, imagining what I must have looked like. Louie turned us and an upside-down Stefan and Brody came into view. Both looked stunned and baffled at the sight of me. "Oh look, both of my parents are here." I grinned at both of them. "So...how was your day?"

Stefan's eyes narrowed slightly. "I think I'd rather hear about yours."

"Mine was exciting! I found out we smuggle cocaine in coffee! Then I got to try coke for the first time. A whole kilo blew up in my and Dean's faces. He looked like a fucking clown!" I laughed, remembering it. "We should probably call Dr. Ben," I wheezed through the laughter. "To see if I'll be okay after mixing coke and oxy and all the other meds I'm currently taking."

Louie hung his head while Stefan and Brody just blinked at me.

Stefan recovered the quickest. "You tried cocaine?" His dark tone was unsettling. *Oh, shit.* Stefan was pissed.

"It wasn't voluntary," I added quickly. "It exploded in my face and I ingested—no, I mean breathed. Wait, that's not the right word either," I rambled.

"Inhaled," Louie supplied.

I snapped my fingers and pointed at him. "Yup, that's the word. I inhaled all the coke."

Brody finally broke out of his stupor. "She inhaled a kilo of cocaine?" The way his eyes bugged out made me erupt with laughter again. "I'm going to call Dr. Ben," he said, rushing out of the foyer.

"The kilo was ripped," Louie said calmly and went on to explain what had happened while I just hung there in his arms.

Stefan closed his eyes and rubbed his forehead.

I drew their attention by whimpering. "I'm burning up. I don't like it. Is Jamie home? I need Jamie." Because I was hot for other reasons too and my body's needs were riding me hard. "Will someone please find my boyfriend?"

"Take her up to her room and don't leave her alone. I'll call Jameson," Stefan said.

Louie did as Stefan asked and carried me all the way up to my room. He laid me on my bed gently. I immediately perched up on my elbows. I watched him as he ran his fingers through his blond hair. Our eyes locked and I found myself wanting to give in to the magnetic pull pulsating between us.

"We should get you in the shower. A cold one," he said and started for the bathroom.

I had to give him props for his restraint. I wished I could say the same for myself. "Are you going to help me? It can be quite slippery in there."

He stopped walking and turned back to me with a scowl. "I understand the coke has crossed the wires leading from your brain to your mouth, but you're not making this fucking easy, Maura. Do you think I'm happy about wanting my best friend's girl? Just being near you tempts me to betray him." Frustrated, he raked his fingers through his hair again. "You said you hate yourself for wanting me, well, I hate you for making me want you."

I sat up slowly, until I was sitting upright on the edge of the bed. My eyes dropped to the floor as his words sank into my heart like a knife. "Thank you for finally being honest with me."

Louie went so quiet. "You did not just fucking play me?" he questioned angrily.

I didn't respond. It was cowardly to let him think I'd used the game to get the truth from him, but it was better than the alternative. Him knowing the truth didn't matter anyway. He hated me regardless of what I felt for him and I still loved Jamie. I couldn't and wouldn't leave him for Louie. So what was the point? Why did I pick at these feelings I had for him like a scab?

Louie took a step toward me at the same time my bedroom door burst open. Jamie walked in, heading straight for me. His eyes swept the room. Reading the tension between Louie and I, he stopped before he could reach me. "What's going on?" His eyes, once again, bounced back and forth between Louie and I.

"Nothing." I hated that I was lying to him again.

Jamie gave me a look that said he didn't believe me. Louie chose that moment to try and storm out of the room, but Jamie stopped him by blocking his way. "Stop being a fucking coward," Jamie said in a low voice. "You're hurting her with this shit."

My eyes dropped to the floor again. With the drugs still in my system, I wasn't confident I could hide my shame or hurt.

"Maura?" Jamie said softly.

"I love you," I blurted to Jamie before he could ask me what I knew was coming. "I love you so much it takes my breath away sometimes. The thought of losing you...I'd rather die." A tear falling down my cheek was what made me realize my eyes were filled to the brim. "I don't know what's wrong with me," I whispered, and more tears fell.

Jamie knelt down in front of me and cupped my face. He tilted my head gently until my blurry eyes met his. "You have feelings for him."

All the air in my lungs rushed out and panic set my heart into overdrive. My eyes shifted to look over his head at Louie. He stared back at me with a somber expression.

Jamie's hold on me tightened a little. "Hey, take a deep breath. I'm not mad."

"You're not?"

He nodded. "I'm not blind, baby. I know things are tense between you two and I've seen how you look at each other. So whatever you have to say about Louie, I won't get upset and it won't make me stop loving you."

More tears fell from my eyes. "I can't and it's not like it fucking matters anyway. He hates me." My words wobbled. "I hate me."

"Stop. Just be honest, Maura," Jamie pleaded.

"I want to grow old with you," I sniffled. "Me and you against the world. That's how it's supposed to be." I took in a deep, shaky breath. "But I feel like something's missing or like I know there could be more. I miss him. I miss the way he makes me laugh. I miss the comfort of him being there with us. We don't feel complete without him. I don't mean you're inadequate, Jamie. He...he feels different. Not more or less. Just different. I'm sorry if that doesn't make sense, but I don't entirely understand it myself."

Jamie released a breath. "Okay, let me ask you this...do you want to leave me for Louie?"

"No!" I said loudly. The one word was riddled with panic. I

was fucking everything up. He was going to leave me because I had feelings for his best friend. I pulled Jamie's hands from my face and stood from the bed with the intention of retreating to my bathroom.

I made it a step before Jamie's hand clamped onto my wrist. "You don't get to be a coward either." Jamie turned to face his best friend. "Your turn, man."

Louie glared at Jamie. "What do you want me to say? You know how I feel about her and she knows, too."

"It doesn't sound like you were clear enough because she thinks you hate her. Not that I blame her, because you've been avoiding her for over a month," Jamie said harshly.

Louie ran his hands down his face. "I said I hated her for making me want her."

Yup, hearing that a second time doesn't feel any better than the first. "Let me go." I tried to yank my hand free, but Jamie's hold didn't waver.

"She doesn't make you want her. So don't put all the blame on her," Jamie argued.

"Well, she made it really fucking hard to not want her today," Louie snapped.

Jamie's eyes narrowed. "What do you mean?"

Louie and I both grimaced.

Fuuuuck! I will never do drugs ever again!

I closed my eyes, trying to conjure up some courage. "Louie told me about the time you and he shared a woman. I told him that I like to imagine that I'm that woman and masturbate to that fantasy in the shower." Never had I ever wished more in my life that the ground would open up and swallow me than I did in that moment.

Jamie's brows rose, showing his surprise. I could feel my neck, cheeks, and ears turning red. Scratch that, my whole body felt like a tomato.

"I think I'm starting to understand the '*he completes us*' state-ment," Jamie murmured. "Maura, do you just want to have a threesome with Louie because it's your fantasy or are you wanting to be in a relationship with both of us?"

"Can you tell me why you're being so calm about this?" I deflected.

He shook his head. "I'll tell you after you answer the question."

"I honestly don't know. I don't want it to be a one-time thing. *I* don't like the idea of being a one-time thing. It would hurt me if that's all I was to him. Just another conquest."

"You aren't a fucking conquest, Maura. You would never be that to me. I haven't been with anyone since you've been home," Louie argued.

"How would I know that, hmm? You won't talk to me," I snapped.

"Because you made your choice! You chose him. You've always chosen him. I've been in love with you since I was seventeen years old. I've never acted on it because my best friend was head over heels for you. Not that he ever told you because for some fucking reason he felt that he didn't deserve you. It was also clear as day how you felt about him. Then you left, leaving the two of us behind pining for a girl who hadn't chosen either of us. Then you came back, looking even more beautiful. Just hearing your voice again, I knew that if there was ever a chance that you'd choose me, I couldn't step aside for him. That left me no choice but to tell him how I feel about you. He already fucking knew, of course."

"And then I chose Jamie," I added.

Louie nodded curtly. "I wasn't surprised. I'm trying to be happy for you two. Do right by the both of you, but it's so fucking hard."

Feeling extremely lightheaded, I sat back on the bed.

"You okay, baby?" Jamie asked.

I didn't answer because I didn't know how I felt. Instead, I lay back and stared at the ceiling. "Your turn, Jamie. Why are you being so calm? You went apeshit after I gave De Luca a lap dance. I've just admitted I have feelings for your best friend. If the roles were reversed, I'd kill Louie."

"Don't give him any ideas," Louie grumbled. Uncontrollably, I smiled up at the ceiling.

Jamie climbed onto the bed to lie down next to me. "You both are important to me—have been since we were kids," he said. "It affects me too when there's a rift between you two and you both suck at hiding what you're feeling when the other walks into the room. Which is why I've had a while to think about all this. I'm not mad. I wasn't mad when I found you two kissing. Jealous, yes. We were fighting at the time and I was afraid that I wouldn't get you back."

"How do you feel now?" I asked.

He didn't answer right away, and I could see him mulling over what he was going to say. "As you know, I've shared with Louie before. It was hot. If you're just wanting to fulfill your fantasy, I'm all for it. But if you're wanting more from the both of us, then I don't know. How would that even work?"

I shrugged. "I say we take it one fuck at a time. See where it leads us."

Both Louie and Jamie chuckled.

"What?" I asked them.

"High or drunk, you always seem pretty with it. It's easy to forget that you're under the influence. Then you say or do something that's...surprising and we're reminded," Jamie explained.

"No holds fucking barred," Louie cursed, shaking his head, astonished.

"You should have seen what she drunk texted Stefan the other night," Jamie said, smiling. Louie's brows rose, curiosity piqued.

Before Louie could say anything, I steered the conversation

back on track. "Because I'm really fucking high right now, I just want to clarify that you're seriously humoring the idea of including Louie in our relationship?"

Jamie looked over at Louie, who was now looking at the floor. "I know you stay away because you don't want to risk hurting me, man." Louie's eyes lifted from the floor and Jamie continued. "I want you to be happy too, but I can't give her up. I think I can handle sharing her with you because you make her happy and I trust you. You're the closest I've ever had to a brother."

There was a knock on the door, interrupting our conversation.

Jamie got up from the bed. "It's not what either of us imagined, but we should take some time to consider this. For her," he said in a low voice before opening the door.

Josh and Dr. Ben were standing out in the hall. Jamie gestured for the doctor to come in. He stopped Josh from entering and said something to him quietly. I thought I heard him say, "I can't guarantee she won't kill you."

I could hear Josh's response clearly. "The boss wanted me to tell her that he'd be up shortly to check on her."

Jamie gave him a curt nod. "I'll pass it along."

Dr. Ben crossed the room over to me and I sat up to greet him. "Heard you unintentionally snorted cocaine and that you're still on medication from your accident." He grabbed my wrist, feeling for my pulse, and looked down at his watch.

"How do you unintentionally snort cocaine?" I questioned because I could sense his judgment.

"You tell me?" he asked distractedly as he counted my pulse.

I yanked my wrist away. "Jamie, I'm about to throat punch Fabio Junior. I won't hit his face because it'd be a shame to hit something so pretty but his throat is fair game."

Jamie stepped between us. "You're in the wrong house to piss people off," he warned Dr. Ben.

"Look, I'm sorry. She's not the first daughter or wife in this family I've seen this past week because they borderline OD'd. I'd just hate to see that happen to her," Dr. Ben said.

I poked my head around Jamie. "Was my aunt Aoife one of those women?"

"Doctor-patient confidentiality," Dr. Ben said.

I reached under my pillow and pulled out the gun I had hidden there. "What if I threatened you with a gun? Could you tell me then?"

Louie chuckled from across the room and Jamie's head dropped in exasperation before he shook it. "Baby, do you have any idea how long it takes to vet a doctor? You can't kill him."

"I won't kill him if he tells me," I said sweetly.

"Yes," the doc said quickly. "Saw her last night. Dylan called me because he was worried she took too much. She didn't overdose, but it wasn't for a lack of trying."

I knew she was on something the other night!

"I saw Brenna, as well. Not because of drugs. She supposedly tripped down the stairs. She had a couple cracked ribs and a cut on her head that required stitches," Dr. Ben added.

My hand tightened around the grip of my gun. "Why'd you tell me that?"

"She's seventeen, bright, and deserves better. The last time we spoke, you didn't seem too keen at the thought of women being mistreated in this *family*." The doctor gave me a pleading look. Then cleared his throat. "Plus, you threatened me with a gun. It's not like I had any other choice but to tell you."

I want to help her—them. I don't know how to yet. I'm trying to figure it out. I hope I won't be too late.

"I think as long as you're doing everything you can, that's more than anyone can ask for," Dr. Ben said, making me realize I had spoken my thoughts out loud.

I held out my gun to Jamie. "Let's get this checkup over with. I think if I were going to have a bad reaction it would have happened by now."

Jamie took the gun and moved away to go stand by Louie.

Dr. Ben eyed them. "I need to check out the injuries she sustained from the accident. I think she'd be more comfortable with you two waiting outside."

Jamie and Louie looked to me.

I waved, gesturing for them to leave. "Go. I'll be fine."

They left and Dr. Ben asked me to lift my shirt. I did and he looked over my pink scars. I had two. The smallest one was above my hip where I'd gotten shot. The biggest was a line that ran from my sternum to the top of my belly button. It was ugly.

"These look good," he said and gestured for me to put my shirt down. "I read over your records from the hospital. Are you still on the antibiotics?"

"I took the last dose last night."

"Besides the oxycodone, are you taking any other medications?" he asked.

"My birth control. I take the pill every morning."

He nodded and pulled a pen light from his duffel bag. He shone it in my eyes. "Well, you're definitely high. Your pulse is accelerated, which is expected. And like you said, if you were going to have an adverse effect, it would've shown by now. I'm not too worried. Take it easy and maybe have one of those gorgeous men watch over you for the rest of the afternoon."

I thanked him and he let himself out. Jamie returned soon after. He told me that Louie had left and that he needed time to think things over.

I wrapped my arms around his waist and buried my nose in his chest. "Any way I can talk you into taking a shower with me?"

His body shook around me, laughing. "You don't need to talk me into getting naked with you, baby." His strong arms lifted me up by my ass and carried me into the bathroom.

CHAPTER NINE

For the next two weeks, most of my time was spent forming a plan with Rourke to get back at the Aryans. I'd invited Vincent to come stay at Quinn Manor again because we needed his hacking magic. I had him gather as much information as he could on every member in the Aryans, similar to what I'd had him do when I'd been looking into Samuel, but on a bigger scale. There were thirty-seven members of the Aryans in the New England area. We came to find out that the majority of the gang's members lived in Connecticut and their main hang-out-slash-headquarters was a dive bar called the Whiskey Bandit here in New Haven.

The leader of the Aryans and owner of the Whiskey Bandit was named Buck Werner. He was a disgusting individual with a hefty rap sheet to prove it. He'd had multiple arrests for hate crimes and assault, been accused of eight sexual assaults, and been a suspect in four murders. He'd been married five times. Two of his wives had died from drug overdoses. One had a restraining order against him and lived on the other side of the U.S. The fourth had killed herself—supposedly. His current wife was nine-teen, twenty-five years his junior. According to her medical records, she was an ex-junkie who happened to be three months pregnant.

The info on the other thirty-six members wasn't much better than their esteemed leader. A lot of sexual assaults, murder, and hate crimes. Some might have said I had no room to judge. The members of my family weren't law abiding citizens either. I could take pride in the fact that my father wasn't a racist or a rapist. A small blessing from everything I'd learned about the Aryans was that at least eighteen members were behind bars, hopefully being someone's bitch or being passed around the prison yard like a PlayStation controller.

Along with learning all there was to know about each member, Vincent found everything he could about the gang as a whole. They made most of their money from dealing heroin and weed, but recently, they'd started selling guns. *Our guns. Bastards.*

After all the research, a plan was formed. The Aryans had killed three of our own and stolen our guns. We'd have to seek payment for the guns they'd stolen another time. For right now, we were out for blood. Rourke and I agreed that revenge for our fallen took priority.

The plan was to infiltrate the Whiskey Bandit and try to get one of the gang's valuable members alone. Like Buck's right-hand man, Dustin Peters, or Buck's pet assassin, Alex Roth. I'd drunk myself into a stupor in order to read through the horrors in Alex's file. There wasn't any proof, but it was obvious Buck liked to send Alex after his enemies, which included witnesses who would have been key to putting Buck in jail. By the many crime scene photos Vincent had found, I could tell Alex liked to take his time, preferred to use knives, and I'd have bet all my money he had every characteristic of a serial killer.

Neither Alex nor Dustin would let down their guard around anyone, unless it was someone offering a piece of ass. Which meant I was going into the lion's den to bat my eyes and offer to spread my legs to get one of them alone. Rourke argued that it'd be safer to do a drive-by or kill them while they slept in their homes. A drive-by felt messy and both Aryans had families. Alex lived with his sister and Dustin was living with his second baby mama. I didn't want to risk innocents.

Rourke procured what I liked to call a kidnapper van, while Vincent hacked into the Whiskey Bandit's security cameras. Asher volunteered to get us tech equipment that he and Vincent insisted we'd need. Dean was in charge of weapons. And I was tasked with finding wing-women. One didn't just walk into a bar alone and not look suspicious. Nope. I needed to enter with a group of girls. I had Dean and Asher take me to an area of town where the... ladies of the night liked to conduct business. I found four that were young enough to pass as college students. I offered them each a thousand dollars to pretend to be my group of friends, taking the night off from studies to celebrate my birthday. I explained to them that after they ordered a drink or two at the bar, they were to leave. The four of them agreed eagerly and I told them to meet me down the street from the Whiskey Bandit.

All that was left for me to do was to find the perfect disguise and I'd really outdone myself this time.

Push up bras were, in my opinion, a secret weapon. When both Dean and Asher's eyes dropped to the amount of cleavage I had on display as I stepped out of my bedroom, I knew I was right.

"I think I need therapy," Rourke said, scrunching his nose in utter disgust. "I know you're my cousin, but you don't look like my cousin, which made me forget that you're my cousin and I just checked you out right now. I'm going to be sick." Rourke put a hand to his stomach and gagged as he turned away from me.

I laughed. "Your rambling totally sounded like me just now." I glanced down at my outfit that consisted of Daisy Duke jean shorts, ankle boots the color of sand, and a white tank, with a red push-up bra peeking through. I completed the outfit with a new black leather jacket. Long strands of iron-straight tawny colored hair fell from where they were tucked behind my ear. My new wig's length was longer than my real hair and was going to take some getting used to. What was really a trip were the blue colored contacts I had on. "I guess if my disguise is good enough to fool you, then it will be good enough to fool the Aryans."

Dean and Asher both nodded and had yet to look away from me.

I put my hands on my hips. "Close your mouths, boys. You'll catch flies."

"You don't look like you," Dean said.

"Yeah," Asher agreed.

"I was going to wear this for Jamie later, but based on all your creepy reactions, I'm worried he'd like it too much," I grumbled as I flipped my fake hair over my shoulder.

"Jameson has been in love with you since we were kids. Everyone could see it but you," Rourke said. "The guys teased the hell out of him when he first joined the ranks. They'd tell him he was pussy whipped without actually getting the pussy with how he'd drop everything whenever you'd call on him. I remember when you were sixteen or seventeen, he overheard one of Samuel's enforcers saying some lewd shit about you. Jameson beat the guy with a tire iron in front of Stefan, my da, and Samuel. And no matter how much Samuel yelled at Stefan to intervene, he wouldn't. Da said Stefan took one look at Jameson, then said, *I'm sure he has his reasons.* The guy survived but barely and after that, no one would risk talking about you or even looking at you for too long in his presence. Well, except for Louie."

"Louie?" I repeated. Speaking of, he was back to avoiding me, but I was going to give him his space.

"Uh...did you tell Stefan the plan?" Rourke successfully deflected.

I turned away from Rourke to look over the plethora of weapons Dean had laid out for me on my bed. "Sure." Stefan liked to micromanage when it came to me, and Jamie would totally be against the plan altogether. So I might have failed to tell either of them what we were doing today.

"Real convincing, cuz," Rourke deadpanned.

I scooped up a nine-millimeter with a silver slide and a hot pink frame. I held it up and arched a brow at Dean. He smirked at me. I rolled my eyes and ejected the magazine, finding it fully loaded. I matched the gun with a silencer and picked a couple of knives. One was a spring-assisted folding knife and the other was a stiletto switchblade. I tucked the folding knife in my back pocket and placed the other blade and gun into my purse.

Asher shocked the hell out of me when he asked me to remove my top. "I need to pin a mic to your bra," he explained.

"I'll go get Vincent and we'll meet you in the van," Rourke said, dashing from my room. I shucked off my leather jacket and pulled off my top.

Asher was professional, maintaining his full focus on pinning a small black wire to my bra instead of my large amount of cleavage. Dean also kept his gaze averted as he held out a beige doodad the size of a cashew. "Earpiece. It's so we can talk to you."

I took it and tucked it into my ear. "I feel like a super spy."

Asher smiled at my comment as he finished pinning the mic and handed me my shirt. I put it and my jacket back on. I grabbed my purse that had a strap that went across my chest and we headed out.

On the drive there, Asher, Rourke, and Rourke's new enforcer, Owen, were checking over all the automatic rifles they'd brought along in case shit hit the fan. Dean was driving and Vincent was fiddling with three different laptops. A live feed of the Whiskey Bandit was playing on each screen.

"They have five cameras. One pointed outside the front

entrance, one outside the back, two in the main bar area, and the last one in the hall leading to the bathrooms and back entrance," Vincent explained and pulled out two headsets with microphones attached to them from one of his computer bags. He hooked them up to one of the laptops and put one on. "Testing. Testing. Can you hear me?" he said into the mic and his voice came through my earpiece.

"Yes. I can hear you."

"Good. Can you whisper or something into your mic?" he asked.

I cupped my boob to push it closer to my mouth and whispered, "Hello."

Vincent chuckled. "It's working."

"We're pulling up," Dean announced and pulled up to the designated curb where I'd asked my wing-women to meet me. All four were there waiting, and all had dressed in skin fitting pants or skirts that weren't too short. Their tops were low cut but not too revealing. Their makeup was also on the lighter side than what I had seen when I'd first met them. I was relieved because they did manage to look like innocent college girls celebrating a night at the bar and a lot less like they charged by the hour.

I hopped out of the van with a friendly smile because they did look a little wary. "Hi, ladies. Excuse my disguise and my cousin's kidnapper van. I know it's creepy as fuck." Asher held out my purse from inside the van. I took it and strapped it across my chest.

"If you have a bad feeling, just leave," he suggested with worry etched around his aquamarine eyes.

I nodded. Rourke poked his head out of the van next. "Just get whoever you pick out the back entrance and we'll be there to back you up."

"That's the plan," I said.

Rourke closed the side door and the van pulled away. I pulled out four envelopes from my purse and handed one to each of the girls. "I was told not to give you these until after because you might skip out on me. I'm really hoping you won't."

"Then why are you paying us now?" one of them asked as she looked inside her envelope.

"Because I can't guarantee I'll be able to meet up with you after and I wanted to make sure you got paid," I explained.

"Just one drink, right?" another asked.

"Yes. We're going to go into the bar down the street. It's kind of shady and I don't want to go in alone. We're going to pretend it's my birthday and we're celebrating but not too hard because we have midterms. If anyone asks, we're attending SCSU. After you all have had a drink or two, leave. Do not stick around and don't spare a glance back at me because I will be staying behind. Any other questions before we walk down there?"

"Why are you staying behind? What are you going to do?" the youngest of the four asked. She had to be about twenty-one or twenty-two. The others were closer to my age.

"Just say you're looking for someone," Asher said in my ear.

I tried not to react at suddenly hearing his voice. "I'm looking for someone and it's best we just leave it at that."

"I've been to that bar before. You know who it belongs to, don't you?" the youngest spoke up again.

"I do. Are we ready?" I asked.

They all nodded, and we walked down the street toward the Whiskey Bandit.

CHAPTER TEN

As we were coming up on the entrance, one of the girls with curly raven hair hooked her arm with mine. I really should have asked them their names. "So, birthday girl, what's your name, how old are you turning, and are you single and looking to mingle with someone in this bar?"

"Don't tell her your real name," Rourke said in my ear.

No shit!

"My name is Mandy. I'm turning twenty-two and yes, I'm looking to mingle," I lied.

She nodded with a smile and as we opened the door to the Whiskey Bandit, she glanced back at the others. "You hear that, ladies? Our birthday girl is looking to get her freak on tonight," she yelled, clearly making it known to not just the girls, but everyone in the bar. Raven—that was what I was going to call her —barely gave me any time to glance around the room as she dragged me to the bar. "I'll buy Mandy's first drink. Y'all decide who's buying the next one. We need to make sure she really lets loose tonight because tonight is all about her," she told the other ladies, really playing her part well.

Three of them took seats at the bar while the youngest and I stood behind them. The bartender was a grizzled older man with a beer belly. "Did I hear that it's someone's birthday?" he asked us.

Raven smiled at him and pointed at me. "Birthday girl." Then she looked back at me. "Do you want to start off with some shots? I don't care if it's midterms. It's your birthday. You have to take a couple shots."

"Not sure that's a good idea," Dean said.

I smiled brightly. "Tequila." The four girls squealed and clapped their hands.

"Fucking hell," Dean grumbled in my ear.

The bartender placed five shot glasses on the bar and poured a cheap tequila in each glass. Raven paid, then handed me my shot. We clanked our shots and threw them back.

"Dustin Peters is playing pool at the table behind you. Alex Roth is sitting in the corner booth next to Buck. Unless he leaves Buck's side, your best bet is Dustin," Rourke said into my ear, reminding me that they were watching through the cameras.

I finally glanced around the room. It was slightly dim, and it most definitely looked like a dive. The carpet was burgundy and stained. The bar was chipped. Some of the chairs didn't match. It reeked of cigarettes and the slight skunk smell of weed permeated the air. There was only one corner booth, at the far end of the room. Sure enough, Buck and Alex were sitting there with a few other Aryans. My gaze swept to the other side of the room, behind where I was standing, and found Dustin, leaning over the pool table getting ready to make a shot. He hit the cue ball into another, but the other ball missed the pocket he was aiming for. He glanced my way, feeling me staring. We locked eyes. I smiled and quickly looked away as if embarrassed at being caught. I waited a second before glancing back again. This time he was staring at me, waiting, and he smirked when we locked eyes again.

He wasn't bad looking. Long blond hair that was tied back and he had pretty blue eyes. He had on a black T-shirt that showed off his muscles and a few tats.

"Do you know how you're going to approach him?" Rourke asked in my ear.

I went to glance at the camera that was up on the wall behind Dustin, but the colorful jukebox directly beneath it caught my eye and an idea came to me.

"See someone you like?" Raven asked, drawing my attention back to her and the other girls. I gave her a slight nod.

"Would you ladies like another round?" the bartender asked.

"I'll take a beer. Don't care which kind as long as it's in a bottle," I answered. While the other girls placed their orders, I pulled a one hundred and a quarter from my purse. I slipped the hundred to Raven and gestured silently for her to pay. She took it discreetly and handed it over to the old bartender when he came back with our drinks. Raven handed me my beer and I took a small swig. Inhaling deeply, I let my darkness take over with the quarter held tightly in my fist.

It's time to play.

I set down my beer on the bar and strutted the small distance in Dustin's direction. I made it look like I stumbled and let my quarter go flying. It landed on the pool table in front of Dustin as he was about to take a shot. He adjusted his stance and knocked the cue ball around the quarter and he successfully knocked a solid colored ball into the corner pocket. With a sheepish smile, I watched as he scooped up my quarter. He walked around the table toward me while his unabashed eyes raked over me from head to toe and back up. He stopped his approach with a few feet of distance between us and held out my quarter.

"What a gentleman," I said, reaching for the quarter.

He moved my quarter out of reach just before I could take it. "You're not from around here, are you?"

I dropped my hand and put it on my hip. "No." I didn't supply more. I didn't want to make it too easy for him and I could tell he was wanting me to chase him. But I had a feeling—no, I could see it in his eyes—he thought I was just an easy lay and was going to enjoy watching me work hard for his attention.

Not today, Señor Dipshit.

He smirked at me and tipped his head at the jukebox. "As a thank you for retrieving your quarter, you should let me pick the song."

"That's my only quarter. What if you have terrible taste in music?"

His surprise showed before he laughed. "What were you going to pick? Taylor Swift?"

I arched a brow. "And what were you going to pick? Lynyrd Skynyrd?"

"What are you doing, cuz? Pissing him off won't keep him interested," Rourke said.

"Let her do her thing. He's fucking chomping at the bit," Asher argued, and I did my best to tune them out.

Dustin's eyes sparkled with mirth. "You're a sassy little thing, aren't you?"

I moved my hand from my hip to shove it into my back pocket, causing my breasts to jut out. His stare immediately dropped. "Well, you are holding my quarter hostage," I flirted with my own smirk.

"I am."

"I'm willing to negotiate for its safe return," I said in a suggestive tone.

His brows lifted with intrigue. "I'm listening."

Yeah, that's right. I fucking got you. "Aren't you supposed to list off your demands?" I asked, taking a step closer. "I *really* want my quarter back." I looked up into his blue eyes. "I might even be desperate enough to give you whatever you want for it," I whispered.

Heat filled his eyes. "Whatever I want, huh?"

"You see, it's my birthday and I was looking to be a little bad," I said. "So do you want to list those demands here or do you want to take me somewhere a little quieter? You know, so I can hear them better?"

He tried to school his face to appear unfazed but failed. "Are you sure you can handle my demands?"

I snorted, with a cocksure grin. "There's only one way to find out." I held his eyes as I backed away, then turned and walked toward the bathrooms, and past them, toward the back entrance.

"He's following. Don't look back," Asher said. I didn't.

The hall that led to the back entrance was short. The door was within my reach when I was grabbed and pulled into the men's bathroom. It was a small bathroom with one urinal, one stall, and a single sink. Dustin pushed me up against the door and caged me with his hands resting next to my head. A slew of curses filled my ear. I had failed to get him outside, which meant I had to kill him on my own.

His eyes were predatory and lust filled. Facts rushed through my head. He was bigger and stronger. I'd have to kill him with one strike, and it'd have to come by surprise. My gun wasn't an option. I wouldn't be able to get it out of my purse without him knowing. The knife tucked into the back of my shorts was my best option, but he'd have to be close and distracted for me to use it.

I took off my purse and let it drop to the floor. Next, I shucked my leather jacket because I didn't want it getting in the way when I went to reach for my knife. Dustin watched silently, eyes devouring my cleavage. "Are you just going to stare?" I challenged.

One of his hands dropped from the door, circled around my lower back, and he pulled my lower half flush with his front. His apparent arousal pushed into my stomach. I locked my arms around his neck and forced him down to my level because he was a tall bastard. I slammed my lips against his and yanked on his ponytail hard to make him open for me to deepen the kiss. He growled and lifted me up by the back of my thighs. I hooked my legs around his waist and shoved a hand between us to grab him through his pants. "Lock the door," I ordered.

His hands went to my breasts and squeezed hard. I felt panic bubble deep inside of me. My darkness quickly smothered it, and I did my best not to wince.

"No lock," he murmured as he moved away from my mouth and started attacking my neck.

He continued to squeeze at my breasts to the point I knew I'd bruise. I couldn't stop myself from sucking in a breath, but I did suppress the pain-filled whimper that threatened to escape.

He chuckled. "I thought you said you could handle me?" he goaded before he bit my neck hard.

I grasped and yanked on his hair just as hard. "Take me into the stall. Someone might come in."

He looked annoyed but didn't respond. He quickly carried me into the stall and slammed my back against the stall wall. He didn't bother to shut the stall door before capturing my mouth again. He nipped at my bottom lip as he pulled the straps of my shirt and bra off my shoulder. His hand dove into the cup of my bra and he roughly yanked my breast out. His mouth left mine and moved to my nipple. As he sucked on it, I held him closer, pretending like I couldn't get enough, but really, I wanted him fully focused on my breast while I reached for my knife. I let out a few moans for good measure, too.

"Maura, are you alright? We can't see you in there," Asher asked.

My finger locked around my knife and I pulled it from my pocket. "Oh," I groaned loudly as I pushed the button to release the blade. "Kiss me," I begged as I pulled his mouth from my breast. He eagerly obliged and plunged his tongue into my mouth. I put my hand on the back of his head to hold him in place, then I put the knife at his throat and sliced deeply from ear to ear.

His whole body jerked. I locked my legs and arm tighter around him, holding him close because I knew a fight was coming. The closer we were, the harder it'd be for him to get a good hit. Blood spilled from his neck, soaking my entire front. It took him a moment to truly realize what I'd done to him, as if he were in shock. Then he snapped out of it and began to struggle. He tried to push me off him and when that didn't work, he slammed my back repeatedly against the stall wall. I let out a grunt but refused to let go. He hit me in the ribs, and I used my knife to cut at his arm and hand, hoping that would help stop him. I took a hard hit to the head and that really set me off. So I started stabbing him repeatedly on his side. He captured my wrist and tried to turn the knife on me, shoving it toward my face. I quickly leaned out of the way and tossed the knife away. Dustin took advantage of the distance I'd put between us and put his hand around my neck. He shoved me back easily, but my legs were still wrapped around his waist.

Why won't this fucker die already?

The guys were yelling in my ear, demanding to know if I was alright.

We were both soaked with his blood. I struggled to hold his free hand away from my neck, but the one that was already latched on was successfully cutting off my air. I smacked his face and hit his ear. It didn't affect him. I was starting to see spots when his legs gave out and we both fell to the floor. His hand released my neck and I sucked in delicious air.

Dustin's body spasmed, but he didn't come after me. I crawled under the stall wall to put distance between us just in case. I scurried over to the bathroom door where my purse was.

The guys had started begging to know whether or not I was okay. Then threatened that they were coming in after me.

"I'm fine," I croaked as I pulled my gun out of my purse. I sucked in a few more breaths and cleared my sore throat. "The asshole wouldn't die." I glanced back over at Dustin. He wasn't moving and didn't appear to be breathing either.

"You need to get out of there," Asher said.

"You have a little time but not much. Everyone in the bar is steering clear of the bathrooms because they think their buddy is getting laid," Rourke explained.

"Okay," I said and got myself to my feet. Moving quickly, I put my breast back into my bra and fixed my clothes. I put my jacket back on because from my neck down, I was covered in blood. I hooked my purse strap across my chest and glanced back at Dustin's body. I wanted Buck and his gang to know this was revenge. That I was the one who had killed Dustin. I walked over and crouched next to his lifeless corpse. His eyes were partially open, and his throat was still leaking blood. I started patting his pockets, feeling around for his cell phone. I found it in his right pants pocket and quickly tossed it into my purse. My eyes darted back to his bloody neck and a sick idea popped into my head. I swiped two of my fingers over his cut neck, coating them in his blood, then walked over to the mirror above the sink. I drew half a shamrock, went back to his neck to coat my fingers once more, then completed the second half. I rinsed my fingers in the sink but didn't bother trying to clean up the rest of me. I was a horrific sight.

"What's taking so long, Maura?" Dean grumbled.

"Keep your panties on, Grumpy. I'm coming out now," I said and cracked the bathroom door open. I didn't see anyone but could hear voices and music coming from the main area of the bar. I poked my head out next and found the hall empty. I stepped out of the bathroom and dashed for the back exit.

Just as I was about to shove open the door someone shouted out, "Hey!" I refused to stop and shoved the exit door hard, making it swing open wide. With my gun clutched in my hand in front of me, I stepped into the dark back parking lot. A couple of Aryans were standing just outside smoking. My appearance took them by surprise, and I saw that as an opportunity. I lifted my gun and pulled the trigger.

I had the silencer on, but it wasn't exactly quiet. Especially since they yelled out when they saw my gun. I hit one of them in the chest. The other ducked and I missed him. He went to pull out his own gun, but the rapid sound of *Pop! Pop! Pop! Pop!* came and the Aryan's chest exploded with holes. I looked out into the parking lot, finding Asher and Rourke standing outside the van with their rifles aimed at the dead Aryan.

"Get your ass moving!" Dean yelled into my ear.

I ran, weaving through the cars while Rourke and Asher covered me. I made it to the van when Asher and Rourke started firing again, walking backward as they did. Dean grabbed me and pulled me inside. He shoved me on the floor and covered me with his body.

Rourke climbed into the van next, then covered for Asher to climb in last. Owen, who was seated in the driver's seat, shifted the van into drive and floored it. Asher and Rourke didn't stop firing until we were out of the back parking lot and driving down the road. Once the van's side door was slammed closed, Dean got off me and ripped open my leather jacket.

"Where are you hurt?" he demanded, while he frantically lifted my shirt looking for any sign of a wound.

His fingers tickled my side when he tried to roll me over and I giggled. "Stop! It's not my blood!"

Dean froze his search. Once my words seemed to register, he let go of me and he sat back on his haunches. His shoulders slumped. "You look like you showered in blood."

I pulled my bloody shirt down and sat up. The rest of the van was quiet as they took me in.

"Care to share what the fuck happened in there?" Rourke snapped.

"In a second," I said and dug around in my purse for Dustin's phone. After I found it, I went through the contact list for Buck's number. I hit call and put the phone to my ear.

It rang three times before he answered. "Who the fuck is this?" Buck sounded mad.

"I assume you found Dustin's body in the bathroom," I said calmly.

"Again, who the fuck are you?"

"You seem to be under the assumption that I answer to you, Mr. Werner."

"You stupid cunt. When I find out who you are, we're gonna find you and I'm gonna enjoy gutting you."

"I'll save you the trouble," I said. "You see, Mr. Werner, your little gang is in my territory and you've started a war with my family. You've killed three of mine. So I killed three of yours. You also stole from us, which means we're not done with you yet. The last name is Quinn in case you haven't figured it out. Until next time, Mr. Werner." I hung up on him and tossed the phone to Vincent. He quickly ripped off the back and removed the battery.

"You going to tell us why you look like that girl from the movie Carrie?" Rourke asked.

For the rest of the drive home, I explained everything that had happened in the bathroom.

CHAPTER ELEVEN

"A re you sure you're not hurt anywhere?" Dean asked after I was done telling the guys everything. I may have skipped over how rough Dustin had been when he'd touched me. They didn't need to know that. I'd talk to Jamie about it after he was done being mad, because there was no doubt that he was going to be pissed after he found out that I had kissed Dustin and let him touch me. My darkness had relinquished its hold and now it felt like I was re-feeling everything, only heightened, as I thought back on all that had happened. Like the panic Dustin had conjured with his bruising grip when he had touched me intimately. My breasts were extremely sore. Every pulse of pain made me feel sick to my stomach. It sucked, but it was proof that I was stronger. A year ago, being touched like that would have been debilitating.

"Maura?" Dean said, pulling me from my thoughts.

"I'm fine," I said firmly. "Just a few bumps and bruises."

Dean eyed me with skepticism before glancing at Asher, who had been quietly listening and watching me.

By the time we pulled up to the house, I was dying for a

shower. The blood had dried, making my skin sticky, and the scent of pennies was strong enough to gag on.

Stefan was waiting in the foyer with his arms crossed over his chest. He didn't look pleased, which told me Rourke had informed him about what we'd been up to. His displeasure was replaced with worry and wide eyes as soon as they landed on me.

I put my hands up. "It's not my blood. As you probably already know, we hit back at the Aryans today." I sent an accusing look in Rourke's direction.

He shook his head. "I didn't tell him."

"He didn't have to. He and Vincent have been practically living here for weeks and then I saw you leave the house earlier this evening, looking like that." Stefan gestured to all of me with a flippant wave of his hand. I was still in my disguise. The wig I was still wearing had stayed in place, but the ends were crusty from Dustin's blood. "I'm disappointed you both failed to tell me the plan." Stefan turned his evil eye on Rourke. "I'm not surprised she didn't tell me, but I am that you didn't, Rourke."

I stepped between them, diverting Stefan's wrath to me. "He asked me if I told you the plan. I lied and said I did. If you're going to be mad at someone, be mad at me."

"You do understand that I'm the head of this family?" he asked as if I'd forgotten.

"Your status in this family means nothing to me. You are my father. Nothing more. I respect and listen to you because I love you. I'll do what you need me to do to serve this family, but I'll be doing it my way. If people have an issue with that, send them to me. I'll happily make sure they understand. Or you can be the big bad boss that I know you are and tell them to kiss your mobster ass before you make them."

The room was quiet, and I could feel the others' unease. Stefan didn't say anything for the longest time as he studied me.

Eventually, his body relaxed a little. "You look horrific. Are you hurt?"

I pulled off my wig and shook out my hair. "I slit someone's throat while he was trying to touch my tonsils with his tongue. Things got messy."

Stefan arched a questioning brow and waited.

I sighed. "He got a few hits in before he went down. I'll heal."

He nodded.

Footsteps pounding on the tile alerted everyone that someone was running through the house. Louie rounded the corner from the hall, and he came rushing into the foyer. He stopped abruptly as his wide eyes bounced all over me. "Fuck, Maura! One of the guys said you just came home, and you were covered in blood," he said, slightly winded.

I schooled my expression because I wanted to smile. I looked to Stefan. "Can we talk later? I need to shower."

Stefan waved me off and asked Rourke and Vincent to follow him to his study. They left in that direction with Owen following them. I glanced back at my goons. "Go home, guys. It's late and all I want to do is strip and shower for the next few hours because I seriously feel it's going to take that long to get clean."

Dean walked past me over toward Louie on the other side of the foyer. Dean leaned close to him and whispered something. Louie's eyes slightly widened at whatever Dean had said and he glanced over at me.

What the fuck? Dean turned and walked back, intending to leave through the front door.

"Best friends aren't supposed to keep secrets from each other," I chided as he passed me.

He stopped in his tracks and glared at me. "No, they're not." With that said, he and Asher left.

I tossed my wig on the table in the foyer and sighed. "You going to tell me what he said?" I asked over my shoulder.

ASHLEY N. ROSTEK

Louie crossed the foyer and turned me to face him. "He's just worried about you. I had Josh call Jameson when I came running. He's probably breaking every traffic law to get here, but I can hang out with you until then," he offered.

"I'm fine. I don't want you to think you have to be around me because of whatever Dean told you."

His hands squeezed my shoulders and his gorgeous dark blue eyes held mine. "I wouldn't have offered."

I looked away. "I'm trying to give you space, Louie."

"What if I don't want space anymore?" he asked and I met his eyes again, searching for his meaning. A smile slowly formed at his mouth. "You look so different with those contacts in."

"I didn't want to touch my eyes with bloody hands to take them out," I explained.

He tilted his head toward the stairs. "Let's go get you cleaned up."

I stayed in the shower way after it had turned freezing. I had a huge bruise on my side and bruises on my breasts. No matter how much I scrubbed, they wouldn't go away. They made me feel dirty. They brought back bad memories. *I did what I had to,* I reminded myself. It helped.

I shut off the water and got out. After drying my body and wrapping a towel around myself, I walked over to the mirror above the sink. My eyes were immediately drawn to my neck. More bruises. My gaze moved up to my face. From my temple to my ear was also black and purple from where he had hit me.

After combing my wet hair, I left the bathroom in search of some comfy PJs. Both Jamie and Louie were sitting on my couch talking quietly as I entered. Like mine had been, their eyes were drawn to my neck.

120

Jamie's head dropped down, eyes closed, and he took a deep breath. "Christ, Maura," he cursed, slowly getting to his feet, intending to come to me.

I held a hand up to stop him. "Don't," I pleaded, and he stayed where he was. "I need you to listen and I *need* you to not get angry until I'm done telling you everything. I don't have it...I just need..."

"Just tell me," he said, calmly.

I began telling him—them everything. Every. Single. Detail. As I went over how roughly Dustin had touched me and how it made me feel—the memories it conjured—Jamie's knuckles turned white from how tightly closed his fists were. Louie stood and put a hand on Jamie's shoulder, looking equally enraged.

"I want to see." Jamie's voice rumbled. A clear sign that he was straining to keep his fury at bay.

I was having déjà vu. I felt seventeen again, getting ready to show Jamie what Zack and Tyson had done to me. I glanced at Louie, hating that another man I cared for would see my body in such a state. I could ask him to leave, but how could I pass up this chance to see if he could accept all of me?

It was easier now to find the same strength than when I'd been seventeen. I opened my towel, watching Louie's reaction intently. His eyes dropped to my breasts, assessing and absorbing every dark mark with a clenched jaw.

Jamie stalked away and I closed my towel tightly around myself. He gave us his back as he stood in front of our dresser where I had a vase full of yellow and pink tulips and Jamie's framed pictures of the three of us on the top of it. His body was stiff, and he roughly ran his hands through his hair.

Then his control snapped.

He sent everything I had on the dresser crashing to the floor and slammed his fists down on the top of it. I didn't even flinch as

121

I witnessed his rage because it was what I was feeling on the inside.

Louie moved over to me slowly and cautiously brushed the tips of his fingers along my arm. I knew he wanted to hug but was leaving it up to me. I stepped closer to him and bound my arms around his waist. His palms flattened in the center of my back before one slid up behind my neck. I laid my head over his heart and the stressful weight from today seemed to slowly fade.

"He's not mad at you," Louie said.

I knew that.

Jamie whirled around. Seeing me in Louie's arms didn't faze him. "I'm not mad at you, baby. I'm pissed off that I can't kill him. I want to make him pay for not only touching you but for hurting you. Fuck, he more than just hurt you. I can see it in your eyes and hear it in your voice. I can't stand seeing you this way."

"I don't need you to get revenge for me," I said, stepping out of Louie's arms.

"Then what do you need?" he asked, desperation underscoring his words as if my answer would put him out of his misery.

"Love me," I replied. "Hold me like you don't want to let go. Touch me until all I can remember is your touch. Make me feel desired—that no matter how damaged or scarred I get, you will always want me."

Jamie came to me in a few long strides. His hands cupped the back of my neck to pull me close and he kissed me. He poured everything into that kiss. His rage. His desperation. His love. I felt it all as his lips danced with mine.

Breaking away, he rested his forehead against mine. "You are not damaged, Maura. If I have to spend the rest of my life proving that to you, I will." His eyes shifted to Louie behind me. "You want to help me show her how fucking perfect she is?"

Louie didn't respond and I was preparing myself for him to

find any excuse to leave. Then hands smoothed over my hips from behind and lips brushed my ear. "I can do that." The caress of Louie's voice in my ear made my heart speed up. Jamie dropped his hands from my neck and Louie spun me around to face him. "I tried to be a good friend, but I can't seem to let you go." His fingers flexed around my hips. "So if you'll have me, I'm here."

I grabbed the lapels of his suit jacket, pulled him down to my level, and kissed the hell out of him. Without missing a beat, he took charge, pushing his tongue past my lips. His assertiveness made me brace for the panic that I thought was coming, like it always did unless it was Jamie kissing me, but it never came. I felt comfortable. I felt safe. I felt so fucking turned on. The combination of it all made me mad with joy. I slid my hands up and snaked my fingers into his golden hair. I took back control of our kiss and gave back as good as he had given me.

Jamie stepped closer, sandwiching me between them. His hands grazed my breast as he grabbed at my towel. With a swift yank that caused me to gasp against Louie's lips, Jamie tossed my towel to the floor. Jamie's pelvis molded to my backside and his fingers trailed softly over my sore ribs, getting to work at erasing Dustin's phantom touch. He pressed his lips to my shoulder as his hands glided in different directions. One slid up to cup one of my tender breasts and the other dove between my legs. He skillfully strummed my clit as if I were an instrument, coaxing musical moans from me that Louie swallowed.

It wasn't long before Jamie's vigorous strokes drove me insane. My head lolled back onto Jamie's shoulder with a groan. I dropped one of my hands from Louie's hair and hooked my arm behind Jamie's neck. Louie's eyes roamed over every inch of my body. He regarded me with awe and lust, but as he took in my bruises once more, the slightest hint of sadness seeped in.

He leaned forward and brushed his lips over my neck with gentle kisses before moving down to the tops of my breasts. He kissed every mark before he knelt in front of me. Jamie moved his hand from between my legs to my hip. Louie stared up at Jamie. A look passed between them and they surprised me by lifting me enough for Louie to hook my legs over his shoulders. His hands cupped my ass, tilting my hips up as an offering to him before he swiped his tongue along my seam. I whimpered and my hips bucked. My hand that was still latched onto his hair fisted when his tongue plunged into my core and he began fucking me with his tongue.

Jamie's hand that had been cupping my breast moved to my chin. He turned my head to the side and his lips captured mine. While Jamie devoured my mouth, Louie's sinful tongue moved to my clit. It didn't take long before I was on the edge of release. I moaned loudly, spewed obscenities, and pleaded for him to keep going. And oh boy, did he.

Jamie watched my face as my whole body exploded from my orgasm. Whatever he saw on my face, he must have liked, because his breathing picked up.

Louie kept his tongue on my clit until it stopped pulsating. He unhooked my legs with a smug smile and a naughty gleam in his eye. "You coming undone on my tongue is the hottest fucking thing, beautiful."

"You should see her face when she does. Her eyes dilate, cheeks flush, and she lets out these breathy little moans," Jamie said and fluidly scooped me into his arms and carried me over to the bed. He laid me down and began shedding his clothes. Louie did the same and I watched, thoroughly enjoying the view.

Louie had a leaner body than Jamie, but it was still sculpted with muscle. He had a few tattoos here and there. His biggest tattoo was of the French flag and the Irish flag crossed with a huge Celtic cross between them on his right bicep. Jamie and I had gone with him when he'd gotten it. It had been after he'd been offered a position to join the family. To celebrate, he'd wanted to get something to symbolize his Dupont heritage and his new chosen family, us. Louie was French. His mother, Adeline Dupont, had been a prostitute and when he'd been four, she had been murdered. The police had found her body in an alleyway, strangled to death. Because his father was unknown, he had been sent here, to the States, to live with his aunt. Jamie and he had met freshman year of high school and stuck together like glue.

Louie was the first to get all of his clothes off. Jamie had been delayed with putting both of their guns in the nightstand. My gaze drank every inch of Louie in as it descended his chest, past the V at his hips, to his cock. Taking in his hard length, my eyes tried to bug out of my head.

I covered my face with both of my hands. *This isn't going to work.*

"You okay, baby?" Jamie asked.

I shook my head. "Nope." Dropping my hands from my face, I sat up and hugged my knees to my chest. They both held worried expressions. I waved a hand at the one-eyed anacondas hanging between their legs. "My fantasy has been ruined. There's no fucking way you both are having me at the same time. I won't be able to sit properly for Lord knows how long. I signed up for sex. Not an episiotomy. You're going to destroy Lady Town."

Their expressions morphed to utter shock at my frantic rambling. Then they looked at each other and threw their heads back laughing. They laughed so hard, tears formed in their eyes and Louie had to grab onto Jamie's shoulder to hold himself upright.

"Ha ha ha, she said my cock is too big," I mocked in my best guy voice as I frowned. "Laugh it up. I'm sure your egos are fucking loving this."

Louie wiped the corners of his eyes and climbed onto the bed next to me. "We would never hurt you and you know that," he said, leaning in to kiss me. It was short and sweet. He pulled back to meet my eyes. "Trust us."

I nodded and Jamie opened his nightstand. He pulled out a small bottle of lube and tossed it on the bed. I watched as he crawled onto the bed in front of me. He grasped my knees and spread them so he could get close enough to capture my mouth. I fell backward on the bed with Jamie braced over me, kissing me. His fingers glided down the side of my breast. I shivered and hooked a leg over his hip, hoping he'd understand that I was ready for more. He didn't disappoint. Reaching between us, he slowly eased himself into me and began rolling his hips.

Just as I was really getting into our rhythm, his arm circled around my back and he flipped us. "Ride me," he ordered, grabbing me by my hips and rocking them. Putting my hands on his chest, I took control of the pace.

Louie shifted on the bed to kneel behind me. He moved my hair off my shoulder and kissed the curve of my neck. His lips traveled up to my ear. "Lean forward a little." I did. His fingers trailed down my back until they met my back entrance. I stilled on top of Jamie as Louie's finger pushed inside me. I dropped my forehead to Jamie's chest, moaning. Louie chuckled. "I'll take that to mean you like it?"

Nodding, I lifted my head to meet Jamie's eyes. He covered my hand that was resting over his heart with his hand and reached up and tucked my hair behind my ear with his other. It made this moment perfect that they were being so patient and gentle with me. I felt cherished and safe.

Louie moved his finger in and out before adding a second. So far, it felt really good. After he thought I was ready, he positioned himself behind me. Jamie pulled me down to kiss him. I had a feeling it was to distract me. It didn't work. I gasped from the pressure of Louie entering me and my nails bit into Jamie's chest.

He didn't seem to care. Instead, he showered me with kisses on my lips, cheeks, chin, and forehead.

Once Louie was all the way in, he waited for me to relax before he started moving. I felt so full and a little delirious. It was better than I'd imagined. My hips started rocking on their own. I needed release. I needed it bad.

I sat up a little, finding the perfect angle. Louie grabbed me by my shoulder and hip, encouraging me to ride them both. "That's it, beautiful," he panted.

Jamie reached between us to rub my clit. The instant he touched me, I came screaming and contracting around them so tightly, their releases quickly followed mine. Jamie cursed, squeezing my hand. Louie grunted while resting his head on my shoulder.

"We are so doing that again," I said, breathlessly.

They both chuckled.

Louie pulled out of me and climbed off the bed. He disappeared into the bathroom and I fell onto the bed next to Jamie. We just stared at each other with sleepy satiated smiles. Louie returned with a wet washcloth. He opened my weak legs and wiped me clean. He left again to toss the wet cloth in the laundry basket. By the time he returned, Jamie was fast asleep, and I was fighting to keep my eyes open. Louie pulled the covers over us and crawled into bed behind me. He snuggled up close, wrapping his arm over my waist. I felt his lips press against my temple just before I drifted off.

CHAPTER TWELVE

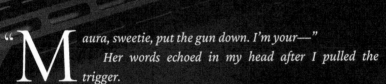

"**M**aura, sweetie, put the gun down. I'm your—"
Her words echoed in my head after I pulled the trigger.

I knew who she was...but I didn't want to believe it.

"Maura, wake up."

My eyes opened to Louie's face hovering above mine. "It's time to wake up, beautiful."

I groaned and sat up. The blanket dropped from my chest, baring my naked breasts, and memories from the night before came rushing back. I wiped away the wet streaks on my face and caught Louie watching me with a tight smile. I could see the questions he held at bay in his eyes. I ignored them.

His hair was wet, and he was mostly dressed for the day. His black dress shirt still needed to be buttoned. *Where did he get the fresh clothes?*

"I have spare suits in Jameson's old room, just in case," Louie said, as if reading my mind. The sound of a drawer rolling open drew my attention to the other side of the bed where Jamie stood, showered and fully dressed for the day. He checked over his gun before stuffing it into the back of his pants.

He caught me staring, leaned over the bed, and gave me a quick kiss. "You better get dressed before your goons get here."

I narrowed my eyes at him. "Only I'm allowed to call them that. Don't make me kick your ass."

Both he and Louie chuckled before Jamie ventured off into the bathroom and Louie got to work on buttoning his shirt.

I threw off the covers and clambered out of bed. The universe decided to give me the middle finger the moment I stood from the bed because my bedroom door swung open with Asher's voice filling the room. "Time to wake up, doll." He strolled right in, carrying a cup of coffee for me like he did every morning. And if that wasn't bad enough, Dean was right behind him. They both froze, eyes wide as they took in my naked body. Then their gazes traveled to Louie in the middle of buttoning his shirt.

I quickly covered my boobs with one arm and va-jay-jay with the other. "I know I'm normally dead to the world at this time of morning but learn to fucking knock!"

They both ignored me and glared at Louie, who stared right back with a bored expression while he finished buttoning his shirt. Dean stepped forward. "I told you to *stay* with her because she was upset, not fuck her!"

"Did you put those marks on her?" Asher asked, his voice turning deep and ominous.

I don't know if I should be grateful or offended by the lack of reaction to my naked body. I sighed and pulled the blanket from my bed to wrap around my body. "I got these yesterday, courtesy of Dustin Peters."

Jamie stepped out of the bathroom, glanced around the room, taking everyone in, then stuffed his hands in his pockets.

Dean and Asher stared at him with even wider eyes.

"I think they were about to try and kick my ass for having sex with Maura," Louie said with a shit-eating grin.

The corner of Jamie's mouth twitched as he looked back at my goons.

Asher snapped out of his shock the quickest, whistled, and grinned at me. "Looks like you had a fun night. Good for you."

Dean sighed and stared at my neck. "You downplayed how badly that Aryan prick hurt you."

I crossed my arms over my chest. "I said he got rough with me."

Dean frowned. "That's an understatement."

I rolled my eyes and held my hand out for the coffee Asher was holding. He handed it over. "Thank you," I said. I took a sip right away and scrunched my nose when the liquid rolled over my taste buds.

"What's wrong?" Asher asked. "It was made the right way. One part coffee. Three parts creamer."

I stared down into my mug. "I think Jeana changed the coffee brand or something. It doesn't taste right," I said and sat the mug on my nightstand.

Jamie crossed the room and kissed my temple. "Breakfast is in twenty minutes."

I turned and gave him a quick peck on the lips. "I'm going to take the world's fastest shower and then I'll be down. Please tell Jeana I'll be eating, and I really, really want pancakes."

Jamie's brows shot up. "You're going to eat breakfast?"

I moved away from him toward Louie. "Seems I worked up quite the appetite last night," I said over my shoulder. I gave Louie a quick peck as well and was rewarded with the bright smile that I'd missed so much. "Are you going to come back tonight?" I asked.

He glanced at Jamie before answering. "If you want me here, beautiful, then I'll be here."

"I want you here," I told him. He kissed me goodbye and he left with Jamie to head downstairs. I showered, then dressed comfortably in leggings and a T-shirt. I had no plans of adulting today. When we went downstairs, my goons veered off toward the kitchen as I went into the dining room. The table was almost full this morning. Stefan, Jamie, Louie, Rourke, and Vincent were already seated and eating.

"Did you spend the night?" I asked Rourke as I rounded the table. He was still in yesterday's clothes.

Stefan looked up from his breakfast at the sound of my voice. His eyes were immediately drawn to my neck and his expression turned dark. "Maura Aisling Quinn!"

I froze where I stood, gaping at my father. *Oh, shit!* He hadn't used my full name in that tone since I was like ten years old. Strangely, it still had the same effect on me. Then I remembered I was twenty-four, I'd killed people, and I sold cocaine for a living. My state of stupor wore off and I took my seat at the table. "It's not as bad as it looks."

Stefan covered my hand with his. "I don't think you should take such risks anymore. We have plenty of trained enforcers and security who are more capable of—"

I yanked my hand away. "Are you saying that because I'm a woman?"

"It's because you are my daughter and nothing will fucking matter if you're dead," he snarled.

"How can I expect anyone to respect me and risk everything for me if I'm not willing to do the same for them?" I questioned.

He shook his head, looking disappointed. "You don't have to be the one to do it all—take all the risks. As a leader, you must learn to step back and rely on others, use their strengths where they're needed."

"It may be that easy for you, but as a woman, they won't—"

He slammed his hand down on the table. "That is no excuse to be reckless! Your ass is already in the chair. You need to show everyone you can lead now, not how to die." He stood from his chair and threw his napkin on the table. "The party is in a week. You still need to get a dress. If you leave the house, you need to take more than Asher and Dean with you."

I opened my mouth to argue.

"I know about the phone call you had with Buck Werner. You painted a fucking target on your back. Your security will be doubled. I will not negotiate on this," Stefan said, his tone brokering no argument, and he stormed out of the dining room.

I slowly turned to glare at Rourke. He was looking anywhere but me. "Of all the fucking things to tell him," I practically growled.

He grimaced.

"I'd go home, Rourke, because I'm debating whether or not I should cut your tongue from your big fucking mouth or maybe sew your mouth shut!" I screamed as I slowly rose from my chair. *He is so lucky Vincent is sitting between us.*

Rourke quickly jumped to his feet, knocking over his chair in the process. "I'm going, I promise! But you should know that Stefan kept me here for hours, interrogating me for every minute detail. I can't get away with shit like you can! I'm sorry, cuz, but he's still the boss and ten times scarier than you."

I picked up Vincent's butter knife that was lying next to his plate. "Are you sure about that?"

Rourke briskly walked out of the room and I sat back down with a heavy sigh.

"That was fucked up, even for you," Jamie said as he continued to eat as if nothing had happened. Louie was at least pushing around his food. Vincent was wide eyed, his breakfast completely forgotten.

I shrugged. "I understand he had no choice, and I didn't exactly tell him not to tell Stefan either. But this will teach him that it wasn't okay to throw me under the bus. In the future, he'll hesitate—he'll think, *How can I do this without screwing Maura because I don't want to betray her?* I get that Stefan is everyone's boss and that puts you all in a damned-if-you-do-damned-if-you-don't situation. All I ask is that you try. If you fail...well, do you think Stefan would punish anyone trying to protect me?"

"Is this you admitting that you believe he loves you?" Jamie asked.

Noah entered the dining room holding a tray. He set a plate of pancakes with syrup and butter on the side. "Can I get you anything, Miss Maura? Some coffee maybe?"

"No, thank you," I said without removing my eyes from my stack of pancakes. They smelled mouthwatering. Noah made his rounds around the table, asking if anyone needed anything else before returning to the kitchen. I got to work by spreading butter and syrup all over my tower of fluffy, cakey goodness. "How can you truly know someone loves you if they never say it? I know Stefan cares and that he's trying to be more my father than the boss. I guess, to answer your question, I'm still not sure."

"He loves you, beautiful," Louie assured.

"You have the weirdest family," Vincent mumbled and returned to eating.

I smiled at him before taking a bite of my own food. *Oh, wow, that's good.* I moaned around my pancake. I caught Jamie trying to hide his smile.

"Huh," Louie said as he eyed me with a slight tilt of his head and then looked at Jamie. "She really does sound like that."

Jamie tried to stifle his laughter but failed miserably. I frowned at the both of them and that seemed to wipe the smiles off of both of their faces.

"Since I need to double my security, can you pick me some good ones?" I asked Louie.

He nodded. "Already on it. I have a few in mind. I'll have them come by this afternoon. When were you wanting to go dress shopping?"

"Tomorrow. I'm taking the day off today. My goons and I have TV shows to catch up on." I turned toward Vincent. "You're welcome to join us, Vin. Unless you were wanting to return home today?"

"I think I should head home. I've been here for weeks," he said.

"If you ever get bored, you're always welcome to come over here," I told him, and we all continued eating.

Later that afternoon, Louie texted me to meet him in the lounge. I peeled myself from my couch and went downstairs with Dean and Asher accompanying me. I walked into the lounge, just off the foyer. It was a large room with soft cream-colored couches, a giant fireplace, and an entire wall full of photos of my family over the generations. A few pictures dated back to when cameras were first invented and were printed on tin plates.

My photo wasn't on that wall. Nope. Mine was hanging over the fireplace.

When I had been three or four years old, Brody had taken me to get my portrait painted by a professional artist as a gift for Stefan's birthday. It was a precious picture, if I did say so myself. Brody had dressed me in a beautiful white gown and had my hair curled into tight ringlets that reached my tiny shoulders. The background of the portrait was stark black, making my pale skin and dress almost look as if they were glowing.

Louie was standing beside the fireplace with two goons I recognized. *Well, there went my good mood.* I'd worked with the two goons before. They were the two who Stefan had ordered to stay behind with me when I'd done my first exchange with Nicoli after Samuel's execution. One of them had told Jamie that I'd kissed the don, and that information had also seemed to make its way to Rourke, as well. I'd asked Asher to find out which of the two was the rat. All I'd gotten was a name before my accident. *Hank.*

Louie smiled at me. "Hey, these guys have worked with you before. I figured they'd..." He trailed off when he noticed me glaring at the two goons standing next to him.

"This should be interesting," Asher snickered behind me.

I folded my arms over my chest. "Find another two."

"Is there something I should know?" Louie asked.

"Dipshit One and Two don't know how to keep their mouths shut. I'll call Finn. That way, you just have to find me one goon who knows how to be discreet. Hell, I'd take Josh or Blake before I'd take either of them," I explained.

Both of the goons scowled at me before one of them stepped forward. "We know how to be discreet. Let us do our job and you just focus on what you know best—being a spoiled girl spending Daddy's money," he sneered. "You need us to babysit you while you go dress shopping, right?"

I took a step closer to him to show I wasn't intimidated. "Let me guess, you're Hank."

He straightened his shoulders. "Yeah, what of it?"

The corner of my mouth lifted. "I'm just putting a face to a name. You told Jamie I kissed Nicoli De Luca. That's not very discreet and I think you should be punished."

Hank laughed and looked back at his fellow goon. "Can you believe this shit?"

The other goon smartly didn't react or encourage his partner. Instead, he glanced at me with a hint of fear in his eyes. Hank turned back to face me with an arrogant smirk. I didn't appreciate that. So I did the mature thing and expressed how his laughing made me feel...physically. My fist shot out and collided with his throat.

He let out a choking noise, grabbed at his throat, and fell to his knees. I threw my fist out again, this time, breaking his nose. Blood poured from Hank's nostrils, splattering on one of the couch cushions before he curled over. I internally winced because I knew Brody was going to be pissed about me getting blood everywhere.

The other goon appeared to be in shock as he stared at Hank on the floor, but quickly recovered and took a step forward. I couldn't tell if he was coming toward me or intended to help Hank. Louie didn't seem to care either way because he stopped him from coming any closer by putting his arm out in front of him. Dean and Asher moved into my peripheral, preparing to protect me if anything were to happen.

I locked eyes with Louie and gestured to Hank. "How can we expect him to protect me if he can be taken down by the boss's spoiled little girl?"

"You cunt," Hank wheezed up at me.

I put the back of my hand to my forehead. "Catch me, Thor. I might faint. His vulgar language is too much for my delicate princess ears."

Asher just stared at me like I'd lost my damn mind. "You have the worst potty mouth I've ever heard, and I used to be in the military." Dean nodded in agreement.

I dropped my hand and beamed up at him. "Aw, thank you. It's nice to know I excel at something." I tilted my head at Hank. "Let's take him for a walk."

Understanding, Dean and Asher yanked Hank off the floor and forced him to follow me out of the lounge. Louie and the other goon also followed as we traveled to the back yard. I stopped next to the pool's edge. "How long can you hold your breath, Hank?"

I didn't get an answer. I watched his eyes lingering on the water before they drifted to me. I almost whistled at the glare he was giving me. The blood running from his nose and dripping off his chin really gave the fury burning in his eyes an extra oomph. *If looks could kill...*

I raised a brow. "Shall we find out?"

Without having to be asked, Dean and Asher kicked Hank's legs out from underneath him, forcing him to his knees by the pool's edge. Hank struggled against them to no avail. My goons got him onto his stomach and Asher's giant hand shoved Hank's head into the water. Hank's body thrashed and the water splashed as he fought to raise his head.

"Don't get involved, Will," I heard Louie order. My eyes flicked over to where he and, I assumed, Will stood a few yards away. Louie was standing in front of Will, doing his best to hold him back.

"She's going to kill him—" Will argued and reached into his suit jacket.

Louie shoved him backward, hard. Will stumbled a little and Louie reached behind his back and pulled his gun. He quickly cocked it and pointed it at Will. "Don't fucking do it, man. Hank made his bed. Don't go down with him."

I wasn't going to kill Hank. I wanted to teach him a lesson and hopefully use this to set an example. *Don't fuck me over.* "Alright, that's enough," I told Dean and Asher. They released Hank and stepped away from him. He rolled away from the pool as he coughed up water.

I squatted next to him. "The next time you gossip about me to anyone, I'll fill your big mouth with bullets."

I stood and walked over to where Louie and Will were standing. Louie no longer had his gun pointed at Will, which was a good sign. Will wasn't much taller than me and he had short ginger hair. I met his light brown eyes. "Rourke also found out about my kiss with Nicoli De Luca. Have any idea how he found out?"

Eyes never leaving mine, he shook his head. "I didn't fucking tell anyone. I don't give two shits who you kiss."

My gut told me he was being honest. "Do you know who I am?"

"The boss's daughter," he answered.

"I am the Banphrionsa. That means I outrank everyone in this family besides Stefan. So if you betray me, I will kill you and no one will bat a fucking eye. Am I understood?"

Will clenched his jaw before he replied simply, "Yeah."

"Good." I looked at Louie. "He may be part of my security. I'll call Finn to help fill in the fourth spot."

"You sure you're comfortable with that?" Louie asked, looking from Will to me.

"I wouldn't have said so if I wasn't. I'm going to leave you Dean to help you deal with that," I said, waving my hand toward Hank.

"You don't have—"

I cut Louie off by standing on my tiptoes and crushing my lips on his. His surprise only lasted for a breath before he took control and pulled me close, shoving his fingers into my hair and wrapping an arm around the small of my back.

The kiss was scorching hot but short. I broke away with a sly smile. He stared down at me with swollen lips. "That was unexpected. Are you sure that was a good idea?"

I didn't care what people thought. It was nobody's business. Unfortunately, my kiss with Louie just now wasn't an announcement that we were sleeping together. It was a test. Dean and Asher were blocking Hank from seeing our kiss, but Will had gotten a front row seat. If word got out that I'd kissed Louie, I'd know if Will could really be trusted.

Before I sauntered away, I locked eyes with Will. "I'll see you tomorrow."

CHAPTER THIRTEEN

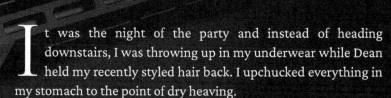

I t was the night of the party and instead of heading downstairs, I was throwing up in my underwear while Dean held my recently styled hair back. I upchucked everything in my stomach to the point of dry heaving.

"Try taking a deep breath through your nose and out through your mouth," Dean advised, to help me stop.

I did. I focused on just breathing until the rolling of my stomach stopped. I flushed the toilet and stood with my hand on my bare stomach. Dean walked me over to the sink and continued to hold my hair back as I washed around my mouth and brushed my teeth.

I took a peek in the mirror for any possible damage. My mascara had run a little from my eyes watering and a few curls needed to be tightened. It was all an easy fix, thankfully.

Because Dean had texted for reinforcement, Asher rushed into the bathroom with a glass of water in hand. "Are you okay?" he asked, offering the glass.

I took it. "I'm already feeling better. I don't know if I'm coming down with something or if I ate something bad. Either way, let's pretend it didn't happen."

He nodded and explained that he needed to get back.

Stefan had hired extra security through the security firm owned by Aiden, Jamie's uncle, for tonight's event. There were going to be a lot of powerful people attending and almost all of them were shady as fuck. I'd suggested to Stefan that Asher be put in charge and give Louie the night off. Asher knew how Aiden's men operated and he'd gotten to know most of our security. Stefan had agreed.

Asher had been very nonchalant when I'd asked him if he'd be interested and replied with, "If you need me to, I suppose I can." I'd had a feeling all our TV binging had made him lazy, but when I'd brought up the bonus Stefan was going to pay him, he'd perked up real quick. "You should have led with that, doll." *Greedy bastard.*

I shooed Dean away so I could finish getting ready. My makeup for tonight's event was dark. I had blood red lips and smoky eyes. My hair was curled and pinned back. I worked quickly to fix my smudged makeup and hair because I was already running really late. I stripped out of my underwear. The black gown I'd bought a week ago wasn't the kind I could wear anything underneath. The sleeves were long but made of loose black sheer chiffon that cuffed at my wrists. The bust of the dress plunged to my sternum and there was a slit in the skirt that went up to the top of my thigh. The back exposed my shoulder blades and zipped down to my butt. I slipped on the dress and called for Dean for help with the zipper.

Dean returned, wearing an all black suit, sans tie. He took me in from head to toe, then nodded. "You clean up nice. It's hard to believe you were in tatty sweatpants just a few hours ago."

I rolled my eyes and turned. "Can you zip me?"

He sighed behind me and zipped up my dress. "You just flashed me your ass."

I huffed. "It's not the first time you've seen my ass and probably won't be the last time either." I smoothed my hands down the front of the dress and turned to face him.

"I was afraid you were going to say that," he grumbled.

I crossed my arms over my chest and frowned at him. "I feel like I should be offended."

"How would you feel if you saw me naked?" he drawled.

I actually thought about it and scrunched my nose. "I see your point. As your best friend, I'd try not to look. Well, not unless you needed me to."

"Why would I need you to look at me naked?"

"You know, as your BFF, I'm obligated to look at anything you might be worried about and offer advice. Like if you have a strange rash or lump on your Vienna sausage or fuzzy walnuts," I explained.

He gave me a disgusted look. "This conversation went sideways real quick. Why would I—did you just refer to my dick as a Vienna sausage?"

I grinned brightly. "And your balls as fuzzy walnuts."

He just blinked at me, then turned around and stalked out of the bathroom.

"Was it something I said?" I yelled after him, fighting back my smile. *Serves him right for complaining about seeing me naked.* I did one last look in the mirror and followed him into the bedroom. I slipped my feet into beautiful red pumps while Dean stood brooding by the door.

"We can't be friends if you're going to refer to my dick as a Vienna sausage," he grumbled.

I bit the inside of my cheek to keep my laughter at bay and walked over to him. I held up both index fingers, parallel to each other. "If you'd give me a ballpark of what you've got going on in your Gentleman's Region, I can compare it to something more adequate. Just tell me when to stop." I began moving my fingers apart. Dean gave me a look that screamed, *What the fuck?* I gave him a doubtful look when my fingers were about a foot and a half apart because, *Come on, really?* "What do you do? Wrap it around your leg?" I asked caustically and dropped my hands.

He snorted and the corner of his mouth twitched. "Gentleman's Region?"

I shrugged. "I call mine Lady Town."

He closed his eyes and his whole face scrunched up. "The shit you say," he mumbled, shaking his head, and he opened my bedroom door with a little more strength than was needed. "It's time to go." He waved his hand, gesturing for me to head out first.

As we got closer to the stairs, music from the party could be heard. Dean and I passed two goons guarding the stairs as we came down. We walked through the kitchen, which was bustling with the catering crew Brody had hired. A waiter passed me, holding a tray of hors d'oeuvres, and the smell made me stagger. Holding my hand up to my nose, I pleaded with my stomach to behave. I quickened my pace, hoping fresh air would save me.

Dean put his hand on my back as we stepped outside. "Are you going to be sick again?"

I dropped my hand and breathed in the cool night air. I shook my head. "I'm alright."

"Want me to get you some water?"

I nodded and watched him head back into the kitchen. I took a moment to look around. The party definitely appeared to be in full swing by the amount of people that were there. The backyard had been completely transformed. The trees were lit with twinkly string lights. The pool had been covered with a platform, which was now a dance floor. A live band played instrumental music. Round tables were set up on the grass on either side of the pool with a tended bar in each section. There were people already dancing, talking at their assigned tables, and mingling around each bar. The catering staff, carrying trays of champagne and hors d'oeuvres, weaved between everyone.

I spotted Stefan speaking to a few people near one of the bars. With the current song coming to an end, I decided to cut through the dance floor, instead of going completely around it. People turned and stared at me as I passed.

About half through the dance floor someone grabbed my hand. "Well, hello, lass. Where are you off to?" His Irish accent stood out and his voice wasn't one that I recognized.

I turned slowly and my nose was immediately assaulted by the strong smell of whiskey. The man who thought it was okay to grab me was short—about my height without my heels on. He wasn't exactly appealing to the eyes with his crooked nose and receding hairline. He clearly didn't have the ego to match if the way he was looking at me was anything to go by. I arched a brow at his arrogant smirk and pointedly glanced down at my captured wrist. He had yet to let me go.

I forced a friendly smile. "Do you make it a point to grab women without their permission?"

He chuckled. "You have fire in ya. I do love fight in a woman."

I let my forced smile fall. "I suggest you let me go, unless you have a thing for being humiliated by a woman, as well." I tried to pull my wrist away, but his grip tightened.

"Why the rush, lass? This was a stuffy party until you walked in. I didn't know Quinn had hired party favors. I'll be damned if you go home with anyone else. I saw you first," he said with a sinister smile.

Fantastic, he thinks I'm a prostitute.

"Let me go," I said firmly and loud enough to be heard by others around us. And by others, I meant Dean, Rourke, and Finn. The Irishman hadn't noticed them standing around us, watching our interaction intently.

His expression hardened as his anger took over. I gave him a bored look as I waited, which in turn set him off further.

"Do I need to teach you your place, woman?" His threat made the guys step closer.

"Try it and I'll send your body back to your family in pieces," I threatened back.

The Irishman didn't like that. He went to strike, but his hand never reached me. Finn and Rourke pulled pistols from their coats and pointed them at the back and side of the Irishman's head. Dean caught the fist aiming for my face. To my surprise, a hand pointing a Glock right between the Irishman's eyes appeared from nowhere. I glanced to my right. Jamie was standing in my peripheral. He was glaring at the Irishman.

"Coleman," the Irishman seethed.

"Let her go, Donnie, and maybe I won't kill you," Jamie said, his tone teetering on the edge of murderous.

"I think you should just shoot him," I suggested. "He thinks Stefan hired me to fuck the guests. I was aiming for beautiful when I bought this dress, not a prostitute. That's the last time I ask my goons for their opinions."

Dean rolled his eyes.

"You look gorgeous, baby. I was heading over to tell you just how breathtaking you are when I saw this bastard grab you." Jamie's words ended with an angry rumbling, because the Irishman had yet to release my wrist.

"I suggest you let go of my daughter, Donnie." Stefan's voice came from behind me. If his tone was anything to go by, he wasn't particularly happy either. It was then that I realized the music had stopped and everyone else had gone quiet.

"What's going on here, Stefan?" another voice asked as they approached. Whoever it was also had a thick Irish accent, and once Donnie heard it, he let me go. My wrist smarted, but I refused to touch it.

Stefan didn't have that problem. He stepped up beside me, grabbed my arm, and pulled back my sleeve. He peered at my wrist and the bright red skin there. "Donnie put his hands on my daughter, Sean," Stefan said, shifting his gaze behind me.

"I didn't know she was your daughter, Stefan," Donnie said quickly.

"Ah, I see, if I hadn't been someone of importance you still would have tried to force me to fuck you and it would have been okay for you to hit me?" I tsked at him. "Tonight is not your night, Donnie."

"What do you want to do with him, cuz?" Rourke asked, pushing his gun into the side of his head. "I'll hold him down while you do your thing."

"What is *my thing,* exactly?" I asked him.

Louie chose that moment to join us. "Feed him his dick, of course." He grinned an evil little grin. "You're The Castrator. I bet two hundred he cries the moment she starts cutting." The men around me chuckled.

"He does look like a little bitch. I bet three hundred he cries way before she starts cutting," Rourke said.

Donnie looked back and forth between Louie and Rourke, a little panicked. "You're joking?"

The men chuckled again.

Louie shook his head. "I've had to clean up the bodies after she was done playing with them."

"You grabbed the wrong fucking woman," Rourke snickered.

"This sounds like a misunderstanding, Stefan. I apologize for Donnie's mistake," said the guy named Sean. I glanced over my shoulder to get a look at him. He was good looking. His hair was the color of cinnamon and he had pretty green eyes with yellow flakes in them.

"Why are you apologizing to him?" I asked Sean. "I'm the one he got handsy with. And furthermore, Donnie should be the one groveling, not you."

Sean looked to Stefan, who was smiling at me. "Sounds like

you have this handled, daughter. Come find me when you're done."

I nodded and Stefan walked away. I looked back at Donnie with a mean smile. *This is going to be fun.* "What should I do to you, Donnie?" I asked rhetorically and Donnie glared at me.

Sean went to reach for me. "Hold on, now. I don't—"

Louie pulled a Glock from inside his tux and aimed it at him. "Don't touch her." His bright smile was gone in a blink of an eye and was replaced with a no-nonsense expression. Sean froze, his hands held up, and then he took a step back.

I returned my attention to Donnie. He did a shitty job of guarding what he was feeling. With what little interaction I'd had with him, I knew deflating his ego and hurting his pride was the best way to get back at him. "You have yet to apologize to me, Donnie. I might not go after your family jewels if you man up and say you're sorry."

His jaw clenched and his eyes narrowed. "I apologize."

I sighed dramatically. "You know what? That didn't cut it. I think I deserve a little groveling, don't you gentlemen agree?"

"Want me to get you a knife?" Dean asked.

"Not just yet," I said and opened the slit in my skirt a little wider, revealing my leg, but most importantly, my flirty red pump. "These are Jimmy Choo. They're fucking gorgeous and make me feel like a princess." I wobbled my foot side-to-side to display the beautiful shoe before setting it back down on the ground. "I feel like your apology would be more genuine if you got down on your knees and kissed my beautiful princess shoe."

Everyone was quiet as they waited. Donnie's anger flared and he made no move to kneel.

"Come on, Donnie. Is your pride really worth your penis? Imagine never being able to have sex again. Because that will be your life. I won't let you die. I'll make it my mission that you survive the...removal. Now, I don't exactly have a good track record with the others living after I mutilated their man sticks, but at the same time I wanted them to die...slowly," I rambled. My spiel may have been a little horrific to Donnie, but he still refused to kneel. I looked to Dean. "It looks like I'll be needing that knife. I'm sure a steak knife can be found at one of the tables." Dean nodded and took a step to leave.

"Wait!" Sean yelled, still held back by Louie's gun. "Donnie, you proud bastard, get on your fucking knees and get this shit over with."

Sean's words did the trick. Donnie knelt slowly with his rage and embarrassment visibly scorching his cheeks. He made quick work of it, dropping his head low to the ground and placing a tiny peck to the toe of my shoe.

I smiled at him after he returned to his feet. "That wasn't so bad, was it?"

He didn't respond and attempted to walk away, but a bunch of guns still pointed at his face were preventing him. I nodded at the guys to let him go. They lowered their guns and took a step back to let him pass. He stormed off with Sean following after him.

"Who is he?" I asked Jamie, tilting my head at Sean.

"Sean Kelly. He oversees the Boston area for the family. He used to kiss Samuel's ass all the time," Jamie answered.

He did look like an ass kisser. "Why?"

"Because he used to report to our Uncle," Rourke supplied. "Before Dylan was appointed to work as his father's second in command, Sean Kelly was gunning for that spot. He was pissy for a long time after the position was given to Dylan. Now that Samuel and Dylan have both been relieved from those positions, I wouldn't put it past him to stick his nose up Stefan's ass, in order to be considered for Samuel's chair."

I frowned. "I run drugs."

Rourke gave me a small smile. "Yeah, but for how long? You're the heir and Sean and his crew are the biggest weed suppliers on the East Coast. He brings a lot of money in for the family. Not as much as cocaine, but still a lot and that makes him more than qualified for Samuel's or Dylan's chair at the table."

"Why am I just hearing of this now?" I demanded, feeling completely blindsided.

Jamie grimaced. "Stefan didn't want to overwhelm you. He wants you to learn everything you can at our home base before you start branching out to the other cities in our territory."

Of course, I'd known our family extended across the New England area and with them, more racketeering. I just hadn't thought their illegal dealings measured up to what we did here in New Haven—the *home base* as Jamie called it.

I sighed and took a moment to admire Jamie and Louie in their tuxedos. Louie's was dark blue with a black bow tie and Jamie's was black with a dark red shirt, sans tie. Both of them looked sexy as hell. *How long do we have to stay at the party?* I was pretty sure I could think of a few excuses to leave early.

"Close your mouth, cuz, before you start to drool," Rourke teased.

Louie and Jamie both smirked at me getting caught ogling them.

I flipped Rourke off and all of the guys chuckled besides Rourke. Instead, he held a tight smile. It had been a week since I'd last seen him—since I'd yelled at and threatened him. Despite how tense things had been left between us, he'd still come to my defense. I moved closer to him, to get a little bit of privacy. "You know I love you, right?"

His smile turned genuine. "You better. I took a bullet for you." His arms gathered me up in a tight bear hug.

"I'm sorry," I whispered low enough for only him to hear.

"Me too," he whispered back before releasing me.

"We need to go find Stefan, baby," Jamie said, taking my arm.

"The Colombians just showed up." I turned to face him and found all their gazes fixed on where guests were entering the party from a path that circled around the side of the house. A group of men dressed in tailored tuxedos and a lone woman in a beautiful red dress were standing at the edge of the party. Conor and a few of our goons were already approaching to greet them.

I let Jamie escort me off the dance floor in search of Stefan. He seemed to know where to go. My eyes roamed over the guests we passed. One guest in particular made me do a double take and come to a halt.

"That stupid bastard. What the hell is he thinking?" Rourke grumbled from behind me, making me realize that he and Dean had been following me. Louie and Finn were nowhere to be seen.

I returned my attention to said bastard, AKA our cousin, and Skank Barbie clinging to his arm.

Dylan had brought Angela as his date to the party.

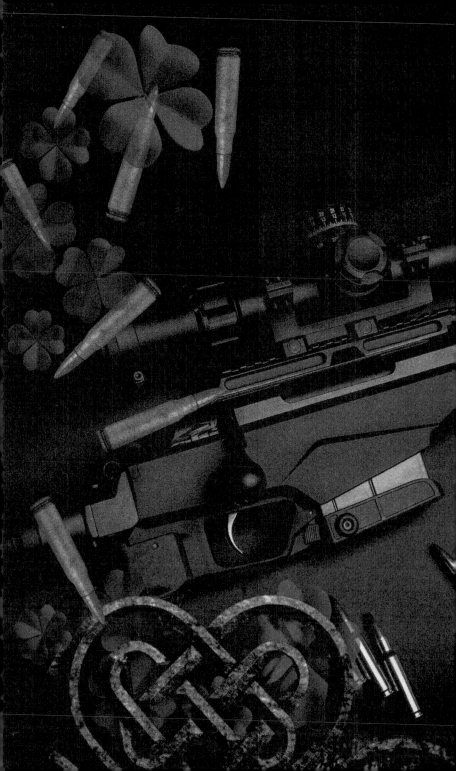

CHAPTER FOURTEEN

"Does he not know what transpired between Angela and me?" I asked Rourke quietly over my shoulder.

He replied, "Everyone does."

Does that mean he knew at the family dinner a month ago?

I held a schooled expression as Dylan and Angela approached us. Dylan's smile was innocent, but I could have sworn a spark of smugness flashed in his eyes. Angela did nothing to hide her glee as she looked from me to Jamie. Unabashed, her gaze raked over him from head to toe. Jamie moved closer to me and placed his hand at the small of my back.

"Evening," Dylan greeted.

I returned his greeting with a smile. "What a pretty date you have, cousin."

"Yes, she is." Dylan mimicked Jamie and moved his hand to Angela's back. It was a protective and possessive gesture, which he made look awkward. "I know you two have a rocky history, but I was hoping we could move on from that."

I didn't understand what Dylan's intentions were with Angela or what game he was playing. Regardless, I didn't have the time to find out. "Enjoy the party," I said with indifference and moved past them, Jamie walking along with me.

"What?" I heard Dylan hiss behind me.

"She's the only one on your side and this is how you repay her? What are you going to do when she's no longer standing between you and Stefan? He only let you live because he didn't want to upset her," Rourke snapped.

"God forbid anyone upsets the princess," Dylan quipped.

Jamie's steps faltered next to me. I knew he was getting ready to whirl around and beat Dylan's ass. I was tempted to let him. Maybe it would knock some sense into Dylan.

I grabbed his hand and made him continue walking. His body was stiff, and his hand squeezed mine.

Rourke raged back at Dylan, but we were too far away at that point for me to make out what he said.

I sighed. "I can't tell if he's testing me or if he hates me."

"He's more trouble than he's worth," Jamie said tightly.

"Maybe."

He brought the back of my hand to his lips. "You need to deal with him before things get out of hand."

"I plan to."

We found Stefan standing with the Colombians under the gazebo toward the back of the property and a good distance away from the rest of the party. Conor was with him, along with about a half dozen goons who circled the gazebo. They let Jamie and me pass.

Stefan's attention shifted to me with a small smile and he held out his hand for me to take. "This is my daughter, Maura." I took his hand and he guided me to stand before the group of Colombians. "She's replaced Samuel."

One man stood in front of the others. He seemed to be in charge. Nothing in particular stood out about him other than that he looked like a wall of muscle. It was the lone woman that drew my attention. She was beautiful with her long jet-black hair. Her eyes were a stunning color of gold with a black rim. Her posture exuded confidence and her golden eyes were scrutinizing. Everything about her stood out, yet she was doing her best to be unseen. She stood slightly behind the wall of muscle and three of the other men in their group surrounded her. It was a protective formation.

"Maura?" Stefan said, pulling me from my thoughts.

"Yes?"

His eyes narrowed. "I just introduced you to Emmanuel," he said, gesturing to the wall of muscle.

I looked at the supposed leader. "It's a pleasure to meet you, Emmanuel." I smiled and took a step closer to the woman, locking eyes with her. I held out my hand to her.

"Maura Quinn."

The men around her stiffened a little as they watched us. The woman stared down at my hand, then returned her eyes to mine and the corner of her mouth lifted.

"Salome Herrera," she said—her accent coming out thick—and she shook my hand. Santiago Herrera was our cocaine supplier. Well, he had been until he had decided to retire. His children ran his empire now. "How did you know?" she asked. *So she was testing us.*

I smiled back at her. "My uncle had many faults, but his biggest was that he was a sexist bastard. I'd bet a lot of money that it was you he had insulted, which in turn soured your opinion of us. I would have told us to get fucked, too."

Her smile grew. "Your uncle thought of me as inferior and always demanded to speak to my brother. Little did he know, I am the head of the Herrera *business*. I wanted to see if Stefan was anything like his brother, but seeing that he's completely let you, his daughter, take control of this meeting, there might still be hope that our relationship may continue."

That's a relief.

In Spanish, Emmanuel said, "She has the same look in her eye as you, Salome. Same spirit."

"I noticed that, too," Salome replied in Spanish as she studied me. "And I have a feeling she's understanding everything we are saying."

"Yes, I can," I said in English, smiling. "I know this was supposed to be a formal meeting, but this is a party. Would you care to join me for a no-boys-allowed drink?"

"Won't your father feel slighted by the exclusion?" Salome asked, eyes drifting to Stefan.

I glanced over my shoulder at Stefan. His hands were stuffed into his pockets and he regarded me with a proud expression. "Not at all. Please enjoy yourselves."

In Spanish, Salome told Emmanuel and the rest of her group not to hover too closely and to behave. Then she gestured for me to lead the way.

Stefan went back to mingling with the rest of the guests at the party, but every once in a while, he would glance over at where Salome and I stood in front of one of the bars. Each member of Salome's group paired up with Jamie, Louie, Dean, or Rourke. They were all strategically positioned where they could watch us from a distance. Jamie was paired with Emmanuel and they seemed to talk with ease. Louie and Rourke tried to talk to their Colombian compadres, but it looked forced. Dean didn't even try.

Salome and I both ordered tequila as we briefly discussed how we—women—ended up in positions of power in a world primarily ruled by men. I was honest and told her that my father had raised me to be smarter than my male counterparts and that I'd hated every minute of it. That made her chuckle with understanding. She said that her father had been harder on her than her brother and it hadn't been until he'd handed over everything to her that she'd understood why. We really didn't talk about business or drugs. As we ordered another drink, I realized that her main objective was to get to know me to better judge whether or not she wanted to continue doing business with us. I didn't mind because I found that I really liked Salome. We were very similar, and it was easy to bond.

"So tell me, which one of these handsome Irishmen has caught your eye? I would have guessed that one," she said, tilting her head in Jamie's direction. "But the way that one..." She pointed to Louie, then pointed to Dean. "And that one look at you, I'm not so sure."

I threw back the rest of my drink and grinned, not at all put off by her prying. Pointing to Jamie and Louie, I answered honestly, "I'm with that one and that one. The other is my best friend and part of my security."

Salome laughed. "I knew there was a reason I liked you. Are you building yourself a harem?"

I shook my head and waved my empty glass at the bartender for another. "I can barely handle the two I already have. What about you?"

With her drink, she gestured to all four of the men she'd brought with her. "The five of us grew up together. I was the only girl in our group, and for the longest time, they just saw me as one of the boys. When I started developing a woman's body, their perceptions changed, and they started fighting for my attention. I couldn't choose because I loved them all." She held a faraway look in her eyes, as if she were walking down memory lane. "It wasn't easy to get where we are now, but we've been together for six years and have two beautiful children."

I held my refilled glass up to her. "Congratulations."

She beamed. "To women in power," she said and clanked her glass with mine.

Soon after that, Emmanuel and Jamie approached us. "It's time to leave, Salome."

ASHLEY N. ROSTEK

Salome pouted a little. "I have to fly back to Colombia tonight," she said. "You were a pleasant surprise, Maura, and I would like to continue doing business." She held out her hand to Emmanuel and he handed over a small black clutch that I just noticed he was holding. Salome opened it and retrieved a business card. "Here is the best way to reach me directly if you ever need me. I'll be in touch."

I took her card and we said our goodbyes.

"Anything to report, daughter?" Stefan said, sneaking up behind me.

I spun to face him. "I like her."

"I'll take it you were able to patch things up?" he asked.

I arched a brow. "Did you doubt that I could?"

The corner of his mouth twitched just before he walked away.

A hand touched the small of my back and I looked up at Jamie. "Dance with me?" he asked.

I did my best not to grin like a loon but failed as he took my hand and guided me out onto the dance floor. He held me close as we swayed to the slow music. I rested my head on his shoulder, loving every moment. "We've never danced before."

"Hmm." He ran his hand up my spine to cup the back of my neck. "What else haven't we done?"

I removed my head from his shoulder to gaze up at him. "Well, we haven't gone on a date."

"So what you're saying is, I've been neglecting my duties as a boyfriend?" he asked with a grin full of affection.

"No, but it would be nice to have a night of fun just the two of us."

"And what would we do on our date?"

I really thought about it. "A whole night away from the house. Take me somewhere I don't have to dress up, like a burger or taco joint. Then I'll want ice cream. If you want to go to a movie, that's up to you, but I want to end the night in a fancy hotel room with a

158

huge tub because I'm pretty sure I can convert you to a bubble bath man."

He chuckled and gave me a quick kiss. "I'll remember that."

The song came to an end. Holding hands, Jamie and I went to leave the dance floor. I scanned the crowd to look for Louie to see if he wanted to dance. Instead my eyes landed on a scene that made my stomach drop before my anger blazed to life within me.

Brenna was here, looking as if she had just arrived, dressed in jeans and a long sleeve sweater. Dylan was holding Brenna by her arm, and it looked like he was going off on her about something. Seeing the fear and pain in her eyes made my feet move without thought. He was hurting her.

"Maura?" I barely heard Jamie say as I took off toward Dylan and Brenna. I couldn't let this happen any longer. I couldn't stand to let him hurt her.

Just as I stepped off the dance floor, I was still about thirty feet from where they stood between two tables when Dylan back-handed Brenna and she fell to the ground.

Consequences be damned, I was going to kick his fucking ass.

Passing the first table, I scooped up a champagne bottle. Dylan had his back to me, and I was using that to my advantage. I swung the champagne bottle hard and broke it over his head. My idiot cousin fell to the ground next to Brenna, unconscious. A woman sitting at a nearby table screamed, and the music died. *Why the fuck didn't she scream when he hit Brenna?*

I moved my rage filled eyes to Brenna. She cowered a little when they landed on her. "Get up," I ordered. I didn't offer to help her. I couldn't. She needed to do it on her own.

It took her a few seconds, but she eventually got to her feet. Tears were flooding her eyes. I closed the space between us. "Don't cry. You can't show them weakness. You must find your strength, because they'll never respect you if you don't."

"I'm not strong like you," she whispered.

"You can be," I assured her. "I can show you." I really did believe she had it in her. "But first you have to trust me and let me help you because I *can* help you. Just say the word and I will get you somewhere safe, tonight. He won't be able to find you. He won't fucking touch you again."

She swallowed nervously and peeked down at her brother. As she stared at him, her expression hardened and determination filled her eyes. "Alright, but I need someone to go to the house to check on my mother. She—it's why I came here...Dylan wouldn't answer his phone." She took a calming breath and squared her shoulders. "She's been using cocaine and I'm worried she's taken too much again."

I nodded. "Okay, I'll get Dr. Ben over to see her right away." I turned to look for Dean. He, Finn, and Jamie were standing behind me. I waved Dean over and got close to his ear. "I want you and Finn to take her home, pack as much as you can of what she'll need, and then take her to Vincent's. Do not let anyone stop you and I will do my best to keep Dylan here for as long as I can," I whispered. Dean nodded, but before he could leave my side, I stopped him. "You might want to stop at Finn's place, too. I don't want him leaving her side until I can make other arrangements. And tell him if anything happens to her, I will hold him responsible."

While Dean explained the plan to Finn, I went back to Brenna. "You're going to go with Dean and Finn. You can trust them. They may look like grumpy bastards, but they got your back."

She gave me a wobbly nod and let Dean and Finn usher her away.

"Can you get Dr. Ben to go check on Aoife?" I asked Jamie. He nodded and pulled his phone from his pocket.

I looked down at Dylan and sighed.

"Oh my God! Dylan!" Skank Barbie yelled as she pushed her way through the crowd that was forming around us and fell to her knees next to Dylan. "What did you do to him, you psychotic bitch?" She rolled him onto his back. He groaned but didn't open his eyes.

Where the hell was she this entire time? As soon as that thought entered my mind, Louie appeared, pushing his way through the crowd.

"Where have you been?" I asked him out loud.

His eyes drifted to Skank Barbie and panic gripped at my heart. As if reading my thoughts, he quickly shook his head. "Not what you're thinking. Trust me. I'll explain later."

I could do that. I definitely had more pressing matters to attend to. "Help me get him inside?" I asked both Jamie and Louie.

They knelt down next to Dylan and started messing with him, trying to get him to wake up. Louie shook him and Jamie slapped him across his unconscious face. That did the trick and Sleeping Beauty's eyes fluttered open. Louie and Jamie got him to his feet. I followed behind them with Skank Barbie walking alongside me— too close for comfort.

"Maura?" I heard Stefan call me. Sean and Brody were standing with him. They watched with curious expressions as Jamie and Louie practically carried Dylan inside.

"Nothing to worry about, Daddy."

"I see. So I heard correctly that you knocked your cousin over the head with a wine bottle?" he questioned.

"It was a champagne bottle," I corrected.

Brody snorted, but quickly covered it up by taking a sip of his drink.

Stefan didn't look surprised or upset, which was a relief. "Alright. Carry on."

I spun on my heel to make my way inside. As I stepped away, I heard Sean ask Stefan, "You're going to let her get away with hitting your nephew?"

I almost laughed at Stefan's reply: "I'm sure she had her reasons."

We ended up in the lounge. Jamie and Louie set Dylan on the couch and stepped away to stand by me. Angela sat next to Dylan and began fussing over him.

"If you're bleeding, try not to get it on the couch. Brody all but ripped me a new asshole for doing that last week," I advised.

Dylan rubbed the back of his head where I'd hit him. "You allow the help to yell at you?"

I relaxed my face and gave him a blank mask. "Brody is my family. I'd mind what you say," I warned.

"Or what? You'll hit him again?" Angela sneered.

I ignored her, staring only at Dylan. "You're pathetic," I said, shaking my head in disappointment.

The muscle in Dylan's jaw ticked. "Where's my sister?"

"There's no need for you to concern yourself with Brenna anymore. I'll make sure she is properly taken care of," I informed him. My lips stretched into a cruel smile at the rage that flared in his eyes.

"You can't just take my sister away," he seethed.

Poor baby was mad that I'd taken away his personal punching bag. That wasn't all I was going to take away if he pushed me. "Yes, I can."

His nostrils flared. "You took her away because I punished her, which I had every right to do. She snuck out of the house. Ever since our father died, she's been acting out—"

"I'm taking her because your home is no longer a suitable environment for Brenna. Your mother has a terrible addiction and you are not fit to take care of a teenage girl," I interrupted, choosing my words carefully. "I'm going to give you two days to get your mother checked into a center that will help her get clean and then I want you to take some time to self-reflect."

"I don't know who the hell you think you are, but you can't

order him around like that," Angela said, and her eyes slid to Jamie. A slow venomous grin tugged the corners of her mouth before she returned her gaze to me. "Just because your life is stale, doesn't mean you can stick your nose in others' business."

"You're waiting for him?" I chuckled. She thought Jamie was going to come running to her once he was done with me. "My, my, someone clearly thinks highly of themselves."

She sneered. "I'm a patient woman. He'll eventually see that you're nothing more than a psychotic bitch with a pussy too stretched out to please him." She lowered her voice and mumbled what sounded like, "I would never allow myself to be raped."

Her words stung and it took a lot of effort not to wince outwardly.

Jamie disappeared from my side in a blur. He moved so fast, his rage consuming him, that we were all stunned as we watched him rip Angela from the couch and shove her up against the wall, holding her by her throat. "What the fuck did you just say to her?" he snarled. "I don't know what your obsession is with me, but I could end you right now and forget you ever existed by morning. You mean nothing to me!"

Tears poured from Angela's eyes and she glanced at Dylan, pleadingly. Dylan made no move to help her.

Jamie's hand squeezed around Angela's neck, forcing her attention back to him. "You think I don't know that she's crazy?" He released an evil chuckle. "If she asked me to gut you so she could wear your insides like a fucking necklace, I wouldn't hesitate. Because *she* means everything to me!"

Angela stared at him in shock and Jamie regarded her as if she were the most pathetic human being he'd ever laid eyes on. "Why are you surprised? Just because I was nice to you doesn't take away who I am. Who all of us are."

I looked over at Dylan. He'd been really quiet until then. I held my hand out to Louie and without me having to ask, he handed over the gun I knew he had on him. I cocked it and aimed at Dylan's head. "Did you tell her that I was raped?"

He shook his head frantically. "No. I have no idea how she knows."

I should just do it. End the burden and the headache. But for the first time, I found it hard to pull the trigger. Regardless of his sins, he was still my cousin—my family. Every memory I had of him growing up flooded my mind. Had Stefan faced this moral dilemma before he had killed Samuel?

"Please, Maura. I'll do as you say," he pleaded, shaking like a leaf. "I know I've been acting out and I'm sorry. I just...I feel like my life is falling apart. My father is dead, my mother can't go a moment without being high, and you're right, I'm not fit to raise Brenna."

I lowered the gun. "I want you to take your whore and enjoy the party for at least another hour. Do not leave a minute before. I also think it would be best that you stay away from Brenna for the time being."

Dylan nodded and slowly stood. He glanced over to where Jamie had yet to release Angela.

"Are you sure?" Jamie asked me. "I'll kill her, baby. I'd fucking kill anyone who talked to you like she did."

Angela's mascara had run down her cheeks and her skin had turned ghostly pale. "I think she's suffered enough tonight," I said.

Jamie released her before Dylan grabbed her by the arm and practically dragged her out of the room.

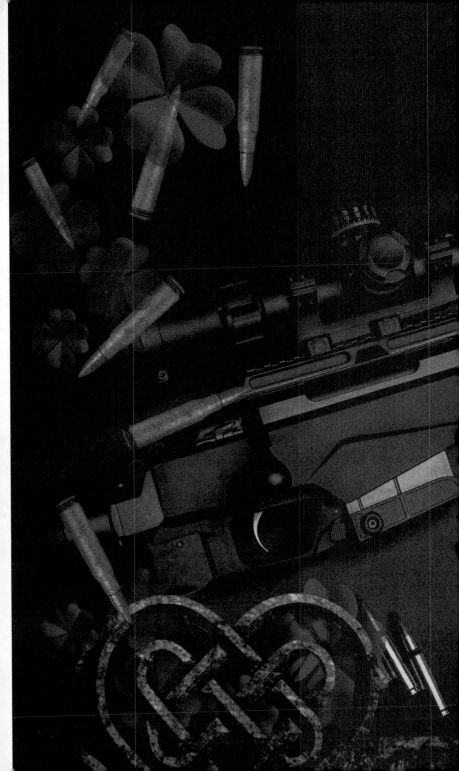

CHAPTER FIFTEEN

I told Jamie and Louie I'd meet them outside because I had to use the restroom. I wanted at least one dance with Louie before we called it a night and he had yet to explain where he had gone off with Angela earlier.

After relieving myself in the bathroom down the hall from Stefan's study, I walked back toward the party slowly. I was tired and my feet were starting to hurt. *One more dance and maybe I can convince one of my guys to carry me up to our room. I can think of some naughty incentives to bribe them with.* The thought made me smile and distracted me enough that I didn't notice someone creeping up behind me.

I was shoved into the wall. I didn't have enough time to brace myself. My entire body ricocheted off the wall, but I didn't bounce back far before I was pushed again and held against it. I hit my forehead hard enough that my vision turned spotty. It was disorienting.

A strong and calloused hand held me by the back of my neck, while the other hiked up the skirt of my dress. I became very alert when that hand slid between my legs, calloused fingers pushing at my entrance, and hot breath hit my ear. "This will teach you to know your place, lass."

I recognized the Irish accent. *Donnie.*

Finding my wits, I began to struggle, pushing back with my hands against the wood wall. I was able to put a few inches of space between me and the wall. Just as I was about to turn, to either break his hold or face him in order to have a better chance of fighting back, he let go of the back of my neck and ripped one of my hands away from the wall. I fell forward as he yanked my arm behind my back. He twisted it at the wrong angle, forcing me to cry out in pain.

He laughed at the sound I made. That fueled my anger and I began to struggle by squirming and squeezing my legs closed around his hand. He pulled up on my arm and I screamed.

"Open your fucking legs," he ordered.

"I'm going to make you and everyone you've ever cared about beg for death!" I roared, refusing to give him what he wanted.

He chuckled. "What are you going to do, sic Daddy—"

Pop!

The distinct sound of a pistol with a silencer fired and Donnie's words were cut off. His hands released me as his body collapsed to the floor. I turned and found Louie holding a gun at his side. His eyes were dark and stormy as he stared down at Donnie's body.

I cupped Louie's face and molded the front of my body with his, needing him.

I will not shatter by what almost happened.

I will not succumb to the panic.

I was frantic.

I was battling for my sanity.

Louie's eyes shifted to mine and I kissed him. I attacked him with desperation. Another man had touched me, tried to force himself on me. I needed Louie to touch me—to erase the feeling Donnie had left behind.

Louie broke away and stared down into my eyes. "Are you alright?"

I shook my head. I cupped him through his pants and pressed my lips to his neck, praying he'd get the message of what I needed.

"Maura?" He pulled my hand from his cock and took a step back. He frowned at me.

"Please," I begged and tried to get closer.

He held me back. "Talk to me, beautiful?"

I fisted his shirt with my free hand. "I can still feel him. I need you to erase him. Please...please, love me, Louie." I felt weak and pathetic. My desperation was the only thing keeping me going because I knew he could make this awful moment fade away.

His understanding showed. Releasing my wrist, he snaked his fingers into my hair to pull me close and captured my lips. I pushed him backward until his back hit the wall, roughly. He dropped his gun and it thudded on the carpeted floor. I shucked his tux jacket off. He let that fall to the floor as well. I pawed, nipped, licked, and not gently. He accepted it all, offering all of himself for me to take what I wanted—what I needed.

"Cameras," he murmured between kisses.

I broke away to look around quickly. Stefan's study was across the hall. I dragged him inside and slammed the door shut. We returned to kissing as we stumbled through the room. My ass hit Stefan's desk. I hopped onto the edge, spread my legs for Louie to step between them. I reached for the button on his slacks. He was already hard and straining against the zipper.

"Fuck me, Louie," I demanded breathlessly as I released him from his pants.

He yanked the slit of my skirt open and then hooked my leg over his hip. I wrapped my arms around his neck and held him close as he pushed inside me. I groaned loudly at the abrupt intrusion. He gave me a second to adjust around him before he pulled back and began slamming into me.

My nails bit into the back of his neck as I held on. He hoisted my leg even higher, changing the angle, and he began hitting that perfect spot. My moans turned loud as my orgasm started to build and his mouth covered mine, swallowing them.

I broke away from our kiss and threw my head back, crying out in ecstasy as I came undone in his arms. His pumping sped up as I squeezed around him. His entire body shuddered and he buried his face in my neck when his own release hit him.

"Christ, I fucking love you," he groaned.

I buried my fingers into his golden locks and hugged him close. It was what I really needed to hear in that moment. Especially after what had happened in the hall. "I love you, too."

"What the hell are you thinking, Maura?" an angered voice asked. Louie and I both tensed. I looked over Louie's shoulder, finding Stefan standing by the door, eyes wide. Brody was behind him, looking equally shocked. Two of Stefan's goons, one of them being Hank, lingered just outside the door staring in.

I dropped my leg from Louie's waist. He slid out of me and tucked himself back into his pants before turning to face Stefan. I hopped down from the desk and stepped around to stand in front of Louie. "Donnie attacked me in the hall. Louie killed him."

Stefan's eyes bounced back and forth between Louie and me and, for some reason, anger began to harden his features.

I sighed, realizing what conclusions he was jumping to. "Jamie knows—"

"I never thought you'd be this stupid," he talked over me. Something about his tone put me on edge. He took a step toward me. "I won't let you start a war within this family because you decided to open your legs for another man."

I reeled back.

Stefan stormed over to me and grabbed my arm—the one Donnie had almost broken. It was still a little sore, so I yelped when he began dragging me away. "What are you doing?" I questioned as I dug my feet in the ground.

"I can't believe you would do this to Jameson and with his best friend. We have a code, Maura. I will not have them killing each other because you decided to be a whore," he seethed, pulling me toward the door. *Where the hell is he taking me?* With the monstrous look in his eye, I wasn't sure I wanted to find out.

I fought against him, trying to yank my sore arm free. "You need to listen. You don't understand," I pleaded with him. Brody and the goons moved out of the way as he overpowered me and forced me from his study. "Stop it, Stefan. You're hurting me!"

Louie came up behind me and glared at my father. "I respect you and have always looked up to you as if you were the father I never had, but if you don't let her go—"

Louie didn't get to finish his threat before Hank and the other goon pulled their guns.

"Take him down to the basement. I'll be down there as soon as I'm done dealing with her," Stefan ordered, and the goons closed in on Louie.

"No! Just listen to me, damnit!" I practically screamed.

"Stefan, you're hurting her," Brody said. He looked torn. He wanted to help me but didn't want to undermine Stefan.

Stefan ignored him, his grip tightening—painfully—to the point my instincts took over and I smacked him across his face. "Let me go!"

The hit surprised him, but his hold on me didn't relent. I went to hit him again. He was ready for me that time and caught my wrist. With a look of disappointment mixed with fury, he bent my wrist back.

I let out a pain riddled scream.

"Maura!" I heard Louie yell.

Someone stepped into my peripheral and a fist slammed into Stefan's cheek. The force behind the punch made him release me and stumble back. Arms enveloped me and I looked up into hazel depths. *Jamie.* His eyes and hands roamed all over me, checking to see if I was okay before he turned a hardened expression on Stefan. Jamie pushed me behind him, and he stared down Stefan, who was rubbing his face as he glared at Jamie.

"So it's like that, is it?" he asked Jamie.

"Did you honestly expect me to stand back and do nothing?" Jamie shot back, his body strung tight. "I don't know what the fuck is going on, but I'd take a moment to look around."

Stefan glanced past us and I turned to look as well. The hall was full of goons. Asher and two of his fellow colleagues from Aiden's security firm had shown up along with Josh and Blake. Everyone had their guns pointed at each other. Asher and his buddies had theirs drawn on Josh, Blake, and Stefan's personal goon. Hank had his gun pointed at Louie's back, who was facing against the wall with his hands held behind his head. Brody was standing next to Stefan's study door, wide eyed.

I looked back at Stefan, with the overwhelming feeling of betrayal and sadness. "Stefan walked in on Louie and I having sex." My tone was emotionless and drone-like. I just wanted to clear everything up so I could escape. "Stefan caught us and wouldn't let me explain."

Stefan's anger lessened as his confusion took over.

Jamie sighed. "We should have told him sooner."

"It was none of his business," I seethed as I tucked my hand inside the back of his suit jacket for his gun. "And if he had listened to me, this whole fucking situation could have been avoided." I pulled the Glock from where he had it tucked into the back of his pants and I stalked over to Hank, who still held Louie at gunpoint. I put the barrel of Jamie's Glock up against Hank's head. "Drop it," I ordered, my darkness taking over and replacing my bland tone with strength.

Hank didn't budge. "I don't take orders from whores."

"Stefan, tell your goons to stand down or I'm going to put a bullet into this one."

"Are you giving me an order, daughter?" Stefan questioned.

I turned to look back at him with an expression hard as fucking stone. "What were you going to do to Louie down in the basement?"

Jamie's head whipped in Stefan's direction, eyes full of shock and disbelief. Stefan's gaze didn't waver from me. He also didn't answer, which was an answer enough.

"I see," I said. "I love them. I'm fucking them. Sometimes separate. Sometimes together. I didn't tell you because it's still new and none of your fucking business. I don't butt into your relationship." I pointedly looked in Brody's direction, silently telling him I knew. "I've respected your privacy and trusted that you'd tell me when you were ready. You couldn't trust me enough to let me explain. Not even for one fucking second. In fact, this entire situation has shown me where I stand with you. We had a deal, Stefan. Father first. Boss second. You broke our deal. You hurt me unjustifiably. According to your precious code, retribution is owed to me." An evil smile pulled at my mouth. "Let's play a game, Stefan."

He squared his shoulders, not backing down.

"I'm going to ask you a question. If you answer honestly, you'll save your goon. If you lie, I'll shoot him. Either way this turns out, your debt to me will be paid."

"Ask away," he said calmly, but I could tell his control was holding together by a hair.

I locked my eyes with his. "How many times have you told me that you love me?"

Silence blanketed the room.

I could see the muscle in Stefan's jaw clench. His body was so still, I had the impression my question had sucked all the air from his lungs because he didn't even look like he was breathing.

"I thought as much," I said and pulled the trigger. The shot was deafening in the small hallway. I never looked away from Stefan. Even when Hank's body hit the floor.

"Our deal is no more now. You can stop forcing yourself to be a father. But know, you've lost your daughter. You just want to be the boss. Fine. Then I'm going to just be a mobster."

I turned to a shocked Jamie. "I want to stay at Louie's."

He recovered, looked past my shoulder at Louie, and nodded. "I'll follow you there in a minute."

I turned around and Louie already had his hand held out waiting for me. I took it. We had to weave around everyone in the hall. They lowered their guns slowly as we passed. We walked away and didn't look back.

CHAPTER SIXTEEN

Louie had been quiet since we'd left the house. My hands had started shaking during the drive to his condo. I wrung my fingers, hoping to make it stop to no avail as I waited for Louie to unlock his front door.

Once inside, Louie asked, "Can I get you anything?"

I took a seat on his couch. Tonight's events kept threatening to replay in my head.

Stefan had tried to take Louie to the basement.

Jamie had hit Stefan.

I had hit Stefan.

Louie knelt in front of me and took my hands in his, stopping me from twisting and pulling on my now red fingers. *Can he feel them trembling?*

"What do you need?" he asked.

I didn't want to talk about what had happened tonight. If I did, I'd cry, and I refused to waste my tears on Stefan.

So I was going to bury my hurt and sadness for now with the intention of revisiting those feelings tomorrow when I was stronger. "A shower."

He nodded and led me by the hand to the bathroom. "Do you want company?"

I squeezed his hand. "I always want your company."

Louie shed his tux, letting the pieces fall to the floor, and unzipped the back of my dress. We took our time washing each other. He peppered my body with kisses as he did. As though to remind me that he loved all of me no matter what I might have been thinking of myself, especially after what Donnie had almost done to me.

It wasn't until we were out of the shower and I was climbing into Louie's bed, wearing one of his shirts, that Jamie arrived. He looked exhausted with his tux coat missing and his sleeves rolled almost to his elbows. His shoulders were slumped slightly. A clear indication that what had gone down tonight was weighing on him.

He didn't say anything as he toed off his shoes, crawled from the foot of the bed, and lay on top of me. His head nestled over my navel and he let out a heavy sigh. I lazily ran my fingers through his hair. Louie stood by the side of the bed, drying his hair with a towel, watching us.

"You never told me where you were with Angela at the party," I said to Louie.

He dropped the towel from his head. "I wasn't with her. She was trying to fucking corner me and I had to keep dodging her. I pretty much played hide and seek during the entire party."

Jamie and I snorted at the same time and our bodies shook as we tried not to laugh.

Louie frowned. "It's not funny."

It really wasn't, but just imagining them playing cat and mouse was a much needed chuckle. I cleared my throat and fought not to smile. "Sorry."

"I saw what Donnie did to you," Jamie said quietly.

My fingers froze mid stroke through his soft brown hair. "On the cameras?"

"We had to show the video footage to Sean to prove that Donnie's death was justified," he explained.

Oh. I went back to stroking his hair, but he stopped me and brought my hand down to his mouth. He kissed my palm. Dried blood and cuts along his knuckles caught my attention. "What happened here?" I asked him as I tilted his hand to get a better look. He hadn't hit Stefan hard enough for that to happen.

His body tensed. "Donnie had sent one of his buddies to the control room to distract Josh from seeing Donnie attack you on the cameras."

"I'm going to need to find a replacement for Josh, I take it?" Louie asked as he climbed into bed next to us. He slid his arm behind my neck so my head rested on that perfect spot where his shoulder met his chest.

"I didn't kill Josh," Jamie said tightly. "I can't say the same for Donnie's sidekick."

We fell into a numb silence, unmoving as we held each other until we eventually drifted off to sleep.

I was woken the next morning by the strong urge to throw up and the fear that I wouldn't make it to the toilet in time. I shot out of bed, crawling over Jamie in the process. He let out a loud grunt when my knee met his stomach. I didn't have time to apologize as I ran into the bathroom and purged all the tequila I had drunk from the night before into the toilet. *Yuck.* I wouldn't be drinking that for a while.

My hair was pulled away from my face and a hand rubbed the small of my back, soothingly. After a few dry heaves, I flushed and leaned against the wall. Jamie knelt next to me and pressed the back of his hand to my forehead. "Did you eat something bad last night?"

"Just tequila."

Jamie sighed and rubbed his face. "When was the last time you ate?"

I grimaced. "Yesterday morning."

I felt his disappointment ripple through his body before it showed on his face. "I wonder if I spank your ass hard enough, you'll remember to take better care of yourself," he grumbled.

He did not just...

"If you ever spank my ass outside the bedroom, Jameson Coleman, I'll punch you in the dick."

A snort trailed into the bathroom and we both looked toward the door. Louie was standing there, holding a glass of water, smiling down at the two of us. "I'd pay to see that." He held out the glass of water to me. "You alright, beautiful?"

I took the glass from him. "I'm already feeling better."

"I know you probably don't feel like it, but you should eat a little something," Louie suggested.

I thought about it and was surprised to find that I was actually hungry. "Okay."

"I'll go see what I have," Louie said.

Jamie narrowed his eyes at his best friend. "Kiss-ass."

Louie gave him a shit-eating grin before heading to the kitchen. I got to my feet and rinsed my mouth in the sink. Jamie watched me silently until I turned and faced him. He had a mischievous glint in his eye that made me nervous.

Without giving him my back, I moved toward the door. Once I was standing just outside the bathroom, I smiled triumphantly and flipped him off.

The corner of his mouth tugged up and his arm snapped out to grab me. A startled yelp rang from my lips and I ran. As I booked it out of the bedroom into the living room, I could hear Jamie's chuckle from where he still remained in the bathroom.

I helped Louie prepare breakfast. He had everything to make pancakes, scrambled eggs, and bacon. The three of us ate quietly at Louie's little dining room table. I gobbled down all of my pancakes and bacon, but couldn't bring myself to touch any of my eggs, at least not without upchucking all of my breakfast.

By the time we were done eating, I had let down my guard around Jamie. As I was taking my plate and fork to the kitchen, I passed where he was sitting. A hand came down on my ass, a loud slap echoed off the walls, and my entire body bristled.

That bastard.

Louie's shoulders were shaking with silent laughter. Jamie held a daring and smug-as-hell expression that made me want to smack it off his face. *And that's just what I'm going to do.*

I scooped up a fistful of uneaten eggs off my plate and smooshed them right onto the center of his face. Louie's head fell back with roaring laughter while Jamie sat there stunned, eggs dropping onto the table.

"Sorry it's not cake this time, *baby*," I cooed. "And don't expect me to lick it off of you either."

Jamie shot up from his chair and lunged for me. I jumped out of his reach. His predatory eyes held mine as he wiped eggs from his face. Still holding my plate in one hand and my fork in the other, I debated chucking them at him as I took a small step back.

The devilish grin he held promised another slap on the ass. "You better run."

I didn't hesitate. Not that it did me any good. I made it four steps into the living room when his arms locked around my stomach from behind. I screamed as I was lifted off the ground, my legs kicking the air.

I barely heard Jamie's chuckle over the sound of the front door bursting open and slamming against the wall, followed by Stefan and Brody storming in.

Jamie and I froze as we watched Stefan and Brody's wide eyes bouncing everywhere before settling on us.

Louie came up beside us, looking as surprised as I felt.

Stefan cleared his throat. "We heard a scream."

Jamie set me on my feet and took my plate and fork from me.

"What are you doing here?" I asked with as much indifference as I could muster.

Stefan put his hands into his pockets as he stared only at me. He had a nasty bruise on his cheek from where Jamie had hit him. Seeing it made everything that had happened last night flood my mind.

When he didn't answer right away, Brody glared at the back of Stefan's head and hissed, "Stefan."

It was an effort not to show my shock. I'd never heard Brody use such a tone with my father before.

Stefan's shoulders noticeably tensed. "Can I have a moment alone with my daughter?"

Did he just ask versus order?

"I'll be out in the car," Brody announced just before walking out and closing the front door behind him.

Jamie and Louie looked to me for my approval before going into the bedroom.

Nothing was said for the longest time and I watched as Stefan looked around the room, absorbing every detail. "I've only been here once, when Jameson first bought it."

I crossed my arms. "Brody made you come here?"

"He threatened to leave me if I didn't," he said casually. That had to be the first personal thing he had ever admitted to me. I didn't know if I should feel happy about getting a glimpse past his impenetrable walls or angry that it took Brody threatening him to come talk to me. What was worse was that I cared either way because why should I waste my energy on someone who wouldn't waste theirs on me? I was an obligation to Stefan. Nothing more.

His eyes flicked to me. "How long have you known?"

I made sure there was zero emotion in my voice. "How long have I known that you're gay or how long have I known about you and Brody?"

Even though his blank mask was unwavering, his body was tense and still as a statue. *Is he uncomfortable?*

"Brody told me last night how you had discovered us and that you weren't surprised."

"Is that why you're here? To find out how long I've known your secret?" I studied him. "You're here to do damage control. What are you going to do? Threaten me so I won't tell anyone?"

"How can you read everyone so easily, yet you are so blind when it comes to me?" He let out a heavy sigh. "I guess it's my fault...no, I know it's my fault."

Maybe if he talked to me or didn't always mask what he was feeling, I wouldn't have had to assume everything with him. He was damn right that he had no one else to blame but himself.

"I didn't come here to find out anything. I was just curious." He stalked over to the couch and took a seat.

"Then why are you here?" I asked again.

"My first instinct is and always will be to protect you," he said. "When I saw you with Louie I thought...if the family had found out that you were unfaithful to Jameson, they would have ostracized you. All the support you've gained? They would have abandoned you. They would have deemed you nothing more than a cheating whore and Jameson would have had every right to kill Louie."

"Everyone knew Samuel was an adulterous bastard and yet no one batted an eye," I argued.

"Samuel wasn't sleeping with a claimed woman. He sought women outside the family."

Beyond annoyed, I huffed. "It wouldn't have mattered if I had found a man outside the family. Everyone still would have viewed me as a whore."

He didn't dispute that. "Women have always been held to a different standard than men. You've always known this."

I shook my head, mumbling, "Fucking hypocritical bastards."

"If you want change, then you need to play the game and get your ass in my chair. I've done what I can in my time to lay the path for you, weeding through the leaders of this family, searching for those who'd be open minded to change and eliminating those who would not. I'd saved your uncle for last. Not because he was my brother, but because I wanted his downfall to be humiliating."

My brow furrowed. "Why?"

"I'm not ready to share that story." What appeared to be sadness flashed in his eyes. "I knew from the very beginning what Sam had been up to—the deal he made with De Luca and that he was lining his pockets. I didn't want to go after him right away. I bided my time, trying to think of the best way to take him down. Then you came home."

Fury swept through me and into my voice. "You used me?"

"No," he bit out. "I laid an opportunity at your feet to prove yourself. It was a bonus that you—a woman—ousted Sam and his crimes. It was the perfect humiliation."

I needed to sit down. He was frying my nerves with all the honesty.

"I'm sorry, Maura," he said in a low voice. "For not listening to you last night. I allowed my need to protect my daughter to take over me."

Holy shit.

I had to swallow once, twice to keep myself calm. "What was

your plan last night? With me and Louie? You ordered Louie to be taken down to the basement. Were you going to kill him?"

He leveled his gaze with mine. "I was taking you to Brody's office, intending to lecture you for your stupidity. Then I was going to go find Louie. I would have threatened him. Knowing that he'd never want to hurt his best friend, he'd agree to give you up until you properly ended things with Jameson. I planned to kill my security after that. As we both know, Hank likes to run his mouth, and I couldn't risk what they had seen getting out." There was nothing but honesty in his eyes.

I crossed my arms over my chest and looked to the ground. My eyes burned as the dam I had created last night to hold my emotions at bay broke. *He apologized.*

I sniffled, but I was able to keep my tears from falling. "I don't know how or when I started assuming you were gay. Maybe it's because I've never seen you look at women or try to have a relationship with one. There was that one maid you slept with, but I saw your regret and disgust toward her afterward. I guess as your daughter, I pay attention to you more than anyone else. Well, besides Brody."

"Why didn't you tell me after you discovered Brody and I?" he asked gently.

"I wanted you to tell me when you were ready. I had hoped that one day we would get to a place where we could talk to each other—tell each other things."

"Was that why you were waiting to tell me about your new dynamic with Louie?"

"I wanted time to enjoy our happy bubble before everyone tried to pop it with their small-mindedness," I answered.

He leaned forward, resting his elbows on his knees with his hands clasped together. "You admit that your relationship is...unorthodox."

I arched a brow at him.

"I'm not judging you," he quickly added. "I want to make sure you understand that not everyone is going to be accepting."

His words angered me because I knew his worry stemmed from the insecurity he felt about his own relationship.

I took a seat on the couch and turned slightly to face him. "Have you forgotten who you are—what you raised me to be?" He waited expectantly for me to continue. "We're mobsters...murderers." I let out a dark chuckle. "Hell, we're monsters. It doesn't matter what the family thinks about whether I cheat, that you're fucking a man, or that I'm fucking two. If anyone has an issue with it, we remind them who we are and what we can do because fear is our tool, not our shackle."

I caught a quick twitch of surprise as I recited his rule about fear. "I used to tell you that when you were little," he said, looking away from me.

That was true, but the rule had been recited to me every night like a broken record. I chewed on my lip, debating until I decided to take the leap and just tell him what had haunted my dreams. "I've been having this dream..." I started, then went on to tell him how my nightmare started with me hearing a woman scream. The more I told him, the more I noticed his back getting straighter, body going rigid, and his fists clenching. "I know it's impossible, but I think that the woman is my mother."

Stefan stood from the couch and walked to the center of the living room, giving his back to me. I thought I heard him release a shaky breath before turning back around with another one of his unrevealing masks. "How long have you been dreaming that?"

"Almost every night since I killed Zack and Tyson."

"Your mother died in a car crash when you were six weeks old," he said, reiterating what I'd been told my whole life.

I nodded. "I'm sorry if I upset you with my morbid nightmare. I just wish I knew how to make it stop."

"I'm not upset with you," he assured. I could have sworn I heard a hint of defensiveness in his tone.

"Did you really love her even though...were you two happy together?" My voice came out low.

Stefan didn't answer right away, as if he needed to consider how he wanted to answer. "Our marriage was a business deal made to strengthen the relationship your grandfather had with a gun supplier in Ireland. It was before we switched to your uncle Conor's family. They sent your mother to live here when she was sixteen. I was nineteen at the time."

"I'm not going to touch the arranged marriage bullshit, but why did they send her so young?"

"So we could get to know each other before we married when she turned eighteen. It worked. We became friends, and then more. I won't lie and say our marriage was perfect. She knew that I preferred men, but I did what I could to uphold my vows and make her happy."

I couldn't imagine what my mother must have been feeling when she had been sent to live in a stranger's home at such a young age. I supposed I could take comfort in knowing that they had cared for each other and tried to make the best of a shitty arrangement.

"Will you come back home?" he asked, pulling me from my thoughts. I had a feeling that was his own way of asking if I would forgive him.

"I have to," I said and pulled on the hem of Louie's shirt that I was still wearing. "I need clothes for tonight's dinner."

He did nothing to hide his annoyance. "Yes, our dinner with De Luca."

CHAPTER SEVENTEEN

I was running a little late to tonight's dinner. *Story of my life.* We were traveling in two Escalades because tonight was more than just a dinner—it was an exchange of money and drugs as well. Finn, Will, and the two goons who had been dutifully watching over our cocaine were riding in one car. Dean, Asher, Brenna, and myself were riding in the other.

Brenna was joining us tonight because Finn had brought her. When I had asked him why, he had grumbled, "If she's my responsibility, then she has to tag along with me to take care of my other responsibilities." He wasn't thrilled, to say the least, but I think his irritation had more to do with his life being uprooted and having to stay at Vincent's.

Vincent hadn't been happy with me either. I had received a text shortly after Brenna, Finn, and Dean had arrived at his place last night, saying,

> A heads up would have been nice

Oops.

I felt terrible. Which was why I had sent Asher and Dean over this morning with an expensive apology-slash-bribe in the form of a Nissan GT-R that I knew Vincent had been saving up for. The next text I had received from him had said that Brenna and Finn could stay as long as they needed.

I had also sent over a credit card and cash for Brenna and Finn to use for whatever they needed. My next task regarding Brenna was to get her enrolled into another school. Online was preferred, mostly because I was worried she'd be snatched from a school. Dylan might have promised to leave her alone, but I trusted him as far as I could throw him at the moment.

"How was your first night at Vincent's?" I asked Brenna.

"It was good. Vincent was really sweet and let me sleep in his bed while he and Finn camped out in the living room. I bet my father is rolling around in his grave." When she spoke of Samuel, her words were angry and bitter.

"Daddies like to protect their little girls as long as they can from boys," I said, doing my best to keep the tightness from my voice.

Brenna snorted. "The only thing he cared about was protecting my hymen so he could marry me off to a De Luca for an alliance after I turned eighteen."

I shouldn't have been surprised, but I still blurted, "What?"

She stared intently out the window. Her expression had hardened. "I'm guessing you didn't have to go to the doctor to be examined monthly to make sure you remained untouched?"

An uncomfortable silence settled in the car, especially from the front seat where Dean and Asher were. I met Asher's eyes in the rearview mirror and they were as murderous as I assumed mine were. The thought of her being violated monthly made my already queasy stomach drop.

"Did Dylan know?" I forced out as calmly as I could.

"He cracked my ribs because I made the mistake of thinking

that I no longer had to go to my monthly appointments now that our father is dead."

I hated how normal she made Dylan beating her seem. Like it was just another day in the Quinn household. I'd known things weren't good for Samuel's wife and daughter, but hearing it...

"Pull over," I breathed. Dean turned in his seat to give me a questioning look.

"Pull over!" I bellowed.

Asher jerked the car off to the side of the road. I was jumping out before he could even put it in park. I just barely had enough time to gather my hair and vomit by the rear tire. Headlights illuminated where I was bent over as the second Escalade pulled up behind us.

Between purges, I watched Dean's shoes come from behind our car to stand with me. He took over holding my hair and huffed. "You know, this is why I didn't pursue a career in the medical field. This shit is disgusting."

I wiped my mouth with the back of my hand. "Your sparkly personality would have gotten you fired on your first day."

He frowned. "You're still not feeling good."

"I've been feeling like shit all day."

"Maybe you're pregnant."

I rolled my eyes because I'd been on the pill since I'd turned eighteen. "Yeah, that's not possible." I put my hand on my queasy stomach and let out an annoyed sigh. "I don't have to tell you that what she told us doesn't leave this car."

"No, you don't have to tell me." He scowled at the ground. "Your uncle and cousin are pieces of shit and Dylan deserved to die right alongside his father."

"The sad thing is that they aren't the only pieces of shit either...Sean and Donnie. There are probably more women with lives worse than Brenna's."

"Do you plan to change that?" His question felt like a test.

"If I have to tear down my family's empire and rebuild it myself, I will."

He nodded with approval.

"I'm going to need you, Asher, and Finn to work with her," I said, tilting my head toward the car. "Teach her what you can about weapons and self-defense until I can hire people outside the family who I can trust."

He agreed.

"Let's get this over with and go home." I wasn't looking forward to tonight's dinner with Nicoli at all.

Dean and I climbed back in the car and as we continued on to the restaurant, I entertained the thought of me possibly being pregnant. Thinking back to my last period had me chewing on my lip. It had been practically nonexistent, and I had chalked it up to stress.

I pulled my cell from my purse and texted Dean.

> I want to stop by the pharmacy on the way home.

Staring out the window, I refused to see Dean's reaction after reading my text. Out of the corner of my eye, I caught him turning in his seat to look at me, but I pretended not to notice.

* * *

The restaurant chosen was Adrian's, the fancy Russian steakhouse where I had stabbed one of Sasha's men. This time when I walked inside, I didn't bother stopping at the hostess counter. I strolled right in toward the private dining room in the back of the restaurant. The beading on my gold cocktail dress shimmered in the dim lighting. It was form fitting, long sleeved, and cut off at my knees. The best part of my attire was, of course, my strappy gold heels that wrapped halfway up my calves.

Coming upon the black painted doors, I noticed that the antique two-way mirror had been replaced since I had shot through it. *I hope I don't have to stab anyone tonight.*

Dean opened a door and Asher and Will went inside the private dining room before me. Brenna, Finn, and the other two goons, whose names I needed to learn, were guarding the cars and the cocaine.

"You're late," Stefan said right as I walked into the small room. Everyone stood from their seats. Stefan was at one end and Nicoli at the other, both taking each head of the table like kings. Jamie had chosen the seat to Stefan's left, like always. Next to Jamie and to the don's right was Ivano De Luca, Nicoli's younger brother. Goons from both families stood along the walls, silent and watchful.

"Fashionably," I quipped. The entire right side of the table was vacant. I had the choice to sit to my father's right or the don's left. My gaze swept over everyone, landing on Nicoli last.

He greeted me with a devilish smirk as his eyes raked down my body and back up. "With how gorgeous you look in that dress, I'd say it was worth the wait."

I made it a point not to look at Jamie. The don's words were flattering, but it was just another tool of the game. He would undoubtedly prod and push to get us to react in a certain way to reveal something we didn't want him to know. I knew this because I had planned to do the same. Now that I was here, I felt too worn out to play games. "Are you saying I wouldn't have been worth the wait if I had shown up in jeans and a T-shirt that said, 'Eat a Bag of Dicks'?"

I caught Ivano's surprise before he snorted and quickly tried to cover it up by clearing his throat. Stefan's blank mask was in place, but his eyes sparkled with unreleased laughter. I finally glanced at Jamie and he held a proud smile. I returned my attention to Nicoli. He wasn't perturbed in the slightest. If his grin and intense gaze were anything to go by, I would have said I entertained and fascinated him.

"It's not every day a woman renders me speechless," Nicoli said.

I normally would respond to that with a witty remark. Instead, I just smiled. "If you promise to be a gentleman, I'll sit next to you."

The mirth in Nicoli's eyes dimmed just before they narrowed in an assessing way. If I hadn't been paying attention, I wouldn't have noticed. He gestured to the chair to his left. "You have my word."

We all took our seats. The waiter came in to give us our menus and to take my drink order. I decided on water. It earned me bemused glances from both Stefan and Jamie.

"Do you not drink?" Nicoli asked.

"I do," I replied, not willing to offer any more than that. No one needed to know that I wasn't feeling well. I moved my attention to Ivano, who had been obediently quiet. I perched my elbow on the table and rested my chin on my fist as I stared at him. Feeling my gaze, his eyes flicked up from his menu to meet mine. The corner of my mouth lifted. "Your brother has neglected to introduce us."

From what I knew, courtesy of all the info Stefan had provided me on other crime families in and around our territory, Ivano and I were the same age, twenty-four, making him ten years younger than Nicoli.

Ivano lifted a brow and I found myself smiling fully. "It seems an introduction isn't necessary, Maura Quinn," he said.

I nodded. "I suppose you're right, Ivano De Luca."

The waiter returned with my water and went around the table to take everyone's food order. The men ordered steaks, which this restaurant was famous for. When it was my turn to order, I went with salad and soup.

Again, Stefan glanced at me, confused. Jamie, however, gave me a look of understanding and slight worry. It had been only this morning that he'd been holding my hair back while I'd hugged the porcelain throne.

An awkward silence fell upon the room after the waiter left. I couldn't help but chuckle.

"Care to share what you find so amusing, daughter?" Stefan asked.

"Were you men this quiet before I showed up?"

Their silence was my answer and I chuckled again.

"Did you get the flowers I sent you while you were in the hospital?" Nicoli asked me, attempting small talk.

"Yes. Very sweet of you and not to mention stalker-ish. You not only knew I was in the hospital but also that tulips were my favorite," I replied dryly.

"I doubt I'm the only stalker at this table," Nicoli said and took a sip of his drink.

He had a point. "Since we're admitting to stalking..." I turned my attention back to Ivano. "Have you asked Alessia to marry you yet?" I might have had Vincent do a little more research on the De Lucas than what Stefan had originally given me. The main reason I had recognized Ivano right away was that I had found his and Alessia's relationship was similar to mine and Jamie's. Alessia's father had been good friends with Nicoli and Ivano's father. They had grown up together as close friends until Ivano and Alessia had started dating toward the end of high school. Ivano had bought an engagement ring six months ago and had yet to ask her when I'd been reading over his file while stuck on bed rest two months ago.

Ivano did nothing to hide his surprise, followed by a glare. Nicoli was losing against the battle not to smile as he looked from his brother to me.

"Maura," Stefan said, admonishingly, which prompted Jamie to snort.

"At least I asked instead of having to sift through his personal life again to find out," I argued.

Both Jamie and Nicoli laughed.

"Out of all the things you've probably learned, that's what stood out to you—my little brother's love life?" Nicoli shook his head.

Ignoring him, I met Ivano's eyes. "If you tell me, I'll do you the same courtesy. You may ask me a personal question, which I will answer honestly."

The laughter stopped abruptly.

Ivano's brow damn near touched his hair line. "I asked her two weeks ago and she said yes."

I beamed. "Congratulations."

He tipped his head with gratitude, then asked, "Why does your family call you The Castrator?"

I felt Jamie and Stefan stiffen and it didn't go unnoticed by Nicoli and Ivano either.

I was very curious to know how he knew that. They obviously had better spies then we did. If Stefan hadn't explained prior to tonight's dinner that the private dining room at Adrian's was not only sound proof but every inch was inspected for bugs before we'd arrived, I wouldn't have felt comfortable answering. "The first time I killed someone, I castrated him. I wanted him to suffer a slow and painful death. The third time, I unloaded thirteen rounds into a man's groin because again, I wanted him to suffer."

"How old were you when you had your first kill?" Ivano asked.

"Seventeen," I answered freely. Both Ivano and Nicoli appeared impressed.

Nicoli peered across the table at Stefan. "I'll admit that I'm amazed at how well you kept her out of the public eye and led everyone to believe that Jameson would succeed you."

"I never confirmed that I would hand over the family to Jameson." Stefan shrugged. "I suppose I never denied it either."

Nicoli nodded, then looked at Jamie. "You don't have any issues with taking orders from your woman."

That time I stiffened.

Jamie leveled a look with the don. "Maura always has and always will march to the beat of her own drum. Why would I want to stop her from being who she is? Pride?" He shook his head. "She's worth more than my pride and she'd gut me in my sleep if I ever did try to control her."

"And does the third member of your *ménage a trois* feel the same?" Nicoli asked.

Jamie did a good job at hiding what he was truly feeling. Before coming tonight, I'd pulled him close and reassured him that I had no romantic feelings for Nicoli. Then I'd explained to him how important it was to me that we settle the feud with the De Lucas and that if we had a shot of doing that—I knew in my gut—Nicoli was the one who would be able to help us do it.

I let out an evil little chuckle. "Just ask what you want to really know, Nicky. I'll respect you more for it."

He smirked, telling me that I had done something that he found entertaining again.

Before he could answer, I said, "But if you're also going to ask personal questions, I get to ask you one next."

He leaned back in his chair. "Is that what we're going to do tonight, play twenty questions?"

My hand fisted under the table, the only sign of my unease, because I was about to take a huge risk. "Why did you agree to do business with Dylan? I've done my research on you and you've been approached by other suppliers who would have charged you less. I can't say the quality is as good as ours, but still...why choose Dylan?"

He didn't answer. However, I could see the wheels turning as he mulled over how he wanted to respond.

A little more. It could be seen as weak to reveal your hand and show the slightest vulnerability. At the same time, for trust to form, someone had to give a little.

"Our families have been feuding for generations." I gave all four of them, including Stefan and Jamie, a hard look. "I *will not* be dragged into it. I have enough shit to deal with as it is and I'm sure you do as well." I directed the last part to Nicoli. "I don't like to surround myself with people I don't trust. If we're going to be doing business, Nicky, I'd eventually like there to be trust between us."

He schooled his face. "You want an alliance?"

"I'd rather have trust." I smiled a little. "Maybe one day we could go see a Yankees and Red Sox game and I wouldn't have to worry about you shooting me when your team loses."

Despite themselves, all four of them smiled.

"You want to be friends?" Nicoli asked with a hint of amusement.

I shrugged. *He better not make me regret this.*

Nicoli looked back to Stefan. "What are your thoughts? You are the head of your family, yet your daughter has done all the talking."

"I think it is better for you and my daughter to take the lead on this *trust*. You are both young and haven't become jaded by what has transpired between our two families like I have. I'm a prideful man, but I have the good sense not to stand in the way of what is right for my daughter and my family."

Nicoli was silent for a moment, thinking. "I agreed to do business with Dylan because I'd hoped it would lead to peace between our families. But we all know how that ended. I found myself stuck with a decision to make. Cut ties and risk our feud blowing up again or continue doing business with Dylan and have things stay somewhat peaceful."

"I probably would have done the same," I admitted honestly. "Looks like I owe you a personal question."

Nicoli's devilish smirk returned. "I'll ask it on the date you owe me."

I snorted and shook my head. He really was incorrigible. "I don't know if I should think up something extravagant to do so you'll end up spending a shit ton of money or make you take me to McDonald's."

Without missing a beat and completely un-riled, Nicoli replied, "Whichever you decide, let me know."

Conversation flowed a lot smoother for the rest of dinner. Afterward, we did our exchange. I ordered Brenna not to get out of the car. Even though we had discussed trust, that didn't mean I trusted Nicoli yet and I didn't want to take any risks with Brenna.

Our goons swapped bags of cocaine for bags full of money while Nicoli and I stood next to each other, watching as they confirmed everything was all in order. I was beyond ready to be off my feet and be home curled up in bed.

"You look moments away from eating the pavement," Nicoli said.

I stilled and did my best to recover from my surprise. I wasn't quick enough. He had been watching me and I could tell he read every thought that ran through my head.

His eyes narrowed. "You're pale and the only thing you touched at dinner were the crackers that came with your soup."

"I'm just tired," I lied. Something sparked in his golden eyes that gave me the impression that he didn't believe me.

Thankfully, our goons pulled our attention by telling us everything was good. I walked toward my car, away from Nicoli, and said over my shoulder. "Until next time, Nicky."

He watched me walk away. "Until next time, Maura."

CHAPTER EIGHTEEN

Will, Dean, and Asher followed me into the pharmacy. "I would have preferred to do this on my own," I grumbled.

"You know why you can't," Asher said patiently. They followed me into the feminine hygiene product aisle, which also contained condoms and a large selection of pregnancy tests. When I stopped walking in front of the tests, Asher blurted, "Oh, shit."

"Well, that explains why she puked on the side of the road," Will commented.

Dean whipped around to glare at him. "If you fucking say a word of this to anyone, I'll gift her your tongue."

Will glared at Dean. "I'm not going to say shit to anyone."

I tried to ignore them as I read over all the different brands. *Which one do I fucking pick?*

Frustrated, I grabbed three boxes of three different brands that had two tests in each. As we made our way through the store, I spotted a snack aisle. I teetered in that direction. Even though I'd been sick to my stomach all day, Twizzlers, Oreos, and hot Cheetos were calling my name.

Asher offered to help me carry the snacks. Dean grabbed something from one of the shelves and held it out to me. It was a bag of gummy worms. I smiled as I took them.

"We never did get those gummy worms that night you kidnapped me," he said with a smirk.

I laughed and headed for the registers. Coming out of the aisle, I almost ran into someone.

A hand came down on my shoulder. "Whoa, there."

I recognized the voice before I looked up to confirm who it was. Detective Brooks.

"Miss Quinn," he said, eyes going wide. Then his gaze dropped to the tests in my hands and his surprise showed again. Thankfully, he politely didn't say anything. Instead, he looked past me, over my shoulder, and his eyes turned cold.

"Gallagher."

"Brooks," Dean grumbled back. They stared at each other. It was clear that something was being exchanged. Dean's jaw clenched and I swore I caught the tiniest smirk twitch at the corner of Brooks' mouth.

"Well, it was nice seeing you again, Detective. Have a good night," I said and, not waiting for a response, I walked away toward one of the registers.

I waited until we were driving home before I asked Dean, "How do you know Detective Brooks?"

He stiffened next to me. "We went to high school together."

That's it? That's all he's going to tell me?

I fiddled with a gold bead on my dress. "Did you know there is a clause in the BFF contract that you're supposed to confide in me if something is troubling you and I'm supposed to listen?"

He stared out his window. "Is that so?"

"I take my BFF contract very seriously. So if you need me, trust that I'll help you."

He responded with a nod, a clear sign that he was done talking. I looked forward and saw that Asher was staring at me through the rearview mirror again. His eyes drifted to Dean before returning to the road. He had been listening.

When we got to the house, Asher held my door open for me to climb out. With just the two of us on one side of the car, he leaned close. "Want me to look into it?"

I nodded, hoping that whatever he found would be nothing. I didn't want to snoop around in Dean's life, but my gut was screaming at me that something wasn't right, and I had an obligation to protect my family. *Just in case.*

According to the instructions on the pregnancy tests, which I had to read quickly in the bathroom before Jamie and Louie suspected anything, it was best to test with your morning pee. It also said that I could either risk pissing on my hand while I tried to aim for the absorbent end of the stick or I could play scientist by catching my liquid waste in a cup and dipping the stick in it. I figured, why not do both.

I had no idea why I was trying to be an overachiever so early in the morning without caffeine, but I managed to do it. I still wasn't able to drink coffee. If I couldn't have coffee because of a possible parasite...*oh, maybe I have a parasite and not a human being growing inside of me. Please! Please be a parasite!*

After a few tests were soaked with my pee, I set them on the bathroom counter.

Dean and Asher were waiting on the couch in the bedroom. Jamie and Louie were downstairs at breakfast. I'd told them I was going to skip breakfast today.

I stared at the tests as I waited. It didn't take long for the results to show. One right after the other, they showed positive.

One of them even spelled it out for me, whereas the other had two dark pink lines.

"Shit! Shit! Shit!" I began pacing. *How the fuck did this happen?* I knew how it happened. But I was on the pill. I took it every morning without fail because I *did not* want kids. Never had.

I was starting to panic.

What am I going to do?

I have to get rid of it.

Could I?

Should I?

What am I going to tell Jamie? Damnit! And Louie?

"Maura?" Dean said, knocking on the bathroom door.

I dashed for the door and swung it open. "I need Brody!" I said loudly in a panicked voice.

"I take it the results weren't what you wanted?" he asked.

"Just get me Brody. Discreetly," I ordered and slammed the door closed.

At first, I didn't know why Brody's name had popped into my head, but as soon as I thought about it, I realized that I had always gone to him when I'd been sick or had a feminine emergency. To me, this fell in both categories.

It felt like forever before there was a knock on the door. "Maura?" I heard Brody's voice from the other side of the door before he poked his head inside. He saw me standing by the counter with my arms folded across my chest. I gnawed on my lip to help keep my composure. He stepped inside, closing the door behind him before coming over to me. "Are you alright?" he asked, eyes roaming over me for any signs of what might be wrong. The tests on the counter caught his attention and his eyes grew big. "Oh, boy."

I took a deep breath and metaphorically pulled up my big girl panties. "Can you help me make this go away?"

His forehead creased. "Are you sure?"

I went to argue, but he spoke before me. "I'm not saying no and I'm not judging you. I'm just asking if you've actually thought it through. I don't want you to make a big decision like this on temporary emotions only to look back at this moment later with regret."

"You're strangely calm about this," I grumbled.

He shrugged. "It could be worse. You could be sixteen, which was a worry of mine every time I found you alone with Jameson and Louie in this big house with so many bedrooms. I think the only thing that helped me sleep at night was that you were completely oblivious to how they felt for you."

"Sixteen or twenty-four, I don't want kids. I'm religious with my birth control. So I don't know how this happened."

"Then let's confirm that you really are pregnant. I'll make some calls and get you in to see a doctor," he said.

"Okay."

"Are you going to tell Jameson and Louie?"

I shook my head. "I don't want anyone to know. Especially Stefan."

He assured me he wouldn't tell anyone and left to find me a doctor. I numbly and patiently waited for him on my couch. Dean and Asher, smartly, kept quiet.

A half hour later, Brody returned. "Get ready. We need to leave in twenty minutes," he told me.

I rushed to get ready and sent Asher and Dean ahead of me to get Will and bring the car around front.

As Brody and I were stepping off the stairs, heading for the front door, Stefan walked into the foyer.

He eyed the both of us and our outerwear. With it officially being wintertime and freezing out, we both had on heavy coats. "Where are you two going?"

"Would you let it go if I said it was a secret?" I asked him.

"No."

Of course not.

"Christmas is around the corner. I need Brody's opinion on a gift I want to get you. Thank you for ruining the surprise," I lied, and it wasn't hard to sound annoyed. Before more could be said, I quickly dragged Brody out the front door. Stefan was the most perceptive person, other than Jamie, I knew. One wrong look or breath from either Brody or myself, he'd know something was up.

It's cold. I thought as I sat, shivering, on the exam table in a paper gown. *Yeah, keep telling yourself that.*

There was a hard knock on the door before a Dr. Greene, one of the best OBGYNs in New Haven, according to Brody, walked in. He was a seasoned doctor with gray hair and wrinkled hands.

Before he'd had me dress down into a paper gown, we had gone over my medical history. He had asked a lot of questions about my accident, specifically the medications I'd been prescribed. When I'd told him about the antibiotics, something had flashed in his eyes. He'd then explained to me that a type of antibiotic can decrease the effectiveness of birth control and one of the ones I'd been taking was known to do that.

"You ready?" he asked as he took a seat on his little rolling stool.

I nodded.

"Go ahead and lie back," he instructed as he rolled over and pulled out the stirrups for me to put my feet in.

I was very surprised to learn that he had to do the sonogram up my hoohaa and not over my stomach with a long wand that was cold and didn't vibrate. Dr. Greene twisted and quite literally probed me with the wand as he stared at a computer screen. He took screenshots and typed in various things I didn't understand. "Well, based on the measurements and from what you told me about your last cycle, the baby appears to be about nine weeks. We might be able to hear the heartbeat," he mumbled the last part absently before twisting the wand again.

"That won't be necessary," I said quickly.

A fast *thump, thump, thump* sound poured out of the computer's speaker. It was completely and utterly unsettling.

Dr. Green smiled. "Sounds good and strong."

At the end of the sonogram, Dr. Greene printed off a picture and gave it to me. I had no idea what the hell I was looking at. Dead center was a tiny jellybean shaped blob with tiny stubs for what I assumed were arms.

"Do you have any questions?" Dr. Greene asked.

"Yeah." I cleared my throat. "What if I don't want to keep it?"

"You're thinking about aborting?"

I nodded.

"If you decide to do that, I can refer you to a colleague. But you must decide soon. He will only perform the procedure up until a certain stage of the pregnancy. I have a pamphlet I can give you."

I nodded again because I'd lost my ability to form words.

He left and quickly came back with a handful of pamphlets. Some had information I might need if I decided to keep the baby and two were about abortion and adoption. He briefly went over each one and I was beyond overwhelmed. I barely remembered getting dressed and leaving the exam room. Dean and Asher were waiting outside the door in the hall. They followed me to the waiting room where Brody and Will were waiting. No one said a word to me as we left. Not that I had it in me to care.

It wasn't until we were in the car driving home that Brody finally cracked. "Can I ask how it went?"

"Fine."

"Do you want to talk about it?" he pushed.

"No."

The rest of the drive was silent.

"Maura?"

The sound of Louie's voice pulled me out of my zoned-out state. I was pretending to watch TV on the couch, bundled in a cozy blanket. "Hmm?" I asked distractedly, then forced myself to turn and look at him. I found him standing by the bed. *When did he get here?* I hadn't even heard him come in.

He tilted his head slightly. "I asked how you were feeling?"

"Oh. I'm fine," I lied, and it even sounded like a lie. I internally cringed and turned back to the TV.

I felt Louie come up behind the couch. I could feel his eyes boring into the back of my head.

"Are you sure you're alright, beautiful?"

I couldn't look at him. I didn't have it in me right now to fake it—mask my true feelings—because I was drained of everything. Emotionally. Mentally. Physically. "I'm just tired. I think I'm going to go to bed." Another lie.

If he could tell, he didn't let on. He put his hand on my shoulder and kissed the top of my head. "Okay. I'm going to jump into the shower and then I'll join you."

I nodded and he went into the bathroom. It wasn't long before I heard the shower turn on and I made myself get off the couch. I was on my way to the bed when the bathroom door opened. The shower was still running, and Louie stepped out still fully dressed. He was staring down at something in his hands.

My heart took off at a galloping rate when I realized what it was. It was the pregnancy tests. I'd left them on the bathroom counter. *I'm a fucking idiot.*

He looked up from the tests and met my eyes. "Are you pregnant?"

I looked away, finding it really hard to speak.

My silence being his answer, he asked, "When did you find out?"

"This morning," I forced out. "You left the shower running."

I heard him sigh frustratedly before stalking back into the bathroom to turn off the water. I took a seat on the edge of the bed.

He returned quickly and came over to stand in front of me. He shoved his hands into his pockets. "Can you be honest with me as to how you're feeling now? I knew something was up. You refused to look at me and you haven't even asked where Jameson is."

"Where's Jamie?" I asked halfheartedly.

"We'll talk about that later." His jokester personality was gone and the Louie who stood before me was still and serious. I didn't like it.

"I'm not keeping it," I said in a low voice because I was dreading what was coming.

The muscle in his jaw twitched and his expression hardened. "Were you even going to tell us? You turned white as a sheet when I found the tests."

"I didn't want this to cause a rift in our relationship. It's better that I take on this burden myself."

"Why would you think a baby would cause a rift?"

"Because I'm nine weeks. The baby is Jamie's."

"You're worried about me," he said. "If you really think that having Jameson's baby would ruin what we have, you haven't been paying attention."

"I don't want kids. I don't want to condemn a baby to this life," I said, anger seeping in.

"You're not your father," he argued.

I shook my head. "We're still criminals. What if it wants to be a doctor or cop?"

Louie shrugged. "What if it wants to take after its mother? We don't know what the future holds. Times are always changing. You're an example of that. You're a woman and the heir to this family's empire. You've given all our traditions the middle finger, done things your own way, and everyone at Stefan's table respects you for it. So whatever this baby wants to be, you're going to help make that happen and if anyone protests, do what you do best—scare the shit out of them."

He was trying to make me laugh.

It didn't work. "I don't want kids."

"Why?"

Rage burned inside me. I was tempted to lash out at him. I knew it showed on my face because I didn't even try to hide it.

He stood his ground. "I deserve to know what I'm committing to."

"You want kids," I mumbled, sullenly. My anger was extinguished by a tight sensation in my chest. "You want kids and you're going to leave me because I don't."

"I didn't say that. I'm not going to leave you," he snarled. "But I could throttle you right now for trying to hide this from us. You took it upon yourself to decide what Jameson and I can and cannot handle. That's not how this works. And yes, I might have wanted kids. I've never really thought about it, but don't you think that's a discussion we should have? All I was asking was that you explain why you are so against it—to fucking talk to me."

"I'm sorry," I said, sounding tired. I rubbed my hands down my face exhaustedly. "Where is Jamie? He should be home by now."

"You're changing the subject."

"I'm tired and don't want to talk about the jellybean-looking alien growing inside me. Especially if I don't even know if I'm going to keep it."

"You're considering it—keeping it?" he asked cautiously.

I didn't want to get his hopes up by admitting that a small part of me was at odds about what to do. That I couldn't get the jellybean's stupid heartbeat out of my head. "I don't know."

He nodded, his shoulders sagging a little. "We got a lead on Gavin. Jameson is looking into it and probably won't be back until really late."

"What lead?" I asked, grabbing on to the much-needed distraction like a lifeline.

"Gavin was found in West Haven. His body washed up on Prospect Beach. I don't know all the details. Jameson will fill you in on everything in the morning."

Shit.

I sighed and met Louie's blue eyes. "I'll tell him tomorrow."

He walked away, heading toward the bathroom. "I love you," he said tightly over his shoulder.

"I love you, too," I shot back in the same manner and flopped backward onto the bed.

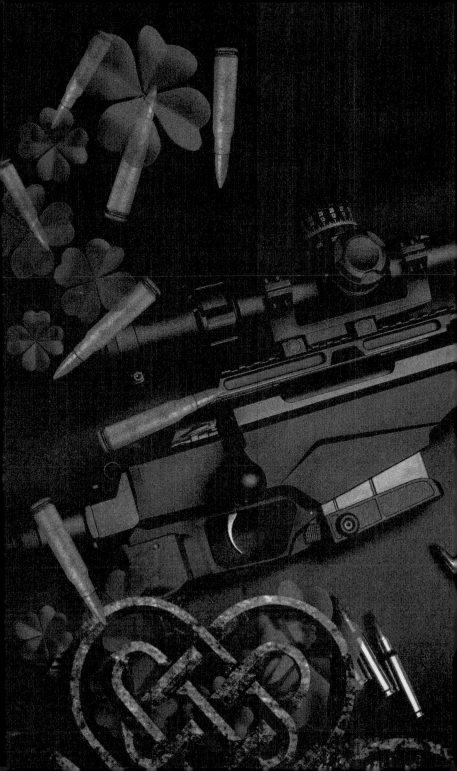

CHAPTER NINETEEN

T he next day I overslept and if anyone had a problem with it, they could kiss my ass. I had been up most of the night, mind racing and plagued with my certain predicament. I told Dean and Asher to fuck off repeatedly every time they tried to wake me. It was like hitting the snooze button on a very annoying alarm clock.

When I was able to drag myself out of bed, I had to run straight to the bathroom to throw up. Morning sickness was starting to be a pain in my ass. I was adding it to my list. I'd decided last night, while I'd tossed and turned, to create a pros and cons list to help me decide if I wanted to keep Jellybean. Was it the best way to handle a life altering decision? *Hell, no.* But I didn't know what else to do. Before I'd gone to the doctor's yesterday, I'd had my mind set that I didn't want to be a mother. After the appointment, I wasn't one hundred percent about anything anymore.

I told Dean and Asher to go home. I wanted to be alone. I thought it best to stay in my room for the day and talk to Jamie that night about everything. I still needed to find out what had happened to Gavin and maybe tell him that he had knocked me up. I just hoped I'd have my mind made up as to what I was going to do when I did tell him.

Throughout the day, I kept sneaking peeks at Jellybean's sonogram picture in my closet, where I had it and the positive pregnancy tests hidden. On my fifth trip to my closet, I broke down.

My list was overflowing with cons—legitimate ones and selfish ones. Such as, I'd never wanted to be a mother. I didn't want to condemn a child to a life of crime. This was a dangerous life. I was gaining respect within the family—what if a baby set me back or ruined my momentum? What if I was a terrible mother? A baby was a huge responsibility. It would ruin my vagina, not to mention my body. Morning sickness. Morning sickness. Morning sickness. I wouldn't be able to have sex whenever I wanted.

I hadn't added a single pro.

Yet, I dared to wonder, what if I kept Jellybean? Would it look like Jamie? Was it a boy or girl? The sound of its heartbeat continued to play on repeat in my head.

The uncertainty of Jellybean's heartbeat and the sonogram was strong enough to stand against all the cons I had. Therefore, I was still no better off and I didn't have a decision. Sitting on the floor of my closet, I sobbed. *What do I do?*

I hadn't planned on going downstairs for dinner, but Stefan sent Josh up to my room asking that I attend. I found out why when I walked into the dining room. It was a family dinner. My aunt, uncle, and cousins were present. The only ones missing were Brenna and Aoife.

My eyes immediately landed on Dylan and Angela sitting next

to him. *Why did he bring her?* He was so far at the top of my shit list, I itched to hit him over the head with something hard again.

Everyone went quiet when they noticed me. I masked my expression as I rounded the table to my seat. I was going to take the high road because frankly, I had too much going on to deal with my cousin's skanky girlfriend.

"Thank you for joining us," Stefan said once I was seated.

I gave him a bland expression with an equally bland response. "Yup."

His eyes narrowed. Thankfully, Noah walked in from the kitchen asking everyone what they'd like to drink.

I tried not to listen as my aunt Kiara, being polite, asked Dylan how long he and Angela had been dating. Angela answered for him. Gushing that it had only been a short time, but they were really happy, and how wonderful Dylan was. The corner of my eye twitched as I fought not to roll my eyes.

By the time Noah made it over to me for my drink order, I was itching for something strong. "Whiskey."

He nodded and made his way over to the liquor hutch.

Louie cleared his throat. He gave me a look I couldn't quite decipher and I returned it with a questioning frown.

Noah set down a crystal tumbler in front of me and I lifted the glass to take a sip.

"Maura," Louie snapped in a low voice, drawing both Stefan's and Jamie's attention because they were the only ones not distracted with conversation.

I paused with the glass an inch away from my lips, realizing what he was trying to tell me. *Shit,* I thought. I wasn't supposed to drink. I set my glass back on the table, annoyed. Not being able to drink was going on the list.

"What's wrong?" Jamie asked.

"Nothing. What happened with Gavin?" I deflected. It seemed

to work on Jamie, but I caught Stefan looking from me to my untouched whiskey glass.

Jamie grimaced. "Let's talk about it later."

Must be bad.

Noah and Jeana came out of the kitchen, carrying plates, and began serving everyone dinner.

The smell of the food reached me before my plate did. My stomach turned and I had to hold my breath as I eyed the seafood pasta dish sitting before me. I battled to rein in my nausea because I needed to breathe. I tried to discreetly put my hand over my nose and mouth as I took in a tiny breath. It didn't help and the smell of fish filled my nose. I jumped from my seat and rushed out of the dining room to the nearest bathroom down the hall. I barely made it to the toilet before I threw up and was so focused on just getting to the toilet in time that I forgot to close the door.

After dry heaving a hundred times, I went over to the sink to rinse my mouth out. I noticed Stefan standing in the doorway behind me in the mirror.

He watched me as I cleaned up without saying a word. Once I'd finished and turned to face him, I'd thought of the best lie I could.

But he spoke before me. "I asked Jeana to prepare dry toast and chicken broth for you."

"Thank you," I said and again was about to *explain*, but he spoke.

"When your mother was pregnant with you, her morning sickness put her in the hospital. She could barely keep water down. Let's hope we can avoid that with you."

Stunned, I lost my ability to respond.

"How far along are you?" he asked. There was no emotion to his voice to reveal what he felt. Just plain curiosity.

I swallowed as I regained my composure. "Nine weeks."

"Do you know who the father is?"

I frowned and crossed my arms over my chest. "Does it matter?"

"No. Just curious," he answered honestly. "Jameson doesn't seem to know."

I shook my head. "I don't know if I'm going to keep it."

He straightened his posture. "You can't make a decision like that without telling Jameson. If it's his, which I have a feeling it is, he deserves a say."

"It's my body. Therefore, it's my decision."

He winced and quickly looked away.

"What?" I asked.

"You sounded just like your mother," he said with an absent look in his eyes.

I did my best to level my voice. "She didn't want me?"

He recovered. "It doesn't matter."

"Yes, it does," I threw back.

"What I meant to say was that you should talk to him."

"I plan to," I snapped.

"Good. Now, make sure you pick up your broth and toast from the kitchen before you head up to your room," he ordered and left before I could push further about my mother.

I did as I was told and went to the kitchen. Despite throwing up less than five minutes ago, I was hungry. But what I wanted was onion rings. Bad. But it was probably best if I took it easy with the bland food.

As I entered the kitchen, the smell of fish hit me again. Thankfully, it didn't overwhelm me with nausea. Just in case, I held my hand under my nose. I saw a bowl of broth and a plate with toast on a tray waiting for me on the island. As I walked across the kitchen for it, the dining room door swung open.

Angela's voice filled the room. "I wonder who the father is?"

I stopped in my tracks and whirled to face her. "Excuse me?"

"Does Jameson know you're fucking his best friend? I saw you together in the hall at the party after you two killed that man," she said and stepped toward me. She put her hand on her hip and gave me a superior smug look. "You kissed Louie and you two screwed in Stefan's study. I wonder what Jameson will do when he finds out that his girlfriend is nothing more than a slut who got herself knocked up by his best friend. Haven't you heard of fucking birth control?"

Fuck the high road.

It had been a stupid move on her part to get within reach. It took little effort to whip my fist out and punch her in the nose. She yelped as her head fell back. She covered her nose with both hands as blood gushed down her chin.

"You crazy bitch!" she yelled in a nasal tone before she tackled me to the ground.

Fear rushed through me. I was worried what the fall could do to the baby. I did my best to maneuver myself and landed on my butt first before my back smacked to the floor. Because I was so focused on protecting my body, Angela got the upper hand. She smacked me across the face before she wrapped both hands around my neck.

She was sitting on top of my stomach with an evil smirk. "How does it fucking feel!"

A shadow appeared over her shoulder. My eyes barely had enough time to see that it was Stefan before he grabbed Skank Barbie by her hair. She screamed out in pain as he ripped her off of me and tossed her ass across the room.

Jamie was kneeling down to help me sit up a heartbeat later. Followed by Louie, who began fussing over me. "Are you hurt? What about the—"

Touching my neck, I gave him a pointed look to stop him.

"Yes, princess, what about the baby?" Angela asked in a sickeningly sweet voice and smiled proudly from where she knelt on the floor, clutching the back of her head. "Please tell everyone how you're carrying Louie's baby," she announced to the room. Everyone had come into the kitchen. My aunt, uncle, and cousins. All looked to me with wide eyes. Angela ended her announcement with, "Sorry to tell you this, but your precious girlfriend is a cheating slut, Jameson."

Jamie's eyes bored into mine, seeking truth. "You're pregnant?"

I went to get to my feet and Louie was quick to help me. I glared down at Angela.

"Really, cuz?" Dylan said, stepping closer. He shook his head at me. "I can't believe you'd do that to Jameson."

I ignored him and held my hand out to Jamie. "Gun," I said firmly. He pulled his gun from where he had it tucked behind him and handed it over.

I cocked it and pointed it at Angela. Before she could react, I pulled the trigger twice, putting two bullets into her chest. Her body hit the floor, blood quickly pooling around her on the tile.

"Fuck, Maura! Why would you do that?" Dylan yelled, clearly distraught. He laced his fingers behind his head as he stared down at the very dead Skank Barbie.

I turned my gun on him, drawing his attention. "Are you questioning me?" I asked him.

He dropped his hands to hold his palms out in surrender.

"You brought a *guest* into my house who not only insulted me, but attempted to kill me. I should kill you. I stuck my neck out for you. I saved your fucking life!" I yelled, making him flinch. "Instead of being grateful and trying to redeem yourself, you conspired with this whore." I tilted my head toward Angela. "Give me a reason why I should let you live."

"I didn't know she was going to attack you, I swear. She was a good lay. That's it. There was no conspiring, I promise," he said, pleadingly.

My hand squeezed around the gun. My gut screamed that I

should do it, but my mind kept flashing back to when we'd been kids. I couldn't do it.

I lowered the gun and stepped toward him. "If you so much as breathe out of line, not even Stefan can save you from me," I warned loud enough that even Stefan could hear the threat.

Dylan nodded.

"Not that it's anyone's business, but I'm in a relationship with both Jamie and Louie. If anyone has an issue with that, please let me know so I can tell you to go fuck yourself," I announced to the room before storming out of the kitchen.

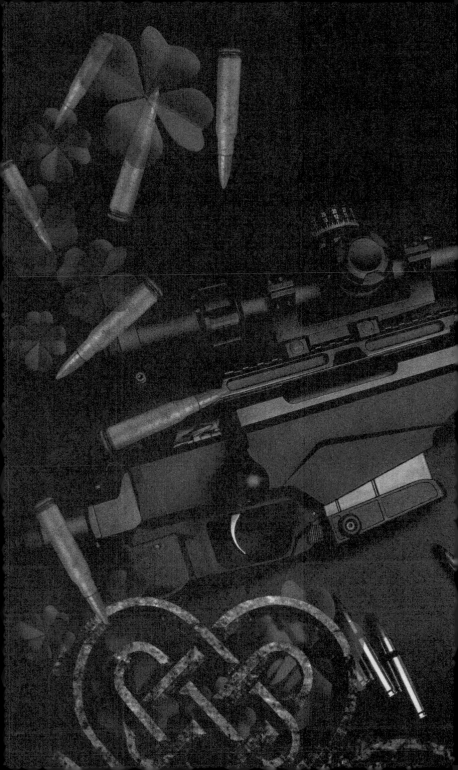

CHAPTER TWENTY

J amie followed me to our room. Louie wasn't with him. I assumed he'd stayed behind to give us a moment. I went straight for my closet and grabbed the tests and Jellybean's sonogram picture. Jamie was leaning against the bedroom door with his arms folded across his chest. His eyes followed me as I left the closet and walked over to him.

I held out the tests. "I found out yesterday morning." He took the tests and looked them over. "Louie knows. He found the tests last night."

"I picked up on that." His eyes shifted to mine. "Were you planning on telling me?"

I took a deep breath. "When I first found out, no. I'd planned on dealing with this on my own, sparing you and Louie the hardship because I had no intention of keeping this baby."

His expression hardened. "I know you don't want kids, baby, but I thought you would at least tell me and let me be there for you. We don't hide shit like this from each other."

"I know and I'm sorry."

He studied me, his harsh glare unrelenting as he did. "You said *had*."

I kept my face blank. "Do you want kids?"

He was a little stunned by the question. "I'd die a happy man if all I had was you for the rest of my life."

I shook my head. "That's not what I asked."

He went quiet, debating. I could see it in his eyes.

I gave him a small smile. "You do, don't you?"

He sighed. "You've never wanted kids. Even when we were younger, you were adamant about it. I've always loved you, so I've never humored the possibility of ever having kids. That was, until we first got together. I thought I fucked up by not wearing a condom. I didn't know how you were going to react to me possibly getting you pregnant. Then I thought, what if you didn't get mad? You'd been gone for six years. Maybe you might have changed your mind about having kids. For a minute, I envisioned what it would be like to have a family with you. And I was good with it. The look on your face when I asked you if I should be preparing for a baby said it all. You hadn't changed your mind. I was a little disappointed, but not enough to give you up. I'm not lying when I say I'd die a happy man if all I had was you. You're enough for me. Kids would just be a bonus."

I held the sonogram out to him. "I went to see a doctor yesterday. I got this there."

He took the black and white picture and the corner of his mouth lifted as he stared down at it. "Do you know who..." He trailed off with a slight wince, but I knew what he had intended to ask.

"Would you love it less if it was Louie's?"

"No," he answered firmly, leaving no room for doubt.

Good.

"If my calculations are correct, there's a huge chance we conceived Jellybean on my father's special table in the chamber."

His eyes lit up before his brow furrowed. "Jellybean?"

Before I could explain, there was a knock on the door. Jamie moved away and Louie poked his head in. He looked from Jamie to me. "Should I come back?"

"No," I said, waving him in. "I need to talk to both of you." They both stared at me expectantly. "I think...I think I want to keep it." My voice shuddered and my hands were trembling. "The one good thing that came from Angela was that when she attacked me, my first instinct was to protect the baby. The feeling was so powerful, and it showed me how I truly felt."

Quiet stretched as the three of us stood there at a loss for what to say until Louie released a breath. "Okay."

"Are you good with this?" Jamie asked Louie.

"I've been preparing myself for the opposite because she was so adamant about not keeping it yesterday," Louie explained. Then his blue eyes held mine. "I would have supported your decision not to keep it, but I'm happy that you changed your mind."

Jamie handed over the sonogram to Louie and he smiled down at it. "I get why you called it a jellybean alien now." He chuckled.

Jamie peered over his shoulder to take another peek and I watched understanding flash in his eyes.

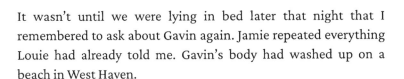

It wasn't until we were lying in bed later that night that I remembered to ask about Gavin again. Jamie repeated everything Louie had already told me. Gavin's body had washed up on a beach in West Haven.

"He was shot in the head and he had restraint marks on his wrists. I spoke to the coroner. There was evidence that he had been beaten repeatedly and they estimated his time of death at two days ago," Jamie said.

Which meant that whoever had taken him had been torturing him for over a month. *What a shitty way to die.*

"Do you think the Aryans are responsible?" I asked. My head was lying on Louie's chest and Jamie spooned me from behind. Jamie had his arm thrown over me and his fingers drew small circles below my belly button. His touch was gentle, yet felt possessive, as if he needed to touch me where our baby was growing.

"I don't know," he responded, his fingers slipping a little lower. "Let's worry about it tomorrow." His voice became deep and husky. He pushed his fingers inside my underwear and delved between my legs.

My breath hitched and heat rushed through me. I ran my hand down Louie's bare chest. Mimicking Jamie, I slid my hand inside Louie's boxers and wrapped my hand around him.

Louie hissed. "Well, hello there."

I felt as he hardened in my fist. I stroked his length, as slowly and torturously as Jamie was stroking my clit. Louie hooked his thumbs on the sides of his boxers and yanked them down to his knees, giving me full access to his thick and beautiful cock.

Jamie was working me into a panting and delirious mess, but I still had enough sense to want to take my time with Louie. While still pumping my hand around him, I pressed my lips over his heart and trailed my tongue down to his nipple. Grazing my teeth over the tip, I smiled at his sharp intake of breath. I continued down his chest and stomach, only stopping to kiss and lick the sculpted mounds of his muscles.

Once my lips made it to the V at Louie's hips, Jamie pulled his hand from my now soaked underwear and got on his knees behind me. Jamie's strong hands grasped me by the waist and easily maneuvered me so that I was also on my knees with my ass up in the air in front of him.

I moved my mouth down to the juncture where Louie's leg met his hip and placed a kiss there. His hips jutted a little, his body wrung tight by my teasing mouth. Knowing where I was headed next, Louie gathered all my hair in his hands so he could watch as I ran my tongue over the head of his cock, making him hiss again. I gave him one more teasing lick, then wrapped my mouth around him. Louie's breathing picked up the further I sucked him into my mouth until he reached the back of my throat. I pulled back, running my tongue along his hard-velvety shaft as I did.

Jamie pulled my underwear down to my knees before he spread me open to look his fill. He cursed. "It's hot as fuck seeing you with your ass in the air like this, soaked and ready."

I released Louie from my mouth to say, "Are you just going to stare all day?"

Louie let out a breathy little chuckle at my challenge.

Jamie's fingers squeezed around my ass cheeks before one hand moved to cup my pussy. His fingers lightly teased my clit, driving me mad with lust. "Do you want me to fuck you, baby?" he asked. I knew what he wanted. He wanted me to beg—beg for his cock.

A defiant smile tugged at my lips. "Yes," I replied simply and swirled my tongue around the underside of Louie's mushroom tip, then sucked him back into my mouth. Jamie's fingers disappeared from my clit and he pushed two fingers inside of me. I moaned around Louie as Jamie's fingers stretched me. His thumb glided over my back entrance, rubbing around it in small circles. My body tensed with anticipation.

"Yes, what?" he growled, and his fingers curled before he began to slide them in and out of me, hitting that special spot inside of me. I clenched around them and pushed back, seeking and needing more.

He withdrew from me, leaving me feeling empty.

Frustrated, I pulled away from Louie again and glared over my shoulder. "If you keep teasing me, I'll make you watch as I get myself off."

His hand came down on my ass with a loud smack. I jumped from the slight sting, but I didn't get far because his hands locked on my hips.

"The only one getting you off tonight is me," he said darkly and pulled me flush against his pelvis. His naked cock rubbed along my wet seam and my entire body shuddered. I wanted it. I wanted it inside me. I let out a whimper as I rocked my hips, rubbing along him some more. His hands tightened, keeping me still.

"Tell me what I want to hear," Jamie demanded. "And I'll slide into you right now."

Louie took the moment that I was distracted with Jamie to sit up and kneel in front of me. He was still holding my hair and he brushed his knuckles across my cheek as he stared down at me.

"Please," I breathed, staring up into Louie's eyes. "I want your cock." I had said it to both of them and they both obliged.

Jamie plunged into me hard and fast. I cried out and Louie took that opportunity to slide into my mouth.

I ravished Louie with my mouth and tongue while he gently rocked his hips. Jamie was anything but gentle. He pounded into me just the way I liked. But I needed more.

I grabbed Louie by the hips and upped my game of sucking, licking, and dragging my teeth along his shaft. He trusted me, pushing deeper into my mouth. It wasn't long until his cock swelled on my tongue and jets of cum hit the back of my throat. He groaned loud and long as I swallowed every drop.

Jamie had stilled behind me so I could enjoy the moment of Louie's release. Louie pulled himself from my mouth and fell back onto the bed, satiated. Then Jamie began moving again.

The tingling sensation started to grow inside me, but slowly. I dropped my head to the bed and fisted the sheets. "Jamie," I moaned. "Harder, baby!"

He tunneled into me faster and the room filled with my loud

moans, his pants, and the sound of flesh smacking. I screamed into the mattress as my release cascaded through me. Jamie grunted soon after, his body shuddering as he came undone.

We both fell on the bed next to Louie, equally spent. My entire body was coated in a sheen of sweat, but they didn't seem to care as they scooted closer, sandwiching me between them. None of us moved until we woke the next morning.

CHAPTER TWENTY-ONE

I found myself irritated at the next family meeting. For one, I was nauseous as hell. And two, Stefan offered Sean a seat at the table. Rourke's hunch had been correct. Sean really had shoved his nose up Stefan's ass, gunning for Dylan's or Samuel's position at the table, because he was now seated in Dylan's old chair.

Conor had decided to move down a chair, claiming Samuel's old seat to Stefan's right. I didn't know if Stefan had asked him to switch seats, or if Conor didn't want to sit next to Sean. Regardless, he looked relieved because Sean and I hadn't stopped staring at each other since I'd arrived at the meeting. I might have been wearing a not so friendly expression while Sean gave me an unwavering smug smirk.

Stefan let out an exasperated sigh. "Maura, are you even paying attention?"

My eyes flicked to my father. "As a woman, I have this fantastic ability to multitask. I may appear to not give a shit about our new deal with the Cartel or that Rourke screwed the maid who was supposed to clean his hotel room in Mexico, but I was still listening nonetheless. I'm waiting for you to explain why he's here," I said, tilting my head at Sean. "What can I say, the suspense is killing me."

Stefan leaned back in his chair. "I want Sean to help you run drugs."

"Oh, really?" I gave him an innocent and curious look. "I'd love to know why you think I'd need help."

"Foolish woman," Sean muttered. "What gives you the right to question him?"

I turned my gaze slowly back to Sean and arched a brow. "Because twenty-five years ago, I won a race."

It took a second for everyone to get my joke, but eventually Louie and Rourke threw their heads back laughing while the rest of the men in the room, apart from Stefan and Sean, chuckled. Stefan held his usual mask, but the glint in his eyes told me he wanted to laugh.

"I don't care that you're his little princess. You will show your respect," Sean sneered.

The room went silent, laughter dying abruptly. Conor cleared his throat. "Did you come to the meeting armed, niece?"

Without removing my eyes from Sean, the corner of my mouth lifted.

"Right. Of course you did." Conor scooted his chair back and stood.

"Where are you going?" Stefan asked him.

Conor smoothed away nonexistent wrinkles on the front of his jacket. "This is a new suit and I don't want to get blood on it when she kills him. I think I'll go stand over there," Conor explained as he pointed to the other side of the table, before making his way to stand behind Rourke. His enforcer also moved to the other side of the room.

Sean looked to Stefan. "There has been talk that letting her question you without punishment has made you look weak."

This time I chuckled and leaned closer to him. "Do you want to punish me, Sean?"

The corner of his eye twitched, a tiny hint that I'd hit a nerve.

"You do, don't you? What would you do to me, I wonder?" I tilted my head as I read every little move he made. The squeezing of his fist and the clench of his jaw. "I bet you'll envision it tonight, when you're alone and have your hand wrapped around your tiny cock. I don't break easily, but I have a feeling that's what you like. It's what gets you off—breaking a woman's spirit."

His eyes narrowed before an eerie calmness took over him. "I didn't think the breaking of spirits was something that would upset you, princess. I thought it was something we had in common." He leaned back in his chair with an arrogant smile. "Heard you cut up two teenage boys piece by piece until they begged for death."

"That's enough," Stefan said.

I didn't want to look away from Sean. He thought hinting at my rape would rile me. He was mistaken.

"I run drugs in this family. *I* repaired our relationship with the Colombians. *I* have a good relationship with Nicoli De Luca, our biggest buyer. None of us at this table are saints, that's for fucking sure, but we trust each other. I don't trust you. You look down your nose at women, therefore I would never trust you to interact with Salome. I'd pay to watch you interact with the don, though. He'd chew you up and spit you out before you even knew what was happening." I looked to Stefan. "So tell me, Daddy, why do *I* need or want his help?"

"You can't do everything on your own. Even Conor has Rourke like Sam had Dylan," Stefan explained.

I waved flippantly. "I have Finn."

"Finn is an enforcer," Stefan argued.

"Again, Salome and De Luca won't work with anyone but me," I shot back.

"He can help you in other areas," Stefan said, his tone turning firm.

"Shouldn't you be taking it easy in your current condition?" Sean added.

Stefan actually grimaced and closed his eyes. He took a deep breath before opening his eyes to look at me. Something in my expression gave him caution. "Maura," he said gently.

Only a few people knew that I was pregnant. So how had Sean found out? By Stefan's reaction, I had an idea. "What. The. Fuck?" I bit out.

Rourke pushed his chair away from the table. "I, for one, don't want to get caught up in the wrath my cousin is about to unleash. I think I'm going to go see what Jeana has planned for dinner. Good luck, Uncle. Sean, it was nice knowing ya." He stood and headed for the door.

"I think I'll join you," Conor said and followed his son, their enforcers leaving with them.

Jamie and Louie didn't move. Instead, they glared at Sean.

Stefan looked from Jamie to Louie to Sean. "Leave us."

The three of them stood in unison from the table and made their way out.

"Maura?" asked Dean, who I'd forgotten was standing behind me.

I didn't remove my eyes from Stefan. "Go."

Once the door closed behind everyone, Stefan's shoulders slumped a little. "Before you get yourself worked up, let me explain."

I leaned back in my chair and waved—gesturing for him to go ahead.

"I didn't know you were pregnant when I considered giving Sean a seat at the table. Since what happened with Sam and the Aryan attack, we've lost a lot of men in a short amount of time. Not to mention, by getting back at the Aryans, we've officially declared war. I need to restrengthen our ranks here in New Haven. At the party, I asked if anyone would be interested in moving here. Some volunteered and I assigned them to Rourke and Conor to replace the men they lost. Sean agreed to move here along with a few of his enforcers if I gave him a seat at the table. I've known him a long time. He may be a bastard, but he's loyal and has made the family a lot of money in Boston. I need you to give him a chance because, now that you're pregnant, we really do need him."

I opened my mouth to argue, but he cut me off.

"You decided to keep this baby. That means you can't continue on as you have been. No more risks. Have you forgotten who we are? How dangerous our lives are?"

"No. I haven't forgotten." I sighed. He had a point. "You should have given me a heads up about Sean."

"I was planning on telling you last night, but you left me with a huge bloody mess to clean up in my kitchen."

A twisted part of me wanted to smile. *Angela had it coming.* "What do you do with the bodies? I've always been curious."

"Our family owns almost every crematorium in the New England area," he answered.

That's handy. "Are we done here? I have plans to go check on Brenna."

He nodded. "How's she doing?"

Better than expected, I wanted to answer, but then I'd have to explain why. It was Brenna's pain to share only if she wanted. "I enrolled her in a new online school. She didn't want to return to the stuffy all-girls school she was attending and I feel online is a safer option."

"How long do you plan on keeping her hidden away at Vincent's? We have plenty of room here."

Originally, I'd sent Brenna to Vincent's because it was the only place I knew to hide her from Dylan in case he fought to get her back. "Even though things have...calmed, I still don't think her coming to live here is what's best for her. Right now, she needs space."

At my request, Jeana kindly made food for me to take over to Vincent's. After loading up a larger amount of food than expected, my goons—including Will—and I headed out.

During the drive, I watched as we passed fast food place after fast food place, longing for onion rings. I was so tired of broth and toast—the only thing I seemed to be able to keep down.

"I want onion rings," I said.

Asher peered at me through the rearview mirror. "Right now?"

"Yes."

Asher pulled up to the next fast food place we saw.

"Do you want anything else? Maybe something a little more substantial?" Dean asked from the front seat. He and Asher knew how bad my *all day* sickness was and how I could barely keep anything down.

"Nope," I replied and requested two large orders of onion rings.

As soon as I was handed the brown paper bag of my greasy cravings, I ripped that sucker open and shoved a whole ring into my mouth. I moaned loud and long, not giving a damn because I was quite literally a woman starved and my tongue was having a foodgasm.

Asher's shoulders shook from silent laughter as he pulled back on the highway. Dean shook his head. "They're that good, huh?"

"Mhm," I hummed as I chewed.

Sitting next to me, Will gaped as I quickly shoved another one into my mouth and moaned again.

I had never been to Vincent's home before. It was a cookie-cutter house in the center of a little suburban neighborhood, not to mention that it was in De Luca territory. I noticed Finn's blue Camaro in the drive and assumed the new G-TR I'd bought for Vincent was in the garage.

I knocked on the front door and tugged the strap of my purse up further on my shoulder. All three of my goons were holding the food Jeana had made. She had made enough to cater a small party.

The front door ripped open to reveal Brenna and she greeted us with a smile.

"What did I say about you answering the front door?" Finn snapped from somewhere inside the house.

Brenna rolled her eyes. "I looked through the peephole first," she shot back over her shoulder.

"I don't care." Finn appeared behind her. "You're still not allowed to answer the door."

Brenna sighed and I could swear she looked as if she were bartering with herself for patience.

Seeing her stand up to Finn instead of cowering, despite what she had been through...her resilience left me in awe.

She caught me staring. "What?"

"I brought food," I said, deflecting.

She opened the door wider, and she and Finn stepped out of the way so we could enter. Finn led the guys into the kitchen, while Brenna and I took a seat in the living room. My eyes were immediately drawn to a disassembled handgun spread apart on the coffee table.

"Finn was teaching me how to take it apart and how to put it back together," Brenna explained.

It was good to know that he had started with her lessons. Dean had said that they had come up with a schedule to start teaching her the skills to protect herself.

"Where's Vincent?" I asked, eyes scanning. The living room was a decent size and the furniture was minimal.

"In his cave," she replied as she tilted her head toward a hallway.

I had no doubt that he was glued to his computer. "Do you have everything you need?"

She nodded. "Vincent has two spare rooms. Thank you for the furniture and everything else. Everyone seems to be doing better now that we each have our own space."

After she had told me about having to sleep in Vincent's room while he and Finn had camped out in the living room, I had done a lot of online shopping. "Can I ask how you are doing?"

She lifted a shoulder. "I'm happy that my mother is getting help, but I don't think I can go back to that house even after she gets better."

"No one said you had to go back."

"So you're not having Finn teach me things so I can fend for myself when I have to return?" she asked, staring down at her lap.

"Don't ever drop your eyes," I said firmly. "If you're going to speak, do it with confidence. The moment you show your fear, you give others power over you."

She leveled her gaze with mine and I gave her a nod of approval. "My protection doesn't have an expiration date. I'm having my goons show you how to defend yourself because I feel everyone should know how to do that and you asked me how to be strong. Learning from them is the first step."

Looking relieved, she said, "Okay."

"While you're living here, I don't want you to think about the family, your mom, and certainly not Dylan. Focus on yourself, stay on top of your schooling, learn what you can from Finn and the others, and think about your future."

Brenna went quiet, absorbing what I had said. I stood from the couch. "We should probably eat the food before it gets cold. Would you mind dragging Vincent from his cave?"

Agreeing, Brenna disappeared down the hall while I ventured into the kitchen. I found all four of my goons standing in there, leaning against the counters, talking amongst themselves.

"Are you four gossiping like a bunch of school girls?" I snickered and smiled brightly at Dean, Will, and Finn's grumpy faces. Asher was the only one who wasn't fazed.

I pulled an envelope from my purse and held it out to Finn.

He took it with a frown. "What is this?"

I set my purse on the counter. "The deed to your house. I paid it off for you," I said and started lifting lids off of the large tin containers of food. It looked like Jeana had made barbecue. There were ribs, chicken, corn, coleslaw, and baked potatoes. To anyone else, I was sure it looked appetizing. For me, the smell made my nose scrunch and my stomach churn.

"Why did you do that?" Finn demanded.

Ignoring his question, I stepped away from the food and started looking in the cabinets for plates. "I know this weekend, you were supposed to have your son. Asher has graciously agreed to come stay here while you take a few days off to be with him." Once I found some paper plates, I grabbed a stack of them and set them on the counter next to the food, then began searching for silverware.

Finn stepped in front of me, glaring.

I frowned. "I did it as a thank you. I know it's a lot to ask you to stay here and protect Brenna."

"It's my job," he grumbled.

I released a heavy sigh. "Did I emasculate you by paying off your house?"

If looks could kill, I would've been a goner with how Finn was scowling at me. "I don't want to owe you anything."

"I don't know how you function with your head so far up your ass," I grumbled, shaking my head. "We may not be blood, Finnegan, but we're still family. Forgive me for wanting you to have one less thing to worry about while you were here." I didn't realize I was crying until a tear dripped off my chin and hit my hand.

Finn appeared taken aback.

I quickly wiped at my face and looked down at my wet hands, baffled. "Congratulations, Finn. I think you managed to hurt my feelings."

A hand came down on my shoulder. It was Dean. Beyond embarrassed, I stepped out of reach of his hand. "Please find silverware and serve yourselves some food before it gets cold," I ordered and went to leave the kitchen. I passed Brenna and Vincent on my way out. "Bathroom?" I asked both of them, not caring who'd answer.

Brenna noticed the streaks on my face, then glared into the kitchen. Vincent pretended not to notice as he said, "Down the hall, first door on the left."

I nodded my thanks and took off in that direction. Just as I stepped into the hall, I paused when I heard Brenna angrily ask, "Which one of you upset her?"

"You're an ungrateful prick," Dean growled. "Would it fucking kill you to ease up on her?"

"I don't understand her. I don't know what she wants," Finn said.

"She's not Samuel. She doesn't want shit from you," Asher snapped.

Not wanting to hear anymore, I went into the bathroom.

Standing in front of the mirror, I took in my wet eyes with disdain. I could barely eat and now I had uncontrollable crying. *Fucking fantastic.* What else was this pregnancy going to do to me?

I splashed some water on my face, willing the tears to stop. Once they did, I intended to go back into the kitchen with a little bit of dignity. I opened the door to Finn waiting in the hall.

With his arms crossed, he leveled his gaze with mine. "I'm sorry and thank you." I would've bet his words tasted like vinegar with how he forced them out.

I schooled my face and accepted his apology with a shallow nod. "Since I have you alone, I need to talk to you about Sean Kelly."

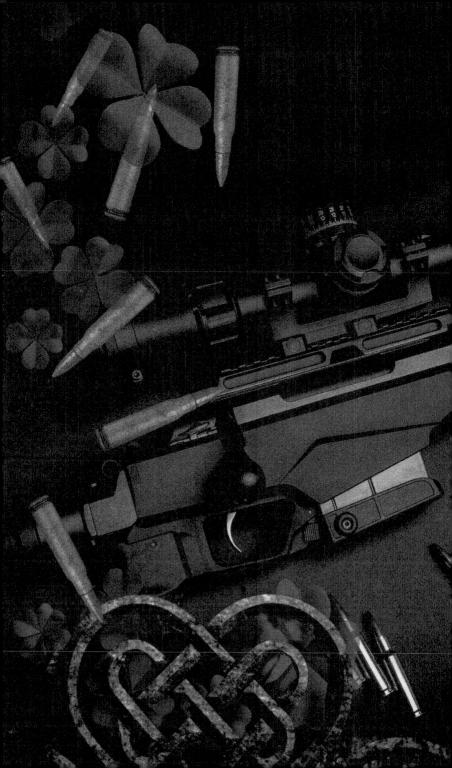

CHAPTER TWENTY-TWO

I stood before my full-length mirror in my bathroom, fighting the urge to cry. I couldn't button my pants. Well, I could, but it was painful. *It's fine, Maura. Gaining weight is normal. A good thing.* I'd just have to wear leggings to my doctor's appointment. Shedding the outfit I'd intended to wear, I headed back to my closet.

Jamie and Louie were going with me to my twelve-week appointment this morning, and both of them were waiting patiently on the couch for me to finish getting ready. Storming out of the bathroom in only my underwear caught their attention.

"What's wrong?" Louie asked.

"I'm getting fat! This baby is going to wreck my body," I snapped before I disappeared in my closet.

Angrily, I snatched a short, loose dress from where it was hanging and some leggings from a drawer and began yanking them on.

I was pulling up the leggings over my ass when Jamie leaned against the door frame, watching me. "You done having a pity party?"

I flipped him off with the meanest look I could muster. "Fuck you!"

The corner of his mouth twitched, and he pulled back his sleeve to look at his watch. "We have time," he said and stepped into the closet.

Eyeing him as he approached me, I asked, "For what?"

He knelt to the ground in front of me in his black tailored suit. As he smoothed his strong hands over my hips, my heart rate sped up. The icy rage in my veins melted, instantly. The heat in his eyes threatened to turn me into a puddle. He smirked up at me. "Take off your pants and you'll find out."

We ended up being a few minutes late to my appointment. Having Jamie's head buried between my legs, his tongue making me writhe on the closet floor, had been so worth it. It had extinguished my sour mood, which I supposed had been Jamie's goal.

During my appointment, Dr. Greene had eyed Jamie and Louie, obviously wondering who the father was. I could see that he was tempted to ask, but he stayed professional and continued on like it was normal for two men to stare intently at the ultrasound monitor and ask a million and one questions.

After my appointment, Jamie and Louie had to go do mob shit and I needed to do some shopping. I loathed the idea of wearing maternity clothes, but I was quickly reaching the point of not having a choice. I invited Brenna to tag along. According to Finn, she was dying to get out of the house.

My goons and I drove to the mall in Milford. The three of them didn't seem thrilled about spending the afternoon shopping and Finn had grumbled over the phone about it when I'd told him to meet us there. Asher parked the Escalade next to Finn's blue Camaro in the parking lot. Both Brenna and Finn waited next to his car as the four of us exited our vehicle. Brenna smiled at me, appearing...better, much better. Like the weight of her pain wasn't as heavy to carry. It had been almost a month since I'd taken her from Dylan. She was doing well in school and was excelling at everything my goons were teaching her.

"Want to get milkshakes first?" was the first thing she said. It was obvious she was excited to be out and about. I'd have to make it a point to plan more outings with her.

I smiled. "Absolutely."

She hooked her arm with mine and we headed inside toward the food court. Asher and Will scanned the court while Dean and Finn kept with us as Brenna and I approached an ice cream counter. Brenna ordered a strawberry shake and I got a chocolate peanut butter one. The smell of greasy food from the next food counter hit my nose. I put my hand to my stomach because it immediately started rumbling.

Dean took a step closer to me and whispered, "Do you feel sick?"

I shook my head. "I smell onion rings."

He rolled his eyes and walked over to the next counter. Onion rings hadn't stopped being my number one craving. Well, that and peanut butter. They were the main things Jellybean wouldn't make me throw up.

The other night, Rourke had joined us for dinner and had watched me, disgust adorning his face, as I had dipped my onion rings in peanut butter before eating them.

"We really need to find something healthier for you to eat, Maura," Stefan had said.

"Peanut butter has protein in it," I'd pointed out before shoving another onion ring into my mouth.

"It doesn't matter what she eats, as long as she does. She hasn't been able to keep anything down all day," Jamie had grumbled. Him coming to my defense had made me so happy, I had started crying.

They all had stared at me in shock, unsure what they should do, like I was a freak in the circus with one eye and three breasts. "I don't know why this keeps happening." I had sniffled and quickly wiped away my tears. "It's all Jellybean's fault."

After we got our shakes, we found a table to sit at so I could eat the onion rings Dean had gotten me. After one heavenly sip of chocolaty peanut butter goodness, I took off the lid and dipped an onion ring into the shake.

Brenna watched me with fascination as she sipped her own shake. "Your spawn has you craving crazy things, huh?"

I chuckled. "Yup."

"Would it be rude if I asked if it was Jamie's or Louie's?" she asked.

"If you were anyone else, yes. But regardless, I won't tell. They both view it as their own, even though they know the truth as to who the father really is, and that's all that should matter."

She smiled. "That's really awesome. I'm happy for you."

"Thank you." I leaned back in my chair, nibbling on another onion ring. "How's school?"

"It's going good. It's nice not having to wear a school uniform all the time or dealing with snobby bitches."

Stefan had sent me to a private school, but it hadn't been an all-girls school. So I could only imagine how much it must have sucked. "Have you thought about what colleges you want to attend?"

She stared down at her milkshake. "What if I don't want to go to college?"

"What is it you want to do?"

I could tell she was choosing her words carefully. She straightened her shoulders and met my eyes, doing her best to exude strength. "I want to work for the family. I want to work my way up the ranks and earn a seat at the table, just like you. I want to do what my father and brother failed to do—to help this family thrive for the better. I want to be respected. I watched my father beat my mother for as long as I can remember, and as soon as I grew boobs, he started hitting me. I used to think there was no escaping this life and that it would get even worse after he married me off, because they too would beat me and probably rape me. I refuse to be treated like that ever again and I don't want it to happen to anyone else either. Stefan has caused a rift by naming you as heir. I've heard my brother ranting about it with others. They know change is coming and they don't like it. Saving me most likely added fuel to the fire. So I want to help."

I stared at her intently as I absorbed her words. "You want to become a mobster, huh?"

"I do," she said with surety.

I wanted to talk her out of it. The thing with teenagers, though, was if you fought them on something, they tended to want it more. "Alright. I'll help you, but under one condition."

"What?"

"You still have to go to college," I said, and she scrunched her nose. "I went to college and I use what I learned there every day. You can go to school during the day and do mobster training in the evenings."

"Deal," she agreed.

We went in and out of stores for the next couple of hours. Poor Dean's and Finn's arms were full of bags, but in our defense, they'd offered to carry. I was having a great time bonding with Brenna by doing something as mundane as shopping. I'd almost forgotten how nice it was to hang out with another girl. I hadn't since Tina. Her betrayal had left me a little jaded when it came to seeking out another girlfriend.

"Let's go look in here," Brenna said and practically dragged me into a baby store. "Oh my gosh! Look how adorable this is."

She beelined for the baby girls' clothes and pulled a tiny pink tutu off the rack to show me.

It was really cute. "I don't know what I'm having yet," I mumbled as I touched a tiny blue suit for a baby boy.

"You can get something that's unisex. Buying for a baby is supposed to be fun and exciting," she said before leaving me to look further into the store. A wall of tiny baby shoes caught my eye. Smiling, I made my way over there. I picked up a tiny pair of crocheted lamb slippers. The tag said they were for a newborn.

"Is there something that I can help you find?" a feminine, heavily Irish-accented voice asked, and my entire body broke out in goosebumps. I turned to face the source and I felt an over-whelming sense of déjà vu. I met gray eyes that felt oddly familiar, yet I couldn't place them. The lady had chestnut brown hair and was really thin. She was older, fifties maybe, and under a heavy layer of makeup I could still see freckles splashed across her nose and cheeks.

"Are you alright, miss?" she asked and touched my upper arm. "You're a little pale."

Her touch seemed to snap me out of my stupor. "I'm sorry?"

She smiled and it felt forced. "Did you need help finding something?"

"Oh!" I shook my head. "No, I'm just looking."

"Are you looking for yourself or for someone else?" she inquired.

I knew in the back of my mind that I was acting strange, but I couldn't take my eyes off her. If she was uncomfortable, it didn't show. "Uh, myself."

Her eyes widened slightly before recovering with another forced smile. "Congratulations. How far along are you?"

"Three months."

"Pregnancy seems to agree with you. Mine was very rough. I

had severe morning sickness up until I delivered," she said, with a faraway look in her eyes.

Jeez, I hope that doesn't happen to me. "Boy or girl?" I asked.

Her brow puckered and she looked away. "Girl. I lost her a few weeks after she was born. She'd be about your age now."

I put my hand over my little bump. "I'm so sorry for your loss." The woman shrugged and faced me with another fake smile. The sound of my phone ringing saved me from the awkward moment. I dug my phone out of my purse and the caller ID told me it was Stefan. "Excuse me. It's my father," I said politely, and I put the phone to my ear. "Hello?"

"Where are you?" His voice put me on edge instantly.

"At the mall with Brenna," I answered at the same time the woman stepped closer to me.

"It's so nice of your father to check up on you," she said somewhat loudly and her accent came out thicker than it had before.

"Who are you with?" I barely heard Stefan ask.

The woman's lips curled into a genuine smile. "It was a pleasure meeting you, Maura."

I watched her walk out of the store, completely bewildered.

"Who was that?" Brenna asked as she came up next to me holding a teddy bear.

"I thought..." I trailed off as I looked around the store. *Does she not work here?* Dean, who had been standing with Finn by the store's checkout counter, noticed me looking around. He gave me a questioning look before he pulled his phone from his pocket. His attention dropped to his phone to read, I assumed, a text.

"Maura!" Stefan yelled, drawing my attention back to the phone.

"I'm here. What's going on?" I asked.

"Come home now," he ordered.

"Okay," I said.

"Is your security close?" he asked.

"Yes."

I heard him let out a heavy breath. "Good. See you soon." He hung up before I could say goodbye.

I stuffed my phone back into my purse and noticed Dean and Finn walking briskly through the store toward us.

"Something's wrong. We need to get back home," I said as they approached.

Dean nodded. "I know. We need to leave now."

Brenna and I set the bear and baby slippers on a shelf on our way out of the store. Dean took the lead, walking ahead of us, and Finn followed closely behind. Asher and Will were waiting just outside the store and both dropped their phones from their ears as we exited the store. Without stopping, Asher and Will flanked Brenna and I, boxing us with protection.

Asher told us to wait by the mall's entrance while he and Finn went to get the cars. They weren't parked far away. I could see my Escalade and Finn's Camaro from where we stood. Asher and Finn had barely stepped off the curb when a boom sounded and made the ground shake. A strong and hot wind hit my entire body, shoving me backward off my feet. My body collided with another and their arms wrapped around me, maneuvering us so that they took the brunt of the fall as we both hit the ground. The impact was jarring, but not as painful as it could have been.

"Are you alright? Are you hurt anywhere?" I barely heard someone ask because my ears were ringing. I rolled onto my back and came face to face with Will. He was the one who had caught and protected me.

"I'm fine," I said and quickly sat up, searching for everyone else. The parking lot was engulfed in a dark cloud of smoke and fire. Both of our cars were burning.

Dean rolled onto his knees from where he'd been lying on the ground a few feet away. Getting his bearings, his eyes landed on me first. "You good?"

I nodded.

Asher and Finn both groaned as they rolled over from where they'd been lying in the street. They had a few bumps and cuts but appeared to be okay. I found Brenna last. She was lying on her back and wasn't moving. Her face was turned away from me, but I could see blood staining her blonde hair. "Brenna!" I called out as I crawled over to her. As I got closer, I could tell she was breathing. Kneeling next to her, I gently shook her shoulder. "Brenna!"

Her face scrunched up and she let out a groan before her eyes fluttered open.

I sighed with relief. "Don't move. You hit your head."

Finn came over and knelt on her other side. "Is she okay?"

"I think so. I want to take her to the hospital, now," I said.

He nodded. "Asher called for an ambulance, and Dean and Will are updating the boss and Jameson."

As he said that, I could already hear sirens in the distance.

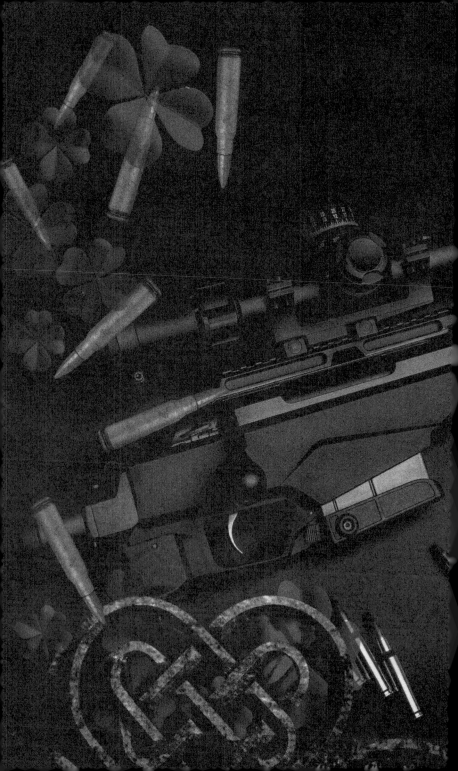

CHAPTER TWENTY-THREE

I t was advised that I also go to the hospital to get checked out. I didn't have a scratch on me, but my body was sore. Brenna and I got to be in the same hospital room. While they stitched up her head, they did an ultrasound of the baby. Brenna had a mild concussion and, thankfully, Jellybean was perfectly fine. I'd have to thank Will later.

The cops showed up at the hospital just as soon as we did. They hovered outside our room, waiting to question us as soon as the doctors were done treating us. I was hoping Stefan or Jamie and Louie would get here before we had to talk to them, but that didn't happen. Just before they came into our room, I gave Brenna a look of warning. *Don't tell them anything.* Understanding, she nodded.

Two guys dressed in blue walked in. Their questions weren't that bad. It honestly felt like they just wanted to get our statements and leave. Both Brenna and I answered mostly with "I don't know." The questioning was over before I knew it and the tension that had a tight hold on my body slowly began to ease.

However, my relief was short lived, because the moment the

two cops closed their little note pads, there was a knock on our door and Detectives Cameron and Brooks walked in.

You have got to be kidding me.

I hopped off my hospital bed and moved over to Brenna's side of the room. I plastered a polite smile on my face. "Detectives," I greeted as I sat on the edge of Brenna's bed, subtly placing myself between her and them.

"Miss Quinn," Detective Brooks greeted back with a small smile.

"Is there something I can help you gentlemen with?" I asked.

"You tell us, Miss Quinn. A few months back, your car was used for target practice, and now another car of yours has been blown up. Put these two incidents together and I'd say someone wants to kill you," Detective Cameron said.

"Bravo, Detective," I said with blatant sarcasm as I slowly clapped. "Thank goodness New Haven has such bright and intuitive law enforcement. I would've never been able to put two and two together to come up with that conclusion."

Detective Brooks surprised me by smirking. When he realized I saw he looked away.

Detective Cameron gave me a dry look, reminding me not to underestimate him. "Do you have any idea who might be trying to kill you?"

I shrugged. "Nope."

Cameron's eyes narrowed as he studied me. "I think you do."

I smiled and stood from the bed. "You're throwing that word around again, Detective," I said as I approached him. "Saying you *think* implies that you're unsure. It's rude to accuse someone of something when you're not entirely sure." I held his eyes as I reached for his tie. I felt his body go tense through his shirt as I straightened the knot that had shifted to the right. "You should consider wearing a clip-on in your line of work. It would be so easy to grab you by this and strangle you with it."

Cameron's bland facade withered, and his expression hardened as he continued to scrutinize me.

"Are you sure you can't think of anyone who may have a grudge against you? What about your father?" Brooks asked.

I flicked my attention to the young detective with an innocent look. "Why would anyone want to hurt my father?"

Cameron snorted. "I highly doubt you're that naive. Everyone knows who and what your father is."

I arched a brow. "Why don't you enlighten me?"

Cameron looked more than ready to tell me, until his attention moved to look behind me. He stepped to the side to get a better look at Brenna, who had been quietly watching us. "What about you? Did you see anything or anyone?"

She shook her head.

"What were you two doing together and how do you know each other?" Cameron asked, flicking his fingers between Brenna and me.

Brenna's demeanor shifted to that of a teenager, full of attitude. The way she looked down her nose at him reminded me of the stuck-up bitches I'd gone to high school with. It made me proud. "We're cousins and we were shopping."

Cameron didn't seem pleased with the way Brenna was snubbing him because his voice turned grumbly. "What stores did you shop in?"

Brenna rolled her eyes. "We went to all the stores. Haven't you even been to the mall? That's kind of what you're supposed to do."

"What did you buy?" he pressed.

"Do you have a point you're trying to get to, Detective? Because I don't see how you knowing that we bought bras and panty sets from Victoria's Secret pertains to someone blowing up my car," I snapped.

Cameron ignored me. "Did you see your cousin talk to anyone suspicious or maybe give them something?"

I put myself in front of Cameron, blocking him again from Brenna. "What the hell are you getting at?"

"I've noticed you've been spending a lot of time at McLoughlin's, your uncle's bar. I've seen a lot of interesting people visit him there. The kind who are known to have dealings in drugs. Want to tell me why you keep showing up there?"

Well, that was both informative and alarming at the same time. He'd let it slip that he knew what McLoughlin's was used for. That meant it was time for a new place to store the cocaine. He'd also told me he'd been watching me, which was fucking creepy. "It's a bar owned by my family. The drinks are cheaper."

"So you go there to drink?" he reiterated.

"Well, it's what they serve," I said.

"Aren't you pregnant?" Brooks asked, breaking his silence.

It took a whole lot of effort not to react. "I'm still waiting to hear the point behind this questioning and how it has to do with today."

"Pregnant women aren't supposed to drink alcohol," Brooks added.

I let out an annoyed sigh. "So my doctor tells me." The corner of my mouth twitched as I tried to contain the shit-eating grin I wanted to give Brooks. "But I never said what I drank."

That seemed to piss him off. *Nice try, baby cop.*

I walked around Cameron toward the door and opened it wide. "I think we're done here." Dean and Will were standing out in the hall and perked up when they saw me. I gestured with a wave of my hand for the detectives to leave. They didn't move, which pushed my hormonal pregnant buttons. "You're not here to ask me about today's incident. All you want to do is accuse me of shit. Therefore, we won't be answering any more questions without my lawyer present. So please, fuck off."

"We'll be in touch, Miss Quinn," Cameron grumbled as he passed me. I watched as he beelined for the officers who had taken my and Brenna's statements, standing by the nurse's desk. Detective Brooks' walk slowed as he passed Dean. They glared at each other and I almost missed the tiny tilt of Brooks' head.

I quickly looked away, pretending I didn't see anything. I stepped into the hall and approached Will. "Thank you for protecting me. I don't want to think about what would've happened if you hadn't caught me when the blast sent me flying."

Will gave me a curt nod. "Just doing my job."

Out of my peripheral, I noticed Brooks leave and turn down another hall. "Still, thank you," I said.

"I'll be right back," Dean said to Will, and my stomach sank as I watched him turn down the same hall as the detective.

"Watch over Brenna," I told Will and followed after Dean. As I went to turn down the hall he and Brooks had ventured down, I had to jump backward before I was seen because they both were standing right there. I leaned my back against the wall and peeked around the corner a little to see if I could listen to their discussion because they were whispering.

"You volunteered for this assignment, remember?" Brooks seethed at Dean. "You've been working for them for almost a year and you expect me to believe you haven't heard or seen anything?" Brooks put his hands on his hips and shook his head. "They flipped you—no, *she* flipped you. You've changed since you started working for Maura."

"I told you that she has nothing to do with this," Dean said angrily.

"She has everything to do with this," Brooks snapped loudly. "I warned you not to fuck me on this. We erased your entire history as a cop so you could go undercover. All you have is me to pull you out of this when we take the Quinns down. Who's to say I won't leave you to rot with them?"

"We both know you don't have shit. It's why you've been a huge pain in my ass, begging for any scraps you can get your hands on. I told you I'm out and I'm not going to give you shit. Stop fucking calling me." After saying his piece, he went to walk away, but Brooks stopped him by grabbing his shoulder.

"You're out when I say you're out, and if you don't get me what I want, I might let it slip to the Quinns that they have a cop working for them."

The muscle in Dean's jaw clenched as his eyes bored into the floor.

"That family you're so loyal to will kill you without a second thought." Brooks chuckled and released Dean's shoulder. "Your life is worth more than pussy, especially Maura Quinn's." Dean gave him a murderous glare and Brooks returned it with a smirk. "I'll give you a week to find something I can work with," Brooks said and walked away. Dean just stood there looking completely lost.

Feeling equally lost, I pulled away from the corner and leaned my head back against the wall. That was when I noticed Asher standing next to me with his arms folded across his chest, also leaning against the wall. Meeting his eyes, I could tell he had heard everything I had.

Dean was a cop.

"Fuck," I said under my breath.

Dean came from around the corner at that moment. He noticed Asher first before his gaze landed on me. It took less than two seconds for his surprise to switch to a defeated demeanor.

"I'm not Stefan," I bit out and my voice cracked, because my hormones were taking over. "You didn't trust me." That time my voice wobbled. *Shit, I'm going to cry.*

Dean's shoulders slumped. "Please don't cry," he pleaded, making me realize I had spoken out loud.

"I'm not crying because of you, you selfish, grumpy dick hole,"

I snapped, making Asher snort next to me. Dean frowned at him. I fanned at my watery eyes.

"The baby is making me cry."

"I wanted to tell you..." Dean trailed off.

"But you didn't," I practically growled. "You are so lucky there are police nearby because I want to stab you. Like in the thigh or somewhere it will hurt like hell and will hurt again when they have to stitch you up. And you bet your sweet ass that I will lie to the doctors and tell them you're a recovering drug addict so they won't give you anything for the pain!"

Dean's eyes went wide and he took a step back. "I know you well enough to know *that's* not the baby talking."

I lifted my fist intending to punch his lying ass, but Asher stepped between us and held me back. I tried to still swing at Dean, hoping to at least hit him somewhere. He took another step back, out of my reach.

"Gah! I'm so mad at you!" I snarled.

Asher lifted me off the ground and took a few big strides down the hall further away from Dean. "Okay, it's time to take a deep breath because you just threatened to stab a cop."

I quickly covered Asher's mouth with my hand and glanced around us.

Thankfully, there wasn't anyone within earshot. I looked up with narrowed eyes at Asher, who was staring down at me, patiently waiting for me to remove my hand. "Don't say what he is out loud again. If Stefan finds out, he's as good as dead and there will be nothing I can do to save him."

Asher pulled my hand away from his mouth and looked over his shoulder at Dean. "I guess that means she doesn't want to kill you."

I leaned to the side to look around Asher at Dean. "You will tell me everything. And by everything, I mean *everything*, Dean

Grumpy Gallagher. Be it your favorite color or your damn shoe size, I don't care how fucking little it is, you will tell me."

He released a heavy sigh and gave me a curt nod.

I wiggled out of Asher's arms and took a step away. I hadn't removed my eyes from Dean. "I'm hurt because my friend didn't trust me to help him, not because of who he is—was, or whatever."

"I'm sorry," he finally said.

I folded my arms across my chest. "You better fucking prove it because now I only have a week to figure out how to deal with Brooks and save your ass."

Stefan, Jamie, and Louie showed up at the hospital not long after my discovery of Dean's secret. I was in a foul mood by the time they arrived. Wanting to give me space, Brenna went to raid the vending machines with Finn down the hall. Stefan, who looked relieved when he saw me, was the first through the door and was unfortunately the one who I blew a gasket on.

"Where the hell have you been?" I demanded. Stefan's steps faltered, blocking Jamie and Louie from coming in. "My car blew up over two hours ago."

Stefan arched a brow at me, not pleased at all with how I was speaking to him.

I looked past him to Jamie and Louie standing outside the door. "I could have been hurt or something could have happened to our baby and it took you hours to get to me? What the fuck?" Could I have been calmer about asking them? Yes. Did I care at the moment? Nope. My best friend had lied to me. Forgive me for feeling a little sensitive at the moment.

Jamie and Louie squeezed through the door and around

Stefan. I stared them down, hard, and they smartly didn't approach further.

"If anything were to happen to any of you, I would have dropped what I was doing and broken every traffic law to get to you. Why the hell do I not deserve the same? Am I not as important to you as you are to me? Because if so, I need to know right now."

"I knew you were unharmed. Will kept me updated as to how you were doing, and I called and spoke to your doctor here at the hospital," Stefan said.

"We weren't in a position to up and leave, baby," Jamie added.

I went over to my purse sitting at the foot of my hospital bed and pulled out my phone. "Oh my gosh, look at this." I mocked shock as I wiggled it in front of me. "Did you guys know I had one of these? You could have fucking called me, instead of my doctor and security." I grabbed my purse because I was blowing this popsicle stand. "I'm pregnant, hungry, and you all are on my shit list. So someone better get me the hell out of here, get me a Southwestern burger with extra onion rings and a peanut butter milkshake, and explain to me what the hell is going on."

I didn't give them a chance to respond and weaved around them to leave the room.

Stefan got Brenna and I discharged from the hospital at record speed, and on the drive home, Louie and Jamie got me my burger and milkshake. I asked Finn and Will to take Brenna back to Vincent's. I didn't trust any of Stefan's goons to take her and not have it get back to Dylan where I was hiding her. Stefan had brought four Escalades to transport us all home. Will, Finn, and Brenna left in one car. Stefan and a few of his goons took another.

Jamie, Louie, Dean, Asher, and I took one. Another four goons took the last Escalade.

It hadn't escaped my notice that Stefan had increased the number of goons around him. I held my questions at bay while I ate on the way home. I finished the last of my burger as we drove up the long driveway and Asher parked the Escalade in front of the house. I told Dean and Asher to go home and that we would talk tomorrow. Dean looked somber, but Asher dragged him away.

"What do you need to talk to them about?" Jamie asked as we walked inside the house. I gave him a hard glare and walked away toward Stefan's study. Jamie sighed, "Right, I'm still on the shit list."

"I told you we should call her," I heard Louie whisper to Jamie.

"I thought you were implying that *you* were going to call her," Jamie whispered back.

When I made it to Stefan's study, the door was open. I walked right in, ready to get some answers, but I stopped dead in my tracks just a few steps into the room.

What in the actual fuck?

My mouth fell open as I took in the entire room. Photos had been thrown and taped up everywhere. The walls, Stefan's desk, the floor. They were all covered, and not with just any photos, but photos of me—of my entire life shot from afar, like someone had been watching me. There were pictures of Stefan carrying me when I'd been eight months old at my grandfather's funeral and of me at school from elementary to high school. There were some of me shopping with Brody for clothes, going to the movies with Jamie and Louie, and getting ice cream with Stefan. The floor seemed to hold a lot of the most recent photos of me at college with Tom and Tina. Then there were ones from after I had returned home, of me and Jamie kissing outside of Anarchy,

Stefan and I at the park the night he had tested me and I had stabbed one of Sasha's men.

I looked to Stefan, who for once wasn't sitting at his desk, but was sitting on his leather couch with a drink in his hand. He had taken his suit jacket off and tossed it onto the arm of the couch. He was leaning forward, head downcast with his elbows resting on his knees. He ran his fingers through his hair, tiredly.

"I debated whether or not I should let you see this," he said without looking at me. "But I don't think I can keep this hidden from you anymore."

"I don't understand what you're saying. What is all of this?" I demanded.

He finally looked up to meet my eyes and my breath hitched. He was unveiled, revealing his anger, sadness, and what I could have sworn was worry. "Go look on my desk."

Cautiously, I did as he asked. Like the rest of the room, the top of his desk was covered with photos. These photos, however, had something written in a dark brownish red on them. The smell of pennies filled my nose, telling me that it was blood. As I rounded Stefan's desk, I got a better look at what the photos were and what the writing said.

Taking in each photo, my heart began pounding harder and harder in my chest, to the point it hurt. My lungs constricted, making it difficult to breathe. It was as if I'd forgotten how to inhale. There were more photos of me, but there were also a few I wasn't in and that was because I'd been in the bathroom. The night I had been raped was laid before me. They started with me dancing at the party, then of me heading upstairs to look for an unoccupied bathroom. Then there were photos of Zack and Tyson standing outside the bathroom I had been using with their heads bent together. The person who had taken the photos looked like they had been hiding in the room the bathroom connected to. The closet, maybe? Wherever they had been hiding, they had shot the moment I had opened the door and Zack and Tyson had barreled in, pinning me down to the ground, just before they had kicked the door closed. There was a shot of when they'd left after they had raped me and I'd been lying on the floor with my skirt shoved up around my stomach. The last two photos were of me leaving the bathroom and getting into Jamie's car, looking beaten and pale as a ghost. Written across the photos was, "You couldn't protect her, like you couldn't protect me."

"Baby?" Jamie said softly from where he and Louie stood on the other side of Stefan's desk, watching me. I turned away from the photos, fighting desperately with my mind to not drift back to that night.

A hand touched my shoulder and I jerked away from it. "Please, don't touch me right now," I said breathlessly because getting air was still a struggle. I was determined to work through my panic on my own. *I can do this. I'm stronger than the pain that night caused—the haunting memories that still loom in the back of my mind even after seven years. I can't let it cripple me anymore.*

The tightness around my lungs eased and I inhaled deeply and exhaled slowly. The thundering in my heart calmed and I regained control of myself. With my head held high, I turned to face everyone. Both Jamie and Louie were standing close, patient and ready to be there for me. "Someone better start explaining what the hell is going on."

CHAPTER TWENTY-FOUR

The four of us moved to the chamber with Jamie's laptop. I took a seat in Rourke's spot with Jamie and Louie sitting on either side of me so I could see whatever it was they wanted to show me on the computer. Stefan sat in his usual spot, currently drinking his second glass of whiskey.

Louie opened multiple videos from different areas recorded around the house and property for me to watch. The first videos were of the front gate. I watched as Blake, one of the grounds security, drove through the gate. Blake was good friends with Josh and Dean and I had met them all at the same time right after I'd returned from Hartford. I remembered during our first encounter Blake had flirted with me, while Josh had acted respectfully and Dean had glared at me.

"Blake showed up late for his shift this morning. We think he purposefully waited until we were all away from the house and only staff were here. Not even Brody was here," Jamie said.

"How do you know Blake did this?" I asked.

Louie pulled up another video on the computer and the control room appeared. Josh was sitting, leaned back in a desk chair watching the CCTVs. Then, in came Blake. He had something in his hand and I couldn't make out what it was until he leapt onto Josh, who had greeted him with a friendly smile. The hypodermic needle became clear as day when he stabbed Josh in the neck with it. Josh collapsed to the floor, unconscious within seconds. Blake took a portable radio and a gun from the cage before leaving the control room. Louie hit some keys again and video from the camera outside the control room started. Blake closed the control room and broke his key off in the lock. Louie switched over to another video from the camera outside Stefan's study. Blake passed Stefan's study and went to the room right next door, which was Brody's office. Blake opened the door and two masked men walked out carrying two large suitcases, followed by the woman who had approached me at the baby store today.

"Oh, fuck," I blurted as I watched the three strangers make their way to Stefan's study and disappear inside while Blake stood guard in the hall.

"They got in through Brody's office. It's the closest to where the staff park their cars and it has a window. They were in Stefan's office for over an hour without anyone knowing because whenever anyone called into control with the radio, Blake claimed to be taking over for Josh. You should keep watching, though," Jamie said and fast forwarded the video a little. Blake pulled out a piece of paper, unfolded it, and held it up to the camera. It read, "They have my kid. They're going to kill me after this, but please save him." On the very bottom of the paper was an address.

I pushed the computer away. "Were we able to save the child?"

"We found him tied up and alone at Blake's condo, but it took a while. We didn't know if it was a trap or not. That's why we didn't get to the hospital right away. As for Blake...his body was found down the street from the house. According to a witness, the people in the car with him made him pull over, shot him in the back of the head, and tossed his body out of the car before one of them hopped into the driver's seat and took off. The cops came straight here after they figured out who he was and who he worked for. By that point, we had discovered what had happened. Jameson and I took off just before the cops showed up and shut down the manor, preventing anyone from leaving. They questioned Stefan and interviewed all the staff here. It took hours, which was also why he couldn't get to you right away," Louie explained.

Well, now I felt like an asshole for biting their heads off. "Fine, I'm a tiny bit sorry for being a bitch." I looked to Stefan. He didn't look good and was staring off into space. "That woman was with me when you called me," I said.

Stefan's eyes flicked to me. "I know. I heard her." He threw back the last of the whiskey left in his tumbler.

"You know her," I said as I studied him. I hadn't seen him this unkempt since I'd been raped. "I guess that explains how she knew my name because I didn't tell her."

Stefan plopped his empty tumbler on the table and the sound of it clanking on the wooden surface echoed in the room. He looked at Jamie and Louie. "Leave us."

Jamie and Louie stood and left the room. Stefan put his elbows on the table and ran his fingers through his hair again. "I'm really surprised you haven't figured it out," he grumbled, locking his eyes with mine.

"I took you to see a therapist once when you were nine. They said that you had traumatic suppressed memories. I was relieved and saw it as another chance for us to move on again. Then you told me about your nightmares, and I knew that I'd eventually have to tell you the truth. I was hoping it wouldn't be so soon because once I tell you the truth, I'm going to lose you."

I stood only to sit in Jamie's chair, so I could be closer. I grabbed his hand, to offer comfort to him and myself because I had a ball of dread rolling around in the pit of my stomach. "Daddy, you're rambling."

He squeezed my hand. "Everything I've done has been to protect you."

"Just spit it out," I snapped.

"Your dreams aren't nightmares, they're suppressed memories. That's why they feel so real and make you cry."

I let go of his hand. "You said she died in a car crash when I was six weeks old."

He nodded. "Would you believe me if I told you I lied to protect you from the truth?"

"That depends on what the truth is."

"Your mother was addicted to cocaine, no thanks to my brother and father who bribed her with it so she would spread her legs for them," he said angrily. I was horrified and I had no doubt that it showed. "I shouldn't have told you that." He sighed frustratedly. "Your mother never wanted you. All she cared about was her next fix. When we found out she was pregnant, I thought I had a chance to save my wife from spiraling or possibly over-dosing one day. I thought you would be the saving grace she needed to get over her addiction and she would realize that too once she was sober.

"I checked her into a facility to help her detox and stay clean for the duration of her pregnancy. She hated me for it and never saw that I was trying to help her. She never wanted to get better, or so she told me, repeatedly. I tried to visit her every day and took her to every doctor's appointment. After she gave birth to you, she didn't want to have anything to do with you. She wouldn't hold you and would get hysterical every time you cried.

"When she came back to the manor, I had her things moved into a separate room and kept you in mine, away from her. In less than twenty-four hours, she was high again. I'd given up on helping her stay clean at that point and focused on taking care of you instead. She didn't like that. She turned belligerent, like a spoiled child not getting the attention they wanted, and voiced how she wished you never existed. I didn't think she would act on her jealousies, but I was wrong. When you were around two weeks old, I came home to find your nanny's throat slit and your mother in the bathroom with you. She said she wanted to give you a bath. The tub was almost filled to the brim, you were fully clothed, and I walked in just as she dunked you all the way under the water. I snapped. For the first time in my life, I raised a hand against my wife. I hit her hard enough to render her unconscious. I was angry enough at what she intended to do to you that I broke my promise to my mother to never harm a woman I cared about. Like my father repeatedly did to her and my sister.

"To punish her, I checked her back into the medical facility for another month and didn't visit. I'd hoped it would show her the lengths I'd take to protect you and she'd realize what she had done was wrong. It didn't. She returned home when you were six weeks old and, somehow, she snuck out of the house with you in the middle of the night. She tracked down a dealer and offered you up as payment for drugs. The dealer knew who she was, because in the time she had spent in the facility, I had put word out that if anyone sold to her, I'd kill them. Despite my threat, he sold the cocaine to her and brought you back to me, explaining what had transpired. She didn't return to the house for three days and when she did, she acted like you never even existed. I played along with her because in those three days I'd come up with the best solution for us. I didn't want to kill my wife, but I couldn't trust her to be near you.

"I asked her for a divorce. I offered her a million dollars to sign the papers right then and there, and then to leave. I told her I didn't care where she went, so long as she didn't return. And if she did, I would kill her. She refused me at first, but as soon as I asked where you were, she lied poorly, saying you were at a play-date. I played along again and asked for the address, so I could go pick you up. She rambled off a random address as she quickly signed the divorce papers, then grabbed the money and took off."

"But she came back," I mumbled.

He nodded. "Twice. The first time, you were four, and she tried to snatch you at a park. While I was at work, Brody had taken you to the playground there to play. You were playing in the sand and had asked him for juice. He turned away from you to retrieve it from the lunch he'd packed, not thinking there was any risk, especially with our security nearby. In the seconds it took him to grab the juice and turn back around, she had scooped you up and run. Brody tackled her to the ground before she could get away and our security took over. That was the last time you were ever allowed to go to the park."

I slumped back in my chair, shocked.

"I had every intention of killing her, but as soon as I saw her again, I couldn't. She begged me not to and my guilt ate at my resolve. I had failed her as her friend, her husband, and she was still your mother. I asked her what it would take to make her disappear. She told me three million. I paid her, even though I knew deep down I should have just killed her.

"She returned again when you were almost nine. She didn't attempt to kidnap you, but went about taking you in a different way. She showed up in the middle of the night with a lawyer, or so she claimed. She said she was taking you, that you were her daughter and she had rights to you. I invited her and her *lawyer* to my study to talk. I decided to play along with her ruse and listened to her go on and on about how she wanted to be in your life, she was clean, and that she wanted to take you back to Ireland to live with her. Little did she know that she had signed away her rights when she'd signed the divorce papers. And I had been keeping tabs on her since the last time she'd tried to take you. She had gotten mixed up with one of the Mexican cartels. She and her new boyfriend, who was pretending to be her lawyer, blew all the money I paid her and still ended up owing money to the cartel. She didn't want to be in your life. She came to use you to get more money out of me.

"I refused her. The boyfriend pulled a gun on me and told your mother to go find you. I already had a gun in my hand, hidden behind my desk. He made the mistake of looking at your mother and I took that opportunity to shoot him. He bled out on my floor while she sobbed pathetically over his corpse. That was when you showed up. Seeing you there put me in a rage because all the time, money, and energy I'd spent in protecting you from the burden and pain that was your mother had all been for naught. I had failed you.

"I didn't want her to hurt you and knew she'd try to sink her claws into you as soon as she saw you. So I had to show her that you were mine and that she would never be able to use you against me. Like in your dream, I did pull you into the room. Her hair wasn't dyed black, though, and you knew who she was immediately. But you didn't shoot her, Maura, I did. I gave you the gun and I did ask you to choose between us. You chose me, but you were shaking so much the bullet missed your mother when you fired the gun. But you pulling that trigger served its purpose and showed her that she'd never be able to sway you against me. I took the gun from you and shot her in the chest. I had our security dump her at the hospital. It was my last show of mercy because I was done caring whether she lived or died. I got a message to the cartel she owed money to and told them where they could find her if she lived. I called the hospital the next day and found out that she had survived, but had disappeared less than an hour prior. I assumed the cartel had gotten ahold of her because she disappeared without a trace."

I was at a loss for words. Stefan stared absently at the table and I could see the shame in his eyes. I grabbed his hand again and squeezed it. It hurt that he had lied to me. At the same time, I knew telling me had been really hard for him and hearing about the lengths he'd taken to protect me from her and the pain of knowing her, even if I ended up hating him, showed me how much I meant to him. Maybe actions really did speak louder than words. I ached to hear him say that he loved me, but if actions were all that he could give me, then maybe I could accept that.

"I wish you had been honest with me about her, but I under-stand why you weren't, strangely. I have a feeling it's because I'm about to become a mother," I said, then released his hand. "It's extremely fucked up that you tried to make me shoot her. I was eight and I don't know how or if I can forgive you for that." I stood from my chair. "I'm tired and I don't want to know anymore tonight. We'll finish talking about this tomorrow."

He let me leave. That night was the first night in seven years I didn't dream.

CHAPTER TWENTY-FIVE

I t took damn near the whole week to figure out a way to
handle Detective Brooks. I debated killing him. But it would
raise too many questions from both Stefan and Detective
Cameron. I had a feeling the bastard would glue himself to my ass
if his partner mysteriously disappeared.

That left me no choice but to give Brooks what he wanted.
Information.

If anyone in the family found out...

Not even Stefan would be able to save me.

Being a rat was an automatic bullet to the head.

"Maura," Stefan said, pulling me from my thoughts.

I peered across the table to where he sat. *Shit.* I had zoned out
in the middle of our family meeting. "Yes?"

"Sean says you're refusing to tell him where you're storing the
recent delivery from the Colombians." Stefan's tone wasn't accusing, but factual. We'd barely interacted since he'd told me about
my mother. He was wisely giving me space and time.

"And she lied about when it was delivered," Sean added, his
irritation lacing his words. I may or may not have lied and said
our shipment of cocaine was to be delivered yesterday when it

had really come two days ago. I wondered how long Sean had waited down at the docks until he had figured it out.

It was hard not to smile. "As I've already told you, Sean, Detective Cameron let it slip that he knew about McLoughlin's. I was worried about what else he might have known, which is why I acted fast and switched things up."

"You still could have told me of your plans," Sean argued.

I suddenly found my nails very fascinating. The paint on my middle finger was chipped. It had to be a sign that I used it too much. I certainly wanted to use it then. "It's never wise to speak of such things over the phone. You never know who might be listening," I lied, and I didn't care that it was obvious.

"Then you shouldn't have any issue telling me where you're hiding the shipment now and when you plan to meet with De Luca," Sean sneered, thinking he had bested me.

I grinned. "I plan to meet with the don tonight."

Sean scowled, face turning slightly red when I didn't offer up anything else.

Rourke coughed to cover up his laughter.

"Maura," Stefan said gently.

My smile dropped as I looked at my father. "Yes, Stefan?"

His hand that was resting on the table clenched before he dropped it to his lap. "Where are you hiding the shipment?"

"I don't know," I replied simply.

Louie snorted, then cleared his throat. Stefan gave him a sharp look.

"Sorry," Louie mumbled.

Stefan sighed. "What do you mean you don't know?"

I wore a mask of innocence. "Well, I've had such a busy week with almost being blown up and finding out that my mother is alive. You could say I've been feeling delicate, especially in my current condition. So I decided to take your advice and not take on everything myself." I shrugged and I caught Stefan tense up when I mentioned my mother. "I delegated some of my responsibilities to Finn." I looked at Sean. "Have you ever heard of pregnancy brain? It causes women to be forgetful at times. I suppose that's why I didn't even think to ask you for help. I just completely forgot about you." He had already tried to use my pregnancy against me. I figured I might as well use his ammunition to my advantage.

"Pregnancy brain," Sean repeated dryly. Then he looked to Stefan for backup.

I almost laughed when Stefan said to me, "Moving forward, try to remember to include Sean in your plans."

"Of course," I agreed, smirking at Sean. "We're meeting him tonight at his club, Show 'n Tail, in Bridgeport."

"If no one has anything else to add, let's call it a day," Stefan said, dismissing everyone. As I went to stand, his eyes locked with mine. "Maura, a word. Alone."

I glanced back at Dean and gave him the okay to leave.

Stefan was quiet until we were alone. "How are you?"

I frowned. *Really?*

His face turned downcast. "What can I do?"

I had to look away from him. His guilt would eat at my resolve and I wanted to hold onto my anger a little longer. "Give me time." After lying to me all my life, that was the least he could do.

"Alright. But before I can do that, I need to know why you asked Josh to make you a copy of the surveillance footage of your mother breaking into the house."

My gaze moved back to him, my face an unwavering blank mask. "I have my reasons for requesting it."

"Are you trying to look for her?"

"No." I held his eyes, willing him to let it go. When they narrowed slightly, I knew there was a good chance that he wouldn't.

During the drive to Bridgeport, I requested that Dean sit in the back seat with me. Asher was driving my new Escalade and Will rode in the passenger's seat. Finn, Brenna, and the two goons whose names I'd learned were Nate and Brandon were riding in the Escalade behind us. Sean and his posse were in their own car following behind them.

I pulled a file from my purse and handed it to Dean. "Give this to Brooks," I whispered.

Dean flipped open the file and saw pictures of my mother inside and a CD with the video footage of her in my house. Dean gave me a confused look.

"Her name is Riona. She's the daughter of an Irish arms supplier. Not ours. She has ties with a Mexican cartel and she's responsible for Blake's murder. I'm sorry, I know he was your friend," I said in a low voice that could only be heard between the two of us.

He stared down at the file with a clenched jaw. "Who is she?"

"My mother."

His eyes shot from the file to meet mine in surprise.

"Just tell Brooks that she's an enemy to the family. It's not exactly what he was wanting, but it should appease him for now and gain us time to figure out a permanent solution."

Dean shut the file. "I can't give this to him. If Stefan or anyone else finds out that you gave me this—"

"Let me worry about that," I insisted and stared out my window. It was dark out. The only light came from the distant city as we drove further and further from it. "I'm well aware that my moral compass is broken. I think the only thing keeping my soul from turning completely black is my love for my family and the lengths I'd go to for them. You're part of my family, Grumpy.

Don't deny me the chance to embrace the one thing that's good in me."

"Alright," he whispered.

Nicoli had closed down Show 'n Tail for our exchange. Music still played in the dim club, but the dancers and other employees were gone. The don was leaning on the bar with a tumbler of amber liquid placed in front of him. Five of his goons were strategically standing around the room, watchful and ready.

I stalked over to him, doing my best not to appear annoyed that Sean was following. He'd brought four of his lackeys with him and he'd gotten pissy with me when I'd told him he could only bring one inside with him. I'd made Brenna stay in the car again, with Nate and Brandon watching over her.

I slid onto the bar stool next to Nicoli. He was texting on his phone and had yet to look away from it to greet me. I scooped up his drink and took a small sniff of it. It was whiskey. *Perfect,* I almost purred out loud and brought the tumbler to my lips. I downed his entire drink in two gulps.

The corner of Nicoli's mouth lifted as he typed away on his phone. "Pregnant women aren't supposed to drink."

I snorted. *Fucking stalker.* "It's been a long week."

"I can relate," he said, setting down his phone, then reached over the bar to grab a bottle of whiskey. He took his tumbler from my hand, refilled it, and threw the whiskey back in one gulp. "You brought a guest."

I forced a smile and Nicoli frowned at it. I swiveled around on my stool to face Sean. He was standing there with his lackey and Asher. Dean and Finn were at a table with two of Nicoli's goons going through the process of the exchange. "Yes. This is Sean Kelly. Sean, this is Nicoli De Luca," I introduced them.

Nicoli turned and put his hands inside of his pockets as he stared at Sean with a bored expression. "I know who he is. Why is he here?"

Nicoli's question was intended for me but Sean answered. "Maura and I will be working together—"

"So?" Nicoli cut him off.

"I thought I should introduce myself since I'll be tagging along during these...*exchanges* and will take over when Maura's impending motherhood hinders her availability," Sean said.

"You've got to be fucking kidding me," I mumbled, unintentionally. The fucktard was already planning my exit and his takeover. What was worse was that he didn't care how transparent he was about it.

Nicoli didn't acknowledge my slip. He continued to scrutinize Sean with a hint of disdain. "The deal I have is with Maura and a stipulation of that deal is that I'm to work only with Maura. You hold no power in the Quinn family. I have no interest in doing business with you."

I had to bite my lip, hard, to keep myself from smiling.

Sean held a dumbfounded expression that nearly did me in. "Maura won't always be able to—"

"Why? Because she's pregnant?" Nicoli interrupted him again. "Meeting with me isn't exactly strenuous and I can be accommodating when I want to be. If I must go to the hospital while she's in the middle of delivering her baby to get my drugs, then so be it."

"You better bring booze because we're both going to be traumatized after witnessing me push a watermelon through my vagina," I quipped.

Nicoli smiled despite himself and turned back toward the bar, silently dismissing Sean. "That's not how I imagined I'd see your vagina. Way to ruin my fantasies."

I couldn't help it. I threw my head back, laughing.

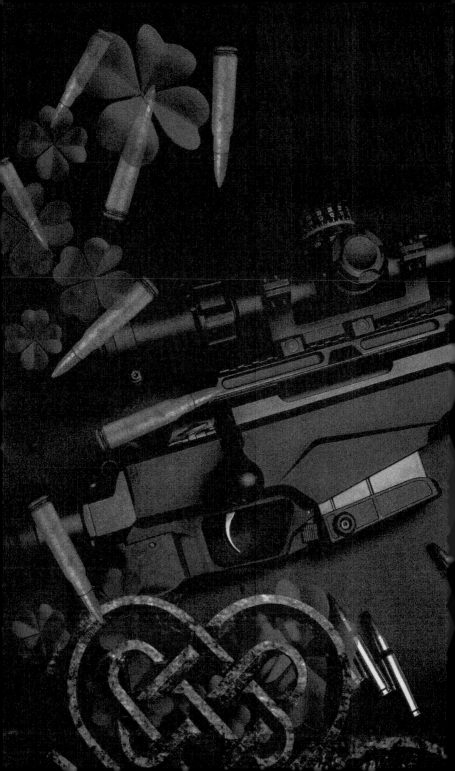

CHAPTER TWENTY-SIX

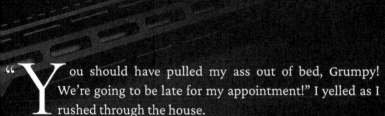

"Y ou should have pulled my ass out of bed, Grumpy! We're going to be late for my appointment!" I yelled as I rushed through the house.

"You would have shot me if I'd tried that," he grumbled behind me.

Asher chuckled next to him. "We'll get there on time."

I slowed once I reached the stairs. "Brody, we're leaving!" I yelled out when I didn't see him in the foyer. He was going with me because Jamie and Louie had mob shit to do.

Both Brody and Stefan stepped into the foyer.

My father watched me as I made my way down the stairs. His demeanor was guarded, and he eyed me with caution. Even though it had been almost a month, I hadn't completely forgiven him yet. I reached the landing and approached them. "Are you ready?" I asked Brody.

Brody cleared his throat and elbowed my father.

Stefan straightened his shoulders and asked, "Would you mind if I came too?"

I did my best to not show my surprise. He'd been trying to get me to forgive him this past month and I was astounded by the amount of effort he was putting forth. He'd been doing his best to give me space, sided with me in every bickering match I'd had with Sean, and paid for all the baby crap Brody had insisted I needed.

He was also paying for the room across the hall from mine to be converted into a nursery. I wished I could blame it entirely on his stubbornness that kept him from giving up, but I knew deep down that he was trying to prove to me what my forgiveness was worth to him. "I'd like that," I said.

He gave me a small smile and gestured for me to take the lead. I walked out of the house to where Will was waiting with two Escalades and four of Stefan's goons. We took both cars and made it just in time for my appointment.

Brody and Stefan went into the room with me while Dean and Asher waited in the hall. I sat on the exam table and Brody took the only guest chair. Stefan stood with his hands in his pockets, studying a pregnant anatomy poster. We didn't wait long before my doctor walked in. He greeted me with a warm smile, but it dropped as soon as he saw Stefan.

Dr. Greene caught himself and re-plastered a smile on his face. "I see we have new faces with you today. Parents?"

"Yes, these are my parents," I replied before Stefan and Brody could knee-jerkingly deny it. Dr. Greene didn't seem to care that they were gay, why should they? He didn't even care that I had two boyfriends.

"How have you been doing?" Dr. Greene asked me as he opened my medical chart.

"I still have *all-day* sickness, but it's not as bad as before and I think I felt the baby move," I answered.

He nodded as he read whatever was written in my chart. "You're at sixteen weeks, so it's very possible you could be feeling him or her already. I see here we got the results of your prenatal screening. Everything looks excellent. No genetic abnormalities.

With this type of blood test, we're able to determine the baby's sex as well. Did you want to know, or did you want to wait? Or I can tell someone of your choosing for a gender reveal?" he said, gesturing to Brody and Stefan.

I perked up and I looked over at Stefan, for what, I didn't know. The answer? Guidance? I wished Jamie and Louie were here.

"You can wait until Jameson and Louie come with you next time," Stefan suggested, obviously seeing my internal debate.

"Or you can find out now and you can surprise them later tonight with a gender reveal gift. We could stop somewhere after this and pick up a pink outfit or blue outfit, depending on what the baby is. You can wrap it and give it to them later to open," Brody quickly added.

His eagerness made both Stefan and I smile. "You're dying to know, aren't you?" I teased.

Brody huffed. "Of course I am. I've already ordered a bunch of stuff, but it's all in neutral colors."

Stefan shook his head. "The decision is Maura's."

Brody glared at him. "Like you aren't dying to know."

Dr. Greene chuckled, reminding me that he was there.

I gave him an apologetic smile. "I'd like to know."

"Are you sure?" he asked.

I nodded.

He smiled brightly. "You're having a girl."

"Oh." It was all I could think of to say. I'd have preferred a boy. Mostly because a boy's life in this family wouldn't be as hard. But Jellybean was a girl. I had a lot of work ahead of me if I didn't want her to go through the same shit I had. I rubbed my hand over my belly, praying I could protect her, and reminded myself I wasn't alone. She had two daddies who would kill for her.

At the thought of Jamie and Louie, I wanted to hurry along with my appointment so I could plan their surprise.

After we left the doctor's office, Brody and I went shopping and Stefan returned to the house. Both Brody and Stefan had gotten to see Jellybean when Dr. Greene had done the ultrasound. Brody had beamed the entire time and Stefan had held a small smile.

Brody dragged me to a bunch of baby stores, but the best one was an adorable baby boutique. We spent quite a bit of time and money there, buying everything I would need and then some. A lot of it was ordered from a catalog and would be delivered at a later date, such as the crib, stroller, and other big baby stuff. All of it was purchased on Stefan's credit card.

I decided the nursery would have a baby lamb theme because I'd fallen in love with those baby lamb slippers I had seen at the mall. Brody was bummed because he had wanted a ballerina theme that we'd seen staged in one of the baby stores. It was obvious he was really excited about Jellybean and it was infectious.

For Jamie and Louie's gender reveal surprise, I found this pink onesie that was made for a gay couple with a baby girl that I felt fit perfectly—written on the front of it was, "I love my daddies." The cashier read the front of it as she rang it up and gave me a strange look. Brody and I fought not to laugh.

Once we got home and my goons helped me carry all of my purchases to the nursery, I told them to go home. I was exhausted and was more than likely going to nap until dinner time. Plus, Jamie and Louie were on their way home and I wanted to give them their surprise alone. If I was lucky, I could convince one or both of them to cuddle me while I took a nap.

Dean, Asher, and Will took off and I went into my room. With the curtains closed, it was dark. Not that it mattered. I'd grown up in this room with the furniture in the same exact places. I could walk through it blindfolded and still know where I was.

Stepping into the darkness, I flipped on the lamp next to the couch and dropped my purse and bag with the onesie in it on the coffee table. I sat on the couch to unzip my boots so I could get them off my aching feet. As I was taking off my last boot, I heard the floor creak behind me. The hairs on the back of my neck rose and my instincts told me to move. I stood quickly and turned while walking backward around the coffee table, putting more space between myself and whoever was in my room.

A man was standing behind the couch, half hidden in shadow. I noticed the big hunting knife in his hand first. Then I took in his coal black hair, cold blue eyes, and realized I recognized him. He was Alex Roth, the Aryan assassin.

I had a gun in my purse, three feet out of reach in front of me on the coffee table. I wasn't confident I could grab the purse, dig the gun out, and aim it before he could get to me. I had to think of something else. I put my hand to my belly protectively. "I'm pregnant," I said, despite knowing it didn't matter to him, but a small part of me hoped.

He didn't even blink.

Think, Maura, I thought as I took another step back, reaching the TV hanging on the wall over the fireplace. *The fireplace!* Without looking down, I knew there was an iron rack of wood by my foot. It had been getting colder out and all of the rooms with a fireplace had been stocked with logs. And next to the rack of wood was an iron set of tools for the fireplace.

"You need to take a minute to think about the repercussions of what you're about to do. My family will wipe out your entire gang and everyone close to you and them if you kill me," I said as I finished forming a plan in my head.

His fist squeezed tighter around the knife and I knew he was coming. I dropped and pulled a log of wood from the rack and by the time I stood up, he was coming for me. I threw the log at the lamp just as he leaped over the couch. The log hit its target, the lamp crashed to the floor, and the light went out. Unless the assassin could see in the dark, I had a slight advantage. I grabbed what I hoped was the fire poker from the tool stand and ran for the corner of the room. I smoothed my hand down the heavy tool and found a pointy end. *Thank fuck.*

Standing there quietly, I debated whether I should make a run for the gun in my nightstand, the bathroom, or the door. I took a moment to listen because if I could determine where he was, I'd have a better idea of where I could go.

Something shattered on the other side of the room and I knew it was my new vase of flowers on the dresser that Jamie had bought me to replace the one he had broken. My best chance was to head for the door. I crept as quietly as I could. I was halfway there when my bare foot stepped on glass from the lamp. The pain of it slicing through the bottom of my foot made me want to cry out and it took everything in me not to make a sound. A lot of good that effort did, because the sound of the glass crunching in the silent room...I needed to move. I ran for the door.

Through the thundering of my heart, I could hear the pounding of his steps behind me. I wasn't going to make it. So just before I reached the door, I turned, and I shoved the poker forward. I felt it stab and heard a grunt, but I didn't stick around to make sure. I got my bedroom door open and was bathed in light. Ignoring the pain in my foot, I pushed on down the hall. I thought I heard a thunk on the floor before my hair and shoulder were grabbed from behind. I was thrown, hurtling toward the wall. Not wanting to hit my stomach, I pivoted so I spun on my foot and my back collided with the wall instead. The impact was a little disorienting, but I shook it off and got my footing in order to take off running again.

Alex appeared in front of me.

I had no time to react.

All I felt was pain.

My eyes dropped, finding him holding the hilt of his hunting knife against my stomach. *Where's the blade?* I got my answer when the assassin slowly pulled back on the hilt, revealing a bloody blade extending from where it had been embedded in my lower stomach.

"My baby," I whimpered, as I brought shaky hands to the stab wound. Blood immediately covered them. I looked back up at Alex. He had taken a step back with his hand pressed above his hip where I had stabbed him with the poker. He looked up and down the hall, making sure we were alone. The strength in my legs disappeared and I fell to my knees. I crumpled the rest of the way to the floor, landing on my side, my hair covering my face. I made myself lie there as still as I could, hoping he'd think he had accomplished what he had come here to do and would leave.

It felt like forever until I finally heard his footsteps retreat back toward my room. *Just a little longer, Maura.* I waited a few more seconds before rolling onto my back. Tears clouded my vision and poured out of my eyes. My hands were sticky with blood and I couldn't stop shaking.

Where is everyone? I turned my head to search for a camera and found I was lying in a blind spot. Pushing through the pain, I bent my knees and tried to scoot myself into its view. It took so long, moving inch by strenuous inch. Halfway into the camera's sight, I gave up and sobbed.

I wasn't going to make it.

My baby wasn't going to make it.

It pissed me off, that this was it. I'd never been afraid to die, but I didn't want to lose my Jellybean.

In one last ditch effort, I sucked in as much air as I could, and I screamed. It was piercing, pain riddled, and I didn't stop until all my air was gone and my throat was raw.

I didn't know if anyone would hear me in this giant house, but at least I had done everything I could. I put my hand back to my stomach when I felt myself fading. I was chasing the rabbit and he was leading me down a dark hole. Within the vast darkness, a voice whispered that they'd take all my pain away.

"Maura!" I heard in the distance and I felt the floor beneath me vibrate. I hadn't known I'd closed my eyes, and I forced them open just in time to see my father skid onto the floor by my side.

His wide eyes scanned over me rapidly and he put his hand on my stomach. "No! No! No! You're going to be alright. It's going to be okay." He was frantic. "I want a fucking ambulance here now!" he roared at the goons moving around us.

"Daddy," I breathed.

He brushed some of my hair out of my face. "I'm here."

I fought to keep my eyes open.

"Maura?" Stefan said, shaking me.

I couldn't protect my baby, I tried to say before my eyes slid closed and I fell into a pit of nothing.

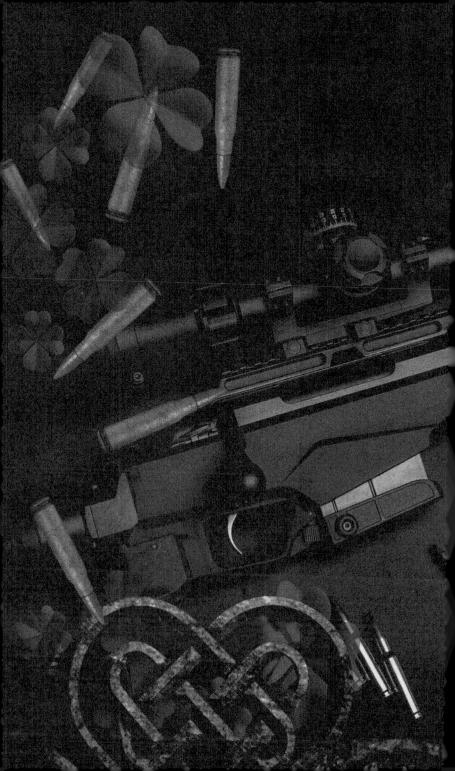

CHAPTER TWENTY-SEVEN

I lost my Jellybean.

I survived.

I wished I hadn't.

I couldn't look at Jamie or Louie, even though they hadn't left my side, because it was my fault that she was gone.

I had failed to protect our daughter.

I was shattered beyond repair.

The only thing that pulled me to my feet was my rage...my need for blood.

I was going to fucking bathe in it.

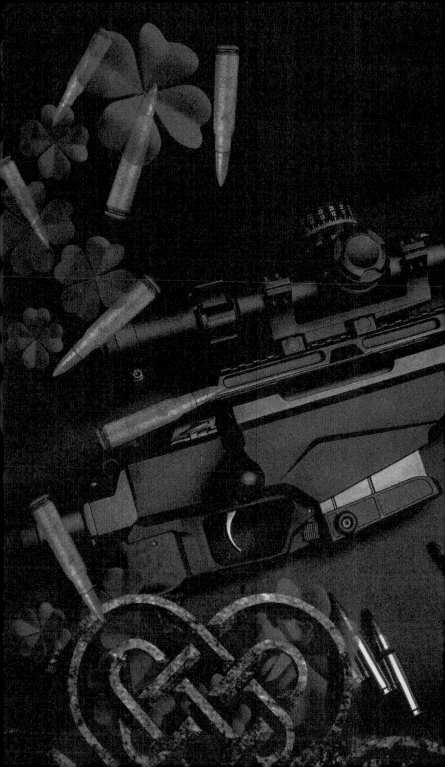

CHAPTER TWENTY-EIGHT

T *hree months later...*

"Remember to breathe," Asher said from where he lay between Brenna and I. Inhaling, I did my best to ignore the rock that was digging into my rib as I stared down the scope of my sniper rifle at the target one hundred and fifty yards away. It was an alien blob figure I had drawn on a poster and nailed to a tree. I aimed for the center of its head and exhaled just before pulling the trigger. My rifle fired and a moment later Brenna's fired.

I pulled back from the scope and looked to my right. Like Brenna and I, Asher was lying on his stomach, perched up on his elbows with binoculars held up to his eyes.

"Maura, headshot. Brenna, right in the Adam's apple," he said, smiling. Lowering his binoculars, he pushed up from the ground to sit on his knees. He picked up his stopwatch from where it hung around his neck. "Get ready to dismantle in three...two...go."

Brenna and I shot up from lying on the ground and quickly got to work taking apart our Barrett M82A1 rifles. I'd named mine BFG. *Big fucking gun.* The sounds of snaps, clicks, and metal sliding was all that could be heard as we concentrated. Brenna finished putting her rifle back into its case a few seconds before I did.

Asher stopped his watch, nodding his approval at the time displayed. "Better than yesterday. Good job, ladies. Now, let's see you run back to the cabin carrying those."

Brenna and I stood, brushing dirt and pine needles from our clothes before scooping up our cases and beginning the long run back to the cabin. The cases were heavy as hell, but we had to get used to their weight as we ran. A lot depended on it.

As he ran next to us, Asher's phone beeped, signaling a new text message. He pulled it from his back pocket and without losing speed, he read it.

"They're back," he said.

I nodded, understanding, and picked up my pace.

By the time I reached the cabin, I was sweating, despite the cold air, and my breathing was a little labored. I took the porch steps slowly. Dean opened the front door and took the rifle case from my hand. Exhaustedly, Brenna plopped her ass on the steps and laid her case on the ground. Asher grinned down at her. "You doing okay, baby Quinn?"

Brenna flipped him off.

Dean tilted his head inside the cabin, gesturing that I follow him. He and Finn had just returned from an important errand I'd sent them on. I walked behind Dean into the cabin's somewhat small living room, where Finn was sitting on a large wooden crate that was already filling the room with the smell of coffee.

I wish I could be a fly on the wall when Sean finds out we stole the shipment.

"Stefan's going to kill us," Finn grumbled.

My eyes met his. "You worry too much."

Finn didn't back down. "Say that to Samuel and the other guys you executed."

"Quit bitching," Dean snapped, which didn't help.

"We're not betraying the family, Finn. I would never do that. I will pay the money back," I assured him.

Finn let out a heavy sigh. "I know."

Asher and Brenna came inside and joined us in the living room. Their eyes went straight to the crate.

"We leave tomorrow," I announced. No one responded and I caught all of them looking at each other.

"We'll make sure everything is ready to go by morning," Brenna finally said, taking charge. She'd been doing that more and more lately. I was grateful because I didn't know how I would have gotten by without her these past three months. *I can't believe that's all the time it's been since...*

"Want to ship the coffee beans to Sean as a way of saying 'fuck you'?" Finn asked, bitterness and resentment lacing his words. I didn't blame him. My blood hadn't even dried on the carpet when Sean had swooped in, trying to take over. He had shut Finn out, telling him he wasn't needed any longer. He had somehow gotten Salome's direct line of contact and told her that I was dead.

Salome hadn't believed him and had sent Emmanuel, one of her lovers, to the States and to the hospital I'd been in.

I remembered him holding a large bouquet of flowers when he'd showed up. "She wants to know that she's alright," I remembered Emmanuel saying to Stefan, who had been refusing to let him into my hospital room. It'd had nothing to do with Emmanuel, it had been what I had asked of Stefan. No visitors. At that time, I hadn't been...capable of doing more than just lying there on that uncomfortable hospital bed, wondering why I hadn't died and wishing I could have because it would have been better than the anguish that had been ripping my soul apart.

Forcing myself to focus on the present, I responded to Finn, "I'm all for pissing Sean off." My words lacked their usual oomph.

They noticed it, too. It was why they all went quiet and exchanged looks again. They did it every time I did something that showed the pieces of me that were gone. A huge part of me had died three months ago, right along with my baby. Now, all that was left was my darkness, my rage, and the pain that couldn't be suppressed by either.

I left the living room before my thoughts could tread into forbidden territory and went down the hall to Vincent's room-slash-Batcave. His door was open, so I knocked on the frame before leaning against it. Vincent was typing away in front of a wall of computer screens.

Without looking away from whatever he was doing, he shouted over his shoulder, "Yeah?"

"It's time," I said.

His fingers froze over his keyboard and he swiveled around in his chair to face me. "When do we leave?"

"Tomorrow morning."

He nodded. "I'll reserve our hotel rooms in New York."

"I'll leave you to it." I pushed off the frame and went into my room across from his. Once inside, I shut my door and lay down on my bed. My gaze immediately went to the ceiling. Pinned to it, directly over my bed, were pictures of every Aryan in Buck's gang. It was strange, yes. But each night as I lay there and my pain threatened to consume me, I'd stare up. Seeing their faces added fuel to my rage and strengthened my resolve. I was going to make them all pay.

There was a knock on my door before Dean let himself in and closed the door behind him. He sat on the bed next to me with his back resting against the headboard. I watched as he reached into his jacket, pulled out a joint, and lit it. He took one puff, then a second, and leaned his head back as if in rapture and exhaled slowly.

Without saying a word, he held the joint out to me and I took it. "Aren't cops supposed to be against drug use?" I asked and brought the joint to my lips. The smoke filled my lungs and, like Dean, I released it slowly.

"I used to smoke this shit all the time in high school. I had to give it up when I signed up for the military and I felt like a hypocrite every time I'd bust someone for possession after I became a cop," he said. "Being undercover gave me an excuse to start smoking it again."

I handed the joint back to him. "What changed your mind?"

Understanding what I was really asking, he went quiet and took another hit. "I was fucking bored and disappointed with my life—my career. When I heard Brooks was looking for someone with weapons and narcotics knowledge for an undercover assignment, I threw my hat in the ring, hoping a change of scenery would help fix what I was feeling. I think Brooks picked me because we knew each other from high school. He was the golden boy back then, always talking about saving the whales or some shit like that. It was a total surprise to learn he'd become a dick. I have a feeling the personality change had to do with his little brother being murdered while Brooks was away at college. It's why he dropped out to become a cop."

I kind of felt bad for Brooks.

"After I learned that my assignment was to infiltrate the Quinn mob in order to obtain evidence to bring your entire criminal empire down, I was actually excited by the idea of getting away with all the illegal shit I was about to do. Everything went according to plan. I got vetted, then interviewed by Louie, and assigned guard duty at the manor. Unfortunately, the thing about going undercover for long periods of time is that it gets harder not to form attachments. I tried really hard to keep everyone at arm's length, but Josh and Blake kept wanting to go out for beers after our shifts. They would share things about their families and their dreams. I'd find myself feeling guilty because I was working to ruin everything for them.

"Then you showed up and you stared at me as if you could see past my lies. It made me nervous. I tried to scare you off by being a prick, but that seemed to have the opposite effect on you." He smiled, remembering it.

"I told Brooks you promoted me to your personal security, hoping he'd pull me out because I assumed there was nothing to be gained from watching Stefan's daughter. Brooks didn't agree and practically drooled at my new opportunity. He wanted me to learn everything I could about you, and I mean really personal shit. Past relationships, who you've had sex with, your shoe size, the type of underwear you like to wear. It was creepy as fuck," he said and handed over the joint.

I took a puff right away because he was right, it was creepy as fuck.

"I told him very little," he assured, guilt showing in his eyes. "The more time I spent around you, getting to know you, the more I started ignoring his calls. Without me realizing it, everything quickly changed. You made me care. You became someone to me."

"Well, let me be the first to welcome you to the dark side," I said with a small smile.

He snorted. "Thanks." I watched as his mood changed from light to somber in an instant. "Are you sure you're ready for tomorrow? Because if you need more time—"

"It's been three months."

"Grief doesn't have an expiration date," he shot back. "You lost a baby and...*them* all within the same week. No one would blame you if you needed more time."

Everyone was very careful not to mention *them* around me.

Dean, Asher, and Brenna had been there. They had witnessed the betrayal. And with the help of Finn and Vincent, they had helped me escape—escape Quinn Manor, Stefan, *them*. "I didn't lose Jamie and Louie. They lost me." Just talking about them filled my veins with fire.

"I know," he said gently. "I'm just trying to say that we're your friends—your family, and that we're here for whatever you need."

It took a moment, but I eventually nodded, and Dean left me alone. Mentioning Jamie and Louie had opened the door I'd tried very hard to keep locked up. Now that it was open, I couldn't stop myself from looking inside.

Waking up in the hospital and finding out that I had survived, and that my Jellybean hadn't...I loved her. I loved her so much and she had been taken from me. What was worse was that it had been my fault. It had been stupid and arrogant to goad Buck like I had.

Had I known...

Regret. It was a black mark on my heart that I'd carry for the rest of my life.

The days I'd spent in the hospital had been the hardest and longest days of my life because all I could do was lie there, drowning in pain. Stefan had insisted that I stay admitted for longer than medically necessary because he'd been worried that I'd kill myself the moment someone wasn't looking. I'd considered it. The thought of escaping the pain had been tempting. But I didn't deserve an escape. I deserved to suffer. So I had lain there in silence, barely acknowledging anyone, and felt it all.

The day I had been due to be discharged and return home, Jamie, Louie, and Stefan had sat around me talking. They hadn't left my side and it had showed in their haggard appearances. Jamie and Louie had struggled every minute to stay strong, but their agony and worry had always been apparent. Stefan had fared better at holding it together. I didn't know how. Maybe it was because he was the boss and he was used to it. Or maybe he'd felt he had no choice.

One of them had mentioned the Aryans and it had pulled me from the fog long enough to listen to what they'd been talking about.

"We can't let this go," Jamie had said, his hand squeezing mine.

"We won't," Stefan had assured. "But let's not worry about that right now. Maura takes priority."

"It's a priority that she's safe and she's not safe here in New Haven," Louie had said, his voice straining to stay calm. "Someone in the family is feeding the Aryans information. We all assumed it when her and Rourke were attacked the first time, but now it's obvious. There's no way that Aryan would have been able to get into her room without being seen on a single camera."

"As much as I want to whisk her away to somewhere safe myself, she won't want to be excluded. Not from this," Stefan had told them.

Jamie had scoffed. "I don't want her to have any part in this. She's been through enough. This is something we need to take care of."

No, my darkness had whispered deep inside me. Having been completely consumed by despair, I'd forgotten all about it.

"And you think she'll let you make that decision for her?" Stefan had snapped.

No. My darkness's voice had gotten louder as if getting closer.

"Look at her!" Jamie had bellowed, his rage unchecked.

No.

"We've already asked Kiara to take her and Brenna to Boston," Louie had said. "She's looking for a house for them to stay in and Jameson has asked his uncle Aiden for extra security to send with them."

Stefan had sighed frustratedly. "I know my daughter. She won't go."

"Then we'll make her," Jamie had snapped.

"No," I had whispered, my darkness taking control. Inside me, it had seemed to wrap itself around my pain, doing its best to shield me from it, leaving me only my rage.

All three of their heads had whipped in my direction but I'd refused to look at them.

Jamie had squeezed my hand. "Maura?"

I'd yanked my hand free from his. "Get out."

I thought they'd been in shock because none of them had moved.

I'd finally shifted my gaze to them, meeting Jamie's eyes, then Louie's. "I'm not going to Boston."

Jamie had been the quickest to recover and his expression had turned cold. "You *are* going to Boston. You—"

"Get out!" I'd yelled. "I don't want you here! Either of you!"

"Maura," Louie had begged.

"Get the fuck out!" I'd screamed, making Louie reel back. His shoulders had slumped before he'd stood and stormed out of the room.

"You don't get to push us away," Jamie had seethed.

I'd glared at him, venom slipping into my voice. "And you don't make decisions for me."

"Jameson," Stefan had barked, stopping him from responding. "Go back to the house. Cool down. She's being discharged soon. You can talk more later."

Jamie hadn't been happy about it but had done as Stefan had ordered.

I'd slowly looked at Stefan and hadn't been surprised to find him masked with a blank face. "I'm moving into the guesthouse." I couldn't have gone back to my room, or even back inside the main house.

He'd given me a shallow nod. "Okay. Is there anything else you need? Brody's on his way here with some clothes for you. If you're hungry, I'm sure he'll be more than happy to pick something up for you."

I'd shaken my head.

I pulled myself from my memories, not wanting to think about what had transpired after and how badly everything had spiraled.

CHAPTER TWENTY-NINE

As I stood before the floor-to-ceiling mirror in my hotel bathroom, I smoothed away the nonexistent wrinkles of my form fitting black suit. I hated how my hands gliding over my flat stomach sparked pain inside me. As if it were a beacon, I touched the spot under my navel—where Alex Roth had stabbed me.

I met my eyes in the mirror. My makeup was dark and on point. My hair was down and straightened. I was wearing the same pant suit I had worn to my first family meeting. The jacket had the perfect plunge that showed off the black lacy bralette I wore underneath. I looked like I had my shit together. My eyes said different. There was no life in them. Just dull, broken despair.

I walked away from the mirror over to the bathroom vanity where I'd left a satin jewelry box. Flipping open the lid, I unsnapped the buttons holding the shamrock necklace Stefan had given me. It had mysteriously appeared in my jewelry a while back. I had chosen to ignore its presence because I'd thought Stefan had been trying to buy my forgiveness for spying on me the entire time I had been away at college.

I clasped it around my neck and the rose gold, diamond

pendant rested just past the swells of my breasts. I couldn't care less anymore as to why Stefan had given it to me. It was now a symbol of my revenge and I was going to make sure all my enemies knew it.

We pulled up to Alessandro's—a restaurant owned by the De Luca family. I was here to speak with the don, not that he knew I was coming. Vincent had tracked Nicoli's phone and tapped into the street cameras around the area to make sure that he was here. Which was how we knew he had been inside having dinner for the past half hour.

Asher and Dean hopped out of the Escalade and stood by my door, waiting for me to exit.

"Drive around until we need you," I told Finn and Brenna, who were sitting in the front. I locked eyes with Finn. "If anything happens, don't come back for me. Just get to the hotel, get Vincent, and get the hell out of here."

Finn nodded and I stepped out of the car. Asher walked ahead of us to open the door for me. I took the lead and walked into the restaurant.

Without stopping, I strutted past the hostess and into the restaurant. The dining room was large and open. Italian music played in the background, the walls were painted a rusty red, and the table linens were solid black. All the way in the back and kind of closed off by sheer black curtains was a long table that sat ten. Nicoli was sitting at the head of that table with seven others dining with him. Five were men and two were women. I recognized Ivano right away and his fiancé, Alessia, sitting next to him.

As I approached, I spotted three tables with two goons sitting at each one. All of them stood once I was mere feet from the main table. I stopped in my tracks and stared straight ahead at the don, who had yet to notice me because he was distracted by a pretty blonde sitting to his left. Ivano noticed me and tapped Nicoli's arm, while the rest of the table quieted and glared in my direction.

Nicoli finally pulled his attention away from the blonde to give his younger brother a questioning look. Ivano tilted his head toward me. The don's golden eyes locked with mine.

I arched a brow. "Hello, Nicky."

He leaned back in his chair and the corner of his mouth lifted. "You never cease to amaze me."

"I like to keep you on your toes," I said.

It looked like he was fighting hard not to laugh. "What can I do for you, Maura?"

"I need to talk to you, and I have your delivery," I answered.

"You could have called first," he said.

I shrugged. "I think you know why I didn't call."

He nodded slightly. "Stefan is offering a lot of money to anyone who can find you."

One of the guys sitting at the table turned to Nicoli and asked in Italian, "This is the Quinn bitch?"

Before Nicoli answered, I replied in Italian, "Yes, I'm the Quinn bitch." I returned my attention to the don. "May I join you?" I took one step forward and all of the Italian goons reached for their weapons. Out of my peripheral I saw Asher and Dean inch closer to me. I raised my hands. "Easy, boys."

"They will need to search you," another Italian man at the table said in English.

I gave Nicoli a look that said, *Really?* He shrugged. We'd never done this song and dance before. His family—the ones who helped him run his Mafia—were all at the table, so I supposed I understood to an extent. Stefan would probably frisk Nicoli too if he were ever invited to a family meeting.

I reached for the buttons on my jacket and worked to unfasten them. "They can look but they can't touch," I said and opened my jacket to reveal my bralette and my scarred, pale stomach to the table. I watched as Nicoli's eyes roamed, unabashed, but when they landed on the long pink scar that started under my belly button and disappeared into my pants, his expression tightened. I spun around and lifted the back of my jacket to show I had nothing hidden there either, besides my shamrock tattoo. I turned full circle and fastened my jacket. "If you want to do a cavity search, you better fucking buy me dinner first."

Nicoli gave me a cocksure smirk. "If that was a real offer, I'd buy you whatever you wanted."

I actually wanted to genuinely smile—a feeling that had eluded me these past few months—but I held it at bay. "May I sit now, Casanova?"

Nicoli nodded at his goons and they backed off. Without having to be told, Alessia and the blonde woman stood and excused themselves. I pulled out the empty chair directly across from the don and took a seat.

"You've got a lot of scars for a pretty thing," said the Italian man sitting to my right.

The first thing I noticed were the rosary beads wrapped around his wrist, and that instantly told me who he was. His name was Dario Moretti and he was infamous for strangling his enemies with his rosary—not that the cops could pin any of the murders on him. He was also Nicoli's right hand man. I supposed he was to Nicoli as Jamie was to Stefan, which made him the deadliest person at the table.

I leaned close to him. "And you're wearing some interesting jewelry for a scary man."

His dark eyes narrowed. "I don't believe you think I'm scary."

"That's because she doesn't," Nicoli stated as he returned to eating.

The rest of the table followed suit, apart from Dario. Nope. He seemed more interested in me. There was an unused wine glass sat to the side of the place setting in front of me. I picked it up and held it out to Dario. I could tell I intrigued him because the corner of his mouth twitched as he reached for the wine bottle in the center of the table.

He filled my glass with the red liquid. "I would have pegged you for a whiskey drinker."

"Actually, I prefer tequila, but the wine will do," I said and took a sip.

"You don't know who I am, do you?" he asked.

I gave him a sly smile. "Dario Moretti. Age thirty-three. You have a younger brother named Mario, who is sitting next to you. Both of your parents have passed. You have a passion for old school cars, and you drive one with suicide doors. Your sex life is decent. You definitely have a thing for blondes and big breasts, but you avoid relationships, which is understandable. Would you like to know your credit score?"

Nicoli chuckled and Ivano snorted. Dario glanced at them with a frown.

I looked to Mario, sitting next to him. "Would you like to know what I've learned about you, young Moretti?"

He glared at me. "You spied on us?"

I shrugged and took another sip of my wine.

"Why don't you seem surprised by this?" Dario asked Nicoli.

"I told you about the dinner I had with the Quinns and how Maura knew personal things about Ivano. She's probably researched everyone at this table," Nicoli said.

Dario's attention returned to me in a studying manner. "Seems a little unfair that you know everything about me, yet I know very little about you."

"I suppose you're right. Hmm..." I tapped my chin. "I'm twenty-four. My birthday is coming up soon, so mark your calendars. My favorite food would have to be tacos. I have a bachelor's in behavioral psychology. My sex life sucks at the moment, but I only have myself to blame for that. I have enough daddy issues to make a shrink's head implode. I'm a control freak, I'm stubborn, and I have a really bad Irish temper." I glanced around the very quiet table. "Would anyone like to know anything else?"

"And you would just tell us?" Mario deadpanned.

"I'm pretty sure she would," Nicoli told him. "Maura has a thing for honesty."

I smiled at the young Moretti before taking a huge gulp of my wine.

"Why is it understandable?" Dario asked me.

It took a second for me to realize what he was asking. When it clicked, I set down my wine, reached over, and ran my fingers over his rosary beads. "Would you like to play a game, Dario?"

He frowned.

"I'll tell you why you avoid relationships if you let me guess why you like to kill using these beads," I said.

He nodded.

I noticed the cross was missing from the beads. "Well, I'm tempted to say you use them as a *fuck you* to the Almighty."

"Do you not pray to God?" he asked.

I huffed. "I'm going to hell so what's the point? I've done too many bad things to be redeemed and I'm not going to stop doing bad things even if it would redeem me. I've accepted who I am and what my fate might be. By the lack of a cross at the end of your beads, I'd say you've come to terms with your fate as well."

He smiled a little, but everything else about him was unreadable. I tilted my head as I studied the beads. They were beautiful and a little on the feminine side. "You know, strangling someone is an interesting choice. It takes time, but the moment they stop fighting, time slows and for a few heartbeats you feel the life leaving their body. It's quite a high."

"You sound like you speak from experience," Dario asked.

I answered with a small smile. "These were your mother's, weren't they?"

Dario's eyes hardened, giving me my answer.

From what Vincent could dig up for me, I knew Dario's mother had been strangled by his father and then his father had hung himself. The coroner had found strange indentations on his neck that hadn't matched the rope that he had supposedly used to hang himself with, but nothing had really been done with that information. Dario had been seventeen at the time.

"Your father was your first," I whispered.

Dario didn't answer, but the reaction in his eyes spoke volumes. His gears were turning quickly, obviously realizing that I had figured it out.

"I know someone like you. They too had to endure something painful when they were seventeen and they killed those who had wronged them in the most painful way possible. Revenge is bittersweet. It's only satisfying until it's over. Then you're left wishing you could kill them again, just to feel that small moment of control and peace once more." I glanced down at the beads again. "You like to recreate how you killed your father because you're searching to feel that moment. Maybe you feel it or maybe you're the definition of crazy. The thing is, no matter how many times you pretend you're killing him, it won't bring back what he took from you."

Dario leaned closer. "It's still satisfying even if it only lasts a moment."

I knew that. It was why I was here.

Dario looked at Nicoli, who had been watching Dario and I interact. "You're right, Nic. She's different. Maybe there is hope for our two families to make peace."

"Aw, Nicky, have you been talking about me?" I teased.

"Why are you here, Maura?" Nicoli asked.

I schooled my face. "I'm here to make you a deal." I held my hand out to my goons. They were standing no more than a few feet away. Asher retrieved a folded piece of paper from his pocket and put it in my hands. I handed it to Dario, who passed it down to Nicoli. "Instead of money for your next...*order,* I want what is on that list instead."

Nicoli unfolded the paper and read the list. "Your family is the largest arms dealer on the entire east coast of the United States. Why are you asking me for this?"

"I'm not here as a Quinn," I said.

"Yet you're using fifty kilos of Quinn powder as currency," he shot back. "Your father is going to kill you."

I smiled. It wasn't a happy smile, but a sinister one. "I doubt it. Regardless, it's my business."

Nicoli threw down my list on the table. "It becomes my business if I'm taking the risk of losing my pipeline."

I sighed. "Did you know our Colombian supplier sells to me and not Stefan? How do you think I obtained your order even though I've been away from home for months?" I stood from my chair. "The only thing you're risking, Nicky, is pissing me off. Think about my offer, then come find me," I said and walked away, back through the restaurant and outside into the busy city.

I was sure it wouldn't take him long to locate the hotel where I was staying.

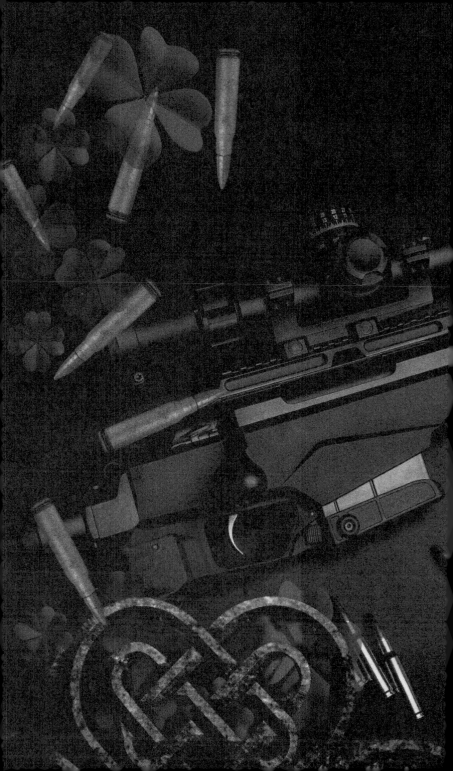

CHAPTER THIRTY

"Do you think De Luca will come through?" Brenna asked from where she was lying on the bed that she had claimed in our hotel room. She and I were sharing a room, while our goons shared two others. Finn and Vincent were in the room across the hall. Dean and Asher were next door. There was a door that connected their room to ours that Asher insisted stay open in case we needed them. It was cracked at the moment to give us a little privacy.

Sitting on my bed, I flipped through the channels on the TV, not finding anything good to watch. It had only been a few hours since I had met with Nicoli and I found the waiting around harder than it should have been. Without having something to occupy my time, my thoughts kept trying to wander.

Deeming it a lost cause, I turned the TV off and gave my full attention to Brenna. "I'd like to think that he will, but I still have doubt and haven't been able to let go of my caution when it comes to him. Our families have a long history of animosity. Trust is going to take time."

Brenna fiddled with her long blonde hair and picked at the

ends. "Is that why you make me stay in the car every time you meet with him?"

"Yes and no. I want you to hold onto your invisibility for as long as you can, because once you're a known player in this dangerous game we all play, there's no going back."

"You think I might change my mind?" she asked accusingly.

"You might," I said as gently as I could. "You haven't taken a life yet."

She sat up, anger radiating from her. "You think I won't be able to handle it?"

"Would it be a bad thing if you couldn't?"

"I guess we'll find that out soon, won't we?"

Sadly, that was true. It was another boulder of guilt I'd have to carry around—dragging her into all of this.

I sighed and also sat up so I could level my gaze with hers. "I'm not doubting you, Brenna. I will support you in whatever decision you make. I just want you to be sure that this is the right path for you, okay?"

She nodded reluctantly and began fiddling with her hair again. "I want to cut my hair."

An aura of eagerness had come over her that gave me pause. "Right now?"

"Will you cut it for me?" she asked.

I gaped. "Have you lost your mind? I can't cut your hair."

"I know this YouTube video we can watch that'll show us how." She smiled. "Come on. It'll be fun."

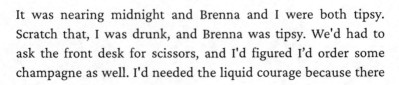

It was nearing midnight and Brenna and I were both tipsy. Scratch that, I was drunk, and Brenna was tipsy. We'd had to ask the front desk for scissors, and I'd figured I'd order some champagne as well. I'd needed the liquid courage because there was not only a pile of blonde hair on the floor, but red hair as well.

I'd given Brenna a few small glasses of champagne while I'd drunk right from the bottle. Was it a good idea to cut hair while drinking? Most definitely not. But I had to say, cutting our own hair had turned out to be a success. Brenna had gotten to be the guinea pig and go first. The video we'd watched had had us tying our hair in four parts and putting the ties where we'd wanted to cut. Brenna's hair had reached the middle of her back, and after I'd gone *snip, snip,* her hair had become shoulder length. It looked really good, if I did say so myself.

Then she had talked me into letting her cut mine. It had probably been the champagne talking because my drunk ass had agreed and decided to go as short as she had gone.

"I love it!" Brenna cooed as she ran her fingers through the short length. "I want to put some curls in it," she said before running out of the bathroom to retrieve her iron while I just stared in the mirror and began chugging champagne.

At least ten inches of my hair lay on the floor. It was a drastic change. I was panicking slightly until I ran my fingers through it, then looked side to side. *I guess it looks okay.*

Brenna returned with her curling iron and Dean following right behind her. His eyes widened with surprise when he saw me. Then they drifted to the pile of our hair on the floor.

"Well? Do you like it?" I asked him.

"It looks different."

Brenna shot him a glare.

"A good different," he corrected, then looked to the ceiling. "Why aren't you wearing clothes?"

I looked down at my bralette and matching lace panties. "I didn't want to get hair on my clothes."

Brenna giggled as she plugged in the iron, the champagne clearly kicking in.

ASHLEY N. ROSTEK

"I was just checking on you two. I'll let you ladies get back to whatever it is you're doing," he said and turned on his heel to leave.

I found myself liking my hair more and more as Brenna styled it with loose curls.

"What made you decide to get a shamrock tattoo?" she asked.

"A lot of alcohol."

She snorted.

After Brenna was done styling my hair, she began working on hers and I went to change into my sleepwear. As I stepped out of the bathroom, there was a knock at the door. I went back into the bathroom because it was where I had left my gun.

Brenna also grabbed hers from where it lay right next to mine on the bathroom counter and we each cocked our Glocks simultaneously. I silently approached the door and looked through the peephole. Nicoli and Dario were standing in the hall.

I unlocked the door and greeted them with a frown. "It's the middle of the night."

Both of their eyes slid down my body and Nicoli gave me a naughty smile. "And I apparently have perfect timing."

Fuck! I'm in my underwear. I didn't let my embarrassment show or let my confidence waver, which was very hard because I was really buzzed.

"I like your hair," Nicoli complimented before his gaze shifted to look behind me.

I glanced over my shoulder and found Brenna standing a few feet behind me. She was staring at Nicoli and Dario with a blank expression. However, her eyes gave away that she was curious.

"Go next door," I ordered.

Brenna looked at me. "I'm not leaving you alone with them."

It took a lot of effort not to go off on her, but I supposed it was too late now.

They'd seen her.

I pushed open the door, a silent gesture for them to come in. I turned and beelined for my suitcase. Lying on top of it was a baggy shirt I'd planned on wearing to bed. I scooped it up and quickly put it on. It covered me to mid-thigh.

Nicoli and Dario stepped inside and Nicoli stopped in front of Brenna. "You look familiar," he said. Brenna didn't shy away from his intense stare and gave him an unimpressed look. Nicoli smirked and moved further into the room. "You Quinns recruit young."

I arched a brow at him. "You have no room to talk."

Nicoli walked over to the small seating area by the balcony door and sat in one of the armchairs. Dario also paused in front of Brenna and eyed the gun in her hand. "Do you even know how to use that?"

The corner of Brenna's mouth lifted slowly. "Want to find out?"

Dario let out an evil chuckle and walked across the room to take his place by his boss.

I set my gun down on the dresser and leaned against it so I wouldn't sway. The champagne was hitting me hard. "Why the late visit, Nicky?" I asked.

"You told me to come find you when I had a decision," he said.

"And what did you decide?"

Ignoring my question, he glanced back at Brenna. "What is your name?"

Here we go. "It's up to you if you want to tell him but know that he will find out one way or another now that he has seen you," I said to her.

She held the don's stare again. "I kind of want him to work for it."

A proud smile stretched across my mouth. *Good girl.*

"But I could be persuaded to tell you, if you agree to the deal Maura offered," she said to him.

Nicoli appeared amused before he looked at me and his expression turned serious. "There were some interesting requests on that list you gave me."

I kept my mouth shut, not willing to divulge.

"Who are you planning on starting a war with, Maura?" he asked.

"I'm not starting anything."

"So much for honesty," Dario scoffed.

My eyes moved to him. "I'm not starting a war...I'm finishing one." I crossed my arms over my chest, hoping that would help hold my rage at bay because I was itchingly close to exploding.

Nicoli sighed heavily and stood. "You still owe me a date. Have dinner with me tomorrow night, alone. After, we'll do our exchange."

My eyes narrowed. "That's a lot of trust you're asking of me."

He closed the distance between us. "It's no more than what you're asking of me. How do I know for sure that your father won't retaliate if I agree to this deal?"

He had a point. "Fine." If he killed me, I'd fucking haunt him.

Nicoli walked toward the door, with Dario following him. Nicoli paused in front of Brenna again and smiled down at her. "You owe me your name."

She glared up at him. "Brenna."

Nicoli's eyes lit up with recognition. "Samuel Quinn's daughter."

Brenna's glare deepened upon hearing her father's name.

"Touchy subject, little Quinn?" he goaded.

She made me proud when her unimpressed facade returned. "Not at all." She looked him up and down. "I just find it boring when old men talk a lot."

I had to bite my cheek to stop myself from laughing. Then I

heard Dario snort and I lost it. Laughter erupted from me. Nicoli was only thirty-four, but her snub was funny as hell. Everyone stared at me and I forced myself to stop, cleared my throat, and said, "Sorry."

If she had offended him, Nicoli didn't let it show as he watched me regain composure. "I can already tell that she'll surpass her brother, especially with you mentoring her." He bid us a good night, and he and Dario left.

Dean and Asher pushed open our shared door and walked in. They both looked as if they had been eavesdropping the entire time.

"That was unexpected," Asher said, staring at the door Nicoli had just left through.

"You laughed," Dean said to me.

"I guess that proves I'm not completely dead inside."

Brenna, Dean, and Asher did that thing where they exchanged looks. Ignoring it, I scooped my gun from the dresser and put it under my pillow. "Let's go to bed. We have a busy day tomorrow."

Dean and Asher returned to their room and Brenna turned off the light before climbing into her bed. I lay there until long after Brenna's breathing slowed, thinking about how much I hated how cold and alone I felt in the foreign bed. I tried to convince myself not to move—that I needed to get used to their absence. With an aching heart, I scooted to the center of the bed, then placed a pillow on either side of me.

I hated that I missed them.

A single tear slipped from my eye as I thought back to the last time they had lain next to me. It had been the fourth night after I'd been released from the hospital. I had moved into the guest-house. Not wanting me to be alone and wanting to help in any way that she could, Brenna had also moved in. I had refused to see or speak to Jamie and Louie because they had still been insistent on sending me to Boston while they went off and got revenge on the Aryans.

My life and all the progress that I'd made had seemed to be crumbling around me. Sean had been working to steal my position in drugs. Jamie and Louie had been treating me as if I were made of glass. Stefan had no longer been keeping me in the loop. I had lost my position of power, deemed by everyone as nothing more than a weak female for the *men* to take care of.

Well, almost everyone.

That night, long after I had lain down to go to sleep, I'd woken to the sound of my bedroom door opening. At first, I'd thought it was Brenna or Dean checking on me. Dean and Asher had also been staying at the guesthouse with Brenna and I. With everything that had happened to me, plus Jamie and Louie's determination to send me away, Dean and Asher had refused to leave me, especially in my weakened state.

I was lying on my side, facing away from the door. I still reached for the gun that I had hidden under my pillow. Just in case.

"It's us."

Jamie.

I hadn't rolled over and I'd kept my hand on my gun. "What are you doing here?"

The bed had dipped behind me. "Let's not fight, please. Can we just hold you?" Louie had asked from behind me. Jamie had walked around the bed and sat down next to me.

Too exhausted to fight and too sad to make them go, I had moved my hand from my gun. "Alright."

Louie had curled up close behind me and wrapped his arm around my upper stomach. His nose had brushed the back of my ear as he'd kissed the back of my neck. Jamie had lain down facing me and taken my hand in his. I could see his exhaustion around his eyes, and in them, I could see pain. I'd squeezed his hand and shut my eyes. I would've started crying if I'd stared much longer.

Before falling back to sleep, for a moment, I'd thought things might turn out for the better. Little had I known, I'd find out that their need to sleep next to me had been their way of saying goodbye before they'd tried to make me go to Boston the next morning. Little had they known, my darkness was in control and blood was going to spill.

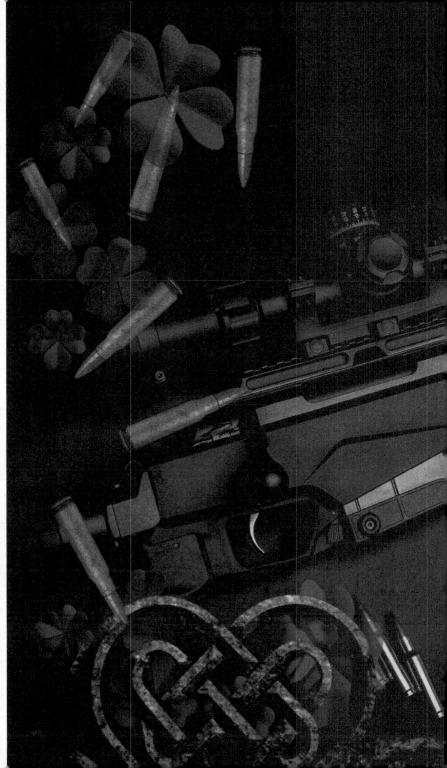

CHAPTER THIRTY-ONE

"He just pulled up outside," Vincent said into my earpiece.

I got comfortable in the leather chair behind what looked more like a sculpture than a desk. Sasha, the pakhan—the boss—of the Bratva here in the States, had a very nice office in Anarchy, the nightclub he owned. One wall was a giant two-way window that overlooked the club's dance floor one story down. On the wall behind his desk were shelves with photos of his Bratva brethren and family and Russian knick-knacks that looked valuable. On the wall directly in front of his desk was a huge TV that showed all the different areas in the club under surveillance.

When Dean, Asher, and I had broken into the club ten minutes prior, Vincent had disabled the cameras and the security alarm. He would do it again when it was time for us to leave. I didn't want there to be any trace of me here that Stefan could use to track me.

I watched Sasha walk into the club via the security cams. He wasn't alone. Eitan was with him, the man I had stabbed in the hand during Stefan's test before he'd officially asked me to join the fold. *This should be interesting.*

I glanced at Dean and Asher, who were standing on either side of the door. They also had earpieces in and had received the heads up from Vincent that we had incoming. They appeared calm. Their stances showed different. They were waiting—prepared for shit to go belly up.

The office door opened, and Sasha stepped in first. He and Eitan were in the middle of talking about ordering more of a certain type of vodka in Russian. Sasha's words trailed and his steps halted when he saw me sitting behind his desk. Eitan also noticed me, then Asher, and went to draw his gun, but Dean came from behind the door and put the barrel of his gun to the back of Eitan's head.

"Don't," Dean warned.

I fixed my attention on Sasha. "I like your office."

"Thank you," he said and stuffed his hands into his pockets. "There are a lot of people looking for you."

I waved my hand flippantly. "I'm taking a vacation from the family."

"Breaking and entering is an interesting way to spend a vacation." His striking blue eyes narrowed. "How did you get in here?"

I mocked innocence. "There was no breaking involved. I simply walked through the front door."

"Sure you did," Eitan drawled.

I let a slow, evil smile form as I looked at Eitan. "How's the hand?"

Eitan squeezed said hand into a fist before he took a step forward. Sasha moved in front of him, blocking him from approaching any further.

"Why are you here, Maura?" Sasha asked.

I stood from his chair and rounded his desk. "I kept your throne warm for you," I teased and moved past him to where he had a couch placed up against the wall, under his massive TV. I took a seat and crossed my bare legs. I was wearing a short, form-fitting black dress with bright yellow heels.

I held out my hand toward his desk. "Why don't you sit, and I'll tell you."

Sasha moved behind his desk and took a seat. Eitan positioned himself in the corner of the room, so that he could keep an eye on everyone.

"You know that I have to tell Stefan that you were here," Sasha said.

"We should call him now. He's offering a lot of money to whoever can find her," Eitan grumbled.

I leaned back, comfortably as if I didn't have a care in the world. "You can try, but you might find that your cell phones don't have any service at the moment."

Eitan scowled and crossed his arms over his chest. Sasha was patiently waiting for me to get to the point.

"I'm here to offer you a lot of money to help me kill a few people, or more specifically, a few prisoners," I said.

Sasha's face blanked, his eyes unblinking. "How many are a few?"

"Eighteen," I answered.

Eitan snorted. Sasha's blank face faltered as laughter filled his eyes. "That's more than a few."

I glanced at Asher, a silent cue. He moved away from the wall as he reached into his coat pocket and pulled out a thumb drive. He held it out to Sasha, who took it and flipped it around in his fingers.

"On that drive you will find files on each of the eighteen men I want taken out... shanked... shivved?" I shrugged. "I don't know the correct prison term. They're serving time in five different prisons. You have...*comrades* also serving time in the same prisons."

Sasha plugged the drive into his computer and gave me an expectant look. The drive was password protected.

"The password is Cheerios," I said.

The corner of his mouth lifted, obviously remembering our first encounter when I'd asked him if I'd pissed in someone's Cheerios by dancing in his club.

Sasha briefly looked over a few files. "They're all Aryans."

I didn't deny it.

"What did the Aryans do to piss off Stefan's princess?" Eitan asked.

A look of understanding came over Sasha. "That's who attacked you three months ago?"

I caught Eitan grimacing.

I held a stone exterior. "Yes."

"You have my condolences," Sasha said, delicately.

I was sensing a *but* coming.

"But if I did what you are asking, I'd be starting a war with the Aryans."

"There won't be any Aryans left to start a war with in two weeks' time," I assured.

His brows rose. "Is that why you left? Did Stefan refuse you your revenge?"

I picked a nonexistent piece of lint off my dress. "They wanted to get revenge for me. I left to remind them not to underestimate me."

"God forbid anyone do that," Sasha said. He too had made that mistake. I hoped he had learned from it. "If I agree to this deal, I won't be pissing in Stefan's Cheerios?" he asked.

I smiled, genuinely. "No, you won't."

He nodded. "Three million."

I gave him a dry look and countered, "One million. They're in prison. It's not like you have to hunt them down or risk getting caught."

"Two point five. My men on the inside will get time added to their sentences."

"One point five. I did my research before I came here, Sasha. Your men won't be seeing freedom in this lifetime even on good behavior."

"Two million is as low as I'll go," Sasha said curtly.

On the inside I was smiling because I couldn't pay him more than two million—the same two million that had been hidden under my bed that I'd made sure to grab before disappearing three months ago.

"Fine, but I want it done three days from now," I said standing.

Sasha's brows furrowed. "Why so specific?"

I smoothed down my dress. "You'll have to wait and see."

"And what do I say to Stefan when he comes questioning?"

"Tell him the truth," I said. "The first million is being wired to your account as we speak."

"Done," Vincent said through my earpiece.

Sasha appeared surprised and I knew he was getting ready to ask me how I'd gotten his account information, but I cut him off. "I'll transfer the second million after all eighteen of them are dead."

"How will I contact you when it's done?" he asked.

"I'll know," I said and walked toward the door.

"We're coming out," Dean said, and only Asher and I knew that he was talking to Vincent.

The power in the club went out, followed by the cameras shutting off on the TV one by one.

Sasha stared at his black TV screen before looking at me. "I guess that explains how you got in."

I gave him a parting smile and left.

We returned to New York with enough time for me to change and get ready for my date with the don. Brenna helped me curl my shortened hair while I darkened my makeup.

"I was able to find you a dress in the city today. It's dark gray. I couldn't find a black one like you wanted," she said.

"That's alright. Thank you for doing that." I hadn't thought to grab anything fancy enough for a date before we'd left Quinn Manor.

Dario picked me up from my hotel and drove me to a high rise that towered over the city. I followed him inside and through the lobby to the elevator. Both the entrance and elevator required a key card to open. It didn't escape my notice that two goons were hanging out in the lobby, pretending not to watch as I walked by.

Dario and I didn't speak as we rode the elevator to the top floor. He appeared bored, which I supposed was a good sign. If this was an assassination, I'd have expected him to look a little more alert.

The doors opened to Nicoli waiting for me in the penthouse's foyer. He was wearing a black-on-black suit. His dark attire made his golden eyes stand out. He really was devilishly handsome.

With his hands in his pockets, he watched me step off the elevator and approach. Dario didn't follow and I looked over my shoulder just in time to watch the doors close with him inside, leaving Nicoli and me alone.

Nicoli took in my long, dark gray dress, particularly the slit that went up to the top of my thigh. Apart from the slit, the dress was modest, with its long sleeves and sweetheart neckline.

"You look beautiful," he said.

I glanced past him, peeking at the rest of the penthouse. All I could see was a modern furnished living room with black couches, white marble tables, and a glass fireplace. "If I'd known we'd be dining at your place, I would have worn sweats."

The corner of his eyes creased, a sign that there was a smile hidden under his blank mask. "If you're uncomfortable with being all dressed up, feel free to...dress down. I wouldn't mind if you wanted to have this dinner naked."

I fought to hide my own smile. If he wanted to play, then fine, I'd play. "You wouldn't be offended if I decided to remove something?" I asked, my voice turning smooth and sultry.

His brows rose. "Not at all."

I pulled up the skirt of my dress and stepped out of my heels. His wood floor was surprisingly warm under my bare feet. I let my smile free as I stared up at him. "There, that's much more comfortable."

His eyes dropped to my bare feet and frowned. "What a tease."

I snorted and walked around him toward the living room. "So what are you feeding me?"

"The dining room is to the left," he said.

Once inside the living room, I took a left and saw that he had an open floor plan. I had a full view of his gourmet kitchen and the area that held an elegant dining table. There were two place settings at the table, and as I got closer I saw that dinner was already served. It was tacos. There were multiple bottles of tequila and already prepared margaritas.

I chuckled. "What a stalker."

"It's not stalking when you share what your favorite food is with not only me but my family," he said and pulled out a chair for me.

I sat in the offered chair and took in the spread of food before me. My mind wandered toward the memory of the time Louie and Jamie had taken me out for tacos right after I had returned home from Hartford. It was like dousing a flame with a bucket of water with how quickly I went from barely keeping it together to depressed. I had to look away from the table and stare down at my hands folded in my lap. I'd unintentionally chased the rabbit and now I was clawing to get to the surface from the black hole I'd fallen in.

"For someone who claims to love tacos, you look awfully sad," Nicoli said as he sat in the seat across from me.

Deep breath, Maura. Grab ahold of your rage and pull yourself together.

I looked up at Nicoli with glossy eyes. "I'm always sad," I whispered and reached for the margarita in front of my plate. I took a few healthy gulps, relishing the taste of lime and tequila on my tongue.

He watched me with an unreadable expression. "If it means anything, I'm sorry about what happened. I even feel bad for Coleman and your other lover."

He's fishing.

I narrowed my eyes. "I'm not in the mood for games. If you want to know something, just fucking ask."

"I tried that last night," he shot back.

I downed the rest of my margarita as I went through every scenario that would end up biting me in the ass if I told him. Eyeing the bottles of tequila, I snagged the Patrón and refilled my glass. "I'm going after the Aryans."

"I had a feeling it was them, but I wasn't sure." He picked up his own margarita and took a sip. His nose scrunched and he set the drink back down. "That's the plan? Wipe out the Aryans?"

I nodded and sipped at my tequila with a hint of margarita. "Don't make me regret this." I locked my eyes with his so he'd see the threat in them.

He rested his elbows on the table. "If I was planning to betray you, I would have poisoned your drink."

I mimicked him by resting my elbows on the table, leaning closer without a tingle of fear inside me. "You'd be doing me a favor." I brought my drink back to my lips to sip from it again.

"You feel that way now," he said with a softness that I found surprising, especially coming from the don of the Italian Mafia.

I stared down at our untouched dinner. "We should eat."

At first, he seemed reluctant, but he nodded, and we began eating.

The tacos were amazing, and we carried on conversing with easy topics. He did try to get details on how I planned to go after the Aryans. I was vague and he got the hint that I didn't want to share. I drank a lot and Nicoli watched each time I refilled my glass without saying a word.

After dinner, we moved to sit in the living room. Nicoli lit his glass fireplace and I found the dancing flames mesmerizing.

"Did you ever envision having a different life?" I asked randomly.

The ice in Nicoli's drink clinked as he fiddled with the tumbler in his hand from where he sat next to me. He had switched to whiskey in the middle of dinner. "I think everyone does."

I set down my empty glass on the coffee table and leaned back on the couch. "I tried to be normal, live the straight and narrow. It was boring."

Nicoli chuckled and set his glass next to mine before extending his arm along the back of the couch behind my head. His eyes met mine and, through my drunken haze, I became very aware of how close we were. "I'm sure it was," he murmured, his stare dropping to my lips.

Don't do it.

He leaned forward and I shot up to my feet. I staggered a little because the alcohol had all rushed to my head. I got my footing and walked across the living room, needing space.

"You don't want me, trust me," I said with my back to him.

"And why is that?"

"There are a number of reasons." My response was met with silence and I knew he was waiting for me to explain. "All I feel anymore is pain and anger. The rest of me is...hollow." I exhaled heavily. "We could just screw. It'd be a welcome distraction. That is, if you didn't run for the hills after you discovered how fucked up I am."

"It wouldn't surprise me if you were a sexual deviant, but I have a feeling that's not the kind of *fucked up* you're talking about."

I shook my head. "Even if I wasn't, you and I still couldn't happen. You have your own kingdom of crime and I have mine. I would not and could not ever submit to you."

"Alliances have always worked before—"

I turned to face him. "Those women were groomed to be subservient. I wasn't."

He wasn't upset but watchful—taking in everything I did or said in stride—like always. He stood from the couch and came to stand next to me. "So what you're saying is that you're a queen who doesn't need a king?" He put his hands inside his pockets and stared out at the city through his floor-to-ceiling windows. "I can respect that."

"We don't have to be bumping uglies to have an alliance."

He smiled. "Won't be as fun."

I smiled back. "No, I guess it won't. We'll make it work, though."

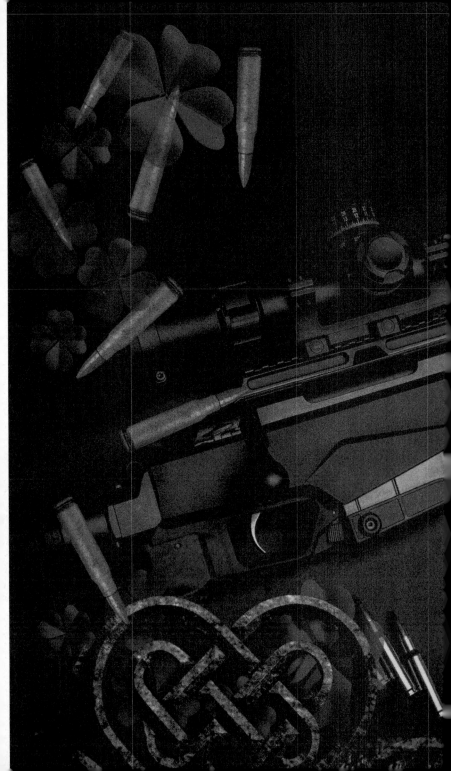

CHAPTER THIRTY-TWO

At three in the morning and under the cover of darkness, Dean, Asher, Finn, Brenna, and I departed toward three different destinations—each a property owned by the Aryans. I was paired up with Dean, and Brenna was paired with Finn. Asher was insistent that he could complete his task on his own. After we were done with our tasks, we were to all meet at the Whiskey Bandit—the bar owned by the Aryans.

"Weapons check," Dean whispered after he parked the black van, which I had purchased with cash. We were down the street from a rundown house where, after a lot of investigation, we knew the Aryans liked to mix up their heroin.

I pulled each of my guns, both equipped with silencers, from the shoulder holster I had on. I released the magazine, rechecking to see it was full, then slid it back in, cocked the gun, and shoved it back into its holster. I repeated the process with my second gun before slipping on a zip up jacket with a hood and repositioning my earpiece to better hear Vincent on the other end.

I glanced at Dean as I put my hand on the door handle. He was in the process of zipping up a black bag carrying enough C4 to completely erase the Aryan heroin house off the face of the

Earth, hopefully along with any Aryan inside at the time of explosion.

Dean met my eyes and nodded, and we exited the vehicle. We kept to the shadows as we moved toward the house. Our black clothing helped keep us hidden. We all, including the others, were dressed in black cargo pants, black long sleeved shirts, black boots, and black beanies.

We halted our approach at the edge of the property line, crouched behind a tall bush.

"We're in position," Dean whispered, talking to Vincent.

There was a moment of silence before Vincent replied, "Alright, the cameras are down and playing a recorded loop for anyone watching. You have ten minutes to get in and out. Good luck."

I pulled one of my guns out and Dean peeked around the bush, getting a position on the two Aryans we knew were guarding the property. He was carrying the bomb and my job was to cover him. We'd gone over the plan for tonight a hundred times and no words were needed after we proceeded from here.

Dean flicked two fingers forward and crept out from behind the bush. I followed and we dashed up the driveway. An Aryan had his back to us as he leisurely walked around the side of the house. Quickly and as quietly as we could, we came up behind him. Dean dropped the bag on the ground right before he reached around the Aryan's neck and put him into a chokehold.

The Aryan struggled, his feet kicking. I quickly reached between them for the Aryan's Glock and yanked it from where it was tucked into the back of his pants. It felt like forever, but after less than a minute, the Aryan stopped struggling and his body went limp. He wasn't dead. Not yet, anyway. The plan was to capture, not kill, if we could. If we had to kill, no bodies could be left behind. It was to look as if we were never here.

Dean laid the unconscious Aryan on the ground and we both

got to work, pulling zip ties from our pockets and tying him up. Dean yanked a bandana from his back pocket and stuffed it into the Aryan's mouth. I picked up our black bag with the bomb and Dean lifted the Aryan from under his arms and dragged him with us as we continued toward the back of the house.

The side gate was open, and I moved ahead of Dean to peek inside. The backyard was a hoarder's wet dream. There was junk everywhere. Car parts, broken furniture, and a lot of discarded liquor bottles. Thankfully, there was a path cleared. I stepped past the gate, slowly creeping further inside.

We were about to round the corner of the back porch when a glass bottle rolled on the ground from that direction. An Aryan, carrying a sawed-off shotgun, followed the glass bottle, completely unaware of us. I lifted my gun, aimed, and pulled the trigger.

It was dark but I could still see the mist that sprayed out from the back of his head onto the torn-up couch directly behind him, which happened to be where his body landed.

Shit.

There was no going back now. We had to keep moving forward. We'd figure out how to hide the blood later. Dean laid the unconscious Aryan next to the dead one on the couch and we made for the back porch.

The wood steps creaked a little as we went up them.

"We're approaching the back door," I whispered into my mic.

Dean crouched so that he was at eye level with the door's lock and pulled out a small kit with tools to pick the lock.

"The alarm is down," Vincent said, and Dean began picking the lock.

With the two Aryan guards down, there shouldn't have been anyone else there, but I'd still need to be on the lookout while Dean set up the bomb.

The lock on the door clicked and he silently turned the knob and pushed the door open. Inside, we were greeted by a dark kitchen. The whole house was an abyss of black and quiet, which I took as a good sign. I followed Dean as he headed for the kitchen sink. He knelt down on the floor in front of it and opened the cabinet doors. Without having to be told, I handed him the bag and he got to work setting up the bomb.

I watched him insert wires into the C4 and set up the timer for when the bomb was supposed to go off. It was a pretty easy set up because everything was premade, thanks to Nicoli and the list I'd given him.

Dean finished setting up the bomb and moved a few old cleaning supplies in front of it to help keep it hidden. He closed the cabinet doors and we backtracked out of the house.

We pulled both Aryans off the couch and were faced with a huge bloody mess to deal with. The upholstery was completely stained.

"Do you think they'll notice if we flip it over?" I whispered.

Dean shrugged and went to one side of the couch. I copied and went to the other and we flipped it backward.

"That'll have to do," he said and pulled the van's keys from his pocket and tossed them to me. "Bring the van up and I'll drag them out front."

I nodded and took off in a jog.

"You guys have two minutes to get out of there," Vincent warned, and I upped my jog to a run.

I was panting by the time I yanked the van's door open and jammed the key into its ignition. Dean was waiting for me with the Aryans in the middle of the driveway. I parked right in front of him, jumped into the back, and ripped open the side door. Dean was already there with the dead Aryan. I helped him roll the body inside and again with the unconscious Aryan. Dean shut the door and I hopped back into the driver's seat. Dean climbed into the passenger's seat and I booked it out of there.

Once we were down the street, I said into my mic, "We're out."

"Okay, the alarm and cameras are back up. The others are also on their way to meet you," Vincent said.

"Good," I replied.

A groan came from the back of the van. Dean and I glanced at each other before he reached into the glove compartment and pulled out a syringe pre-filled with a sedative. Dean pulled off the cap and flicked the bubbles free from the liquid inside before climbing into the back.

The Whiskey Bandit was closed, the parking lot was empty, and there wasn't an Aryan in sight. We met down the street where there weren't any cameras. Brenna and Finn got out of Finn's new white Camaro. His old one had blown up with mine the day we'd gone shopping at the mall. Asher parked his blue truck in front of our van and hopped out.

"We got one," Brenna announced as she approached Dean and I. She was talking about an Aryan.

"So did I," Asher said.

Dean tilted his head at the van. "We have one alive. She killed the other."

I eyed Brenna. "Three will do."

Dean opened the back of the van and pulled out another black bag. He opened it and pulled out three ski masks. He handed them to Asher and Finn, who each put them on.

Dean shoved his mask on and with the black bag in hand, he shut the van's door. "Let's get this over with."

The three of them began making their way toward the Whiskey Bandit, while Brenna and I climbed into the van.

"There's binoculars in the glove compartment," I told her.

She opened it and pulled out two pairs. She handed one to me, and the two of us did our job as the lookouts while the guys set up the last bomb under the bar in the Whiskey Bandit.

We took the Aryans to the family's warehouse on Stone Street—the one where I had killed Zack and Tyson and where Samuel had been hiding all the money he had been stealing from the family. Vincent had disabled the cameras and alarm. The only other security this place had was a chain-link fence that was locked with a padlock. Some bolt cutters took care of that.

The guys tied the three unconscious Aryans to chairs, and then it became a waiting game. They each had been given a sedative and it would be a while before they woke.

It was midafternoon when the first Aryan opened his eyes, groaning. Like a domino effect, the other two did the same. I stood in front of them, waiting. I knew they recognized me because as they became fully conscious, I was met with either surprise or loathing. They were all gagged, so they couldn't spew their detestation, but two of them still grumbled incoherently around their gags.

I didn't say anything to them. I just wanted them to see me—to understand why they were about to die.

Dean, Asher, Finn, and Brenna were standing behind me, silently watching. I pulled my gun from its holster and turned to look at Brenna. I held my gun out to her.

Her hands hanging at her sides clenched before she stepped forward and took the gun from me. This was a test I wished I didn't have to give her. However, if she wanted to be part of this life, she needed to be able to kill.

She stared, blankly, at the three Aryans for the longest time. They stared back at her, then me, their confusion apparent.

I waited, patiently. Brenna could take all the time she needed.

"She's not ready," Finn said from behind us.

I was about to give him a look that would warn him to shut the fuck up, but Brenna aimed the gun.

Pop! Pop! Pop!

She shot them one after another right between the eyes. The girl was very quick and had amazing aim. Even the guys appeared impressed.

She held out my gun and I took it. She turned to face Finn, gave him the dirtiest look, and held out her middle finger. He accepted it all with a proud smirk. She walked away after that and none of us followed, understanding that she needed a minute.

"Help me untie them and get their shirts off," I asked the guys and pulled a Sharpie from my back pocket. Their bodies were going to serve as a message to Buck and the rest of the Aryans. I was coming for them.

At five minutes until midnight, the streets weren't as busy. It made it easier to go unnoticed as we pulled over to the side on one of New Haven's bridges. Just in case, though, we were all wearing ski masks and Vincent, per usual, took care of the street cameras.

Asher opened the van's side door and Brenna and I jumped out, pulling four ropes from inside to tie them on the bridge's railing. Dean, Asher, and Finn worked together to get the now four dead Aryans from the van, each bearing a large shamrock—the same shamrock I'd drawn on the mirror in the bathroom of the Whiskey Bandit after I'd killed Dustin Peters—on their chests. After Brenna and I were done tying the four ropes, we went to help the guys.

"One minute until midnight," Vincent announced into our ears.

Brenna and I dragged one body while the guys took one each over to the railing. We all had to work together to lift the bodies over the edge. After the first body was thrown off the bridge, a loud crack of the rope snapping the dead Aryan's neck traveled up to us.

"Gross," Brenna whispered.

Asher and Finn chuckled, and we continued on to the next body.

Four explosions went off in the distance when we were lifting the fourth body over the railing.

New Haven's night sky lit up with orange light from the blazing fires.

"Time to go," I said.

We quickly piled into the van and drove away.

We all returned to our newly acquired hotel room in New Haven. I'd asked Vincent to get the largest suite the hotel had, so that we could all stay together. He hadn't disappointed. The suite could sleep fifteen. The hotel was really luxurious and there was a club downstairs, which I'd caught Brenna staring at a few times. We all had fake identification and Vincent had made sure his and Brenna's age was listed as twenty-one.

Once inside our hotel room, the guys and Brenna headed straight for the suite's living room. Asher turned on the TV and switched it to the news. The explosions were already being talked about.

I slipped into my and Brenna's shared room and I pulled my burner cell from my pocket. I went out onto the balcony and dialed Stefan's cell.

It rang twice before Stefan answered. "Hello?"

"It's me," I said.

"Maura."

"I've called to tell you that I'll be making some noise in the city. In fact, I've already started."

He sighed. "The explosions, I take it that was you?"

Refusing to confirm or deny, I replied, "I should be done with my vacation in two weeks. After that, I'll come home."

"Running away isn't a vacation, Maura," he snapped.

"You know why I left," I snapped back.

"We were trying to protect you."

"You weren't protecting me. You shut me out and tried to send me away."

"Enough," he bit out. "I just want you to come home."

"I said I'll be home in two weeks. And I need you to guarantee my goons and Brenna's safety. You can punish me all you want, but you won't lay a finger on them."

"You think I'd go after them for helping you run away?"

"No, not because of that. I stole the cocaine and used it as currency. I owe the family a few million. I'll pay it back. If I need to be punished, punish me. Or if my fate is to be the same as Samuel's, then so be it. But you won't touch them or so help me, I will destroy everything this family has built and don't doubt that I will. I have nothing left to lose."

Stefan went quiet for a few heart beats. "I'll pay the family back. No one has to know."

It was my turn to go quiet.

"Don't act surprised," he said. "Sasha said you came to see him. I told him to give you whatever you wanted."

"Did he tell you what I asked him to do?"

"Yes," he answered.

"Then you know what I have to do."

"I didn't need Sasha to tell me what you were up to. I know my daughter." He sighed again, this time sounding exhausted. "Jameson's shoulder healed, in case you were wondering but were too stubborn to ask."

"I don't care," I said with indifference. "I have to go."

"Finish what you need to do and come home."

I didn't respond and hung up.

I leaned on the railing and stared out at the city. Large clouds of smoke were still wafting up into the sky. I had been curious to know how many Aryans we'd taken out in each explosion, but now my mind was consumed with Jamie. My hand squeezed around my phone.

I didn't regret shooting Jamie. I hated why I'd had to.

The morning after Jamie and Louie had snuck into my room under the false pretense of wanting to hold me, I had woken up to them stuffing my clothes into a suitcase.

"What are you doing?" I'd asked.

They'd ignored me and exchanged a look. Louie had finished stuffing the clothes in his hand into my suitcase and begun zipping it up. Jamie had come to the side of the bed, thrown my covers off, and scooped me up in his arms.

I'd groaned from the sharp pain in my abdomen. Jamie had carried me toward the door that Louie had held open.

"Stop!" I'd yelled and grabbed at the door frame as we'd passed through it. "Put me down!"

Louie had removed my hand from the frame and Jamie had continued on.

"No! Stop it!" I'd screamed as I'd thrashed, despite the pain, and knocked over pictures on the walls, trying to grab on to anything I could. "Dean! Ash—"

Jamie had covered my mouth with his hand, and they'd taken me out of the guesthouse. I'd continued to struggle, and his arms had squeezed around me. "Stop it, Maura. You'll hurt yourself."

"Stop!" I'd heard Brenna scream from behind us.

Jamie and Louie had ignored her.

A shot had rung out. They'd both frozen, then turned around. Barefoot and dressed in champagne silk pajamas, Brenna had stood just outside the guesthouse with a gun aimed at the sky. She'd glared at Jamie and Louie as she'd lowered it and aimed it at Jamie. "Let her go."

Dean and Asher had rushed out of the house, each armed. They'd quickly taken in the scene and aimed their own weapons at Jamie and Louie.

"Jameson, put her down," Brenna had ordered again.

"Your aunt Kiara is waiting out front with a car to take you and Maura to Boston where you'll both be safe," Jamie had said.

"She doesn't want to go to Boston," Brenna had argued.

"She doesn't get a say," Jamie had spat.

"Yes, she does," Brenna had snarled. "You may be her lover, but she's Stefan's heir. You don't have the right to make that decision for her."

I would've been proud of her if I hadn't been so fucking pissed.

"What is going on out here?" Stefan's voice had bellowed. He'd appeared from behind Louie. Will and Josh had been with him. Stefan had looked from Brenna and my goons to Jamie holding me and Louie holding my suitcase.

"I thought you were going to talk to her and convince her to leave, not force her," Stefan had said to Jamie.

I'd thrashed again and growled behind Jamie's hand.

"Christ, Jameson, put her down before she gets hurt," Stefan had ordered, and Jamie had done as he'd said.

The moment my feet had touched the ground, I'd slapped Jamie across the face. His face had jerked to the side.

"You bastards," I'd seethed and turned my glare on Louie as well. I'd walked backward until I'd reached Brenna's side, with my hand pressed to my tender stomach.

"We're just trying to protect you," Louie had said, his tone pleading.

"I don't need your fucking protection," I'd snapped.

Jamie's eyes had turned cold as they narrowed. "You're a woman, Maura. What would you know? You already lost our baby. I won't let you get yourself killed too."

"Jameson!" both Louie and Stefan had yelled at the same time.

He blames me. I know it was my fault. She's gone because of me. I had felt myself shutting down again.

"You are a fucking asshole. How dare you blame her?" Brenna had raged.

"I'd shoot you now if she didn't fucking love you," Dean had growled.

Jamie had reached behind his back and pulled out his gun. He'd aimed it at Dean. "You all are rallying behind someone who's incapable of standing up for themselves, even to me. She's going to Boston."

Seeing Jamie aiming his weapon at Dean had seemed to give a spark of strength my darkness had needed to fight against my pain and stoked the flames of my rage. My body had moved without thought and I'd taken Brenna's gun from her. I'd aimed it at Jamie. "How's this for standing up for myself?" I'd asked and pulled the trigger.

Jamie had fallen backward to the ground, clutching his shoulder. Louie had knelt down next to him and helped him put pressure on his wound.

"Maura," Stefan had said cautiously.

I had turned my gun on him. Both Will—my newest goon— and Josh had drawn their weapons. It had been good to see where Will's loyalties truly lay.

I had scowled at Stefan. "You're going to leave me the fuck alone, like you've been doing since I was released from the hospital. I won't be going to Boston. The next person who tries to make me go, I'll kill them." I had looked back at Jamie and Louie. "You fucking come near me again, I'll kill you both."

I'd spun on my heels and walked back into the guesthouse. I'd held on until I'd been inside and out of view before I'd crumpled over in pain. Brenna had been there instantly to catch me before I'd hit the floor. Asher had showed up next, picked me up, and carried me back to my room.

"I'll get her some pain medicine. Do you think we need to call Dr. Ben?" Brenna had asked as she'd rushed into my bathroom, where all my medicine was kept.

Asher had laid me on my bed. I'd lifted my shirt, revealing a bloody bandage. He'd peeled it back to get a look. "Yes. It looks like she popped a stitch."

"Call Vincent and Finn, too," I'd said.

"Are you worried your boyfriends will try and take you again?" Dean had asked as he'd joined us, carrying a glass of water. Brenna had also appeared from the bathroom. She'd spotted the water Dean had been holding and taken it from him, and then taken a seat on the bed next to me. She'd given me the water and the pills she had retrieved.

I'd quickly swallowed them. "No. At least not today. I want Vincent and Finn here because I'm leaving Quinn Manor and I'm going after the Aryans myself. And I'm going to need all of your help to do it."

CHAPTER THIRTY-THREE

W e lay low for the next couple of days, glued to the TV as the news covered the explosions and the four men found hanging on the bridge. The first day, the news was stating that the explosions had been a terrorist attack. That evening, one reporter said he suspected that the hanging bodies on the bridge were related to the explosions and that everything was gang related. That reporter was out sick the next day and the news channels changed their tunes drastically. The four hanging Aryans weren't talked about again, as if it had never happened, and every news station was reporting that the explosions had been caused by an arsonist who'd turned himself over to the police that morning.

I wonder how many strings Stefan had to pull to make that happen?

Seven additional Aryans and five civilians were confirmed dead. Two of the civilians had been workers in the heroin house, one had been the bartender at the Whiskey Bandit, and the last two had been women. One of them had been a girlfriend to one of the Aryans and the other had been a known prostitute, both of whom had been inside the Whiskey Bandit at the time of the explosion.

I had known there'd been a possibility of innocents getting caught in the crossfire and I would undoubtedly carry that guilt forever, but I didn't have the capability to feel it at the time. My darkness wouldn't let me. So I buried it to feel another day.

Vincent had been monitoring the prisons to see if Sasha would come through and he did. The news briefly reported on it, stating that a bunch of prison riots had broken out that had resulted in a *few* deaths. I had a feeling the downplay was also the work of Stefan.

After calculating all the deaths, there were only eight Aryans left to deal with. Within those eight were Buck Werner, the leader of the Aryans, and Alex Roth. My plan was to save those two for last. I wanted them scared. I wanted them to watch their comrades dying all around them. I wanted them to suffer.

As suspected, the Aryans went into hiding. Which is why we had placed GPS trackers on all of their vehicles and hacked their phones. Interestingly, Alex separated himself from Buck, and they both went in two different directions. Alex headed toward Cornwall, while Buck and the rest of the Aryans went to Hartford.

Alex seemed to be the wisest among the bunch, because he ditched his phone right away and found and destroyed the GPS tracker we had on his truck. He must have shared that knowledge, because an hour later Buck's phone was also ditched and the trackers on his and the other Aryans' vehicles were also destroyed. They probably thought that they had outsmarted us, but they'd failed to check the women's cars. The trackers on the cars belonging to Buck's pregnant, nineteen-year-old wife and to Alex's sister were still pinging strong, leading us straight to them.

I sent the guys out to confirm that the locations were legit. Buck and his Aryans were staying in an apartment above a bakery. According to Asher, the Aryans rotated guarding the front entrance by hanging out in the bakery. Dean and Finn found Alex holed up in an old house in a rural area with his sister.

With the confirmed locations, Brenna and I packed up our BFGs—sniper rifles—and left for Hartford. We were to meet Asher on the rooftop of a ten-story building down the street from the bakery. We parked in the back alley and entered the building through the back entrance. It was a long and fucking tiring trot up the stairs.

We set up our rifles while Asher kept watch on the bakery through his binoculars. It was overcast and the air smelled like rain. The sun wasn't due to set for a few more hours. So only the weather was threatening to make our jobs harder. That was, if we could get this done before nightfall.

"You'll need to take them out when they change shifts. It should be soon. They haven't switched since this morning," Asher explained.

"Okay," I said.

"Are you sure you don't want to wait until Dean and Finn get here?" he asked.

"They're over an hour away and we might miss our window," I answered.

He nodded. "Buck will flee from the fire escape behind the bakery. I'll keep watch there and shadow them to their next location," he said and left us to get into position.

The plan was to pick off Buck's Aryan lackeys one by one, keeping him running scared. Once he was all alone, feeling as helpless as I had felt when he'd sent Alex Roth after me, we'd close in on him and then kill him.

Brenna and I stared through our scopes at the bakery and waited.

It was an hour later when the door leading up to the apartment opened and two Aryans stepped out.

"Blue shirt," I called out.

"Gray shirt," Brenna called next and we locked onto our named targets as they headed for the bakery doors.

Brenna pulled her trigger and blood sprayed out of the side of her Aryan's head. I pulled my trigger a second later, but Blue Shirt ducked out of the way and my bullet shattered the bakery's front window.

"Fuck!" I hissed and cocked my gun for another shot.

Brenna did the same.

Blue Shirt was hiding behind a car.

"Come on," I growled.

"We'll get him," Brenna assured.

After an agonizingly long minute, he tried to dash for the bakery doors. Brenna and I both fired. Blue Shirt took a hit in the back of the neck and the center of his back before falling to the ground.

Sirens could be heard in the distance. Brenna and I rushed through the process of dismantling our rifles.

Three shots rang off in the distance. Brenna and I paused for only a second.

"Asher," Brenna said, worry etched in her voice.

We got our BFGs packed up and rushed toward the door. As we sped down the stairs, our heavy breathing and bootsteps echoed off the walls. We burst through the back entrance into the alley. Given how loud the sirens were, I'd have said they were already at the bakery. We needed to get out of here, now.

We threw our BFGs in the back of the van and climbed inside.

"Call him," I ordered as I turned the van on and shifted it into drive.

Brenna pulled out her burner and called Asher. I got the van out on the main road and, as planned, drove away from the scene as inconspicuously as possible.

"He's not answering!" Brenna said, panic overtaking her. She dialed him again and her knee bounced as she listened for him to pick up. When, I assumed, it went to voicemail again, she growled, "Fuck! We have to go back for him."

My hands squeezed the steering wheel, debating.

"Maura!"

"I know!" I snapped and turned the van around.

We couldn't even get within a block of the bakery. The cops had it all sealed off. There was no way in and no way out.

"Call him again," I said as I got detoured away from the bakery.

My burner started ringing. I pulled it from my back pocket and brought it to my ear. It was Dean.

"Dean—"

Before I could utter another word, he asked, "Where are you?"

I told him. He and Finn were in Hartford and they were near the bakery. I explained what had happened and how we couldn't find Asher. He told us to go back to New Haven and that he and Finn would try to find him.

We hung up and I tossed my burner in the van's cup holder angrily.

The rage inside me made me want to erupt. I slammed my hand down on the steering wheel. "Shit! Shit! Shit!"

It was nearing eight o'clock at night and Brenna and I had been back at the hotel for over an hour, waiting anxiously. Right after we'd returned, I had received a text from Dean saying that they had found Asher, he was unharmed, and that he would explain everything when they got back to the hotel.

Brenna and I were sitting on the couch with Vincent while watching the news when the door to our suite opened. Dean walked in first, followed by Finn and then Asher. Seeing that he was unharmed for ourselves, Brenna and I both let out a sigh of relief and each took turns hugging him.

"What the hell happened?" I asked as I crossed my arms.

Asher took a seat in one of the living room's armchairs. "Buck and his child bride fled down the fire escape like we expected, with two other Aryans guarding them. They were supposed to head for their cars parked in the parking garage next door, but they didn't. They broke into the building across the alley. It was some restaurant. I followed on foot. One of them must have seen me because when I went inside the restaurant, the wife was hunched over in the middle of the kitchen, pretending to be in labor. It distracted me. I barely had time to duck when one of the Aryans popped out from behind a corner and started opening fire.

"One of the cooks took a bullet. I'm pretty sure he didn't make it. I tried to follow them through the restaurant, but I lost them in the crowd that was frantically trying to flee out of there. I was circling back to my truck when I was stopped by two cops, asking me if I witnessed anything. I told them I hadn't and that I just heard gunshots. They asked to take down my *information* so that they could question me again later. It wasn't until I went to hand them my fake ID that I realized I must have dropped my burner in the restaurant's kitchen. Dean and Finn found me not long after that."

"I'm glad you're alright," I said. It sucked that we had no idea where Buck was now, but I was sure we'd find him. Preferably tomorrow because right now... "I need a drink."

Asher gave me a shit-eating grin. "It warms my heart that you were worried for me, doll."

I rolled my eyes.

"Speaking of drinks, we could take the night off to let loose and check out the club downstairs," Brenna suggested.

Dean and Finn groaned.

Vincent scrunched his nose. "I don't like crowds. I'm out."

Brenna turned pleading eyes at me. "Please go dancing with me. You know I've never been allowed to do anything remotely fun in my life."

Oh, she's good. Using guilt to manipulate an outcome in her favor. "Alright."

Brenna jumped from the couch and squealed. "Good. Because I found us the perfect dresses to wear in that dress shop down the street this morning," she said and took off toward our room.

I glanced at Vincent with an arched brow. Both of them had gone out for coffee this morning and, thinking back, they had taken a while.

"Don't give me that look," he grumbled. "You couldn't say no to her either."

I smiled. "I'm not mad. I'm happy she's learning to be more assertive." I gave my goons a pointed look. "It's a good thing and we should encourage it."

Dean frowned. "Two Quinn women going clubbing. What could go wrong?"

CHAPTER THIRTY-FOUR

B renna and I danced together in the dark crowded club, losing ourselves to the music. The guys were nursing beers at the bar while they watched over us. The music was hypnotic, and the beat buzzed over my skin. And boy, did I have a lot of skin on display. Brenna's perfect dress she had found for me was very close to a handkerchief. The black fabric was thin, the skirt was very short, there was no back, and the straps were nothing more than strings. The dress left very little to the imagination. My mint green stilettos were gorgeous, though. Brenna's dress was thankfully a little more modest. It was also black and short, but it was long sleeved and had a keyhole neckline.

Hips swaying to the music, I threw my arms up in the air and closed my eyes. I felt light—free, like nothing else mattered. Knowing the feeling wasn't going to last, I was determined to relish every second. It was why I wasn't bothered when hands smoothed over my hips from behind and a body swayed with me. I could tell it was a guy by the feel of his strong hands and masculine scent. It was probably all the alcohol I had drunk that made me brazen. I leaned back against the stranger's chest and hooked an arm around his neck.

Our bodies seemed to mold together, and we moved as if in tune with one another. One of his hands moved to my arm that was around his neck and he ran his finger along the underside of my arm, down the side of my breast, to rest on my ribs. It made me shiver.

I slowly opened hooded eyes and saw that Brenna had stopped dancing. She was staring at me and my dance partner, wide-eyed.

The stranger behind me brushed his nose along my ear and said, "You cut your hair."

I froze, my hooded eyes going as wide as Brenna's. I unhooked my arm and whirled to face him.

Hazel eyes stared down into mine.

Jamie.

How... My heart picked up speed, pumping adrenaline and the urge to run through my veins.

His arms tightened around me as if sensing it. I forced myself to calm. Putting my hands on his chest, I pressed my body against his. His eyes narrowed in confusion, a clear indication that I had surprised him.

He didn't shove me away and it gave me the confidence to do what I needed to next. I trailed a hand up behind his neck. Pulling him close at the same time I pushed up on my toes, I brought my lips to his. His whole body went rigid, and his fingers pressed firmly into my skin. I snaked my tongue out and lightly brushed it across his lips. That seemed to melt him, and he shoved a hand into my hair before taking over, plunging his tongue past my lips to stroke mine.

Knowing I had him distracted, I pulled away slightly and rammed my knee up between his legs. He let out a grunt and fell to a knee. I stepped out of his reach and turned to Brenna. Dean, Asher, and Finn were weaving through the dancing crowd behind her.

I grabbed her wrist and moved to meet them. "You know the plan," I shouted over the music at Dean and handed Brenna over to them. I looked at Asher. "Get Vincent and go. I'll catch up."

Dean and Asher opened their mouths to argue, but I cut them off. "That's an order," I said.

Dean reluctantly handed over a keycard and the four of them left in one direction while I went in another. Jamie being here meant Louie wasn't far. I exited the club and headed for the stairs instead of the elevator. I kicked off my heels and ran up the cold metal steps until I reached the third floor. I rushed down the hall to room three-twenty-seven. It was a room that was rented under my fake alias in case something like this happened. The suite that we all shared was checked-in under Dean's alias, and after we had received our keycards for the room, Vincent had changed all the information in the hotel's computer system to show a random person was renting it instead.

Be it Stefan or Jamie and Louie, they were mainly after me. Room three-twenty-seven was a diversion I'd use to give everyone else time to escape. And if I was unable to escape, at least the others were free to come and rescue me later.

Before entering the room, I stopped by the table up against the hall wall. There was a phone on the table to call down to the front desk if need be and a huge vase with fake decorative flowers. I felt around the underside of the table until my fingers ran over the Glock I'd taped there. I wrapped my hand around its grip and yanked it free. After ripping off the excess tape, I cocked it and unlocked room three-twenty-seven with the keycard Dean had given me.

I pushed the door open slowly with the barrel of my gun. The lights were on. I had purposely turned them all off. Once the door was fully open, I could see Louie sitting in a chair waiting for me. He appeared relaxed, blue eyes watchful as I stepped into the room.

"Are you going to shoot me, beautiful?" he asked, his stare dropping to the gun I had pointed at him.

I refused to acknowledge how my heart ached at seeing both him and Jamie. Not only from the sting of their betrayal, but because I still loved them. I probably always would. I'd given them a piece of my heart and they'd never given it back.

My darkness helped keep me in check...

They think of you as lesser because you're a woman.

They wanted to send you away.

They tried to control you.

They blame you.

My hand squeezed around the grip of my gun, my rage clearing a path to clarity and determination. I lowered my gun. "What are you doing here?" My voice was cold and distant.

"You know why we're here," he said.

I eased further into the room. "I'm afraid that I don't."

The room door opened behind me and I whipped around to see who it was. Jamie stormed in, carrying my heels that I had discarded in the hotel's stairwell. "You dropped these," he snarled and tossed them on the bed. He didn't stop walking toward me and I lifted my gun to stop him.

He halted and glared down at my gun. I smirked up at him.

"You think that was funny?" he growled.

"Did you honestly think I would throw myself at you after what you've done?"

I saw Louie stand up out of the corner of my eye and I was tempted to glance at him, but Jamie would have taken that moment to disarm me.

"It seems we started off on the wrong foot. We only came here to talk," Louie said.

"Bullshit," I bit out.

"We did. I swear," he insisted.

"Even if that were true, I don't want to talk to either of you," I seethed. "So you might as well just leave."

A sardonic smile pulled at Jamie's mouth. "We aren't going anywhere."

I tilted my head. "Why? You had no problem leaving me before. I remember you being pretty insistent on sending me away. You did just about anything to unburden yourselves of the woman responsible for your baby's death."

Jamie winced and stepped away.

"That's not true and you know it," Louie argued. "We wanted to send you somewhere safe so we—"

"So you could what?" I snapped. "Get back at the Aryans for me?" I laughed darkly. "I don't need fucking men to fight my battles for me. The only thing you two ended up doing was make me look weak to the rest of the family."

Jamie's fists clenched. "You were weak."

"I had my baby gutted from me!" I roared. "You couldn't give me a fucking minute to grieve. Instead, you wrote me off. You abandoned me!"

"We didn't abandon you! We were trying to protect you!" Jamie roared back. "You left us. You shot me and disappeared for three fucking months."

"You think I wanted to leave? That I wanted to do this alone?" My eyes filled with tears and I lowered my gun. "I needed you and you tried to send me away." My voice cracked. *Damnit!* "And don't tell me it's because you wanted to protect me. You both knew that once I was able to pull myself to my feet, I'd want revenge. You tried to take that from me, to punish me."

Louie shook his head. "No. We—"

"It's my fault we lost her," I interrupted, not wanting to hear his lies. "Right, Jamie?"

Jamie stared at me with a clenched jaw. I did my best to regain my composure, but a tear fell down my cheek. I quickly wiped it away.

"I don't blame you," he said.

"We never did," Louie quickly added.

I stepped away from them. If I stayed here much longer, all my determination would wither away. "It doesn't matter."

Jamie moved closer. "Yes, it does. I didn't mean any of it. I was hoping that if I hurt you, you'd go. You weren't safe and I was desperate."

My disbelief must have shown because he continued on.

"I know it sounds stupid, but you're a runner," he said. "You tried to run from Louie when you thought he didn't want to be with you. You've run from me I don't know how many times. When it involves emotional pain, you run."

Louie also moved closer. "We almost lost you. It scared us. We were angry and grieving. Did we go about things poorly? Yes. But our intentions were to protect you, especially since we have no idea who is feeding all our secrets to the Aryans."

I shook my head and took another step away from them. I felt like they were closing in on me. I felt trapped. I spun and darted for the bathroom. An arm locked around my waist, stopping me. "See what I mean? You run," Jamie said.

I jammed my elbow into his ribs, and he released me with a grunt. "If you've said all you needed to say, then leave." I dashed into the bathroom, slammed the door closed, and locked it.

"We're not leaving," Louie said from the other side.

I woke the next morning to a warm breath on the back of my neck. I cracked my eyes open to Jamie lying next to me. At first, I felt content, thinking I had woken up before Jamie and Louie for once. Then I blinked and my memories came back to me. I lifted my head and looked around. We were still in the hotel room and I was lying between them on the only bed.

The last thing I remembered from last night before falling asleep was sitting on the bathroom floor, with my back against the wall and my knees pulled up to my chest.

They must have broken into the bathroom while I was asleep and carried me out here. Bastards took my gun too, no doubt.

Their breathing was slow and even. Louie was lying on his stomach and Jamie was on his side, facing me. I sat up slowly, careful not to move too much, then began scooting down toward the foot of the bed. Once I had my feet planted on the floor, at a snail's pace, I stood. Free from the bed, I released a breath I hadn't known I'd been holding.

I tip-toed toward the closet by the front door, where I had a small bag hidden. It held a change of clothes, identification for a new alias, cash, and a key for a car parked downstairs. I slid the closet door open and grabbed the bag. The room door was going to be my biggest hurdle. It made a lot of noise. I put my whole hand over the deadbolt, and it squeaked a little as I turned it.

After that was unlocked, I reached for the door handle and a shadow loomed over me from behind before two hands laid themselves flat on the door on either side of me. The tattoos on the arms told me who it was.

"Are you hungry?" he asked.

I turned to face him. My gaze dropped to his bare chest. *He's been working out.* His muscles were definitely more defined. He was only in his black boxer briefs, so there was a lot of...muscle on display.

Catching myself staring, I forced my eyes up to his. He had a stupid smirk on his face.

"I'm not hungry," I answered.

He moved closer, making me bump into the door. He leaned forward and pressed his lips on my collar bone. I jerked, rattling the door behind me. He chuckled, breath puffing against my skin. "I think you are hungry. Not for food, though."

His words filled my veins with ice. "Don't fuck with me, *Jameson*."

He pulled back to stare down at me. "I'm not fucking with you. Just stating what you're too damn stubborn to admit."

"You wish."

"Enough," Louie snapped, startling us both.

Jamie pushed off the door and took my bag from my hand. Right away, he began digging through it. He pulled out the fake ID and passport, reading over the alias's information. He pulled out the phone next and tossed it to me.

"Call your little team," he said. "Tell them that we'll drop you off in a couple hours."

"Or you could just let me leave," I grumbled.

His expression turned cold. "No. She was our baby, too, Maura. Revenge is not only yours." He walked away and tossed the bag on the dresser.

I stormed further into the room. "So, what? You're going to help?"

"Yes," Louie replied from where he sat on the foot of the bed. He ran his fingers through his blond locks tiredly. "We want to help."

A part of me wanted to be petty and deny them like they had tried to deny me. Then I thought back to how excited they'd been to become fathers. No matter how hurt and angry we were with each other, I couldn't do that to them. Their souls deserved some peace, too.

"Fine." I walked over to the dresser and grabbed my bag. "I'm taking a shower," I announced and headed for the bathroom. I was still in my handkerchief dress and smelled of sweat and alcohol. As I went to close the bathroom door behind me, I noticed the lock was broken.

Bastards. I growled on the inside and slammed the door closed.

CHAPTER THIRTY-FIVE

J amie and Louie insisted on driving me back to the cabin—
the place where we were to all regroup if anything were to
happen. Dean and Asher were already waiting outside on
the porch as Jamie pulled his car up the dirt drive. I hopped
out and they both eyed me, checking for any injuries no doubt.

When I had texted them, explaining briefly what had
happened after we'd separated, they hadn't been happy, especially Dean. He disliked the idea of Jamie and Louie being here.

My goons finished looking me over and shifted hard stares at
Jamie and Louie. I took the steps leading up to the porch two at a
time and the cabin door opened. Brenna walked out with a Glock
in her hand.

She looked me up and down. "You okay?"

"Just peachy," I grumbled and looked at Dean. "Did you move
things around?" The cabin had four bedrooms. Brenna and I had
had our own rooms while Dean and Asher had shared a room and
Finn and Vincent had shared the last. Because the guys didn't
trust Jamie and Louie and felt Brenna and I were most likely to be
taken, we were not to be alone. Finn had moved into Brenna's
room because that was who she was most comfortable with.

Dean had moved his stuff into mine and Asher had moved in with Vincent, leaving an available room for Jamie and Louie to share.

"Yup," Dean responded without taking his eyes from Jamie and Louie, who were making their way up the steps.

"Finn made lunch. Let's go eat," Brenna said, hooking her arm through mine, and pulled me inside.

She went to close the front door behind us, but I caught it, leaving it open an inch. I gave her a look that said that I wasn't dumb and leaned my ear close to the door, to hear what my goons were up to.

"You got something to say?" Jamie asked. His tone alone told me that he was looking down his nose at my goons.

Brenna scooched close, trying to listen with me.

"Just trying to figure out why you're here," Dean replied in a bored and unintimidated voice.

"We're here to help," Louie said.

"She doesn't need your help," Asher snapped.

"No, she doesn't," Louie said, and I could hear his annoyance. "But we're here anyway."

Dean huffed. "You're here to win her back."

Brenna's eyes flicked to me in surprise.

"It's none of your business," Jamie said.

"Where she's involved it is our business," Dean snarled. "Because we were there for her. We helped her stand and reminded her that she was still strong. What did you do? You kicked her when she was down and tried to send her away."

Brenna grabbed my hand and squeezed it.

There was the sound of shoes hitting the porch steps followed by gravel crunching underfoot.

"Jameson," Louie called out.

"If he can't handle the truth, then he doesn't deserve her," Asher said.

"Maura wasn't the only one suffering," Louie seethed. "We lost our baby, too."

"Yeah, but no one blamed you for it," Dean said. "Maura woke up in that hospital blaming herself and the two people who could have convinced her otherwise blamed her, too."

The sound of footsteps heading toward us made Brenna and I scramble to get away, but we weren't quick enough. The door opened and Dean walked in, catching us.

"Eavesdropping?" he asked, shutting the door behind him.

"The entire time," Finn said from behind us. We turned to find him standing by the kitchen door with his arms crossed. "I made lunch."

Brenna pulled on the hand she hadn't let go of and dragged me toward the kitchen. Dean didn't follow and I assumed Asher had taken on the task of showing Jamie and Louie where their room was.

The cabin's kitchen was small and quaint. There was a small round table in the corner of the room that sat four. Two plates stacked with grilled cheese were waiting for us on it. Brenna and I took a seat and dug in. We purposely didn't make a comment on the fact that our grilled cheese was crustless. Finn cut them off out of habit because his son hated crust and mentioning it put Finn in a really bad mood. He missed his son. They routinely talked every other night on a burner Finn had given to him before he'd left to help me, but it wasn't enough. It wouldn't have been enough for me. Over a month ago, when I had been able to see past the vengeful fog narrowing my sight, I'd realized that by asking him to help me I'd been keeping him from his son. I'd tried to send Finn back home. He'd refused. He'd said that he'd made a promise to help me and he wouldn't go back on his word.

"Are you sure we can trust them?" Brenna asked me between bites.

I shrugged. "They had all night while I was sleeping and vulnerable to drag me back to Quinn Manor."

"Maybe they really are trying to win you back," she said.

Finn snorted from where he stood, leaning against the kitchen counter. "Don't try to redeem mobsters, Brenna. You'll always be disappointed. If they've betrayed her once, they'll do it again."

My grilled cheese turned sour in my mouth as my emotions began seesawing. One minute, I was pissed off, the next, I was sad.

"I don't believe that. Mobsters are still human," Brenna argued. "Humans make mistakes and depending on what those mistakes are, they should get second chances."

Finn shook his head. "You're young."

Brenna shot out of her chair. "And you're a jaded asshole," she snapped before storming out of the room.

I leaned back in my chair with a sigh. "I can't say that I agree with her when it comes to my situation but there's nothing wrong with her wanting to find good in others."

"Thinking like that will only get her hurt."

"Maybe, but jamming every bad thing about this world down her throat isn't the way to go about preparing her. She's already had a taste of how bad people can be. Between an abusive father and brother and a crackhead mother, it's a miracle that she's still able to smile," I said, scooping up our plates before getting up from the table and heading for the sink. "The best thing we can do for Brenna is not snuff out the last bit of light she has left inside her, but prepare her for the time that she does come across someone who isn't remotely good and teach her how to outsmart them."

Later that evening, we all gathered in the living room. Brenna and I were loading extra magazines with bullets while we sat on the floor. Finn and Asher were going through our inventory of weapons, courtesy of Nicoli, for what we'd need for tomorrow. Vincent was typing away on his laptop and Dean was cleaning his gun. Jamie and Louie listened and asked questions about our plan moving forward. We were going after Alex Roth.

Vincent slammed his computer shut. "I've got nothing on Buck," he said, rubbing his hands down his face. "I was able to follow him from Hartford to the interstate using street cameras. They showed him heading south. After that, I have nothing. Facial recognition hasn't picked up him or the others that are with him anywhere."

I got to my feet and walked over to him. "No more computer tonight," I ordered and took his laptop. "We'll find him, but right now, you need rest. Go to bed and try again tomorrow."

He brushed a few blue strands of hair away from his eyes and stood. "Okay."

I handed him back his laptop and he went to his room.

"We should all get some rest," Asher said. "Big day tomorrow."

"Some rest it's going to be. Finn snores," Brenna grumbled.

Finn frowned. "Are you still pissed from this afternoon?"

I winced. Finn excelled at putting his foot in his mouth.

Brenna glared at him. "You really shouldn't piss off your roommate. They might kill you in your sleep."

"Roommate?" Jamie repeated.

"You aren't sharing a room with Maura?" Louie asked.

Brenna gave me an apologetic look. "Finn, that's our cue to leave."

Finn didn't argue and the two of them briskly left the room.

"Dean is bunking with me," I replied.

Jamie blanked his expression.

Louie didn't even try to hide that he was mad. "Are you fucking him?" He had been trying to be the peacekeeper up until this point, so I found his jealousy surprising.

Again, I wanted to be petty and hurt them, but it wasn't what we needed right now. Not when we were all going after Alex in less than seven hours. "No."

They both looked at Dean as if they didn't quite believe me. He tried to appear bored. The corner of his mouth twitched, and he shook his head. "None of us trust you not to take her." With that said, he stood from his chair and gestured for me to walk ahead of him. I did and he followed me down the hall to our room. Asher lingered in the living room. I had a feeling he wouldn't retire for the night until Jamie and Louie did.

"I'll take the floor," Dean offered after we got into my room.

"Don't be ridiculous. We can share the bed. You can put a pillow between us if you're worried about your virtue."

He froze, appearing stunned.

"What?"

He cracked a smile and shook his head.

"Tell me," I demanded.

His smile dropped. "Lately, you've been having moments where the old you shows. You just made a joke." He looked away. "I never thought I'd say this, but I missed your sass. It made you... well, you."

I didn't know how to respond to that.

He grabbed a pillow from the bed and tossed it in the middle. "To protect my virtue," he joked, making me crack a smile.

We all loaded up in the van and Asher's truck before the sun rose the next morning. Alex Roth's hideout was a house located in a wooded rural area, near Cornwall. Dean parked the van a mile away on the side of the road. We'd trek through the woods the rest of the way, then spread out into position.

Everyone climbed out of the vehicles. I pulled on a ski mask to my forehead, folding it so it wouldn't cover my face, then rechecked my weapons. I had two Glocks in my shoulder holster, spare magazines in my cargo pants' pockets, and a hunting knife strapped to my thigh. Asher grabbed my BFG and Brenna grabbed hers and they took off to find the best spot in the woods. They were going to be our eyes from afar, while the rest of us would circle around the cabin and move in. Jamie and Louie weren't happy with how involved I was going to be. Dean and everyone had come to my defense and pretty much told them to get fucked.

It might have been excessive for all of us to go after one man, but Alex Roth was the Aryans' pet assassin for a reason. He was smart, lethal, and unpredictable. He'd snuck into Quinn Manor alone, attacked me, and left without being seen.

I waited for the rest of the guys to finish checking over their weapons. Dean, Jamie, Louie, and I would split up in pairs to cover the house while Finn set up explosives under Alex's and his sister Tiffany's cars. We were hoping the explosions would draw them out of the house. If they didn't we'd have to smoke them out a different way.

Once everyone was ready, Jamie and Louie went to the right, Finn down the middle, and Dean and I veered off to the left. The mile long walk was a little strenuous because it was at an incline.

We moved slowly and kept our eyes peeled. With the sun beginning to rise, it was still dim and gray out. I was carrying one of my Glocks with a silencer screwed on. I flicked the safety off once we were about halfway there.

"We're in position," Asher said through my and everyone's earpiece. "The sister is sitting on the porch, boiling heroin in a spoon."

Fan-fucking-tastic.

We all responded in whispers that we copied. Dean and I slowed our approach and began creeping behind trees, being careful not to be seen. The side of the house came into view.

"We have a visual," Jamie said.

"Us too," Dean said next.

"Same," Finn said last.

"We should just shoot her," Brenna mumbled. "I bet that'd draw the bastard out."

I glanced at Dean and we both smiled at her bloodthirstiness.

"No innocents," I said into the mic clipped inside my shirt.

"I doubt the junkie is innocent," she quipped. "What if I maim her? She'll live."

Quiet chuckles from all the guys filled my earpiece and I shook my head.

"And now she's high," Brenna said, annoyedly. "She isn't moving from that spot anytime soon."

I moved to get a better view of the front of the house. I picked a tree to hide behind and peeked around it. Tiffany was relaxed in a rocking chair on the front porch, head thrown back.

The front door opened, and I ducked back.

"Don't move," Asher ordered. "He's looking around."

I stayed still and waited.

"Okay, he's walking over to the sister," Asher said.

I carefully peeked again, just in time to see him undo his pants, whip out his man sausage, and grab the back of his sister's head. She didn't even resist and began performing...oral relations on her brother.

"That's fucking disgusting," Brenna hissed. "Please let me shoot them. My eyes can't take it."

I looked around, debating and playing out different scenarios. "Can you get him in the leg?"

"Yeah, I can," Brenna answered. I could hear her smile in her voice and I was beginning to think we'd created a trigger happy monster.

"We move in once she takes the shot," I told everyone else. They all agreed.

I pulled down my ski mask to cover my face. "Okay, Brenna."

The sound of Brenna's rifle firing echoed in the woods at the same time blood sprayed from Alex's leg and he fell, roaring in pain. Because of how close Tiffany's face was, most of his blood hit her. She let out a delayed scream.

"Brenna, Asher, take out the tires on the cars," I ordered before moving out from behind my tree and advancing on the house.

Shots rang out one after the other, and the tires on the two vehicles parked in front of the cabin began popping and shrinking from air loss.

Dean hovered close as we approached.

"Get my gun," I heard Alex yell at Tiffany. She frantically dashed inside the house.

"Jamie, the sister went inside for a gun," I said.

"I'll go in from the back," he replied.

"I'll go too. Finn, you're with Maura," Dean said and took off.

Finn moved toward me as we ducked behind one of the cars. Louie showed up next and crouched behind the other.

"I want him alive," I reminded everyone.

Louie looked at me. "I know, beautiful."

A shot went off inside the house, followed by a scream and glass breaking.

"Tiffany!" Alex yelled and tried to stand.

I stood from behind the car, aimed for his shoulder, and fired. His shoulder jerked from the shot and he fell back to the ground.

More rustling came from inside the cabin. Then I heard Jamie grunt in my earpiece.

"Jamie?" I called. He didn't respond and without thought I dashed for the house.

"Maura!" Louie shouted and ran to catch up to me.

I rushed onto the porch next to Alex. Our eyes locked. I could barely contain my rage and need to make him pay, but finding Jamie and Dean took priority. I kicked him in the face, making him roll in pain on his side. "Watch him," I ordered over my shoulder. I was getting ready to go inside the cabin when Dean said through the earpiece, "We got her."

My shoulders slumped in relief. "Jamie?"

Just as I asked, Jamie stepped out onto the porch, Dean right behind him. I noticed right away that they weren't wearing their masks. I yanked mine up, ready to question them as to why when my gaze caught on Jamie's arm. It was bleeding.

It looked like he was cut from the crease of his elbow down to his wrist. I went to reach for him but stopped myself. He caught the movement and his eyes locked with mine and I looked away.

"What happened?" Louie asked, pointing at Jamie's arm.

Jamie looked down at it. "The bitch cut me with a piece of glass when we tried to grab her."

I pretended not to listen and went over to where Alex was lying. Finn had his gun trained on him, but Alex only stared at me. Blood dribbled out of his nose into his mouth and down his chin.

Standing next to him, I pulled my mask off the rest of the way. I held his stare with a blank expression. For three months, his face and the way he'd looked when he'd stabbed me had been seared in my mind. No amount of alcohol could make it go away and I'd cried repeatedly, begging for just a moment of peace. Today, I'd replace that memory with one of him suffering and screaming out in agony.

His mouth stretched into a bloody smile. It was meant to intimidate, but I was too busy playing out his death in my head. "Let's tie him up."

CHAPTER THIRTY-SIX

We tied Alex and Tiffany to two kitchen chairs, facing each other in their living room. We couldn't let Tiffany go now because she had seen Jamie's face. He hadn't put on his ski mask. His half-hearted excuse was that he'd forgotten. He hadn't forgotten. He'd wanted her to die. And the sad truth was that if it hurt Alex, I wanted her to die too.

I pulled Dean and Asher aside. "Don't take this the wrong way, but I don't want you guys here for this." I tilted my head at Jamie and Louie. "This is something the three of us need to do on our own."

Asher nodded, understanding, and handed over his truck keys. "We'll tell Brenna and Finn. See you back at the cabin," he said and shoved Dean out of the room before he could argue. "They'll be fine," I heard Asher assure him.

I put the keys in my pocket, and I turned. I eyed Alex and Tiffany, tied and bloody. Tiffany had a pretty bad cut on her temple. Alex was still bleeding from where Brenna had shot him in his leg and where I'd gotten him in the shoulder.

My eyes drifted to Jamie and Louie standing on the other side of the room before I pulled out my hunting knife and went to stand next to Tiffany, facing Alex.

"I warned you that we'd wipe out your pathetic little gang and take away everything you care about. I've pretty much followed through with the first half of that threat."

Alex stared up at me with a defiant, bored look. I took my knife and lightly ran it along Tiffany's collar bone. She flinched and his eyes flickered slightly, telling me what I needed to know. She was his weakness.

"Do you know where Buck is?" I asked.

He didn't answer.

Jamie's fist came out of nowhere and collided with Alex's face.

Alex didn't make a noise and slowly turned his head back to face me. Then his eyes shifted to Jamie and he spit blood on the floor. "You must have been the father of the baby I cut up inside your bitch."

Jamie punched him again.

Tiffany laughed, deliriously. "All Irish babies go to heaven," she sang. I smacked her, my rage getting the best of me. She laughed again. "You should have stayed dead, bitch!"

Things were getting out of hand, fast. I needed to regain control. I glanced at Louie. "Untie one of her hands." He did as I said, and she tried to claw at him. I caught her hand, bent it in a way that I knew would hurt. She yelped, then screamed when I slid my knife across her wrist. Slicing the artery, blood steadily poured from her wrist to the floor. She tried to yank her hand free, but I held it firmly, displaying it for her brother to see.

"She'll bleed out," I said to him. "Tell me where Buck is."

"Ow! Damnit, Alex!" Tiffany cried. "She's hurting me!"

"Shut up, Tiffany!" Alex snapped. "I don't fucking know where he is. Even if I did, I wouldn't tell you."

Despite his bravado there was panic in his eyes. My gut believed that he truly didn't know where Buck was.

I released her wrist and grabbed her by her hair. I yanked her head back, revealing her throat, and brought my knife to it. "How'd you get into my house? Who in my family is feeding you information?"

He shook his head. "I don't know. That's a question for Buck. He gave me the blueprints of all the blind spots in your house and a list of times when the security changed shifts."

I didn't remove my knife from his sister's throat. He looked from me to it, then back to me. "I'm telling the truth."

More fear leaked into his eyes—one of the things I truly wanted from this moment. Next was agony.

"I believe you." I moved my knife to the side of her neck and dragged it to the other side.

"No!" he roared as blood gushed from his sister's neck. I took a step back, absorbing every second of his pain. He fought against his restraints to no avail. He cried and screamed, his face turning red as he watched her choke on her own blood.

We stood there and waited until she was dead and his screaming turned into groaning. Then, I stalked up to him and slammed my knife into his stomach in the same place he'd stabbed me. He gasped and I left it inside of him.

"Your turn," I said to Jamie and Louie before walking out of the house. I didn't care to see him die. I didn't care to see the peace death provided. I was content with his misery being the last thing to remember him by.

Jamie and Louie didn't torture Alex for long until they eventually killed him. Then, they joined me on the porch, both sporting split knuckles. We sat there for a while, feeling the finality of Alex Roth. I wanted to cry, but I wouldn't let myself.

After that, we set up the bombs originally meant to lure Alex out with inside the house and blew it up. Jamie drove us back and the three of us didn't speak the entire time.

We didn't return to the cabin until dark. Everyone was sitting in the living room when I walked in. Feeling numb, I didn't so much as greet anyone. I must have had a look on my face because no one said anything to me either and just watched me pass by. I started stripping off my weapons, not caring where they landed as I headed straight for my bedroom. My shoulder holster and two Glocks were taken off first. They thunked on the floor, then my bloody hunting knife that Jamie had returned to me followed. I kicked off my boots in my doorway and unbuckled my pants. Not caring to shut the door, I stripped on my way to my bathroom. I stepped into my shower in my underwear, turned the water all the way on hot.

I could see the steam coming off the water, but I couldn't feel it. I couldn't feel anything. No rage. No pain. I felt completely hollow. I couldn't stand it.

A hand touched my shoulder, startling me. It was Louie.

He reached inside the shower, getting the sleeve of his shirt wet, and turned down the temperature. "You're going to hurt yourself."

"What are you doing here?" My voice cracked.

His brow furrowed and I could see sadness marring his handsome face. "I wanted to check on you." His gaze slid down my almost naked body.

I grabbed the bottom of his shirt and pulled on it—a silent tell that I wanted him to join me.

He hesitated.

"I just want to feel," I whispered and pulled on him again. He stepped into the shower fully clothed. I molded my wet body to his and let him capture my mouth.

Our lips touching seemed to set something off inside of us. We turned frantic and rushed.

While my fingers worked to unfasten his pants, he reached behind me to unclasp my bra and tossed it on the shower floor. I freed his already hard cock from his briefs and shucked my underwear off. My back was pushed against the cold tile wall and I hooked my leg around his hip. He slammed into me and we both groaned.

With his pants only halfway down his thighs, the fabric of his clothes scraped along my bare skin each time he rocked inside of me.

I slid my fingers into his hair and pulled, making him thrust into me hard. I felt the delicious sensation of pain and I couldn't get enough.

"Harder," I panted. He upped his speed, his pelvis slamming against mine.

It felt good.

I didn't want to feel good.

I wanted to feel pain.

"Harder," I moaned.

He hiked up my leg higher and pounded into me.

I pulled him close so that he wouldn't see the tears filling my eyes. *It's not working.*

"She wants you to hurt her," an angry voice said.

Louie and I froze and stared in the direction the voice had come from. Jamie was leaning against the bathroom door, watching, looking pissed at me.

Confused, Louie looked from his best friend to me. He reeled back when he saw that I was crying. He cupped my face. "Why would you want me to hurt you?"

I refused to answer.

"She wants you to punish her," Jamie answered for me. "Because she feels like she deserves it."

My body tensed.

"Maura, no," Louie groaned. "I'm sorry for everything that I did." His blue eyes bored into mine. "I let my fear get the best of me. If I have to grovel and beg to get you to forgive me, I will. I love you so fucking much." He stepped back, sliding out of me, leaving me feeling hollow and numb once more. "But I can't and won't ever intentionally hurt you."

He tucked himself back into his pants and got out of the shower. He snapped a towel from where it was hanging on the rack angrily before leaving the bathroom.

"If you're going to torture one of us, torture me," Jamie said. "I'm the one who made you think that we blamed you. Not him."

I stepped back under the spray, giving him my back. "Get out." I turned the heat back up on the shower.

"I'm sorry, too, you know. I regret how I handled everything and for what I said. Every minute of every fucking day I wish I could take it all back."

I refused to turn around. I stayed under the water and let the evidence of my new tears wash away. The sound of the door closing was my only sign that he had left. I crumpled to the shower floor and pulled my knees to my chest, sobbing silently.

In the middle of the night, while everyone was sleeping, I crept through the cabin to go sit outside on the porch. I had my burner in my hand. I flipped it open and dialed Stefan's cell. It rang a bunch of times. I was preparing to leave a voice message.

On what might have been the last ring he answered. "Maura?" He sounded like he had been sleeping.

"Hi." My voice was weak and fresh tears rolled down my cheeks.

"Are you alright?"

"Not really." I wiped at my face. "I knew killing him wouldn't

ENDURE THE PAIN

make me feel better, but it gave me purpose. Now that he's dead..." I was rambling and he probably didn't know what the hell I was talking about.

"Alex Roth?" he guessed.

"Jamie's reporting back to you?" *Why am I not surprised?*

"He checks in," he said, vaguely.

"How did you all find me?"

"He didn't tell you?"

"I didn't ask."

"Right after you disappeared, we gave every hotel in the city your picture. Someone recognized you and they called me the day you shot up Hartford."

"I only shot two people in Hartford," I corrected.

"Regardless, cleaning up your carnage this past week has aged me." He sighed and I could hear his exhaustion. "Decorating those Aryans with shamrocks has put a lot of eyes on us. It's as if you wanted to get caught."

"I wish I felt sorry." *But I don't.* My fingers clenched around the phone. "Why did you shut me out?"

"I never shut you out," he said. "I...I didn't want to make the same mistakes twice and lose you for another six years."

"What do you mean?" I asked.

He hesitated. Without being able to see him, I couldn't tell if he was pondering his words or thinking up a way to evade answering altogether. "I banned others from coming to the house and canceled our weekly family meetings. For one, because I don't know who to trust. And two, I didn't want you to feel like you couldn't grieve—that anyone was judging you for it. I purposely didn't update you on business and the family because that was the last thing you needed to be dealing with."

I rubbed a hand down the side of my face. *We really need to work on our communication.* I stared up at the night sky. The stars

391

were so visible. The cabin was about a four-hour drive from New Haven, but I felt like I was a million miles away from home. "I don't know what's going to happen when this is all over and I have nothing left to focus on."

"Come home and we'll figure it out together," he said.

CHAPTER THIRTY-SEVEN

Three days passed without any luck in finding Buck and the remaining Aryans. It was really pissing Vincent off and he barely left his cave/bedroom. We had to practically drag him from it and his computers to eat.

My goons occupied a lot of their time continuing Brenna's *education* in self-defense and weaponry. Even Jamie and Louie got involved and showed her a few things.

I spent a lot of my time working on myself. The day after we'd killed Alex, I'd stayed in bed. The hollowness had lessened as each hour passed, my pain and rage returning. The day after that, I'd felt like I could take a deep breath. I was back to what I'd considered normal these past three months, but the weight of my grief wasn't as crushing.

It was hard to be cooped up with Jamie and Louie around. So I went on a lot of walks to get some space. Dean and Asher alternated in following me. They at least gave me a wide berth when they did. This morning Jamie asked if he could join me on my walk as I was heading for the door. I was ready to say no. The kicked puppy look he held made my teeth grind and I reluctantly said yes. The whole point of my walks was to get away and feel a tiny bit of peace. With Jamie walking with me, it was awkward and silent.

My walk was usually a mile and a half through woods toward the lake. I'd admire the view from the lake's shore for a while. It was easy to just stare at vast beautiful blue water and the backdrop of mountains covered in lush green trees. We both made it to the lake, and he stood next to me, taking in the view.

"I hate that you're standing next to me, yet feel so far away," he blurted, breaking his silence. "I hate that every time you look at me, I see hurt in your eyes. I hate being the one who put it there." The anguish woven into his words stabbed me in the heart. "Everything has fallen apart and I don't know where to begin to fix things, but I can't accept that this is the end for us."

I folded my arms over my chest, hugging myself. "I want to tell you not to accept it, but even if we were to forgive each other, I doubt it would fix things. A huge part of who you loved died that day. I'm not the same person anymore. Maybe what's best for you and Louie is to move on."

"Isn't that for us to decide?"

"I'm a shell of myself—"

"You feel that way right now," he interrupted. Nicoli had said the same thing.

I shook my head. "Things won't get better."

"Yes, they will."

I tore my eyes from the lake to look at him, finding that he was already staring at me. "I can't have children."

His brow furrowed and I could see the questions forming in his eyes.

"The doctor in the hospital told me that there was a chance that I might not be able to carry children. I had it verified last month. The scarring on my uterus is too extensive. If by some miracle an embryo were able to implant itself in a spot that's not scarred, the likelihood of miscarriage is very high. I can't give you or Louie children and I saw how happy you two were at the idea of becoming fathers."

"There are other ways—"

"No!" I snapped. I didn't want to humor the idea of other avenues. I wouldn't survive it if something were to happen again. "It's just me, Jamie. That's it. If who you see in front of you is enough for you, then don't give up on us. But if I'm not, let me go."

I left him by the lake and began the walk back to the cabin.

After dinner, Brenna and I were relaxing on the couch when we heard Vincent yell, "Maura!" He came running down the hall into the living room. "We have a lead." He beamed.

I sat up. "We do?"

He nodded. "Buck's child bride, Amber—no—Amelia, the one that's pregnant." He was so excited he was stumbling over his words. The poor kid really needed some fresh air. "Her sister just checked into the hospital for pregnancy complications."

I knew I must have looked confused, but I waited for him to explain.

"Her sister isn't pregnant, and I hacked into the hospital's cameras and it's Buck's wife. She's gone into labor early and is getting ready to have a C-section. Buck isn't there. I figured if she's getting ready to have his kid, he's bound to show up sooner or later. Or she might know where he is," he said.

"Way to go, Vincent!" Brenna praised.

"Which hospital is she in?" I asked.

"Yale New Haven hospital," he answered.

Brenna frowned. "I bet those bastards have been hiding back home this entire time."

I stood from the couch. "Looks like we're going back to New Haven."

We arrived back in New Haven right after Amelia got done delivering her baby via C-section. Vincent continued to monitor her from the cameras inside the hospital, while all of us pretty much camped outside waiting and watching for Buck to show.

When he didn't show the next day, we knew we had to go about this a different way.

I showered and got cleaned up at the same hotel we'd fled from after Jamie and Louie had found us. I dressed casually in jeans, a green blouse, and a long tan peacoat. My makeup was light, and my hair was straight. I was aiming to look down-to-earth and unintimidating.

I put my wristlet and burner phone in my coat pocket and grabbed the teddy bear Brenna had purchased before heading back to the hospital.

We all agreed I'd go in alone, while they monitored the hospital's entrances and cameras. As I walked through the hospital's halls toward Amelia's room, my earpiece filled my ear with static. *Ow!* I winced and pulled it out. I grabbed my burner from my pocket, intending to call Vincent, but I didn't have any service.

My eyes flicked to Amelia's door, which I was mere feet from, and I debated. Maybe I was out of range and the hospital had bad reception? She was getting discharged tomorrow morning and we might not get another chance.

Mind made up, I continued on. I knocked on her door and waited for her to respond.

"Come in," a young and delicate voice said.

I walked in and saw that Amelia was sitting up in the hospital bed, holding her baby. She was very thin, despite just having had a baby. She was sporting a swollen black eye and split lip. Her hair was black as ink and her eyes were a bright shade of green. *Christ, she's just a kid.*

Her un-swollen eye widened the moment she saw me and she clutched her baby closer.

"I'm not here to hurt you," I said, quickly. "I just want to talk."

My words didn't seem to reassure her. I held out the teddy bear. "I got this for the baby," I said, placing it on the foot of her bed, and took a step back.

She stared at the bear, then me. The baby let out a cry and she rocked it in her arms while patting its bottom. "I don't know where he is," she said.

"Will you tell me what you do know?" I asked.

She looked away, her good eye turned glossy. "I can't. He'll kill us."

I took a seat in the only guest chair in the room. "What is it?" I asked, gesturing to the baby. I didn't even want to acknowledge it, but I needed to find some common ground with her.

"It's a boy."

"Did you pick a name?"

She shook her head.

"What's your plan after you're discharged from here?"

That question seemed to break her, and she started crying. "I don't know. I don't want to go back to him, but he'll find me. I've been clean since I found out I was pregnant. If I go back, he'll make me shoot up again to keep me compliant."

"I could help you. I could get you somewhere safe, with a new identity and enough cash to start over."

She shook her head frantically. "Everything has a price and I already told you that I don't know where he is."

"I'll accept any information that you have."

"If I gave you that, who's to say you won't kill me?"

My gaze dropped to her baby. "You and I were six weeks apart in our pregnancies." I stood and unbuttoned my pants. Lifting my shirt, I revealed the long vertical pink scar under my bellybutton to her. "I had just found out that I was having a girl and returned home to find Alex Roth in my bedroom. He stabbed me, killing my baby girl."

She did nothing to hide her guilt. "I'm so sorry."

I fastened my pants and sat down again. "I don't hurt kids and that baby needs his mother. I give you my word as a Quinn that no harm will come to you or your baby. Just please, help me," I pleaded.

She stared down at her baby and chewed on her lip, debating. She let out a heavy exhale and looked back at me. As she was about to answer, her room door burst open.

My stomach dropped when Buck and three Aryans walked in.

I jumped to my feet and reached behind my back for my gun tucked into the waistband of my jeans.

Because his was already drawn, Buck pointed his gun at me. "Na-ah, bitch. Put your hands up, slowly."

I did as he said and lifted my hands in the air. He approached me with one of his Aryan lackeys, who also had a gun trained on me. Buck put his hand inside my jacket and took my Glock. He handed it over to the lackey, then began patting me down. He paid extra attention to my breasts and butt as he did. He found my burner and earpiece in my pocket and tossed them.

Once he was done, he smirked down at me. I could see why Amelia had fallen for him. He had that bad boy swagger down pat. He kind of reminded me of Patrick Swayze from Dirty Dancing, with his thick brown hair and light brown eyes. The universe really liked to fuck with us, I swore, because it was wrong for a disgusting individual such as Buck to be even remotely handsome.

"You're prettier than your picture," he said and ran his finger down my cheek. "I think I'm going to enjoy breaking you."

I made an effort to look bored.

His smile only broadened, and he finally looked at his wife. "Get up, Amelia. Time to go," he ordered, and the other two Aryans yanked her and the baby out of bed. She let out a whimper and stuffed her feet into her shoes. They didn't even give her a chance to change out of her hospital gown before they dragged us out of the room.

One of the Aryans held a gun to my spine as we walked. I glanced at every camera we passed, praying Vincent was watching and was sending in the cavalry. Buck led us to the cafeteria. We passed the dining room and the line of people for the buffet into the back kitchen area.

"Hey, you can't be in here!" one of the cooks wearing a hairnet yelled. Buck and the Aryans ignored him and continued on to a door in the back that led outside. The smell of trash and cigarettes filled my nose instead of fresh air. A few hospital staff were huddled near the dumpsters, smoking, and didn't even acknowledge us as we walked by.

We rounded the dumpsters and my stomach sank when I saw a white van, with the fourth and last Aryan in Buck's gang sitting in the driver's seat, waiting for us in the parking lot. They were all here.

The sound of tires squealing pulled my focus to the right and speeding down the road was Asher's truck. The Aryan holding a gun to my back grabbed my arm and began dragging me toward the van.

Shots went off and the Aryans ducked. Amelia screamed and jumped inside the van.

"Maura!" I heard Jamie and Louie yell.

I looked over my shoulder. They were both running toward me while Dean and Asher shot at the Aryans, covering for them. I dropped myself to the ground. My captor, unable to bear my weight in one hand and shoot at the same time, let go of my arm. I rolled away and scrambled to my feet. I lunged into a run, only to be yanked back by my hair. I let out a pain riddled scream and I clawed at the fist clamped to my hair.

"I'm not letting you go." Buck's voice poured into my ear. Using me as a shield as he walked backward, he aimed his gun at Jamie and Louie. They saw the gun but didn't have enough time to react and Buck pulled the trigger. Louie's whole body jerked.

"Louie!" I screamed.

Louie's hand went to his abdomen before he bent over and fell to the ground. Jamie slid to the ground next to him and threw his body over his best friend, protecting him.

Dean and Asher moved in, raining fire down on the Aryans to help cover Jamie and Louie.

I fought with everything I had, not caring if my hair was ripped out. I just had to get to Louie.

Buck wrapped his arm around my middle, picked me up off the ground, and threw me in the back of the van, where another Aryan was waiting to catch me. That Aryan locked his arms around my middle and pinned me to the van's floor with his knee digging into my back.

Buck jumped in next and yelled, "Go! Go!" and the van took off.

"What about Wesley?" the Aryan pinning me asked.

"He said he'd hold them off so we can get away," Buck said and only a fool wouldn't have been able to tell that he was lying. His eyes dropped to me. "Drug her and tie her up."

Amelia, sitting in the front seat, stared at me worriedly as she clutched her baby. Buck held his hands out to her. "Let me see him."

She hesitated.

"Let me see him!" Buck roared, making her wince, and she handed over the baby.

The Aryan pinning me put a cloth over my nose and mouth. I

held my breath and tried to thrash, wiggle, do anything that would get my face free. He pushed his knee harder into my back, making me groan, and I mistakenly inhaled.

My eyes became very heavy.

Louie.

He was the last thought I had before everything faded away.

To Be Continued...

Book 2.5
Jamie & Louie Novella

ASHLEY N. ROSTEK

ESCAPE
The Reaper

THE MAURA QUINN SERIES BOOK THREE

ABOUT THE AUTHOR

Ashley N. Rostek is a wife and mother by day and a writer by night. She survives on coffee, loves collecting offensive coffee mugs, and is an unashamed bibliophile.

To Ashley, there isn't a better pastime than letting your mind escape in a good book. Her favorite genre is romance and has the overflowing bookshelf to prove it. She is a lover of love. Be it a sweet YA or a dark and lusty novel, she must read it!

Ashley's passion is writing. She picked up the pen at seventeen and hasn't put it down. Her debut novel is Embrace the Darkness, the first book in the Maura Quinn series.

SOCIAL MEDIA

You can find out more about Ashley and her upcoming works on social media!

The Inner Circle ~ Ashley N. Rostek's Book Group
https://www.facebook.com/groups/arostektheinnercircle/
(THE BEST PLACE TO STAY UPDATED)

FACEBOOK
https://www.facebook.com/ashleynrostek/

INSTAGRAM

https://www.instagram.com/ashleynrostek/

<u>NEWSLETTER</u>

https://landing.mailerlite.com/webforms/landing/j7z0t1

Printed in Great Britain
by Amazon